Also by Douglas Preston and Lincoln Child

THE LOST ISLAND

A GIDEON CREW NOVEL

DOUGLAS PRESTON &
LINCOLN CHILD

GRAND CENTRAL
PUBLISHING

NEW YORK   BOSTON

Grand Central Publishing
Hachette Book Group
1290 Avenue of the Americas
New York, NY 10104

www.HachetteBookGroup.com

Grand Central Publishing is a division of Hachette Book Group, Inc.
The Grand Central Publishing name and logo are trademarks of Hachette Book Group, Inc.

The Hachette Speakers Bureau provides a wide range of authors for speaking events. To find out more, go to www.hachettespeakersbureau.com or call (866) 376-6591.

The publisher is not responsible for websites (or their content) that are not owned by the publisher.

Printed in the United States of America

Originally published in hardcover by Hachette Book Group
First mass market edition: March 2015

10 9 8 7 6 5 4 3

OPM

ATTENTION CORPORATIONS AND ORGANIZATIONS:

Most Hachette Book Group books are available at quantity discounts with bulk purchase for educational, business, or sales promotional use. For information, please call or write:

Special Markets Department, Hachette Book Group
1290 Avenue of the Americas, New York, NY 10104
Telephone: 1-800-222-6747 Fax: 1-800-477-5925

Lincoln Child dedicates this book to his wife,

Luchie

Douglas Preston dedicates this book to

Joshua Richholt

1

THE CONFERENCE ROOM at Effective Engineering Solutions emptied. Everyone left, leaving Gideon Crew alone with Eli Glinn and Manuel Garza in the austere room, high above the streets of Manhattan.

With his withered hand, Glinn motioned Gideon to a chair at the conference table. "Gideon, please, sit down."

Gideon took a seat. He sensed already that this meeting—which had begun with a celebration of his successful completion of the latest project for EES—was morphing into something else.

"You've had quite an ordeal," Glinn said. "Not just the physical manhunt, but the, ah, emotional toll as well. Are you sure you want to jump right into something new?"

"I'm sure," Gideon replied.

Glinn looked at him carefully—a long, searching look. Then he nodded. "Excellent. Glad to hear you'll be continuing with us as our . . ." He paused, searched for a word. "Our special deputy. We'll engage you a suite at a hotel around the corner, so you'll have a place to stay while we find you an apartment. I know how you hate to be away from your beloved Santa Fe, but it's a very interesting time to be in New York. Right now, for example, there's a special exhibition at the Morgan Library—the Book of Kells, on loan from the Irish government. You've heard of the Book of Kells, of course?"

"Vaguely."

"It's the finest illuminated manuscript in existence, considered to be Ireland's greatest national treasure."

Gideon said nothing.

Glinn glanced at his watch. "Then you'll come have a look at it with me? I'm a great fancier of illuminated manuscripts. They'll be turning a new page of the book every day. Very exciting."

Gideon hesitated. "Illuminated manuscripts are not exactly an interest of mine."

"Ah, but I was so hoping you'd accompany me to the exhibition," said Glinn. "You'll love the Book of Kells. It's only been out of Ireland once before, and it's only here for a week. A shame to miss it. If we leave now, we'll just catch the last hour of today's showing."

"Maybe we could go Monday."

"And miss the page displayed today—forever? No, we must go now."

Gideon started to laugh, amused at Glinn's earnestness. The man's interests were so arcane. "Honestly, I couldn't care less about the damn Book of Kells."

"Ah, but you will."

Hearing the edge in Glinn's voice, Gideon paused. "Why?"

"Because your new assignment will be to steal it."

2

GIDEON FOLLOWED ELI GLINN into the East Room of the Morgan Library. Despite its being packed with visitors, entering the magnificent space was nevertheless an overwhelming experience. Gideon hadn't been in the Morgan since its renovation—he always found its treasures too tempting—and immediately became entranced all over again with the vaulted and painted ceilings, the three-story tiers of rich books, the massive marble fireplace, the opulent tapestries, furniture, and thick burgundy rug. Glinn, operating the joystick of his electric wheelchair with one claw-like hand, moved into the room aggressively, cutting the line and taking advantage of the fact that people tended to yield to the handicapped. Soon they had moved to the front of the line, where a large glass cube contained the Book of Kells.

"What a room," murmured Gideon, looking around, his eyes instinctively picking out the many aggressively visible details of high security, starting with the hyper-alert guards, the single entrance, the camera lenses winking in the ceiling moldings, the motion-sensor detectors and infrared laser placements. Not only that, but—in entering the room—he had observed the side edge of a massive steel pocket door, ready to seal the space off at a moment's notice.

Glinn followed his eye toward the ceiling. "Magnificent, isn't it?" he said. "Those murals are by the artist H. Siddons Mowbray, and the spandrels feature the twelve signs of the zodiac. J. P. Morgan belonged to an exclusive dining club that admitted only twelve members, each of whom was given a zodiac code name. They say the arrangements of the signs and other strange symbols painted in the ceiling relate to key events in Morgan's personal life."

Gideon's eye fell to the grand fireplace adorning one end of the hall. Even in its intricately carved recesses he could make out the faint presence of security devices, some of which he had never seen before and had no idea what they did.

"That tapestry over the fireplace," Glinn continued, "is sixteenth-century Netherlandish. It depicts one of the seven deadly sins: avarice." He issued a low chuckle. "Interesting choice for Mr. J. Pierpont Morgan, don't you think?"

Gideon turned his attention to the glass cube that contained the Book of Kells. It was clearly bulletproof, and not the standard blue kind, either, but white glass—he guessed a P6B standard—which rendered it not only bulletproof but blast-proof, hammer-proof, and ax-proof as well. He stared intently into the case, ignoring the fabulous and irreplaceable treasure it contained, his eyes instead picking out and categorizing the many layers of security within—motion sensors, atmospheric pressure sensors, infrared heat detectors, and even what looked like an atmospheric composition sensor.

Clearly any disturbance would trigger the instant shutting of that steel door—sealing the room and trapping the thief inside.

And that was just the security he could see.

"Breathtaking, isn't it?" murmured Glinn.

"It's scaring the shit out of me."

"What?" Glinn looked startled.

"Excuse me. You mean the book…" He looked at it for the first time. "Interesting."

"That's one way of putting it. Its origins are shrouded in mystery. Some say it was created by Saint Columba himself around AD 590. Others believe it was created by unknown monks two hundred years later, to celebrate Columba's bicentennial. It was begun at Iona and then carried to the Abbey of Kells, where the illumination was added. And there it was kept, deeply hidden, as the abbey was raided and looted again and again by pagan Viking marauders. But they never found that book."

Gideon looked at the manuscript more closely. Despite himself, he was drawn in, enthralled by the fantastically complex abstract designs on the page, almost fractal in their depth.

"The page on display today is folio 34r," Glinn told him. "The famous Chi Rho monogram."

"Chi Rho? What's that?"

"*Chi* and *Rho* are the first two letters of the word *Christ* in Greek. The actual narrative of Jesus's life starts at Matthew 1:18, and that page was often decorated in early illuminated gospels. The first word of the narrative is

Christ. In the Book of Kells, those first two letters, *Chi Rho,* consume the entire page."

The crowds began to back up behind them, and Gideon felt someone's elbow giving him a faint nudge.

Glinn's whispery voice continued. "Look at the labyrinth of knotted decoration! You can see all kinds of strange things hidden in there—animals, insects, birds, angels, tiny heads, crosses, flowers. Not to mention Celtic knots of stupendous complexity, a mathematician's dream . . . And then the colors! The golds and greens and yellows and purples! This is the greatest page from the greatest illuminated manuscript in existence. No wonder the book is considered Ireland's greatest national treasure. Just *look* at it."

This was the first time Gideon could remember hearing anything approaching enthusiasm in Glinn's voice. He leaned closer, so close his breath fogged the glass.

"Excuse me, but there are people waiting," came an impatient voice from behind him.

As a little test, Gideon reached out and put his hand on the glass.

Instantly a low beeping sounded and a guard called out: "Hands off the glass, please! You, sir—hands off!"

This stimulated the impatient crowd. "Come on, friend, give someone else a chance!" came another voice. Others murmured their agreement.

With a long sigh of regret, Glinn touched his withered finger to the joystick and the wheelchair moved aside with a hum, Gideon following. A few moments later they were back out on Madison Avenue, the traffic streaming past, cabs blaring. Gideon blinked in the bright light.

"Let me get this straight. You want me to *steal* that book?"

He felt Glinn's hand touch his arm reassuringly. "No, not the entire book. Just that one little folio page we were looking at, number 34r."

"Why?"

A silence. "Have you ever known me to answer a question like that?" Glinn asked pleasantly as their limousine came gliding up to take them back to Little West 12th Street.

3

THREE DAYS LATER, Gideon Crew, fresh from a swim in the rooftop pool of the ultra-hip Gansevoort Hotel, stood stark naked in his suite high above the Meatpacking District of New York, staring down at a king-size bed overspread with diagrams and schematics—which mapped out, in minute detail, the security system of the East Room of the Morgan Library.

The loan of the Book of Kells by the Irish government to the Morgan Library had taken eight years to arrange. It had been fraught with difficulty. The main reason was that in the year 2000, one of the book's folios had been sent to Canberra, Australia, for exhibition. Several pages were damaged by rubbing and a loss of pigment—the vibration of the plane's engines was blamed—and the Irish government was now loath to risk another loan.

James Watermain, the billionaire Irish American founder of the Watermain Group, had made it a personal mission to bring the book to the United States. A man known for his charisma and charm, he managed to persuade the Irish prime minister, and finally the government, to release it—under stringent conditions. One of those conditions was a total overhaul of the security system of the East Room of the Morgan Library, which Watermain paid for himself.

Watermain had initially tried to put the manuscript on display at the Smithsonian. Museum security, however, had proven unwilling to provide the necessary high-tech face-lift, and the effort had fallen through. Secretly, Gideon was pleased to hear this. Although he had dreadful memories of Washington, DC, as a child—after all, that was where his father had been killed—in later years he had gone back occasionally to visit and found the town to be a somewhat boring, even sleepy, collection of handsome monuments and timeless documents. But just weeks before, he'd been summoned to Washington to receive a medal for his recent accomplishments at Fort Detrick. And to his dismay—perhaps because of 9/11, perhaps simply as a result of red tape and the inevitable bureaucratic accretion—what had once been a pleasant and relaxed capital was now more like an armed camp. The Metropolitan Police, Capitol Police, Park Police, State Department Police, US Mint Police, Secret Service Police, "Special" Police (*achtung!*)—in fact, something like two dozen different police forces, he'd learned—now choked downtown with their presence: all armed, and all seemingly with the power to pull over and arrest any luckless driver or visitor. (This according to one of Gideon's cabdrivers, himself formerly on the job.) Looking around at all the redundant cops, with their overlapping fiefdoms, Gideon could practically smell his tax dollars burning away.

The final straw came when he later received a robot

traffic ticket in the mail: some pole-mounted camera-radar had observed him driving up New York Avenue at a few miles over the thirty-five-miles-an-hour speed limit, and—snagging an image of his license plate—had mailed him a ticket for $125. Now there seemed no easy way to protest the ticket short of traveling back to Washington to defend himself. And, of course, the actual event was so vague in his memory there was no way to reconstruct it: had there been a 35 MPH sign posted anywhere nearby? Had he truly been speeding? Where the hell, exactly, was New York Avenue? Many days had passed—how was an honest citizen to recall? So Gideon had done two things: first, paid the fine; and second, vowed not to return to DC for a long, long time. What had, in his opinion, always been a beautiful and abiding symbol of the country's greatness was now apparently obsessed with balancing its swollen budget.

Or maybe, fresh from his trout stream, Gideon was just feeling the pain of reentry into urban existence. But either way, there wasn't a chance in hell he was going back to the Smithsonian.

Now—as his thoughts returned to the present and he circled the bed—Gideon began wondering how Glinn had managed to get hold of the complete engineering, wiring, and electrical diagrams of that security system. Here was every circuit, every sensor, every spec, spelled out in minute detail. Lot of good it was going to do him. He had never in his life seen a security system like this—he had never even *imagined* a security system like this. There were the usual multiple layers, redundant and hardened systems, backup power supplies, and everything a burglar might expect. But that was just the beginning.

The East Room itself was now, essentially, a vault. It had originally been constructed of double-laid walls of Vermont limestone block almost three feet thick. The single entry into the room came equipped with a divided steel pocket door that would drop down from the ceiling and rise up from the floor the instant an alarm was triggered, sealing the room. There were no windows anywhere, light being incompatible with the preservation of books. The vaulted ceiling was of poured reinforced concrete, incredibly thick. The floor was a massive slab of reinforced concrete, covered with marble. To all this original reinforcement had been retrofitted, at the Irish government's request, an outer layer of steel plating and sensors.

At night, the room was completely sealed up. Inside, it was secured by crisscrossing laser beams, motion detectors, and infrared sensors of several wavelengths, including one that would pick up even the smallest hint of body heat. Quite literally, not even a mouse (and probably not even a cockroach) could move inside the room without being detected. There were cameras running day and night, the monitors staffed by highly trained, handpicked security guards of the highest caliber.

During the day, when the exhibition was open to the public, people had to leave behind all their bags and cameras and pass through a metal detector. There were guards inside and outside the hall, and more cameras than a Las Vegas casino. The cube in which the book sat contained an atmosphere of pure argon. Inside the cube were sensors that would immediately go off if they detected a whiff of any other atmospheric gas, even in levels as low as one part per million. If the book was disturbed, the steel doors would seal the room so quickly that not even an Olympic runner could carry it from the case to the exit before it shut.

For days, Gideon had looked for weaknesses in the system. All systems had vulnerabilities, and almost always those vulnerabilities were related either to human fallibility, to programming glitches, or to a system too complex to be completely understood. But the designers of this system had taken those limitations into account. While this system was indeed complex, it was modular, in the sense that each component was fairly simple and independent of the others. The programs were simple, and some layers of security were entirely mechanical, with no computerized controls at all. The redundancy was such that multiple systems could fail or be compromised without affecting the ultimate security of the book.

There was, of course, a way to turn the system on and off, because the pages of the book were turned on a daily basis. But even this had been exceedingly well planned. To shut down the system required three people, each with a simple, independent code that they had memorized. There were no physical keys or written codes or anything that could be stolen. And these three people were untouchable. They were John Watermain himself, the president of the Morgan Library, and the deputy mayor of New York City. While one might be corruptible or susceptible to social engineering, two would be extremely difficult and three impossible.

And what would happen if one of them died? In that case there was a stand-in, a fourth person—who happened to be the prime minister of Ireland himself.

What about fire? Surely in the case of an emergency,

Gideon reasoned, the book would have to be quickly moved. But the specs dealt with that possibility in an unusual way. The book would not be moved in case of a fire. It would be fully protected in situ. The glass cube was designed to be a first line of defense, able to withstand a serious fire on its own; the second line was a fireproof box that rose from inside the cube to enclose the book, protecting it from the most prolonged fire. And the East Room had redundant, state-of-the-art firefighting components in place that would stifle any fire well before it got going. There were similar systems protecting the book against earthquake, flood, and terrorist attack. Just about the only thing it wasn't protected from was a direct nuclear strike.

With a long sigh, Gideon strolled over to his closet and flipped through his clothes. It was time to get dressed for dinner. He had taken, as a loose cover, the persona of a young, hip dot-com millionaire, a persona he had used before with success. He took out a black St. Croix mock turtleneck, a pair of worn Levi's, and some Bass Weejuns—he had to mix it up a *little*, after all—and pulled them all on.

He hadn't eaten anything all day. This was usual. Gideon preferred one elegant and extraordinary dining experience to three cheap squares. Eating for him was more ritual than sustenance.

He checked his watch again. It was still too early to dine, but he felt restless after three days cooped up in this room, staring at diagrams. He had yet to find a hole, a chink, even the slightest hairline crack in this security system. Since he'd started stealing from art museums and historical societies when he was a teenager, he had come to believe that there was no such thing as a perfect security system. Every system was vulnerable, either technologically or through social engineering.

That had always been his certitude. Until now.

Christ, he needed a break. He went into the bathroom, combed his wet hair, then slapped on some Truefitt & Hill aftershave balm to cover up the lingering smell of chlorine from the pool. He left his suite, hanging the DO NOT DISTURB sign on the doorknob on his way out.

It was a hot August evening in the Meatpacking District. The beautiful people were out in the Hamptons, and instead the cobbled streets were packed with young, hip-looking tourists—the District had become one of the chicest neighborhoods in Manhattan in recent years.

He walked around the block to Spice Market, sat down at the bar, and ordered a martini. As he sipped the drink, he indulged in one of his favorite activities, observing the people around him and imagining every detail of their lives, from what they did for a living to what their dogs looked like. But try as he might, he couldn't get into the groove. For the first time in his life, he had run into a security system designed by truly intelligent people—people even smarter than him. The damn Book of Kells was going to be harder to steal than the *Mona Lisa*.

As he pondered this, his mood, already foul, deepened. The people around him—well heeled and sophisticated, talking, laughing, drinking, and eating—began to irritate him. He began to imagine they weren't people, but chattering monkeys, engaged in complex grooming rituals, and that eased his annoyance.

His drink was empty. Long ago he had learned it was a bad idea for him to order a second one—not that he had a drinking problem, of course, but after two he seemed to pass a line that led to a third, and even a fourth, and that would inevitably lead him to seek out one of those sleek, blond, chattering monkeys...

He ordered a second drink.

While he sipped it, feeling marginally better about the state of the world as the alcohol kicked in, a little idea came to him. If it was truly impossible to steal the Book of Kells—and deep down he knew it was—he would simply have to get someone else to take it out of the room for him...with the full cooperation of those three people. This would require a level of social engineering far more sophisticated than any he had attempted before.

And a way to do just that began to materialize in his very crooked, half-soused mind.

His third drink arrived, and he cast his eye about the elegant bar. There was a woman at the far end, not necessarily the most beautiful woman in the room—she was plump and wore glasses. But—what he personally found most attractive in a woman—she possessed a mordant, intelligent gleam in her eye. She was looking around, and it seemed to Gideon that she found this scene as amusing as he did.

He picked up his almost finished drink and walked over. He glanced at the stool. "May I?"

She looked him up and down. "I think so. Are you in the computer business?"

He laughed and put on his most self-deprecating look.
"No, but I am WYSIWYG. Why do you ask?"

"The Steve Jobs uniform—black mock turtleneck and jeans."

"I don't like thinking about what I'm going to wear in the morning."

She turned to the bartender. "Two Beefeater martinis, straight up, two olives, dirty."

"You're buying me a drink?"

"Any objection?"

He leaned forward. "Not at all, but how did you know what I was drinking?"

"I've been watching you since you came in."

"Really? Why me?"

"You look like a lost boy."

Gideon found himself flushing. This woman was perhaps a little too keen in her observations, and he felt unmasked. "Aren't we all a bit lost?"

She smiled and said, "I think we're going to get along."

The drinks arrived and they clinked glasses.

"To being lost," said Gideon.

4

T HE SHOP OF Griggs and Wellington, Rare Books and Manuscripts, was just around the corner from the Portobello Road. It was one of those antiques shops that had moved up from Portobello but had not quite achieved the success it was trying very, very hard to reach. As Gideon entered the shop, he noted a veneer of British snobbery not quite covering up a kind of trashy East End hustle. The shop's proprietor, a young Brit dressed in overdone Savile Row, confirmed Gideon's suspicions when he arrived, his plummy accent almost but not quite smothering a Cockney origin.

"May I help you, sir?"

Gideon, himself dressed in an expensive Ralph Lauren suit, gave the proprietor a dumb-ass American smile. "Well, I was wondering if I could look at that old manuscript page in the window." His Texas accent came out despite the effort to control it.

"Naturally," the proprietor said. "You mean the illuminated book of hours?"

"Yeah."

The man went to the case, unlocked it, and removed the small page. It was enclosed in stiff plastic. With obvious reverence he placed it on a black velvet tray that he whisked out from under the counter, then set the tray within a pool of light from a spot in the ceiling. It was a page out of the gospel, with an illusionistic border of flowers, its central scene showing the Virgin Mary seated under an arch, with an angel descending from a blue sky. Mary was drawing back in fear. It was exquisite in every detail.

"Very lovely," the shopkeeper murmured. "You have a good eye, sir."

"Tell me about it," Gideon asked.

"It's from a Flemish book of hours dating to around 1440—a very fine one indeed. Very fine," the man repeated, his voice hushed with veneration. "It is believed to be by the workshop of the Master of the Privileges of Ghent and Flanders."

"I see," said Gideon. "Nice."

"It depicts the Annunciation, of course," the dealer added.

"And how much is it?"

"We have a price of four thousand six hundred pounds on that very rare page." The man's voice became pinched, as if discussing sums of money were distasteful to him.

"What's that, about eight grand?" said Gideon. He peered closely at it.

"Would you like to examine it with a loupe?"

"A what? Oh, thank you."

As Gideon examined it, the dealer went on, hands clasped, his buttery accent filling the small shop. "As you probably know," he said, his tone implying that Gideon certainly did not know, "the medieval book of hours came from the monastic cycle of prayer, simplified for private devotions. They represent some of the finest works of medieval art in existence. They were incredibly expensive—the cost of a book of hours in the fifteenth century was about the same as buying a good farm, buildings and all. Only royalty, nobility, and the very wealthy could afford one of these books. Just look at the detail! And the color. I especially direct your attention to the blue in the sky—a pigment made with crushed lapis lazuli, which in the Middle Ages was more expensive than gold. The only source of lapis at the time was Afghanistan."

"I see."

"Are you a collector?" the dealer asked.

"Oh, no. I'm just looking for an anniversary present for my wife. She's religious." Gideon gave an indulgent laugh, signaling that he himself was not.

"May I introduce myself?" the dealer said. "I am Sir Colin Griggs."

Gideon glanced up at the fellow extending a small white hand, his chin thrust slightly forward, his back straight. He was about as much a "sir" as Gideon was a lord. He took the hand and shook it enthusiastically. "I'm Gideon Crew. From Texas. Sorry, you can't put any 'sir' in front of my name, I'm hardly even a mister." He gave a belly laugh.

"Ah, Texas, the Lone Star State. You have excellent taste, Mr. Crew. Can I answer any other questions about the item?"

"How do I know it's real?"

"I can assure you it's real beyond all doubt. We stand behind everything we sell. You would be welcome to have it examined by an expert after your purchase, and if there were any doubts we'd immediately refund your money."

"That's good. But . . . well, I have to say this four thousand six hundred pounds is a lot of money . . . how about making it four thousand, even-steven?"

Sir Colin gathered himself up into a ramrod of disapproval. "I'm sorry, Mr. Crew, but at Griggs and Wellington we don't negotiate."

Gideon bestowed a genial, Texas smile on the snobby Brit. "Aw, don't play that game. Everything's negotiable." He took out his credit card. "Four thousand or I'm outta here."

Sir Colin allowed the disapproval on his face to ease somewhat. "I suppose—for someone who appreciates it as much as you do—we could make an exception and lower the price to four thousand four."

"Four thousand two."

The expression on Sir Colin's face indicated that this was a painful and unpleasant discussion. "Four thousand three."

"Sold."

5

After a quick trip back to his hotel room for a change of clothes, Gideon set off with the precious page for the London offices of Sotheby's, where the final test of his scheme would take place. It was a stiff three-mile walk that took Gideon through some fascinating byways, as well as Hyde Park. It was a splendid late-summer day, and in the park the ancient trees were in full leaf, cumulus clouds drifting overhead like sailing ships, the greensward alive with people. London was an extraordinary city, and he told himself he really should spend more time there—maybe even live there.

And then he remembered his terminal medical condition, and such thoughts were quickly forced from his head.

The Sotheby's building was an unpretentious, nineteenth-century edifice of four stories, newly white-washed. The staff were most solicitous when they saw the little illuminated manuscript page he wanted to place with them at auction, and he was ushered into a neat little office on the third floor, where he was greeted by a charming, roly-poly man with gold-rimmed spectacles and a huge shock of Einsteinian hair, dressed in an old-fashioned tweed suit with a vest and gold watch chain, looking like a man out of a Dickens novel. He was considered to be—Gideon had done the research—one of the world's greatest experts on illuminated manuscripts.

"Well, well!" the man said, smelling of tobacco and perhaps even a hint of whiskey. "What have we here, eh?" He held out a fat hand. "Brian MacKilda, at your service!" He spoke as if always out of breath, punctuating his phrases with a *huff-huff* as if catching his wind.

"I've got an illuminated manuscript I'd like to place in auction." Gideon held out the small leather portfolio.

"Excellent! Let's take a look." MacKilda came around the desk, opened a drawer, and pulled out a loupe, which he pressed into one voluminous, winking eye. Adjusting a special lamp—which threw a pool of white light onto a smooth black tray—he picked up the portfolio, took out the plastic-covered page Gideon had just purchased, slipped it out, and stared at it with a few nods, which set his fluffy hair a-wagging, accompanied by grunts of approval.

He then put it under the light. Several minutes went by while he examined it with the loupe, making more animal noises, all of which sounded positive. After that, MacKilda switched off the bright light, reached down into his desk, and removed a small, peculiar-looking flashlight with a square face. He held it close to the page and turned it on. It cast a deep ultraviolet light. MacKilda shone it here and there, lingering only briefly, and then switched off the light. The noises suddenly turned into negative snorts.

"Oh, dear," the man said finally. "Dear, dear, dear." This was followed by some huffing and puffing.

"Is there a problem?"

MacKilda shook his head sorrowfully. "Fake."

"*What?* How can it be? I paid four thousand pounds for it!"

The man turned a pair of sad eyes on him. "Our business, sir, is sadly rife with fakes. Rife!" He rolled the *r* with particular emphasis.

"But how can shining a light on it for five seconds be definitive? Don't you have other tests?"

A long sigh. "We have many tests, many, *many* tests. Raman spectroscopy, X-ray fluorescence, carbon 14. But in this case there's no need to do other tests."

"I don't get it. One five-second test?"

"Allow me to explain." MacKilda took a deep breath, followed by several *huff-huffs* and a general throat clearing. "The illuminators of yore used mostly mineral pigments in their inks. The blues are from ground lapis lazuli, the vermilion from cinnabar and sulfur. Green came from ground malachite or copper verdigris. And the whites were usually made from lead, often in combination with gypsum or calcite."

He paused for more stentorian breathing.

"Now, the point is that some of these minerals fluoresce strongly under ultraviolet light, while others change color in certain ways." He paused, breathing hard. "But look at this."

He shined the black light once again on the manuscript page. The surface remained dark, dull, unchanged. "There, you see? Nothing!"

He snapped it off. "These pigments are therefore cheap aniline dyes, none of which react to UV light."

"But it looks so real!" Gideon said, almost pleading.

"Please take a look at it again, *please*. It's got to be real!"

With another long-suffering sigh, MacKilda turned to it again and in fact did look at it for more than five seconds. "I admit the work is quite good. I was fooled at first. And the vellum looks original. Why a forger with such evident talent would go to the trouble to create an artistic fake like this—and then use aniline dyes—is beyond me. My guess is that it's Chinese. It used to be most of the fakes came out of Russia, but now we're starting to see some out of the Far East. The Chinese are a bit naive—hence the aniline dyes—but they'll catch on, unfortunately."

He shook his head, the hair waggling, and held the page back out to Gideon. "It's most certainly, most definitely, without a doubt, a forgery." And he punctuated this with a final jiggle of hair and a loud *huff-huff*.

6

Julia Thrum Murphy, thirty-two years old, had driven all the way from Bryn Mawr, Pennsylvania, where she was an assistant professor of romance languages, to see the Book of Kells on its last weekend in the States. It was a glorious Sunday afternoon, if a bit warm in the city, and what she had feared turned out to be true: the exhibition was jam-packed.

At the ticket desk, she was informed by a harried attendant that the wait just to get into the East Room was about forty-five minutes. And then there was a long, slow-moving line within the room itself, which might take another thirty minutes or more.

An hour and fifteen minutes. Hearing this, Julia almost decided to skip it and head up to the Cloisters to see the unicorn tapestries instead. But then she decided to wait. This, she knew, would be her only chance to see the Book of Kells outside of Ireland.

So she bought the twenty-five-dollar ticket, checked her handbag and camera, went through the metal detectors, and got in line. As people exited the East Room, more were let in, and the line moved slowly. Finally, after forty minutes, she reached the head of the initial line and was given the nod to enter the East Room.

Inside the room it was almost worse. The crowd moved snake-like between sets of stanchions and velvet ropes that would have done an airport security gate proud. Viewers were given less than a minute to ogle the book before guards began polite murmurings for them to keep moving, keep moving.

An hour-and-fifteen-minute wait for one minute of pleasure. This was a bit like sex, she thought, feeling disgruntled as she moved along through the serpentine line.

Just then, a fellow about her age, a bit ahead of her, passed going the other way in the queue and gave her a smile, a little warmer than mere politeness would dictate. She was startled by his roguish good looks and the combination of jet-black hair and blue eyes: a type her mother would call "Black Irish." As his smile lingered, Julia looked away. She was used to this; it was her good fortune to be born not only with brains but also with a certain willowy beauty, which she maintained with a regimen of Pilates, yoga, and jogging. Even though she was a professor, she was not at all attracted to the crop of flabby, self-important, and often pretentious men who were her peers at Bryn Mawr. Not that there was anything seriously wrong with them: the type, frankly, didn't turn her on. At the same time, it was hard to find a man who was her intellectual equal outside of academia. She could imagine herself marrying a poor man, or even an ugly man—but never, ever, would she marry a man who was less intelligent than she was.

As she thought about this, the line shuffled forward,

and the man who had smiled at her approached again. When they drew side by side, he leaned over and spoke to her, sotto voce: "We've got to stop meeting like this."

While the line was hardly original, she laughed. He didn't look stupid, at least.

He moved on as the parallel lines inched forward. She found herself anticipating his next pass, her heartbeat even accelerating a little. She glanced around the dense but orderly crowd in the East Room, looking for him. Where was he? This was crazy, her getting all a-flutter about some random stranger. She had been celibate way too long.

And then, quite suddenly, it happened. A flash of light, followed by a terrific *bang*, so loud it made her heart leap in terror, and she threw herself to the floor amid a chorus of shrieking and screaming. Immediately, she thought *terrorist attack*, and even as this went through her mind the alarms went off and the room abruptly filled with a thick smoke, totally opaque, that transformed her world into a hellish brown twilight in which she could see nothing, only hear the useless hysterical screams and cries of her fellow museum-goers.

Then came the hollow boom of what sounded like steel meeting steel, immediately followed by the *crump* of another, muffled explosion.

She lay on the ground, cheek by jowl with a dozen others, maintaining a defensive fetal position, protecting her head, as the hysterical screaming continued. She remained silent and, somewhat to her surprise, collected. After a few moments she could hear some shouted orders—security, trying to calm people down—along with sirens and the sudden roar of forced air.

Rapidly the fog thinned out and the light came back up. Almost by magic, the smoke was gone, sucked into forced-air grates now exposed in the ceiling by the withdrawal of painted panels.

The screaming began to subside, and she sat up, looking around to see what was happening. The first thing she noticed was that the glass cube holding the Book of Kells had been cleaved, a corner of the cube dirtied by what must have been a detonation of some kind. The book was not in the cube—it had been stolen. But no, not stolen, because there it was, on the floor next to the cube, open and in disarray.

And then she realized they were locked in: the only door into the East Room was now a slab of stainless steel.

The next thought that came to her mind, with some relief, was that this whole thing was nothing more than a botched robbery.

7

Now the stanchions and ropes served another purpose: they allowed the guards to control the seething crowd, which remained sealed in the East Room while security reviewed the situation.

Julia Thrum Murphy found herself herded, along with everyone else, to one side of the room while the half dozen guards secured and examined the Book of Kells and talked animatedly to their counterparts outside the East Room via radio. It became even more obvious to Julia that this was a botched robbery: the flash-bang and smoke used as a cover, the muffled explosion that split the case, the book removed—but the thief had evidently not been able to get the book out of the room before the steel security doors descended. So he'd dropped it and melted back into the crowd.

Which meant the thief was still locked in the East Room with the rest of them—a fact that was clearly evident to the guards as well. It seemed she was in for a long ordeal. While the crowd had grown more orderly, there was still a degree of chaos, with the inevitable hysterics making scenes, along with some enterprising people who appeared to be claiming non-existent injuries, no doubt hoping to make some money. Several doctors in the crowd had already come forward and were examining them.

A part of Julia was actually beginning to enjoy this. Now a sweating guard moved her and some of the others to another place in the room, and she found herself once again next to the man with the roguish face and dark hair.

He smiled at her again. "Having fun?"

"As a matter of fact, yes."

"Me too. You realize," he went on, "the ersatz thief is still in the room."

Ersatz. She liked a man with a big vocabulary.

"So . . ." The roguish-looking man smiled. "Take a look around. Let's see if we can pick him out."

This was fun. Julia glanced around, scouring the faces of the people. "I don't see any obvious crooks."

"It's always the person you'd least suspect."

"That would be you," she said.

He laughed, leaned toward her, and put out his hand. "Gideon Crew."

"Julia Murphy."

"Murphy. Irish, by any chance?" He raised an eyebrow comically.

"What about Crew? What kind of a name is that?"

"A distinguished name of Old Welsh origin. Distinguished, that is, until a Crew nicked the bailiff's moneybox and stowed away to America."

"Your ancestry is as elevated as mine."

The guards were already lining people up, organizing

them for questioning. A commander—at least he had a couple of stripes on his shoulders—stepped forward and raised his hands.

"May I have your attention, please!"

The general hubbub died down.

"I'm afraid that we can't let anyone leave this room until everyone has been interviewed," he announced. "It would greatly speed things up if all of you would please cooperate."

Murmurings, objections. "I want to get out of here!" one of the hysterics cried, to a scattered chorus of agreement.

The commander raised his hand. "I promise you, we're going to get you out of here as soon as possible. But to do that, we need your help. We've just had an attempted robbery of the Book of Kells, and there are certain protocols that must be followed. So I ask for your patience."

More murmuring, complaining, expostulation.

"So what do you do?" Gideon asked.

"I teach at Bryn Mawr. Romance languages—French, Italian, Spanish, and some Latin."

"Bryn Mawr," he said. "A professor. Nice."

"And you?"

The man hesitated. "Until recently, I worked at Los Alamos National Lab. I'm now on leave."

Julia was startled, taken aback even. "Los Alamos. You mean, where they build nuclear weapons?"

"Not build. Design."

"Is that what you do? Design bombs?"

"Among other things."

Was he joking? No, he wasn't. She didn't know

whether to be impressed or horrified. At least he wasn't just another dumb, good-looking male.

"I know," he went on, defensively. "Maybe my profession sounds a little dumb. But really, I'm an American doing my duty to keep my country safe and all that."

Julia shook her head. "I can just see you talking like that at a faculty sherry at Bryn Mawr. Oh, God, they'd label you a killer."

"And what do *you* think?"

She gave him a level gaze. "Do you care what I think?"

He returned the gaze, and she was a little taken aback by its intensity. "Yes."

He gave this a peculiar emphasis that caused her to blush, and as she became aware she was blushing, she only turned redder. "I'm not sure what I think," was all she could say.

They were silent for a few minutes. She glanced over to where the book had been placed back within its cradle. Several guards were hunched over it, examining it with enormous care—turning the pages with white-gloved hands. They seemed to be getting more and more agitated. Moments later they called out to the commander, who bustled over. A short, intense confab took place, and then the commander spoke furiously into his radio. The crowd, noticing the change, fell into a hush.

The commander raised his arm again. "I need your attention. It appears a page has been cut from the Book of Kells and is missing."

A gasp from the audience.

"The page must still be in this room. So I am afraid to say that no one can be allowed out without being questioned *and* searched. We're obtaining the necessary warrants as I speak. The security door must remain closed until we recover the missing page. I apologize for the inconvenience, but there's nothing else we can do. We cannot let anyone out of this room without a thorough search."

"Wow," said Julia. "The plot thickens."

Gideon Crew was peering around the room, lips pursed, his blue eyes sparkling. "Identified the thief yet?"

"I still think it's you. You come from a line of thieves and you do look a bit of a rogue. And…you look nervous."

He laughed. "And I'm sure *you're* the thief. A professor of romance languages from Bryn Mawr—talk about the perfect cover."

People were now being fed through the stanchions to where the guards had set up a makeshift screening area, behind a bookcase draped with a heavy curtain. Those who had been searched were being led into another holding area, the two groups kept separate. The room remained sealed in steel.

Several people were continuing to protest, and the temperature in the room was climbing. "We're going to be here all afternoon," Julia said. The novelty was starting to wear off. She had a long drive back to Bryn Mawr. Maybe she should stay in the city and drive back on Monday. She would miss morning classes, but at least she had a good excuse. She glanced over at Gideon and wondered, idly, if he had an apartment in the city.

"Seriously, I don't see any obvious crooks in here," he told her. "Just a lot of boring old white people with names like Murphy and O'Toole."

Suddenly there was a shout. One of the guards, who

had been searching the room, was calling out and gesturing frantically. He was kneeling at a bookcase, the glass door of which was open. The commander and other guards went over, and they all bent down to examine something. It looked to Julia like a piece of paper shoved between two volumes. More activity, discussion, and finally—with gloves—the thing was removed. It was a sheet of vellum, and it looked very much like a page from the Book of Kells. It was brought over to the volume, now back on its stand, and a long examination and a second whispered confabulation ensued.

Once again, the commander gestured to the crowd for quiet. "It appears," he said, "that we've recovered the page cut from the Book of Kells."

A large murmur of relief.

"I'm afraid, however, that we're still going to have to question and search each and every one of you before we can open that security door."

A smattering of angry expostulations.

"The sooner you all get with the program," the commander said wearily, "the sooner all of us will be out of here."

A collective groan. "Oh, God," said Julia. "At this rate, I won't get back to Bryn Mawr until midnight. How I hate driving at night."

"You could always stay with me. I've got a suite at the Gansevoort Hotel, with a view of the High Line."

She looked at him and, to her mortification, found her heart rate accelerating considerably at the thought. "Is that some sort of indecent proposal?"

"As a matter of fact, yes. We'll have a wonderful dinner in the hotel restaurant with a good bottle of wine, talk about nuclear physics and French literature, and then we'll go up to my room and make passionate and indecent love."

"You're awfully direct."

"*Vita brevis*," he said, simply. And the Latin, more than anything else, was why she said yes.

8

It was a fresh summer morning as Gideon walked the block from his hotel to the offices of Effective Engineering Solutions on Little West 12th Street. Dr. Julia Thrum Murphy. He felt more than a twinge of regret. As much as he'd enjoyed her company, he couldn't allow himself to get entangled in any sort of relationship with anyone, not with a death sentence hanging over his head. It wouldn't be fair to her. For her part, she seemed quite happy with a one-night stand and had said good-bye to him with no tone of regret. He would have loved to have seen her again—but it was not to be.

He angrily swiped his card and the unprepossessing doors of EES whispered open; he traversed the cavernous lab spaces, with their shrouded models and setups, the white-coated technicians whispering among themselves or making notations on clipboards; and he made his way to the conference room on the top floor of the building. There he found only the dour, nameless man who served coffee, waiting in his uniform. Gideon took a seat, threw his arms behind his head, and leaned back. "Double espresso, no sugar, thanks."

The man vanished. A moment later, Glinn came in, bringing with him an arctic chill. Silently, he directed his electric wheelchair to the head of the conference table, the humming noise of the motor all the while greeting Gideon got. A moment later Manuel Garza, Glinn's bullish aide-de-camp, entered, followed by half a dozen other EES employees. Nobody said a word.

The steward went around and collected everyone's murmured orders for coffee or tea. Once he had left, Glinn pressed a button on the small console beside the table—evidently starting a recorder—and then began speaking in a neutral tone of voice, giving the date and time, the names of those present. After that, he fell silent, his eye scanning the room and ending on Gideon.

"It seems the third time is not the charm, is it, Dr. Crew?" he said.

When Gideon said nothing, Glinn addressed the group sitting around the table. "Dr. Crew managed two successful operations for us, for which we are very grateful. I am sorry the Book of Kells has proved to be his undoing. After the utter disaster yesterday, it will be going back to Ireland this afternoon, by chartered jet, surrounded by unbreakable security."

Gideon Crew listened to this statement with his arms crossed.

"This botched and amateurish operation of Dr. Crew's, I'm afraid to say, has created enormous difficulties for our client. It has caused an international furor in Ireland and the US. We've lost our chance to acquire the Chi Rho page."

Glinn looked around. "In other words, *we have failed.*"

A grave murmur rippled through the room. Glinn's

gray eye turned back toward Gideon. "Do you have anything to say?"

Gideon uncrossed his arms. "Not really. Except that the book hasn't left the country yet. Something still might happen."

Something still might happen," repeated Garza in a voice laden with sarcasm. There was a frosty silence.

"You never know," Gideon went on. "Remember Yogi Berra. 'It ain't over till it's over.'"

Glinn's unflappable composure began to crack. "Spare us the hoary quotations. We must act now to contain the damage from this disaster."

"It's not a disaster yet. The flight to Dublin leaves at six o'clock. That's ten hours from now."

Glinn frowned. "Are you telling us you have a new plan to steal the page that you so conspicuously failed to acquire yesterday?"

"I'm sorry you don't have more faith in me, Eli."

"Because if you do have some sort of plan B, I'm sure we'd like to hear it."

"No, I don't have a plan B. Because plan A is still in progress."

"You call this a *plan?*" Garza broke in. "You attempt to steal the page, fail in the worst way possible, and in the process you get ID'ed, and we can only thank God you weren't actually caught. The whole business is now front-page news across the US and Europe. Some plan!"

"Do you know where the book is now?" Glinn asked quietly.

"No."

More incredulous looks around the room.

"I've had our people do a little digging," Glinn said,

"and I *do* know where the Book of Kells is right now: in an impregnable vault underneath the Citicorp building. The prime minister of Ireland himself is on his way here to escort it back to his country. It will be in his personal possession from the Citicorp vault all the way to a vault at the Bank of Ireland, guarded by the heaviest security the US Secret Service and Interpol can provide, roads cleared of traffic, chartered jet, all the trimmings. And you think you still have a chance of stealing it?"

"Of stealing the Chi Rho page, yes." Gideon checked his watch.

"And just how can you be so sure?"

"Because before the afternoon is out, you will learn—from the news resource of your choice—that the page cut from the Book of Kells in an attempted robbery is a fake, and that the real page is missing and presumed stolen."

There were shocked looks around the table.

"Is this true?" Glinn asked.

"Of course."

"Well," Glinn said after a moment, returning Gideon's look with a faint, cold smile. "Extraordinary. Although you might have spared us the drama."

"Just think of all the drama you've put me through. Besides, I couldn't help having a little fun."

"So, where's the original? Do you have it?"

"No, I don't have it. As I said, I don't know where it is right now. But I know where it *will* be, probably by the middle of the week."

"And then?"

"And then I *will* steal it—for real, this time."

9

Sᴇʀɢᴇᴀɴᴛ Aᴅᴇʟʟᴇᴘᴏɪsᴇ Jᴏʜɴsᴏɴ was in charge of the Third Tier Evidence Vaults in the vast basement complex of One Police Plaza, in Lower Manhattan, almost in the shadow of the Brooklyn Bridge. Sergeant Johnson had been a chain of custody supervisor for ten years, and during that time, in each of those years, she was the supervisor who'd experienced the lowest rate of CoC infractions. For that extraordinary record, she had been awarded an "Integrity" commendation with a dark blue star and a Meritorious Police Duty citation, both of which she wore proudly on the ample front of her uniform. She had fifteen clerks handling evidence curation for her, as well as another dozen assistants and technicians, and she managed them with military precision and correctness. She knew as well as anyone that evidence management was critical to the outcome of criminal prosecutions. While she might not be the most beloved supervisor in the Evidence Vaults, she was the most respected. People were proud to work for her.

It was a Friday, nine o'clock in the morning, and

Sergeant Johnson had been in since seven getting an early start on the computer paperwork of the week, reviewing all the evidence that had been checked out or returned, every movement of every shell casing and hair and DNA swab, whether for trial, lab work, or on-site examination. Maintaining the chain of custody of evidence was of paramount importance, and in the past few years the entire procedure had been computerized, with digital video recording of absolutely everything that was done to a piece of evidence, by whom, when, and why.

Sergeant Johnson was never happy when someone arrived to examine evidence by surprise, and she was particularly irritated that it would occur on a Friday morning. But occur it did. One of her evidence clerks arrived with a tall, thin gentleman in an expensive dark suit, sporting a wiffle cut that practically screamed *FBI*. And sure enough, he was a special agent of the most annoying kind, one of those who thought they were God's gift to law enforcement and that beat cops were a lower form of life.

"I've spent over an hour now getting credentialed," the man said in a sarcastic drawl. "I tip my hat to the efficiency of the NYPD."

With this, he held out his badge and a folder containing his credentials.

Sergeant Johnson never got into it with anybody for any reason. She rose from her desk—her sheer size was often all that it took to quell a sparky personality—gave the man a smile, and took the badge and folder.

"Special Agent Morrison?" she asked.

"That's what it says on the badge," he said.

A real hard-ass. She looked at the ID, which was brand new, and the badge, also new, and then looked at him. He looked new, too. Fresh out of the academy. They were the worst.

"So you're working on the Kells case, Agent Morrison?"

"It's all spelled out in the file."

"And you want to examine the forged page, I see."

"I repeat, it's all spelled out in the request, Sergeant."

"You understand, Special Agent Morrison, that in CoC situations the less evidence handling that goes on, the better. It's my responsibility"—she emphasized the *my*—"to make sure any evidence handling is necessary and justified. I'm telling you this to make sure you understand the procedures."

"I'm sure you will find that my examination of the evidence is not on a whim, and I can assure you the FBI would not be happy if my request were denied."

Sergeant Johnson had dealt with Morrison's type countless times before, and it was almost laughable how predictable he was. Spoiling for a fight even before there was reason for a fight. She opened the folder and carefully examined his credentials and documents. Everything did indeed look to be in order. The FBI had gone through all the proper channels, the only issue being that Agent Morrison was three hours early for his scheduled appointment. But again, that was typical FBI. The reason for the examination was standard and pro forma, evidentially justified and legal.

She approved the documentation, signed it, stamped it, and handed it back. "I will accompany you," she said, rising.

"Fine," said Morrison.

He didn't seem interested in knowing why, so she

added, truthfully, "I do this with many high-profile cases. My testimony can be helpful if the defense raises CoC issues."

"It's your call," he said.

Johnson, the evidence clerk, and the FBI agent proceeded to the elevators and descended to the basement, which had been completely renovated in 2011 as part of a major expansion project. Much of the new space had been devoted to state-of-the-art evidence curation, and entering it was like entering the spotless corridors of a first-class hospital. It was a long walk to the Third Tier Vaults, which housed all the evidence in active, open criminal investigations. It was the most important of the three tiers of evidence storage.

After passing many numbered doors, they came to the appropriate storage room. The clerk deactivated the alarm, and the door opened to reveal a beautiful, clean white room with locked cabinets and a plastic table and chairs. There were cameras in all four corners of the ceiling, which Sergeant Johnson knew were recording their every move.

The clerk put on sterile, powder-free latex surgical gloves, scanned the numbered cabinets, and approached one. She punched a code into a nearby keypad, and the cabinet sprang open. Peering inside, she removed a shallow tray and brought it to the table.

"Do you need to handle it?" Johnson asked Morrison.

"Yes."

"Then you'll need a face mask and gloves, as well." She almost added a hair net to the list, just to be difficult, except for the fact that Agent Morrison had almost no hair. Frowning, Agent Morrison donned the gloves and a face mask, and then sat down at the table. He pulled the tray toward him and looked down at the forged page of the Book of Kells. Johnson, curious, edged closer to take a look. *What an amazing-looking thing,* she thought, *so intricate.* It would have been nice to see the original—before it was stolen.

Morrison reached into his suit and removed a notebook, which he laid down on the table beside him, and began taking notes in pencil (pens weren't allowed). He placed a loupe to his eye, examining the page silently. The time began to drag on, and on, and on. Five minutes went by, and then ten. What on earth was he looking at? She glanced at her watch but decided to say nothing. She was fairly sure Morrison was no expert, and the ridiculous examination was nothing more than the man feeding his own swollen ego.

She and the evidence clerk exchanged a glance.

And now, finally, Agent Morrison picked the page up and examined it while holding it closer to the light, squinting at it and turning it this way and that. Again, the examination went on interminably. Again Johnson exchanged another glance with the clerk, more exasperated this time. Her legs began to ache from standing, and finally she eased herself down into a seat; the clerk, with evident relief, did the same. Would this never end?

Yet still he examined it. Now he was taking more notes, writing rapidly in his notebook in an illegible hand, acting like the expert she was sure he wasn't.

Suddenly there was a clatter and she rose from the chair to see that the agent had clumsily knocked his notebook off the table, which was now lying spread out beneath it, with loose papers scattered all about. He had jumped up, the page in hand, and was bending down to pick up the notebook, his back to her. She was about to call out to him to put the damn page down while he collected his things but then he turned, still holding the page in one gloved hand, while with the other he fixed the rifled pages of his notebook, putting them back in order.

With a disapproving stare Johnson sat back down, while the agent went back to his examination, taking still more notes.

"Done," he said at last, placing the page back in its tray.

Without a word, Johnson creaked once again to her feet. The clerk put the tray back into the cabinet, made sure it was locked; they signed out and proceeded out of the room and back down the long white corridors. All routine.

Sergeant Johnson didn't realize they had a problem until three hours later, when the real Special Agent Morrison arrived for his appointment—right on time.

10

Gideon went straight from One Police Plaza to the EES offices on Little West 12th Street. Glinn and Garza met him in the cavernous engineering space, and Gideon followed them past elaborate dioramas, mainframe computers, and heavily scribbled whiteboards to a room in the back. It contained a state-of-the-art chemistry laboratory. A stooped technician with a lugubrious face was awaiting them.

Glinn's wheelchair whispered along the polished concrete floor, and the door to the lab slid shut behind them.

"Do you have it?" Garza asked.

Gideon removed a notebook from his suit and opened it, displaying the small, jewel-like page. Glinn reached out and took it, staring at it with great intensity. The man's normally expressionless face was almost comically excited, the good eye glittering, his every movement sharp and precise. After staring at it for several minutes, he signaled the technician, who came over, latex-gloved hands bearing a tray onto which Glinn placed the page.

He turned back to Gideon. "Tell us how you did it," he said, unable to disguise the eagerness in his voice.

"Well," Gideon began, "after looking over the specs, I realized the security in the East Room of the Morgan was pretty much perfect. There was no way I was going to get the page out myself. So I had to figure out a way for someone else to take it out for me."

"How?"

"First I had to stage a spectacular, and apparently botched, robbery."

Glinn nodded.

"I went on the final Sunday, when I knew the East Room would be packed. I set off a weak flash-bang with smoke, to scare and temporarily blind the room. Then I went to the case and attached a device that detonated a small shaped charge, which in turn split the bulletproof cube containing the book—not unlike cleaving a diamond."

"A shaped charge designed by you, no doubt, given your work at Los Alamos with implosion bombs." Glinn waved a withered hand. "Go on."

"After splitting the case, I took out the Book of Kells, cut out the Chi Rho page, and gave it a very brief chemical treatment. Then I left the book on the floor and hid the page elsewhere in the room. It all took less than sixty seconds. The room cleared of smoke, and then things proceeded like clockwork. They discovered the book was missing a page; they searched for the page; they found it. At this point, the job had all the hallmarks of a botched robbery. They questioned and searched everyone who had been in the room—one of them had to be the thief—but found nothing, not on me or anyone else. They didn't look as hard as they might have if the page had remained missing. They thought they had the entire book."

Gideon smiled. He was coming to the good part. "But I knew that, at some point, they would have an expert conservator examine the cut page. Just to make sure it wasn't damaged or in need of special attention. They might have even decided to test it to see if it was real or not. At any rate, the Chi Rho page I'd cut out immediately failed a UV examination, indicating it was a forgery."

"Very good."

"How did you know they would do this?" Garza asked.

"Because I bought a real illuminated manuscript page in London, gave it my special chemical treatment, and brought it into Sotheby's. There it was pronounced a fake by one of the world's greatest experts on illuminated manuscripts."

"Very good."

"So—as soon as they found the page was a fake—they realized they weren't dealing with a botched robbery, but a *successful* one. Clearly, they concluded, the thief had brought a fake page into the room to substitute for the real one and hid it in the room, to make everyone *think* it was a botched robbery and that nothing had been stolen. You see, I had to make them think the real page was actually a fake. It had to fail the standard UV test."

"Clever," said Glinn. "So what was this 'special chemical treatment' of yours?"

Gideon reached into his pocket and removed a small spray can. "La Spiaggia Scent-Free Ultra Sunblock, SPF 70."

Everyone in the room stared at the small canister.

"The ingredients are titanium oxide, zinc oxide, and octyl methoxycinnamate—all broad-spectrum UV blockers. All it took was a quick spritz on both sides of the page and the deed was done. And when I was searched and the guards found the canister of sunblock—which of course they did—they thought nothing of it."

Glinn nodded his approval.

"So when the page—covered in sunblock—was subjected to the standard UV tests, nothing happened. None of these glorious medieval mineral pigments fluoresced as they should have if the page was real. The page was therefore assumed to be a fake, made with aniline dyes! And now the powers that be realized—or so they thought—the thief had gotten away with the real page, leaving behind this substitute."

"Brilliant," murmured Glinn.

"Thus, the 'fake' page became evidence in a criminal investigation. As such, it was sent to the evidence vaults underneath One Police Plaza. And this morning, Eli, thanks to your phony credentials and your scheduling data from the FBI database, I was able to get into the vault and switch the fake *real* page with a *real* fake page. It was just a matter of prestidigitation, at which I excel, done under the table, out of sight of the video cameras. Now they have the fake that they always thought they had, and we've got the real page. And no one is the wiser—save for the fact that two Agent Morrisons visited the evidence labs today."

Glinn clasped his withered hands together, almost as if he were praying. "This is amazing. *Amazing.*"

"Thank you. And now, I'd like to know why this page is so important."

"And so you shall." Glinn turned. "Dr. Stanislavsky?"

"Vee are ready, Dr. Glinn," said the Munster-like technician, picking up the tray with the page and bringing it over to a series of other, shallow trays filled with liquids, akin to developing trays, each with its own thermometer. He took the manuscript page, laid it on a screen with a handle, and immersed it in the first liquid.

"What, exactly, are you doing to it?" Gideon asked, alarmed.

"You shall see," Glinn replied.

After timing the bath, Dr. Stanislavsky raised the screen and placed it in a second bath, again timing it.

The bath became cloudy.

"Hey, what's going on?" Gideon asked, staring at the clouding water. It looked to him like the ink on the page was dissolving.

The technician raised the screen. The colors of the intricate Chi Rho image were now running all over the place, along with a heavy white underpainting.

"What the *fuck*?" Gideon yelled, taking a step forward. Garza laid a firm, restraining hand on his arm.

The page went into the third tray, a laminar flow bath. Gideon could see, through the shimmering surface of the moving liquid, that the Chi Rho image was vanishing, dissolving . . . and then it was gone. With a deft motion the technician plucked the page from the bath with rubber-nose tweezers and held it up, dripping fluid.

It was blank.

11

Y OU SON OF a bitch!" Gideon cried as Garza tightened his grip. "I can't believe you just destroyed—you fucking *destroyed*—that priceless work of art!" He jerked his arm away from Garza, took another step toward Glinn.

Unperturbed, Glinn held up a hand. "Wait. Please reserve judgment until the end."

Breathing hard, Gideon fought to get himself under control. He couldn't believe it. He had been conned into participating in a horrible act of destruction. This was unbelievable, despicable. He would go to the cops, tell them all about Glinn and the theft. What did he have to lose? He was going to be dead in ten months anyway.

Still using the tweezers, the technician laid the now blank sheet under blotters to absorb the excess moisture, and then put it on a glass stage, part of a large machine.

"That," said Glinn calmly, nodding at the machine, "is an XRF analyzer. X-ray fluorescence."

As the technician busied himself with the machine, Glinn continued. "Are you familiar with the term *palimpsest?*"

"No."

"In the Middle Ages, manuscript vellum was a very costly material. Only the finest skins could be used—sheep, calf, or goat. The best came from fetal animals. The skin had to be prepared by skilled experts—split, soaked, limed, scudded, and stretched. Because it was so expensive, monks often reused vellum from old books. They'd scrape off the old text, resoak and wash the vellum, and use it again."

"Get to the point."

"A *palimpsest* is the ghostly shadow of that earlier, original text. Some of the most important and famous Greek and Latin texts are today known only as palimpsests, having later been scraped off and written or painted over for other purposes. That's what we're looking for here."

"There's an older text underneath the Chi Rho painting?"

"There's something under there, but it's not a text."

"For God's sake, did you have to *destroy* it to see it?"

"Unfortunately, yes. The Chi Rho page had an ultraheavy underpainting of white flake, a medieval paint made with lead. We had to remove that to see what was underneath."

"What could possibly be more important than what was there?" Gideon asked angrily. "You yourself said the Book of Kells is the finest illuminated manuscript in existence!"

"We have reason to believe what's underneath *is* more important." Glinn turned back to the technician. "Ready?"

"Run it."

Stanislavsky nodded.

The technician raised the stage on the analyzer, adjusted some dials, and punched a command into a digital keyboard. A faint, blurry drawing sprang to life on the embedded screen. Slowly, like a master, Stanislavsky adjusted various dials and controls, fine-tuning the image. At first it looked like a random series of dots, lines, and squiggles, but slowly it came into sharper view.

"What the hell is that?" Gideon asked, peering more closely.

"A map."

"A map? To a treasure?"

"A map to something better than a treasure. Something absolutely, utterly, and completely extraordinary. Something that will change the world." Glinn's gray eye fixed itself on Gideon. "And your next assignment is to go get it."

12

Gideon and Garza followed the wheelchair of Eli Glinn as it glided through the long, silent upper corridors of EES, heading to an area Gideon had never been in before. They passed through a door leading into two small rooms, dimly lit. Gideon, still struggling with surprise and residual anger, looked around. The first room was a gem-like library, its mahogany bookcases filled with rich leather bindings, winking with gold. A Persian rug covered the floor, and at the far end stood a small marble fireplace, in which burned a turf fire. There was a rich smell of leather, parchment, and buckram. In the middle stood a refectory table and chairs. The room beyond was exactly its opposite: a sterile white-walled laboratory, all stainless steel and plastic surfaces, lit by stark fluorescent lighting.

Glinn motioned toward the table. "Please, sit down."

Gideon complied silently, and Garza took a seat opposite him. A moment later a lab-coated technician came in carrying an enlarged digital reproduction of the strange map that had been hidden beneath the Chi Rho painting.

With a nod from Glinn, he laid the map out on the table, then withdrew.

Glinn opened a sideboard beside the fireplace, revealing various cut-glass decanters and bottles and a small refrigerator. "Would anyone care for a drink?"

Gideon shook his head.

Glinn poured himself a measure of port in a hand-blown tumbler. He brought it to the table, took a sip, gave a small sigh of satisfaction, and laid his claw-like hand down on the map.

"I'd like to tell you a story about a man named Saint Columba."

Gideon waited.

"Columba entered the Clonard Monastery in Ireland around the year 550. He was a big, powerful man, strong and self-assured, not at all the stereotypical image of a humble monk. He was also charismatic and intelligent, and he quickly attracted notice. His mentor at the monastery was a monk named Saint Finian. As the years passed, Columba's fame and circle of friends grew. However, over the course of a decade, the two men—student and teacher—gradually came into opposition. In 560, they got into a terrific argument over who had the right to copy a rare psalter. Both had fiery tempers, and both had powerful friends. The dispute escalated, drawing in others, until it culminated in a fight—a battle, in fact. A horrific slaughter ensued, in which as many as three thousand people were killed. It became known in history as the Battle of the Book. The church was horrified and, blaming Columba, decided to excommunicate him. But Columba pleaded with them. He managed to avert excommunication by agreeing to go into exile in the savage hinterlands of Scotland and convert three thousand pagans to atone for the three thousand killed in the battle.

"So he and a group of monks departed by sea from Ireland to Scotland, carrying with them Columba's priceless collection of manuscripts. They landed on a lonely island off the coast of Scotland, in the heart of the tribal lands of the Picts. There, Columba founded the Abbey of Iona."

Glinn paused, slowly lifting the glass full of tawny liquid to his thin lips and taking a long sip.

"Enter our client. I regret that I cannot reveal his identity. Suffice it to say he is a man of unimpeachable integrity who has only the good of humanity as his goal."

"Or so the client assures us," Garza rumbled.

Glinn turned to Garza. "So I assure you. You well understand, Manuel, our requirements about client confidentiality."

"Of course. But as chief of operations for this project, I'd like to know who I'm working for."

There was a brief, uncomfortable silence. Finally, Glinn cleared his throat and went on. "Our client is, among other things, a collector of medieval manuscripts. In his searches, he came across an incomplete set of documents kept at Iona: *Annales Monasterii Columbae,*' annals of the monastery of Columba.' It was a sort of daily journal of the goings-on at the monastery. They were written in Latin, of course. It was a very rare find, as these sorts of records almost never survive.

"The *Annales* told a curious story about a monk who found an old Greek manuscript among the monastery's stores of secondhand vellum. The vellum had already been scraped, ready to be bleached and reused. According to the journal, however, the old Greek text was still legible. The monk read it, was amazed, and brought it to Saint Columba."

Glinn plucked a sheet of paper from his jacket pocket and referred to it. "The manuscript in question was an early Greek geography, and it described various legendary wonders of the world. Among these was a most intriguing place: an island 'far in the West, where the earth meets the sky.' The geography went on to mention a 'great cave overhung with laurels on the face of a cliff far above the sea.' There, the manuscript claimed, a 'secret *remedium* could be found, the source of eternal healing.' The manuscript contained directions to this location, which was 'beyond the land of Iberia, two thousand *dolichoi* west of Tartessos.' Iberia was the name the ancients gave to Spain, and Tartessos was believed to be an ancient city at the mouth of the Quadalquivir River. A *dolichos* was a Greek measure of distance equaling about a mile and a half. In short, this was a location far, far beyond the boundary of what was then the known world."

"Two thousand *dolichoi* west of Spain?" said Gideon. "That's three thousand miles. That would put this cave in...in the New World."

Glinn smiled and replaced his glass on the table. "Exactly."

"So you're saying these Greeks *discovered* the New World?"

"Yes."

Gideon merely shook his head.

"The old Greek manuscript gave this wondrous island a name: Phorkys, after an obscure god of the sea. Columba believed that God had placed this manuscript into his hands for a reason. He and his monks, being

Irish, were already expert seafarers—and they had excellent ships. So Columba ordered an expedition to seek out Phorkys and bring back the *remedium*, the healing balm.

"According to the journal, the monastery outfitted three ships, and a group of seafaring monks sailed from Iona, initially bound for the Mediterranean, preparing to follow the directions in the old Greek manuscript. They were gone for years. Columba eventually gave them up for lost. Finally, one sorry ship returned with half a dozen survivors. The monks had quite a story to tell."

Glinn paused dramatically, his eyebrow raised, then went on in his gray, neutral voice.

"It had been a terrible journey. They traveled beyond the Straits of Gibraltar, only to have their ships caught in a storm in the Atlantic and driven southwestward, wrecked among some unknown islands that were, most likely, the Cape Verdes. They built new ships and set sail again. This time they encountered ideal weather, favorable currents, and steady trades that carried them across the sea to 'unknown islands off a savage coast.' Following the directions in the old Greek map, they finally reached Phorkys. Here they were beset by 'the most dreadful monsters and giants,' who guarded the healing balm, referred to in the *Annales* as 'a secret physic, the jewel of the deep-delved soil.' Many of the monks were slain by these monsters."

Glinn paused again to slowly savor another mouthful of the port. He was enjoying retelling this story.

"Nevertheless, the surviving monks defeated the monsters long enough to steal a *cista*, or 'chest,' of the physic. Returning to the abbey, they presented it to Columba. He was overjoyed and ordered the monks to draw a new map, a *Christian* map, showing the route to Phorkys. And he ordered the old, pagan map destroyed."

He stopped, eyes glittering. "And that is the map we now possess—thanks to you."

"That's quite a legend," Gideon said drily. "So ancient Greeks, and then Irish monks, visited the New World long before Columbus."

"Yes. But that's not the main point. The last surviving fragment of the *Annales* tells that the monks used this *cista* full of the physic to heal themselves of 'grievous wounds, afflictions, diseases and infirmities.' Columba himself took the physic, and as a result lived such a long and vigorous life that he was able to fulfill his mission and convert those three thousand souls.

"But at the end of Columba's life, the monastery fell on hard times. They were repeatedly attacked by Viking marauders. Columba, terrified that the Phorkys Map would fall into the wrong hands, ordered it hidden 'beneath layers of gold and lapis and other colors of the greatest brilliance.' Not long after that fact was recorded in the *Annales*, the monastery of Iona was destroyed by the Vikings. Many of the monks were butchered, and the rest fled back to Ireland—to take refuge in the Monastery of Kells. The map was never spoken of again."

Glinn drained his glass, replaced it on the table.

"Enter my client. He was sure the map described in the *Annales* still existed. But he couldn't find it. So he came to me."

He removed a silk handkerchief from his pocket and dabbed his lips, carefully refolding it and slipping it back in place.

"The problem proved an elementary one. When the

monks fled Iona ahead of the marauding Vikings, they carried with them their most holy relics. Among those was a book, a wondrous illuminated gospel. Which became known—after its new home—as the Book of Kells."

He paused significantly.

"Recall Columba's instructions: to hide the map 'beneath layers of gold and lapis and other colors of the greatest brilliance.' Naturally, I concluded it had been painted over and bound into the Book of Kells. But which page? That was even easier. One of the pages of the book had already excited scholarly interest because it appeared to be of a different material than the others."

"The Chi Rho page," Gideon said.

"Exactly. The Book of Kells was written on the finest vellum available—fetal calfskin. But the vellum of the Chi Rho page is different—stronger and thicker. And the Chi Rho page is the most heavily painted page in the entire book. The vellum was first painted with flake white—which has lead as its base—which was totally unnecessary: the fine vellum was snow white to begin with. It seemed obvious to me the Phorkys Map was hidden under the paint on that page. And thanks to you, we've now found it."

He tapped the enlargement of the map with a crooked finger.

"Which brings me to your new mission: to follow this map to Phorkys."

Gideon was no longer able to keep the sarcasm from his voice. "And find the secret to eternal life?"

"Not eternal life. *Healing*."

"Don't tell me you actually *believe* that legend?"

"I do."

Gideon shook his head. "I'm not sure who's more gullible—you or this mysterious client of yours. Greeks discovering the New World. Monsters guarding some kind of magic medicine."

Glinn said nothing.

Now Gideon rose. "I thought you had a real mission for me. It's bad enough that, thanks to me, a priceless masterpiece has been destroyed. Now you want me to head off on some wild goose chase? I'm sorry, but I want no part of this."

Without a word, Glinn removed a manila folder from his briefcase and laid it on the table, giving it a gentle push toward Gideon. It was labeled PHYSICAL ANTHROPOLOGY, IONA. "This is a confidential report on an archaeological excavation of the graveyard at Iona Abbey. Archaeologists recovered the remains of quite a few monks, many dating back to the time of the Phorkys Map."

"So?"

"The archaeologists found skeletons of monks who had suffered dreadful injuries, many no doubt at the hands of Viking marauders. Arms chopped off, skulls split, eyes gouged out. They found evidence of birth defects, deformities, various illnesses. But here's the rub: the skeletons had healed up almost perfectly. These monks had recovered from wounds, deformities, and illnesses that should have been permanently disabling or even fatal."

"Medicine is replete with amazing recoveries," said Gideon.

"Perhaps. But that report notes that some of the monks *had regrown entire limbs.*"

There was a dead silence. Gideon finally said, "I don't buy it, Eli."

"When a frog or lizard loses and regrows a limb, the process leaves unmistakable, unambiguous signs. You can see where the bone was severed, where it began to grow back. The new limb is often smaller and weaker than the old one. The bone is newer, fresher, younger. This is *exactly* what the physical anthropologists found when they examined the skeletons of some of these monks. It's all here, in this folder. The science is impeccable. They are mystified. Their research continues. But we . . . *we* know why these monks healed."

Gideon simply stared in disbelief. Now he was sorry he hadn't accepted a glass of port.

Glinn opened the folder, displaying an array of electron micrographs of bones. "See for yourself. The dig was sponsored by the Scottish government and—not surprisingly, when they discovered this—was immediately hushed up. That of course was no impediment to EES. So you see, Gideon, this isn't a wild goose chase after all. The monks truly did find a *remedium*, a physic, that could make the blind see, the crippled walk, limbs regrow."

Once again the crooked finger tapped the paper with its long witch's nail. "This is no legend. *The skeletons don't lie.*"

13

A LONG SILENCE gathered in the room as Gideon stared from Glinn to the folder and back again. The head of EES was deadly serious—and, it seemed, as sane as ever.

Glinn finally broke the silence. "Let's have lunch before we examine the map in further detail. We should give our experts a little time to make an initial examination. But rest assured, now that we have the map they'll be working on its decipherment flat-out, twenty-four seven. Our client is most anxious to get his hands on that drug."

"And do what with it?" Gideon asked.

"He will see to it that the drug is researched, tested, developed, and shared with the world."

"And you trust him? This medicine, if real, would be worth billions to whoever brings it to market."

"I can absolutely assure you: he has no intention of profiting financially from this. He will create a nonprofit foundation to bring the drug to market. Now I'll order in lunch for you two."

"You're not joining us?" Gideon asked.

"I have much to take care of."

On the spur of the moment, Gideon followed Glinn into the hall. "I need to...ask you something."

Glinn paused, turning the wheelchair around to face him, and arched the eyebrow on his one good eye inquiringly.

"This drug...I can't help but wonder if it might cure my AVM."

Glinn gazed at him quietly, his face unreadable. "Impossible to say. Also impossible to say is whether it would heal me." Glinn held up his withered hand and made a gesture encompassing his crippled legs, eye, and arm. "But it seems you and I have a powerful, *personal* motive to succeed, do we not?"

Gideon watched the wheelchair move away down the corridor. His initial skepticism had begun to give way to mental turmoil. Glinn, who was well aware of Gideon's terminal condition, and what the *remedium* might mean to him, hadn't been the one to bring it up. But quite obviously he'd known just how powerful a motivation it would be.

An hour later, Gideon and Garza followed the wheelchair through the halls of EES, descending to the first floor. Gideon hadn't been able to get the story of the physic out of his mind. *Perfect healing. Regrown entire limbs.* But his initial excitement had dimmed. No medicine, however powerful, could heal the congenital tangle of blood vessels in his brain that doctors had said would kill him in less than a year.

They entered the cavernous central space of EES, and he was glad of the distraction. The firm was always busy with obscure projects, but it seemed to Gideon that today it was busier than usual. Everyone worked industriously in the hangar-like room, mingling, chatting, looking over each other's shoulders. Glinn had once explained that such a work environment broke down compartmentalization and encouraged spontaneous collaboration. As they made their way across the floor, one mysterious project in particular attracted Gideon's attention. Every time he'd entered EES this project had grown in size, but as it did its nature grew more obscure. Today half a dozen engineers were swarming about a detailed, three-dimensional model of the ocean floor. It looked like an advanced deepwater drilling project.

Glinn greeted one of the engineers as they passed, a young Asian woman who was studying a dusty manuscript written in what appeared to be Greek. When they reached a door in the far wall, he touched its adjoining keypad and the door opened to reveal a private laboratory. Within, a small, restless man with a tonsure of unruly white hair seemed to be holding forth loudly to a figure on a computer screen—apparently, via Skype—speaking in a language Gideon did not recognize. The tonsured man took no notice of their arrival and continued his argument until at last he closed the window on the display in exasperation.

"Oh, these *Latvians!*" he said to no one in particular.

He was one of the very few employees Gideon had seen at EES who was not wearing a lab coat. Instead, he was dressed in a plaid jacket of questionable taste, complete with a mismatched bow tie and an egg-streaked shirtfront.

"Allow me to introduce Dr. Chester Brock," Glinn said,

"former professor of medieval studies at Oxford and one of the world's experts in medieval manuscripts and maps. Dr. Brock, may I introduce Dr. Gideon Crew, who obtained the map for us."

"I say, Glinn," Brock said querulously, after giving Gideon a graceless handshake, "I can't work in a shed. I need more space."

"But you declined the common room," Glinn replied in a fatherly, indulgent tone. "I'll see if I can't find you something more comfortable. For now, though, I'd like you to give Dr. Crew a briefing on the map."

Brock continued to scrutinize Gideon with goggle eyes. "You're not a medievalist, I hope." For such a small man, his voice was surprisingly deep.

Gideon wondered why he hoped that, but before he could answer, Glinn said: "Dr. Crew is a physicist. You're our only medievalist. Why would we need another?"

"Why, indeed?" said Brock, mollified. "Very well, come with me." He led them through the cramped lab to a table. The Chi Rho page, now perfectly dry, lay on a tray on the table beneath a digital overhead projector. Brock tapped some commands into a laptop and an image of the map appeared, greatly enlarged, on a flat panel mounted on the wall. With some deft digital manipulation, Brock was able to sharpen the map into crisp detail.

It wasn't anything like a real map. The mapmaker had made no attempt to locate geographic landmarks or create a two-dimensional representation of the landscape. Instead, it was a sort of continuous ribbon, with a series of parallel strips sprinkled with little pictures of islands or other images, many accompanied by short descriptions in Latin.

"That map will never get the AAA seal of approval," said Gideon.

"This *map*," Brock said with a sniff, "is based on a type of Roman atlas called an *itinerarium*. During the empire, travelers needed to find their way along the road system the Romans built. They used maps like these: stacks of line segments of the journey, with towns, villages, forks in the road, and landmarks all indicated. There was no attempt to reproduce the landscape—they were simply guides from landmark to landmark. It appears that this Phorkys Map is the early-medieval equivalent, only transferred from land to water—a sort of primitive sailing chart." He pointed to the ribbon of lines. "I've only just begun to analyze the map, of course, but this line, broken up into segments, would appear to indicate the sailing route. And these little figures indicate various landmarks the traveler should take note of along the way. Take this one, for example. We've numbered all the landmark symbols on the map, and this one is number four."

The plump, sausage-like finger pointed at a tiny picture of an island rising from the sea, barely more than a rock, containing two twisted trees that looked like horns. A deft series of keystrokes magnified the image on the screen.

"The attached inscription says: *Perge ad orientem insula Diaboli, tunc pete meridiem*. That is: 'Seek the east side of the island of the Devil, and then go south.'"

"That's pretty vague," said Gideon.

"Indeed," said Brock. "Particularly when you consider those two trees are surely long gone. Here's another example, which we've labeled clue five." He indicated a second tiny drawing, which showed a passageway between two bodies of land, a sort of strait, one with a split rock on one shore that vaguely resembled a cross. "The legend for this image says: 'Your path is through the strait of the cross.' That's it. No compass rose, no indication of distance. Note, however, that there are a total of exactly nine images, or clues."

Gideon squinted at the map. "I've got to admit the draftsmanship is amazing."

"The Irish monks were geniuses at the art of miniaturization. Most of the work was done with single-haired brushes."

"So where is this mysterious island located, exactly?" Gideon asked.

"Ah! The million-dollar question..." Brock paused, his green eyes goggling. "And the answer would appear to be: somewhere in the Caribbean."

"Caribbean? How do you know?"

"I've already identified with some certainty the third landmark in the map, here. *Columpnas Herculis transiens*—the Pillars of Hercules. That was the universal name in the ancient world for the Strait of Gibraltar. Unfortunately, most of the other landmarks seem to be obscure, quixotic, and deliberately misleading."

"Why 'deliberately'?"

"Because it says it right here: 'Only those favored by God may follow this map.' The monks would have made it difficult to follow, to ensure that only those whom God helped could do so. The rest would perish."

Glinn interjected. "Dr. Brock's begun feeding the details into the large geographic database we maintain here at EES."

"But what makes you think they reached the Caribbean?"

"Because from the Cape Verde Islands, where according to the *Annales* the monks were shipwrecked and had to rebuild their ships, the Canaries Current heads south and southwesterly along the African coast, where it turns west and becomes the Northern Equatorial Current. The trades blow steadily with the current. Our computer models already indicate that the two combined would have taken the monks along the precise route Columbus followed on his third voyage. That would have carried them straight into the Caribbean."

Glinn pointed at the screen. "As evidence, all these little islands in this part of the map could only be located in the Caribbean."

"I've also identified the starting point," said Brock.

"Isn't he a marvel?" Glinn said with evident pride.

Brock shrugged this off. "It's here, in what would be the eastern Aegean Sea." He zoomed in on the first picture at the top left of the map, showing four hills in profile, along with a tiny, stylized drawing of a horse.

"*Ibi est initium*," said Brock, reading the accompanying Latin inscription. "'There is the beginning.' The four hills are a well-known landmark on the coast of Turkey."

"And the horse?"

"No idea why there is a horse—not yet, that is."

Gideon's eye wandered along the route. "What about that inscription at the end?"

"I was just getting to that," said Brock. "First of all, we can see the phrase *Hic sunt gigantes*: 'Here there be giants.' And then: *Respondeo ad quaestionem, ipsa pergamena*."

"Which means?"

"It would appear to be a riddle," said Brock. "It literally means: 'I, the very page, answer the question.'"

"And what is the question?" asked Gideon.

"Yes, indeed, that itself is a mystery. I would say the question would be: What is the nature of this cure? Is it plant, animal, insect, or something else?"

Glinn spoke. "It seems to me the answer would be somehow hidden on the page, most likely in one of these little drawings. The map tells us how to get there, but the answer to the riddle tells us what to look for."

Toggling his wheelchair, Glinn turned toward Gideon. "We've made some important deductions in the last hour. But as you can see, there's still much we need to learn. Even so, there's no reason to wait—in fact there are many good arguments against doing so. As a result, we've already begun work on chartering and outfitting a boat in the Caribbean. You'll be on a flight the day after tomorrow."

"Wait, hold on. I'm no sailor!"

"You'll have a licensed captain on board."

"I don't like the water." Gideon decided not to mention that he was prone to seasickness.

"You'll adjust," Glinn said. "You're just the man for this assignment."

"I suppose that's what your computer model tells you?"

"As a matter of fact, yes. A journey like this will take improvisation. You're the master of improv."

"I'll improv my way right into Davy Jones's locker."

Glinn looked at him appraisingly. "I'm surprised at you, Gideon. This journey won't be like your other assignments. You're going for a cruise in the Caribbean. There's no danger, no physical challenge."

"Are you forgetting about the giants?" Gideon asked.

Everyone laughed.

"Our initial estimate is that this Phorkys will be found somewhere in the southern Caribbean," Glinn said. "If, for example, the Irish monks picked up the Caribbean Current near Barbados, it would have carried them through"—he paused a moment—"the Windward Islands, and then parallel to the coast of Venezuela and Colombia, perhaps even as far as the Mosquito Coast of Nicaragua and Honduras."

"That's a huge area to cover."

"Yes. Encompassing hundreds, even thousands, of islands. And of course the map is full of dirty tricks. It's intentionally misleading."

Gideon had to admire the speed with which they had deduced so much about a map that was so obviously obscure. "In other words, we might be wandering around for weeks," he said. "Sipping champagne, sunbathing, and visiting every single island and surveying the beach—just in case."

"Now you're getting into the spirit of it," laughed Glinn. "Trust me, compared with your last assignment, this one's a walk in Central Park."

14

G̲ideon exited the lab into the cavernous space, Garza following behind him.

"Nothing like that good old railroaded feeling, eh?" Gideon asked.

"I wouldn't complain if I were you. A cruise in the Caribbean? I'll take the assignment, thank you."

"He gets on my nerves."

"Welcome to the Glinn's-a-pain-in-the-ass club."

As they walked through the enormous lab, Gideon glanced over at Garza. He knew Garza didn't much care for him, especially his brash, lone-wolf way of doing things. He in turn found Garza to be uptight and rule-bound. It was true that the two of them weren't exactly buddies. But maybe it didn't have to be that way.

"How about a drink?" he asked impulsively as they went through the double set of doors leading to the street.

Garza paused to look at him. The offer had taken him by surprise. "Well . . . sure."

*   *   *

Spice Market was crowded, as usual, but they were able to grab a small table in the corner. Gideon ordered a Beefeater martini, Garza an IPA.

As the waitress left, Gideon looked at Garza more closely. He was a small, dark, heavily muscled man, with tightly curled black hair fringed white at the temples. His eyes had an intelligent gleam in them.

"How long have you been working at EES?" he said to break the ice.

"Twelve years. Ever since Eli and I got out of the military."

"Military?"

Garza nodded. "I was an engineering specialist on Glinn's team."

"What kind of team?"

"Special Forces. Came up through Airborne, then the Rangers."

"What kind of work did you do?"

"We blew things up, mostly."

"What kind of things?"

"I'd tell you, but then I'd have to kill you."

Gideon chuckled. "If you've tagged along with Glinn all these years, you must enjoy working for him."

"*Enjoy* isn't the word. Let me put it this way: the man's an honest-to-God genius, and he's fair. That's a rare combination."

The martini and beer arrived and they broke off as each indulged in his respective drink. As Garza raised his bottle, Gideon—out of habit more than anything else—noticed the man's wristwatch. "Nice watch."

"Think so?"

"Oh, yeah. Blancpain L-Evolution Flyback Chronograph. With a red-gold caseband."

Garza eyed him. "Most people don't know anything about Blancpain watches."

"With that carbon-fiber bracelet, it's one of the finest watches made. Worth, what, fifty grand?"

"I wouldn't know. A grateful client gave it to me."

Garza paused. "What makes you the expert?"

"I used to be a high-end thief and scumbag, remember?"

"Right."

"Tell me something," said Gideon. "What is this big project Glinn's been working on ever since I came to EES? You know, that underwater model that everybody's crawling over."

Garza took a long draw on his beer, draining a third of it before setting down the bottle. "Glinn should be the one to tell you about it."

"Come on. I've signed NDAs up the wazoo. It's obviously no secret within the confines of EES—I thought that was the whole point of the open lab."

"True." Garza waved over another IPA. "That project . . . it's Glinn's Moby-Dick."

"How so?"

The fresh beer arrived, and Garza took the opportunity to drain it down almost by half. "Well . . ." He hesitated for a moment, seemed to come to a decision. "You remember Palmer Lloyd, the billionaire who went nuts a few years ago?"

"Sure do."

"You may also remember he had plans to open a museum, which got shelved after he went to the funny farm."

"I remember the auction of all the stuff at Sotheby's. Unbelievable collection."

"Yeah. Well, five years ago—before all that went down—Lloyd hired EES to, ah, *expropriate* the world's largest meteorite from Chile for his museum."

Gideon put down his drink. "I never heard about that."

"Of course you didn't."

"Tell me about it."

"The meteorite had been found by a prospector on an uninhabited island called Isla Desolación, at the tip of South America. Twenty-five thousand tons. Long story short: we went down there, secured the meteorite, loaded it on a chartered supertanker, got chased by a Chilean destroyer, and were wrecked in a storm. The meteorite went to the bottom in two miles of water and three-quarters of the crew died, including the captain. That's when Glinn became…obsessed."

"Were you on the ship?"

"Yes. What a nightmare." Garza took another long pull of the IPA.

"And so Glinn's still trying to recover it?"

"No. We're not trying to recover it."

Here Garza ordered a third beer and fell silent, waiting for it to arrive.

"If you're not trying to recover it, what are you doing?"

"We're trying to kill it."

"Kill—?"

"It wasn't a meteorite, after all."

"What was it?"

"Sorry. I've already told you too much. If you want to

know more, ask Glinn. I will say, though, that we've lost some great projects because of this damn obsession."

"But not the Phorkys Map."

"Phorkys. There's something odd about this project. For a minute, Garza's thoughts seemed to go far away. "Eli used to share with me even the most sensitive details of every project. But this time, he's playing his cards close. He won't even tell me the name of our client. I'd like a guarantee that it's someone who's going to do right by this discovery—not some corporation that'll just turn it into a billion-dollar profit center."

"I feel the same way."

"It makes me wonder if the client is unsavory."

Gideon shook his head. "Glinn has talked about these computer programs of his that can predict human behavior. Is that for real?"

Garza's third beer arrived. "Yes."

"How does that work?"

"Eli founded Effective Engineering Solutions as a company specializing in 'failure analysis.' We'd get hired to come in after some cluster-fuck. Our job was to figure out what went wrong, and why. Not a nice business, because often you end up blaming your own client."

"Making it hard to get paid."

"Oh, Eli always gets the money up front. The bigger problem is that, once we've completed our work, sometimes the client wants to deep-six the report. And the people who prepared it."

"Tough business."

"You're not kidding. But Eli's the toughest man I know. Any normal person would have died from the injuries he sustained on that shipwreck."

Gideon shifted in his chair. "So what about these computer programs?"

"Eli developed them. The human factor is always the most important in any engineering project. So these programs can predict, to a certain extent, human behavior. He calls it QBA—Quantitative Behavioral Analysis."

"Sounds like science fiction."

Garza laughed. "It started out *as* science fiction. Glinn got the idea from reading Isaac Asimov's *Foundation* series. Remember Hari Seldon and the discipline of 'psychohistory'?"

Gideon shook his head. He hated science fiction.

"Asimov invented a new science that combined history, sociology, and statistics. Psychohistorians could make predictions about the behavior of groups of people. With QBA, Glinn took psychohistory out of fiction and made it fact. His programs make predictions, not about groups, but about how a *single* person will react, in a given set of circumstances." He took a sip of his beer. "You can bet that both you and I have had thorough QBAs done on us."

"How comforting."

"In an odd way, it is. Eli knows more about you than you do yourself."

Gideon thought back to the time when he first encountered Glinn—and the extraordinary amount of information the man had already dug up on him, including his terminal condition. "So how did Glinn get from failure analysis to engineering?"

"Failure analysis is one side of the coin," Garza said. "Engineering is the science of *not* failing—of doing something right. It isn't enough to figure out how to do something right. You also have to figure out how *not* to do something wrong. You have to analyze every possible path to failure. Only then can you be sure of success."

"Like the meteorite disaster."

"That was our only failure—although I concede it was a big one. Up to that point EES had never failed, ever. It was our trademark."

"So you're confident we'll succeed with Project Phorkys?"

Garza stared moodily at the IPA bottle, and then chuckled to himself. "A simple Caribbean cruise? With Glinn's fanatical attention to every detail, every possible avenue of eventuality? Oh, yeah, Gideon. We'll succeed, all right."

15

V ᴇʀʏ ʟᴀᴛᴇ ᴛʜᴇ following night, Eli Glinn sat in his wheelchair, alone in the silent vastness of the central EES laboratory, thumbing through a tattered, burned, and half-destroyed book of poems by W. H. Auden. It was almost five o'clock in the morning, and his entire body ached with the old ache that never left him.

Tucking the book into a pocket, he directed his wheelchair out of the laboratory and to the elevators. The doors opened, and he placed his hand on a digital reader; a moment later the doors closed again, and an LED display indicated the elevator was ascending to the penthouse.

When the doors reopened, Glinn rolled out. Three years earlier, finding that his infirmities made commuting difficult, Glinn had turned the uppermost floor of EES headquarters into a small penthouse and roof terrace, designed to accommodate his physical limitations. The apartment allowed him to retreat when he felt like it, and to reappear at the most unexpected moments, day or night, to supervise or review what was happening in the various labs and offices. He rarely left the building—it was too taxing. More to the point, Glinn no longer felt comfortable with strangers. There were too many pitying glances, too many people who spoke to him in a certain gentle tone of voice, too many small children who hid behind their mothers' skirts and pointed when he appeared.

The wheelchair whirred into the apartment over polished slate floors. A soothing array of cool gray walls met the eye, the space Zen-like in its spareness and asceticism. There was virtually no furniture; Glinn was wheelchair-bound and he almost never had visitors to his private space, eliminating the need for sofas or chairs.

Glinn brought the wheelchair to one of the apartment's few tables, picked up a remote control festooned with dials and various-colored buttons, and turned on the gas fire. Gesturing again with the remote, he aimed it at a pocket door, which slid open with a hiss, leading to his master bedroom. Another click of the remote started the water in the whirlpool bath, and a fourth click caused a row of scented candles to flicker on.

With great economy of movement and the help of two powered platforms and a robotic arm, Glinn undressed and was lowered into the churning, steaming whirlpool. This was not a luxury; it was a necessity in dealing with his broken body, to soothe away the pain that accumulated over the course of the day.

As he lay back in the water, he once again picked up the well-worn collection of W. H. Auden and began to read the famous poem titled "In Praise of Limestone." After another moment, he put the book aside. It had been recommended to him by a woman: the only woman in his life. Or rather, almost in his life, as their relationship had terminated prematurely with her brutal death in the sinking of the supertanker *Rolvaag*.

That had ended forever any possibility of romance.

Not that there had been much emotional content before that, either. He had been orphaned at two when his parents were killed in a fiery plane crash, the cause of which was never properly determined. It was the first secret project he had undertaken at EES, the results of which were banal—the plane had suffered a fuel-line rupture—but at least it had afforded him closure.

After his parents' death, a string of foster families had followed, and Glinn closed himself up as tightly as a bud on a frozen tree.

In the military, he'd had little need for friends, lovers, family, birthdays, Thanksgiving dinners, presents under the Christmas tree, or Friday-night parties. A loyal team that would obey his every command was enough. It satisfied his modest needs. The only thing he needed in life—which he needed absolutely—was the challenge of solving extremely difficult problems. He had a thirst for great challenges, the more demanding the better. As an intelligence operative, he could blow up almost any bridge or structure, he could break into just about any computer, he could design the most complex op and pull it off. Once, in an advanced cryptanalysis class at the academy, the professor assigned them a problem. It was a nasty sort of trick: unbeknownst to the students, the problem, known as the Michelson Conjecture, had never been solved. Glinn worked on the problem for forty-eight hours straight and brought in the solution at the next class.

The challenge of the impossible was the fuel that drove

him through the military, the founding of EES, and life it-self.

And then came the Lloyd Museum catastrophe, which killed the only woman he could ever imagine loving, and put him in a wheelchair.

With a sigh, Glinn picked up the book again and re-sumed reading the poem:

> *I am the solitude that asks and promises nothing;*
> *That is how I shall set you free. There is no love;*
> *There are only the various envies, all of them sad.*

Finishing the poem, he lay back in the bath, his thoughts gravitating to that strange phrase on the ancient map. *Respondeo ad quaestionem, ipsa pergamena:* "I reply to the question, the very page."

Was it the key to the nature of the mysterious "physic"? It would do them no good to find Phorkys and then not know what to look for.

I reply to the question, the very page. The answer to the riddle was there, on the page itself—it had to be. Lying in the bath, visualizing the map in his mind's eye, Glinn searched it, then searched again, roving over the lovely miniatures, the dotted lines, the tiny inscriptions.

The answer was there, and he would find it. Of that he was sure.

16

T HE SPARSE CLOUD COVER around them vanished as the Gulfstream approached its destination. Sitting in a gray leather seat, Gideon gazed out the window at the seascape below. Ahead, as they approached the southern end of the Windwards, he could see the distant coastline of Venezuela, with the ABC islands in the distance: Aruba, Bonaire, and Curaçao. All around lay the turquoise Caribbean, speckled with islands, hundreds of them: grains of land set in the turquoise blue, many uninhabited. He wondered which of them, if any, would turn out to be Phorkys.

Garza, coming up the aisle, touched his shoulder lightly. "Gideon? We're ready for Eli's transmission."

He rose and followed Garza to a partitioned area in the rear of the aircraft, where a large blank screen dominated one wall, a small array of seats in front.

The EES employee he had briefly seen at headquarters had come along on the flight; apparently, she would be helping conduct the briefing. Amy, Garza had called her. She was small and slight but quite attractive, Asian looking, with exotic green eyes, glossy short black hair, and a pert, athletic body. He noted in passing the wedding band on her finger. He wondered where the pilot of their vessel was; decided he was probably already on board in Aruba.

The woman drew a curtain over the aisle, and a moment later the lights went out and the screen sprang to life. And there was Eli Glinn, looking back at them from the conference room at EES headquarters.

"Greetings, Gideon," he said, his voice surprisingly clear over the satellite connection. "Hello, Manuel. And hello, Amy. The pilot tells me you're somewhere over the Caribbean as we speak."

"An hour out of Aruba," said Amy.

"Excellent. You have your briefing folders and all the information we can provide you at this time. During the mission, we'll stay in contact through sat phone and computer. The yacht we've engaged for you is fully equipped with a high-speed satellite uplink, email, Wi-Fi, you name it. And it's fully stocked with comestibles. Once you're settled, Garza will return here and we'll continue our analysis of the Phorkys Map. As we uncover more information, we'll feed it to you."

"Very good," said Gideon.

"We'll have people standing by at EES headquarters at all times, but Manuel will be your point man. And now, just a couple of parting words, if I may."

"Shoot," said Gideon.

"While I wouldn't characterize this as an easy mission, Gideon, it doesn't present the kind of challenge your earlier assignments did. For one thing, it's the Caribbean. If things go wrong, we can always abort, extract you, and try again later. There's no time limit on the mission beyond our client's eagerness to see it completed. It's true that we're moving into the hurricane season. But with forecasting as powerful as it is today, you should have plenty of advance notice about bad weather."

"I understand," said Gideon.

"Now: any questions?"

There were none.

"Well then: good luck, you two."

There was another brief silence. And then Gideon said: "What?"

Glinn paused, the eyebrow of his one good eye rising.

"What did you mean, 'you two'?"

"You and Amy, of course. You're partners."

"Wait a minute," said Gideon, "who said anything about a partner?"

"I mentioned you'd be traveling with a licensed captain," Glinn said, his voice neutral. "That's Amy. You'll be making this journey together."

Gideon stared at her and then back at Glinn. "Is this another of your QBA schemes? Introducing us at the last minute like this?"

"You'll find her to be a most useful companion. In addition to having a hundred-ton master's license, Amy has dual PhDs in sociology and classical languages."

He looked at Amy and found her looking back with a faintly sardonic smile on her face. That she was evidently in on the surprise irritated him even more. "What is this, *The Dating Game?*"

"In a way, yes," said Glinn. "You will be posing as a young, well-heeled married couple on a pleasure cruise. Garza has a wedding band for you."

"Garza?" Gideon turned on him. "You knew about this, too?"

Garza was grinning and holding up a little blue box. He flipped it open to reveal a gold band nestled in silk. "Try it on. Size eleven, right?"

Gideon flushed with annoyance. "And here I thought she was just a glorified stewardess."

"Funny, and I thought you were the lavatory attendant," said Amy, eyeing him coolly.

Gideon stared at her and then had to laugh. "Touché. Okay, I deserved that. But I still object to being the only one kept in the dark."

Amy continued looking at him. The stewardess crack, it seemed, had gotten under her skin. Well, he felt aggrieved, too. She'd known all along they were going to be partners—and had said nothing.

"All right, Manuel, give me the ring," Gideon said. He slipped it on and held it up. "So we're married?"

"Don't think any benefits are going along with that ring," Amy replied tartly. She had a low voice with just the faintest hint of an accent.

"I do everything with a reason," said Glinn. His face had become smooth, placid, disinterested. "And there was an excellent reason for this particular partnership. Trust me, you both have skills that will complement each other."

Gideon looked from Glinn to Amy. She couldn't have been more than five feet tall, and he doubted she weighed more than ninety pounds. "What if we don't get along?" he said.

"You won't."

Amy said to Glinn: "Your QBA program predicted we wouldn't like each other?"

"It did."

"Your program works," she said drily.

"You will, in time, understand why you make good partners. After you land in Aruba, a car will take you to Savaneta, a village on the southwest coast, where your yacht is berthed. It is a port favored by wealthy yachtsmen, quiet, quaint—a good place to begin your cruise while attracting the least amount of attention. Not that we expect any attention; it pays to be cautious. I leave it to you to work out together your marital history. Manuel has arranged everything else. Manuel?"

Garza spoke. "The boat's a Hinckley T55 MKII motor yacht. The *Turquesa*. Very elegant. Amy's familiar with its operation and can fill you in on the details. It has two staterooms, a length of fifty-five feet, and a top speed of thirty-six knots. We've hustled to retrofit the craft with some specialized equipment you might need for the journey. Again, Amy has been briefed on the details."

Gideon turned toward Glinn. "Just the two of us on this boat? What about a wait staff? Cabin steward? Butler? Lavatory attendant?"

"The beauty of the Hinckley is that it requires no crew. It's a simple boat to operate, dual jet drives, joystick operation. You'll be cruising in fairly sheltered waters. One thing, Gideon: Amy is the captain. She's in charge. That's the way it is on a boat. You follow her orders. Understood?"

Gideon swallowed. "Understood."

"At the same time, Amy, Gideon has exceptional qualities for this mission. You will seek his counsel."

Amy nodded silently.

"Now, tomorrow you will cruise due west from Sa-vaneta. Thanks to careful perusal of the latest satellite imagery, Dr. Brock has managed to identify one other lo-cation on the Phorkys Map—the sixth clue, neatly bypass-ing the still-undeciphered images four and five, which we assumed were somewhere in the Cape Verde Islands but because of clue six are now moot. *That*—clue six—will serve as your starting point."

A picture flashed up on the screen of a tiny, precise drawing from the map, magnified greatly. It depicted what looked like a black bottle against a white hump. The ac-companying Latin phrase read: *Nigrum utrem, naviga ad occidentem.*

"'Black bottle, sail west,'" translated Amy.

"Exactly," said Glinn. "Fifty nautical miles west of Aruba lies a desolate cluster of islands—rocks, re-ally—known as Los Monjes del Sur. The southernmost island has a huge basaltic sea stack in the shape of a leather bottle. That picture on the map reproduces the sea stack against the outline of the island quite remarkably."

"And how do we find this place?" Gideon asked.

"Amy has the coordinates."

"And from there?"

"The next clue on the map, image seven, is this."

A picture flashed on the screen, a tiny, upside-down U with an odd projection on the right side, like a knob. The Latin inscription read: *Sequere diaboli vomitum.*

Gideon glanced at Amy for a translation.

"'Follow the Devil's vomit.'"

"Of course," said Gideon. "Finally: an obvious clue."

"That one has us stumped, too," said Glinn. "It's our hope the two of you will figure it out when you come across it, and that this will lead you to the next clue, and so on."

A chart flashed on the screen, and Glinn went on. "As you will see from the charts, if you sail due west from Los Monjes, you will encounter a very remote headland known as La Guajira, part of the coastline of Colombia. This entire section of coastline is harsh desert, uninhabited. We believe the 'Devil's vomit' landmark will be found along this coast somewhere."

"I take it this is well off the normal cruising routes."

"Yes. In fact, west of La Guajira, you enter a part of the Caribbean where few ever go. It's not at all a postcard picture of lush islands and white beaches. This is a remote, untraveled sea of barren, uninhabited islands, with tricky currents and few places to land. The coastline of Colombia is unfriendly. Lot of drug smuggling. And if you continue west, you will eventually hit the Mosquito Coast of Nicaragua and Honduras—not exactly the Côte d'Azur."

"And you call this a pleasure cruise?" Gideon asked dubiously.

"You just need to exercise common sense—and be careful," Garza said.

"So what, exactly, is our excuse for cruising in this Caribbean desert?"

"You're adventure travelers," Glinn told him. "In your briefing books, you have our analysis of the map so far. You also have copies of the map itself. We've devoted a Cray XE6 Opteron 6172 computer to working exclusively at deciphering that map. It is essentially scouring the world's databases of pictures and map elements for clues. But the pictures and clues in the Phorkys Map are so obscure, so peculiar, it's quite possible you'll have to figure some of them out as you go. Now, if there aren't any more questions, I'll sign off. May I recommend the Flying Fishbone in Savaneta for dinner? The Bouillabaisse à la Marseille is excellent, paired with a Puligny-Montrachet. That would be a good place to be seen—and for you to establish your cover."

The screen went blank.

17

THE DINNER HAD been excellent and the half bottle of Montrachet had improved Gideon's outlook, tempered only slightly by Amy's announcement that she was a tee-totaler. It had been a quick dinner; Gideon had felt disinclined to chat and Amy was practically mute, eating so fast he had hardly begun when she was shoveling the last forkful of fish into her mouth. He was beginning to feel as if he'd been victimized by an arranged marriage of sorts. Vintage Eli Glinn. And now—as they climbed aboard the gorgeous, sleek yacht, berthed at a fancy marina—Gideon stole another glance at Amy. He was usually good at reading people, but he felt like he didn't understand her at all yet. She seemed about as accessible as the Kremlin. He vowed to keep an open mind and stay cool.

It was ten PM and the marina was starting to settle down, many of the big yachts ablaze with light, people eating late suppers or drinking cocktails on the decks. It was a warm evening, with the gentle sound of water lapping the hulls, the clink of rigging on masts, the whisper of wind, the murmur of voices, distant cries of gulls.

Gideon paused on deck to breathe in the fragrant air. Despite the awkward company, this wasn't so bad.

"I'd like to give you a tour of the boat," said Amy. "So you'll know where everything is."

"Good idea, thanks."

"When we get under way, we'll be sharing responsibilities. You'll be the first mate, of sorts. You'll have to know how to take the helm, operate all the navigational systems. I'll show you a few simple knots and how to cleat a line. It's not really that hard."

Gideon nodded. As they entered the pilothouse, he reached for a light switch, flipped it on. "Uh-oh. No juice."

"The power's off," Amy said. "Turning it on is the first thing you do." She showed him the battery dial, then turned it to HOUSE. Lights went on. He followed her to the helm and listened while she lectured him on how to use the radar, chartplotters, sonar, and VHF radio. Next, she went through the wipers, fuel gauge, fuel consumption, temperature gauges, oil pressure, the wheel, throttles, shifts, and joystick. Gideon nodded, hands clasped behind his back, murmuring his understanding, not retaining a quarter of it.

"I know it's a lot to absorb all at once. Once we're under way, it'll get clearer."

"I hope so."

"There's some very special scientific equipment on the boat," she said, flipping her raven hair back. "Sidescan sonar, a small ROV and controls, towing gear, scuba equipment with tether line reel, tank racks and air compressor, pingers, sand strobes, water dredges and jets, that sort of thing. We may never need that stuff, so I won't bother showing it to you unless it becomes necessary. But here's something that is very necessary." She pointed to a device built into a nearby bulkhead. "It's the sat phone we'll be using to communicate with EES. There's also a spare portable phone stowed away in the cabin that we'll be able to use on land."

Next, Gideon got a tour of the engine room, with more obscure dials, gauges, and dipsticks. Then came the galley. This was something he could relate to—stovetop, microwave, dining nook, along with a workstation with giant-screen satellite TV, laptop computers, all surrounded by mahogany, teak, and brass. There was even a climate-controlled wine cabinet—filled with wine bottles.

Gideon could kiss Garza for that.

"Glinn tells me you cook," said Amy. "That's something useful."

Gideon didn't quite like the tone of the remark, but let it pass.

"The staterooms are through there." She made a vague gesture.

"Could we see them? If you don't mind."

She pushed through the door. A short corridor divided the two rooms. "Yours is starboard, mine's port."

"Starboard and port. That's right and left, right?"

"Yes."

Gideon couldn't resist. "So we're not sharing the same stateroom?"

"You snore."

Gideon laughed. "I do not."

She looked at him, unamused. "That's the reason why we don't sleep in the same room, if anyone should ask. You snore."

"I think *you* should be the snorer."

Finally, for the first time, Amy smiled. "Do I look like a snorer?" She paused. "Gideon, we have to be realistic about this. Look at you—tall, awkward. I'm sure you *do* snore."

Gideon swallowed his irritation. Okay, so she had a dry sense of humor. That was at least one mark in her favor. Maybe.

Time to move to ground he was comfortable with: identities and disguises. "Speaking of our backstory," he said, "we'd better start figuring it out. I was thinking that—"

But Amy was already removing a notebook from her case. "It's all here."

"But—"

"Glinn and I have already worked out all the details of how we met, fell in love, the whole works."

"Jesus. I can't wait to hear *our* story." He followed her into the galley, deflated.

"Have a seat."

Instead of sitting down, he went over to the wine cabinet, opened it, and perused the bottles. It was a superb and expensive selection. He felt another rush of gratitude toward Garza. He selected a French Bordeaux. "I'll need a glass of wine if I'm to hear the heartwarming story of how we met and fell in love."

"Feel free."

He uncorked the bottle, poured a taste into a glass, swirled it about, sipped. It badly needed air, but he badly needed a drink.

She primly opened the notebook. This was feeling odder by the minute. *Go with the flow,* Gideon told himself.

"Okay. Your name is Mark." She reached into her case. "Here's your wallet, with driver's license, credit cards, passport, the works."

"Glinn never said anything about a new identity."

"You can't lie about yourself these days. If you go by Gideon Crew, any moron with an Internet connection could figure out in five minutes this whole thing is a sham."

"That's not the point. I prefer to create my own identities." Gideon took a goodly drink from the wineglass.

"Glinn assembled most of this for us and asked me to brief you. You're Mark Johnson. Which makes me Amy Johnson. Amy's a common enough name—I might as well keep it. My maiden name was Suzuki. I'm half Japanese—which happens to be true, by the way."

"Mark Johnson? How dull. I would have preferred a name like Ernest Quatermain."

"Mark Johnson has the advantage of being Internet-anonymous. There are too many Mark and Amy Johnsons online. And Suzuki is one of the most common Japanese surnames. Now for the marital details. We met in college. MIT, senior year. I was majoring in classical languages, you in physics. We took a class together—the theory of computing."

"How romantic. Tell me about our wedding night."

She ignored the comment. "We got married in Boston the year after graduation. You're a banker, I'm an attorney. We live on the Upper East Side of New York. We have no kids. We're both into physical fitness, skiing, and of course yachting—me more so than you."

"What's our song?"

"Song?" She looked up. "Hmmm. How about 'Opposites Attract' by Paula Abdul?"

"I'm going to shoot myself; we're so boring. Make it 'Atomic' by Blondie."

"Very well." She jotted a note in her notebook. "This cruise is an anniversary dream come true. We're exploring this part of the Caribbean because we're looking for privacy and adventure, getting away from the crowds. We're a little naive and don't realize these waters are frequented by drug smugglers. We rented this boat, of course, paying for the trip out of my year-end bonus."

"Your year-end bonus. Don't I make enough money?"

"I make more than you do."

"I see. So what bank do I work for?"

"That's the kind of detail you don't want to go into—not that it's likely to come up. Stay generic and avoid saying anything that might individuate us."

"Stay generic with whom? Just how many people are we going to meet?"

"You never know. These are simply precautions. As for most everything else—other questions regarding interests, political beliefs, religions, and so forth—we'll tell the truth."

Gideon looked at her oddly. An idea just struck him. "This isn't the first time you've done this."

"No, it's not."

"So who are you, really? And what line of work are you normally in?"

"Those details would only confuse you. Just stick with the cover story and forget who I really am."

He looked at her left hand. "Are you really married, or is that ring a fake like mine?"

She held it up. "All right. You get one more detail. It's a fake, like yours. I'm not married, never have been."

Gideon shook his head, poured himself another glass of wine. "Are you sure you don't want a glass? It's opening up—a wonderful wine."

She shook her head. "No thanks."

Gideon momentarily wondered whether Glinn had told her about his terminal condition. Probably not. He also wondered if Amy didn't have some medical condition of her own to motivate her. It would be just like Glinn to find someone he could exploit like that.

She shut her notebook. "Any questions?"

"Yeah. Where are the guns?"

She pointed behind him. A pair of mahogany doors opened to a metal cabinet. It was unlocked. He pulled the doors open to reveal a small arsenal of weaponry: assault rifles, handguns, spearguns, a Heckler & Koch PSG 1 sniper rifle with a five-round detachable magazine. There was even an RPG and a rack of handheld incendiary and fragmentation grenades. Gideon whistled, reached in and removed a Colt .45 1911, ejected the magazine. Fully loaded. The piece had been customized, fully rounded for tactical use, fitted front and rear with combat sights with tritium inserts. A beautiful, expensive custom gun.

"You know how to use these?" Gideon asked, putting it back.

"That's my 1911 you were toying with. So yes."

"We could start a war with these weapons."

"Hopefully we'll never need to even open this case."

Gideon turned and looked steadily at Amy. She returned the gaze, her face neutral, thoughts inscrutable. "I wonder just where Glinn found you," he said.

Another rare smile. "You'll never know."

18

GIDEON AWOKE TO the sounds of thumping and grunting coming from Amy's stateroom. She was doing calisthenics. He glanced at the portholes—not even light yet. The clock said five thirty AM.

Rolling out of bed, he pulled on a bathrobe and stumbled into the galley. He was delighted to find a small but expensive Italian espresso machine and grinder tucked into one corner. A few cupboards down he found the beans. He ground them and prepared the machine, wondering if his teetotaling "wife" would be a prohibitionist in the caffeine department as well. He was damn glad he wasn't married to her for real.

As he filled a tiny cup with hot espresso, a *ristretto*—the way he liked it—he appreciated even more Garza's attention to detail.

A moment later the galley door opened and Amy came in, dressed for the day in a work shirt and white pants. "I'll take a double, black, no sugar," she said, passing through. "Bring it to me at the helm, please; I'd like to get under way."

Gideon sipped his own coffee while grinding the beans

for hers. He made the double and brought it up to her as the twin engines of the yacht rumbled to life. She took it without comment while poring over a book of charts open on the dashboard next to the helm. He could hear an electronic-sounding voice on the VHF reading out the weather report, winds, and wave heights.

The boat backed away from the berth with a growl, and a minute later they were heading out of the marina and into open water. It was a calm day, fluffy clouds floating above and a rising sun sparkling off the water. As they cleared the port, she accelerated, the speedometer needle creeping up to twenty-five knots. Aruba dwindled on the horizon, the mainland of Venezuela dropping away on their left. Soon they were cruising in open water.

"Los Monjes is about fifty-five nautical miles away," Amy said. "We'll be there in two hours."

Gideon nodded. "Anything you want me to do, Captain?"

She glanced at him. "Another espresso."

"Coming right up."

He made another espresso. While he didn't particularly enjoy taking orders, he had to admit this was a cushy mission. It was also nice in a way, having somebody else making the decisions for a change. He brought up the espresso and she shot it down as quickly as the first.

The boat thundered across the water, sending back a long, creamy wake. For the first hour of travel, the sea was dotted with other yachts, mostly sailboats, but as they went on, the vessels became less frequent until there was nothing but blue sea. So far he'd felt no symptoms of seasickness—thank God.

Gideon did the rounds as he was instructed by Amy:

cleaned the head, downloaded email, called up the weather on the Doppler radar, checked the sat-phone printer for messages from EES. Amy, while not exactly warm and friendly, was courteous and professional. And she was clearly very, very smart. Gideon liked that.

On schedule, a distant hump appeared on the horizon, followed by another, farther away and to the north. They approached the more southerly island, a whitened, barren rock about a quarter mile long, with a ruined lighthouse on top, surrounded by cliffs and pounded by the sea. As they came around the end of the island, the Black Bottle appeared: a sea stack of basalt, standing about fifty yards off the tip of the island, roiled by white surf. Amy called up the tiny drawing of clue six from the Phorkys Map on her navigational computer. As the boat circled the island, the sea stack moved into position, the black rock standing out against the white rock of the island.

Suddenly she reversed throttle and the boat rumbled to a stop.

"Incredible," said Gideon. He could hardly believe how perfectly they matched.

"Get the camera, please, and take some pictures." Amy seemed almost more surprised than he was.

While Amy held the boat steady in the swell, Gideon snapped a number of photographs with a digital Nikon camera that EES had provided and took a short video.

"I'll download everything and send it to Glinn," he said. "Along with a report."

"Good. And fill in the log the way I showed you, indicating position, engine hours, fuel, water, weather conditions, and a narrative entry. And then you might make us breakfast. Bacon and eggs, please."

"Aye aye, Captain."

Gideon went below. At the workstation in the galley, he emailed the photos and report to Glinn over the satellite uplink. He could feel the movement of the water becoming rougher, the boat pitching and yawing as it rode the waves. To his great dismay, he began to feel queasy.

He stood up, put on a frying pan, and began cooking bacon. The smell filled the galley despite the fan and—rather than sharpen his appetite—made him feel worse. He cracked a couple of eggs, scrambled them, added some cheese and fresh chives from the well-stocked refrigerator. When it was done, he set a place for one at the kitchen table, put on the food, and went above.

"Breakfast is ready."

"Good. You take the helm."

"Me?"

"Yes, you. Use the wheel, not the joystick. The joystick is for maneuvering in the harbor. Keep the heading at two hundred and seventy degrees—the electronic compass is right here—and keep an eye out for floating debris. That's the one thing you really need to worry about out here. We're in deep water, no reefs, no other boat traffic. As we approach the mainland, you may note a change in the color of the water. I should be back before that."

With great trepidation, Gideon took the wheel while Amy went below. The boat rumbled along. The flow of air through the open windows was refreshing and began to drive away his incipient nausea. The chartplotter showed the location of the boat, and overlaid on that was radar data. The sonar indicated a depth under the keel of several hundred feet. The speed was fifteen knots, the heading two hundred seventy degrees. The vessel seemed to be riding well, at least to his inexperienced feel.

So far so good.

A moment later Amy reappeared. "Taking the helm."

"Already?"

"You don't waste time eating on a boat. I noticed you didn't cook anything for yourself."

"I'm not hungry."

"I'll take another espresso," she said. "Before you do the dishes."

Gideon swallowed his annoyance. Was this really the way they did things on a boat? Maybe he was just being sensitive. No matter, he was going to follow orders and remain pleasant. He went below and reached for some more coffee beans.

"On deck," came a sharp voice from the intercom.

He came up. Amy pointed west. A low, dark line lay on the left-hand horizon.

"That's the South American mainland," she said. "As we go west we're going to graze the coastline of the upper Guajira Peninsula of Colombia. My idea is to cruise along the shore—as the Greeks would have done, and the Irish after them—looking for whatever the Devil's vomit might be. In the early days of sailing, before the compass, sailors kept within sight of shore whenever possible. So the vomit should be found along this coastline."

"Looking for vomit. Great. Knock yourself out. By the way, what's the next clue after that—number eight?"

Amy brought it up on her navigational computer. The picture showed nothing more than a flat line, rising into a second, sharp line, which pointed in turn toward a rounded line. The clue read: *aquilonius*.

"*Aquilonius?*" Gideon asked. "What does that mean?"

"'Northerly.' But let's not get ahead of ourselves."

The water had turned a dirty greenish brown. As the coastline loomed closer into view, he left the dishes half done and brought out the binoculars. A distant line of surf appeared in the glass: a long brown beach with a sea of sand dunes behind.

"That is one desolate coast," he murmured.

"It's one of the worst coastlines of the entire Caribbean—treacherous as anything. The offshore sandbars shift continuously."

"I see a wreck. A big one." His binoculars focused on the remains of what appeared to have been an enormous container ship, skeletonized and broken.

"According to the charts, that's *El Karina*. There are wrecks all along this coast."

"We'd better be careful."

"The *Turquesa* draws only three feet and the hull is made of Kevlar. We're not in much danger."

Gideon said nothing. The queasiness was returning in force.

They moved into a course parallel to the coast, and Amy slowed to five knots. She kept clue seven displayed on her nav-computer.

"By the way," Gideon said, "when I was looking at the weather just now it noted there's a low pressure system developing east of the Cape Verde Islands. The long-term forecast says it might develop into a storm heading into the Caribbean."

"This time of year, there's always a low pressure system developing in that area. The vast majority of hurricanes trend north. Very few brush the coastline of Colombia."

"Just thought you should know . . . Captain."

She nodded. "Keep a sharp lookout for something that might resemble an inverted U—a cave, rock formation, anything."

The coastline was low and featureless, but as they moved along it began to grow rockier, with headlands and black volcanic sea stacks rising up among the sandy wastes. The wind picked up, blowing hard from shore, carrying with it veils of orange sand that stained the water. The air smelled of dust, and as the sun rose the heat became intense. They continued creeping along at five knots, about five hundred yards offshore.

"These swells are bad," Gideon said, trying to ignore his nausea. The slow speed made the motion worse.

"That's because we're in shoaling water."

"How long is this coastline?"

"About sixty miles from here to Cabo de la Vela. Then it curves back south. I feel fairly confident the Devil's vomit will be along here somewhere."

Devil's vomit. If the swells kept up, Gideon thought grimly, he'd have some vomit of his own to offer the coastline.

The day wore on as they cruised along the endless, barren coast. In one deep bay, sheltered by two headlands, they saw a large boat at anchor, streaked with rust. Gideon examined it through the binoculars.

"Lot of new electronics on that mast," he said.

"Probably drug smugglers," said Amy. "Too bad—I was hoping we could anchor in that bay for the night." Gideon continued examining the boat. "Looks like they see us."

"Of course they see us. Let's hope they've got bigger fish to fry."

The sun was now setting into a scrim of blood-red sky, made hazy by dust. The wind grew even stronger, now blowing hard from the east. The brown sea was covered with whitecaps.

"There's a headland called Punta Taroa about five miles ahead," said Amy. "According to the chart, there's a sheltered bay just behind that."

Gideon could make out the headland: a massive pyramid of black rock pounded by surf, with a string of sand dunes running away from it inland, in the shelter of a serrated ridge. He looked for something that might resemble the U but could see nothing.

They rounded the point and—as shown on the chart—a shallow bay appeared, with a crescent of orange sand running up into ribbed dunes in fantastical shapes.

"It's pretty exposed," said Gideon, thinking of the drug smugglers.

"It's the best we're going to find. We'll do a blackout and set four-hour watches."

Amy brought the boat in behind the headland, moving slowly and examining the depth finder, the dual diesels rumbling.

"Here's a good spot," she called out.

She showed Gideon how to draw the pin on the anchor. In a narrow cove behind the immense rocky bluff, in twenty feet of water, she released it. It ran out and the boat swung around to face the wind, the anchor, as she put it, "setting nicely." As she killed the engine, the sun dropped behind the dunes and, bloated and wavering, sank out of sight. A dull orange light enveloped everything.

Ten minutes later, as Gideon was airing a bottle of Malbec and whipping up a dinner of lobster risotto, he heard Amy on the intercom.

"Gideon? Go to the gun cabinet and fetch me my 1911. And grab a sidearm for yourself. We've got company."

19

Respondeo ad quaestionem, ipsa pergamenta.

In his aerie high above the Meatpacking District of Manhattan, Glinn gazed from a plate-glass window that looked westward over the High Line park to the dark back of the Hudson River, reflecting the lights of Jersey City. It was just after three o'clock in the morning.

"I respond to the question, the page itself." *Ipsa pergamenta,* the page itself. . . .

Glinn had not studied Latin, but Brock had spent hours with him going over every possible meaning, submeaning, double meaning, and alliteration in each word of that sentence, parsing it with Talmudic intensity. To no avail. Now Glinn's mind felt congested. He'd been chewing this over too long.

The page itself. . . .

To clear his head, he took out another book of poetry: Wallace Stevens. He opened the book at random. The poem his eye settled on was titled "Not Ideas About the Thing But the Thing Itself." The page itself, the thing itself. A nice coincidence.

He read through the poem once, twice, then laid the book aside.

Not ideas about the thing, but the thing itself; I respond to the question, the page itself

And that was when he had the revelation. It wasn't a riddle at all. It was a literal statement of fact. *Ipsa perga-menta.* The page itself or—quite literally—the vellum or parchment itself, the physical parchment, would answer the question.

Could it really be that simple?

It made perfect sense. The vellum of the Chi Rho page was different: thicker, finer, whiter, cleaner than the rest of the Book of Kells. The secret lay *in the vellum itself.*

There, in the dark, he blushed with chagrin. The answer was so obvious he had missed it completely.

He directed his wheelchair to the elevator and descended to the main floor. The back laboratory for Project Phorkys was empty. Glinn motored to the safe that held the Chi Rho page, punched in the code, and removed it. Laying it on a clean glass stage, he selected a sterilized surgical knife from a set of tools resting in an autoclave and, working with great care, cut a millimeter-square piece from a blank corner of the page. Using tweezers, he placed the square into a test tube and sealed it, labeled and racked it.

For a long time he stared at the square piece of skin. Then he muttered, under his breath: "I wonder . . . I wonder . . . just what kind of *animal* you came from."

20

G IDEON STUFFED THE two pistols into his waistband, feeling a bit like a pirate, and ascended to the pilothouse. In the twilight he could make out the boat they'd seen earlier just a few hundred yards off, coming into the bay, its running lights on, heading slowly in their direction.

Gideon slipped the 1911 to Amy, who tucked it into her pants and pulled out her shirttails to hide it. She pulled down the VHF mike and hailed the ship, identifying herself as captain of the *Turquesa* and asking, in a neutral voice, for identification in turn.

"This is the *Horizonte*," came a male voice, speaking perfect, American-accented English. "Captain Hank Cordray. We don't mean to bust in on your privacy, but you don't often see cruisers along this coast."

"What are you doing in these waters, if I may ask?"

"You may ask. We aren't drug runners, if that's what you were thinking." An electronic chuckle followed this. "We're a pair of documentary filmmakers. Myself and my wife, Linda."

"Really? What are you making a documentary about?"

"Pelicans."

A short silence. "Pelicans?" Amy said into the mike. "We haven't seen any around here."

"Not around here, but past Cabo de la Vela there's a lagoon known for them. That's where we're headed."

Gideon began to snicker. Drug traffickers, indeed. Amy waved a dismissive hand at him.

"We hope to anchor in this bay, if you don't mind. There aren't many decent anchorages along this coast."

"No objections," said Amy.

"And if we aren't interrupting anything, we'd like to pay you a courtesy visit at your convenience. As I said, these are lonely parts and we haven't seen anyone in days, aside from our hired crew."

"You'd be welcome," said Amy. She glanced at her watch. "We're about to eat dinner—how about in an hour?"

"Very good."

Amy racked the mike and glanced over at Gideon. The old boat was slowing and turning, preparing to drop anchor. A moment later Gideon heard a splash and the rattle of the anchor chain going out.

"Pelicans," he said. "And here we thought they were drug runners. I'd better go below and finish cooking if we're going to entertain. You want me to put your pistol away?"

"I'll keep it, thanks. You should keep yours, too."

Gideon looked at her. Her brow was furrowed with skepticism. "You still suspicious?"

"I don't know. That's an awfully large boat for a pair of filmmakers."

"He sounded pretty harmless to me."

Amy was silent.

"Why allow them on board, if you're worried?"

She glanced at him. "It'll give us a chance to check them out. And not allowing them to visit would be such a breach of cruising etiquette it might convince them that *we're* drug smugglers. Which in turn might encourage them to call the Colombian coast guard—who, by the way, are known for shooting first and investigating later."

She picked up her binoculars and scrutinized the ship, anchored about two hundred yards away. Gideon could see various figures moving about on deck. She was silent for a long time then lowered the binoculars with a frown.

"Rough-looking crew."

"How many?"

"Four. Listen…while you're working on dinner, send an email to Garza, urgent. Ask him to look up the details of a boat named *Horizonte*, hailing out of Maracaibo."

"Will do."

She looked at the charts. Glancing over her shoulder, Gideon could see the lagoon Captain Cordray had talked about, some thirty miles down the coast. "And ask Garza if there are pelicans in Bahía Hondita, La Guajira, Colombia."

Gideon went below, sent the email, and finished preparing dinner. Amy came down and they ate in silence, Gideon helping himself to wine. She drank Pellegrino. He had never seen anyone eat so fast, and with so little appreciation of her food. She just shoveled it in.

"How do you like the risotto?"

"Good."

The dinner was over way too soon. Amy pushed away from the table. "All right, let's get them on board. You got your sidearm?"

Gideon patted his Beretta.

She looked him over, narrowing her eyes. "It's a problem, these tropical clothes. Anyone can see we're packing."

"Maybe it's good they can see."

"Maybe."

He heard the ping of incoming email and checked the computer. Garza had come through: the *Horizonte* was a cheap charter vessel out of Maracaibo—that was all he could discover. And there were pelicans in Bahía Hondita. A lot of pelicans.

They went up into the pilothouse. Amy got on the VHF and made the invitation. Moments later the boat's launch was lowered from stern davits into the water. The sky was clear and dark—no moon, but countless stars. As the launch hit the water there was a fizzle of bioluminescence. An engine started up and the launch came their way, leaving a phosphorescent wake. In a moment it had pulled up to the swim platform. Gideon looked at them intently in the dim light from the pilothouse. The captain, Cordray, was short and a little soft looking, almost geeky, with a wispy goatee and thick glasses. The wife was taller and leaner, with a hard-bitten look—as if life had not been easy for her. The launch was driven by a man who, in another century, would have looked quite at home on a pirate ship—shirtless, heavily muscled, covered with tattoos, his long brown hair tied back in a thick ponytail. He had a dark, nasty-looking face with scars.

Gideon helped the woman—Linda—out of the boat and onto the swim platform. The man got out on his own. The driver turned the launch around and headed back to the *Horizonte*.

"Come and have a drink," said Amy, shaking hands and introducing herself, seating them outdoors in the stern cockpit. "Mark, bring out some candles and wine."

A little miffed at her tone—in front of strangers no less—Gideon fetched the hurricane lamps and the wine. It was poured all around, glasses were clinked.

"That's quite a boat for a pair of filmmakers," said Amy. "What is it, seventy-five feet?"

"Seventy," said Linda. "Terrible fuel consumption. But she was cheap and came with a crew. You should see our crew. Scary-looking bunch, but they're gentle as kittens."

"Or so you hope," said Gideon.

Linda laughed, looked around. "Speaking of boats, this is quite the yacht you've got here. A Hinckley, no less."

"We're celebrating our fifth wedding anniversary", said Gideon. "Chartered it out of Aruba."

"Well, congratulations." Linda shook out her bleached-blond hair. "Strange place to go cruising, though."

"We wanted to get off the beaten track," said Gideon. He noticed that the man, Hank, hadn't spoken. But his eyes were roaming everywhere, taking in every detail. "You know these waters well?" he asked Linda.

"Oh, yes."

This was encouraging. "Are there any . . . unusual land-marks along the coast worth seeing?"

"Such as?"

"Oh, I don't know. Interesting rock formations. Caves, maybe? That sort of thing."

He found Cordray was now looking intently at him.

"There's a lot of wrecks," Linda said slowly. "You inter-ested in wrecks?"

"Not really. More into natural formations. Rocks, caves, sea stacks."

Another drag and another sip. Gideon noticed her nails were very long and very red. "Caves? Why caves?"

"I'm interested in caves."

"You scuba divers?"

"Ah, not really."

"You got a scuba setup here."

Gideon shrugged.

There was a pause before Linda spoke again. "There are some caves in the bluffs along Punta Gallinas, about ten, fifteen miles down the coast."

"Thanks, we'll check them out tomorrow," said Gideon.

The man, Hank, rose. "May I use your head?"

"I'll show you where it is," said Amy. The two vanished into the pilothouse.

Linda watched the two leave, then laughed. "If I didn't know better, I'd think you two were smuggling drugs!"

Gideon managed to laugh along with her. "Why do you say that?"

She waved her hand at the mast. "Two supersize radars, two GPS antennas, microwave horn, VHF and ELF, satellite uplink. You're equipped up the wazoo!"

"Came with the boat."

"So what's the top speed?"

"They tell me thirty-six knots."

"Thirty-six? I bet you could do forty-five on a flat sea. Hell, you could probably outrun some of the patrol boats of the Colombian navy!"

Amy returned with Cordray. They took their seats again and Cordray drained his wine. "You folks are sure traveling in style," he said. He had a soft, whistling sort of voice. "Nice suite of electronics. Not to mention sidescan sonar with a tow apparatus. You looking for something on the seafloor?"

"It came with the boat," said Amy.

At this, Linda cackled: a raspy, smoke-cured sound. "Funny, that's just what your husband said. *It came with the boat!*" She shook her head. "Well, we'd better get going, leave you two in peace." She pulled a walkie-talkie out of her pocket. "*Jose? Listos.*"

A few moments later the launch arrived and the couple departed, motoring back to their boat, waving good-bye. Gideon waited in silence, watching as they boarded their vessel. Amy poured her untouched glass of wine over the side, then motioned Gideon into the pilothouse.

"They're more suspicious of us than we are of them," Gideon said.

"Using the head was just an excuse," said Amy. "That guy didn't miss a thing."

"They could have stayed anchored right where they were when we first passed them, in that bay down the coast. Instead they came after us."

Amy nodded.

"Think maybe they're drug traffickers, pissed that we're in their territory?"

Amy shook her head. "My guess is they're up to something else—something no good."

Gideon went to pour another glass of wine, only to be surprised when Amy's hand stopped him.

"I need you to be sharp. We're going to run an armed watch tonight. Two on, two off."

"Why don't we just hoist anchor and take off? We could easily outrun that tub."

"No. Who knows how they might react? They might report us to the Colombian coast guard—and we really, really don't want them looking for us."

21

GIDEON LOUNGED IN the stern cockpit, having taken the midnight-to-two-am watch. The wind had picked up and was blowing hard from shore, whipping up whitecaps in the bay. Each gust brought stinging sand with it. The air smelled of smoke, and he could taste salty dust on his tongue. It was very dark, the stars now obscured by blowing dust.

Once in a while he picked up his binoculars and looked across the two hundred yards of water to the *Horizonte*. It showed no signs of life. All the lights were out, and the launch was safely hoisted in its davits.

He got up and made the rounds of the boat, hopping up on the deck and completing a circuit outside the pilothouse to the foredeck and back around the other side. He wasn't sleepy and was glad to be on watch instead of tossing and turning in his stuffy stateroom.

The wind gusted again and he closed his eyes, turning away from the biting sand. He thought of the doughty Irish monks sailing this coastline in a tiny curragh or whatever sort of sailboat they had used. It was almost beyond comprehension.

The gust died down and, in the sudden lull, he thought he heard a noise. It was a strange sound, like bubbling, off the left—port—side of the boat. He rose, pulling out his pistol, and moved silently toward it. He waited just out of sight, listening. Another sound of bubbles breaking the water.

A scuba diver.

Moving slowly, pulling an unlit flashlight from his pocket, he leaned over the rail and aimed it at the spot where he could hear bubbles rising. They broke the black surface with a sparkle of phosphorescence. He steadied his gun, switched on the light.

The beam probed the murky water, revealing nothing. How deep was the diver? Was he sabotaging their boat, placing explosives? Was he trying to board? And now, of course, the diver knew he'd been spotted—having seen the light.

Gideon leaned over farther and probed into the murky water with the light. For a brief moment he thought he saw a flash of metal.

It was hopeless to fire into the water. What he had to do was wake Amy and prevent them from being boarded.

Scrambling away from the rail, he climbed onto the foredeck, above the staterooms, giving the deck two hard raps—their prearranged signal—to rouse Amy. Then he climbed onto the hardtop roof of the pilothouse, where he had a view of the entire boat. Keeping his flashlight off—which would just make him a target—he took cover behind the mast and waited.

The wind moaned about the mast, obscuring his ability to hear. His eyes strained into the darkness, looking for the telltale flash of luminescence indicating bubbles breaking the surface. But the water remained dark.

What had Glinn called this assignment? A walk in Central Park. Yeah, right.

Where the heck was Amy? Was it possible she hadn't heard his signal?

Suddenly there was another flash of phosphorescence to his right, followed by another on his left. *Two divers?* He felt his heart pounding. It wasn't a natural phenomenon, not a school of fish. He had seen a flash of metal—he knew he had.

And now he called out. "Amy! *Amy!*"

"*Ella esta aquí,*" came a deep voice from the pool of darkness below him.

He turned on his flashlight to see Amy, in her pajamas, the tattooed pirate holding a gun to her head. He was wearing nothing but a scuba tank—not even a bathing suit. In the darkness the tattoos looked like scales.

Another dark figure rose up, from a hidden position on the swim platform astern. It was the captain—Cordray.

"Drop your weapon or she dies," he said.

22

Gideon stared in shocked disbelief. Somehow, despite his vigilance, the pirate had managed to board and get hold of Amy.

Cordray smiled and flicked the wet hair out of his eyes.

"Don't be a hero, pal. I'll count to three. One, two…"

Gideon held up his hands, gun dangling, thumb in the trigger guard.

"That's a good boy."

Now a third figure hoisted itself out of the water onto the swim platform, again stark naked, immensely muscled, with long hair and a mustache, and more tattoos. He shed his tank and came over the stern, a six-foot shark harpoon in one hand.

"Now come down. Keep the gun in sight."

Gideon slid off the roof, came around the railing. The pirate with the mustache took away the gun and grabbed his arms, yanking them roughly behind. He slapped on a zip-tie. Gideon was thrown onto the deck beside Amy.

Cordray came over and Gideon was, at least, thankful that he wasn't naked. But somehow the pudgy, smallish man—with his thick glasses and damp goatee—looked more menacing than the naked pirates.

"How about telling me what you're really doing here?" he asked Gideon.

When Gideon said nothing, Cordray drew his hand back and smacked him hard across the face. More silence. Another smack.

"All right. We'll find out ourselves." He spoke in Spanish to Pirate, who moved to stand guard over them with a rifle.

Cordray went into the pilothouse, and the lights came on. Gideon could see him through the window, going through the cabinets, pulling things out, looking at them, tossing them on the floor. He went to the laptop computer and turned it on, cursing when the log-in password came up. He picked up the briefing book lying on the table and began pawing through it. A moment later he came out, holding it.

"I *knew* it."

He shoved the open book at Gideon, with a picture of the Phorkys Map. "Oh, God, this is even better than I expected."

Meanwhile, Gideon could hear the sound of the launch, crossing the water between the two boats. It landed at the swim platform and Cordray's wife, Linda, hopped off.

"Look at this!" Cordray cried, triumph in his voice. "It's just what you thought. They're treasure hunters, like us—and they've got *a fucking treasure map!*"

She took it, examined it in the cockpit light. "Unusual." She came up and stared at Gideon, then at Amy. "I think we might need some help interpreting this."

Silence. Amy hadn't said a word. Gideon could feel blood trickling from the side of his mouth. But Cordray hadn't been strong enough to really hurt him. If Pirate or Mustache ever hit him, that might be a different story.

Linda came up close to him and looked in his eyes, breathing rank cigarette breath into his face. "The name's Mark, right?"

Silence.

"Mark, let me explain something. I don't know if you two are really a married couple, or what. I don't give a shit. I do know this: if you don't explain this map to me, my husband's going to do something awful to her. Something really awful."

Her raspy voice was almost thrilling with a sort of anticipation. She was, Gideon realized, actually getting off on this.

"It's not a treasure map," said Gideon. "It's...it's an old Irish map, that's all. No treasure—"

Amy spoke for the first time. "Shut the hell up."

"But—"

Linda stepped back. "Hank, handle this little bitch, will you?"

Cordray stepped forward. *"Dame el arpón."*

Mustache handed him the harpoon. It was a vicious-looking thing, with a savage double blade at the end and an enormous steel hook. He held it up before Gideon and turned it around, slowly.

"This is a flying gaff harpoon," he said, in his soft voice, "and we use it to kill sharks. *Big sharks.*"

He touched the bladed tip. "This is called the dart. You can jam it deep into a shark. But the real business part is this flying gaff. It's razor-sharp. You hook this into a shark's belly and pull. With one stroke, you can disembowel a great white and watch him eat his own entrails." He smiled.

Gideon looked from Cordray to his wife. She was standing back, watching. Her face was flushed, her breathing fast.

"That's exactly what I'm going to do to Amy, here. I'm going to hook her in the belly and pull this through her. Unless you start telling me everything I want to know."

"Don't say a word," Amy told him.

When Gideon didn't answer, Cordray reached over to Amy and ripped open her pajama top. He detached the enormous barbed hook—six inches in diameter—and slowly moved it toward her belly.

Linda watched eagerly.

The gleaming point of the gaff hook just touched Amy's skin, piercing it. Blood welled out. Amy's face remained expressionless.

"Okay," said Gideon. "I'll tell you everything. Just *stop* that."

"Shut up," said Amy.

"Keep talking."

"It is a map to a treasure—a really big one."

"What kind?" the woman asked eagerly. "Pirate treasure?"

"No. Spanish fleet." Gideon racked his brain for what he knew about treasure from the museums and historical societies he'd burglarized in an earlier life. "Back in the early sixteen hundreds, the Spanish treasure fleet was caught along this coast in a hurricane. Several ships were damaged. They had to unload and bury it on this coast. It's still here."

"And the map?"

"Shows where it is."

The woman stared at the map. "It's in Latin. I don't get it."

"A lot of early Spanish government documents were written in Latin," said Gideon, not at all sure that was true. "It's a very difficult map to understand. Deliberately obscure."

"So where's this treasure?"

"All we need to find...is one landmark along this coast. Just one."

"Which is?"

He hesitated. "Devil's vomit."

"*What?*"

"It's the seventh clue on that map. The inscription reads: 'Follow the Devil's vomit.' We don't know what that means. We're trying to find the landmark. That's where the treasure is buried. That's why I asked you about landmarks."

He could see they were buying it lock, stock, and barrel, greedily drinking in every word. And understandably so—for treasure hunters, this would be the score of a lifetime. But he was merely buying time—for what, he didn't yet know.

Linda was looking at the map, hands trembling. "Devil's vomit...what the fuck?"

"Look at the drawing," said Gideon. "The landmark is something that looks like an upside-down U with that knob on the side. A cave, maybe. Maybe you've seen something like that around here."

"Upside-down U...Knob...okay, I see it..." The woman was really excited now.

"That's where the treasure is buried."

She stared and stared. "Jesus Christ. I know this."

"What?" Cordray said.

"It's that rock arch, you know, that cay down the coast—the one with the strange name—Cayo Jeyupsi. That's the outline of it—I swear."

"But the Devil's vomit?"

A hesitation. "Who cares? That's the cay, I'm telling you!"

Cordray peered at the drawing. "Fucking hell. So it is."

The woman turned back to Gideon. "So where's it buried on the cayo? *Where?*"

"Talk." Cordray moved the hook a little. Amy winced.

"We don't know, damn it!" Gideon said.

"Yes you do. Where on the cay? *Where?*"

"I already said we were still looking for the spot. I can't tell you right here, right now."

"Yes you can. You will. What does the map say about the exact location?" Cordray was practically screaming.

"Tell us or I gut her!"

"Take that hook away," said Gideon, "or I'll never talk."

The hook didn't move away.

"He doesn't think you're serious," said Linda Cordray.

"Go ahead—gut her. And then he'll talk."

"My pleasure." The hook began to bite deeper into Amy's flesh.

23

As the gaff hook sank deeper, the trickle of blood became a rivulet.

"You hurt her," said Gideon, "I'll never speak another word, I swear."

"Shut up," Amy told him again. Her eyes were clear, her jaw set. Gideon had never met a person less afraid of death.

"You'll *never* find the treasure," he said.

"Do it," Linda urged her husband. "When he sees her all over the deck, he'll talk."

They were working themselves up, and Gideon believed they really might do it. But maybe he could use their craziness against them.

"It's worth over a billion dollars," he said. "You hurt her, you'll never get it."

That stopped Cordray cold. "A *billion* dollars? Of...what?"

"Five tons of gold. Coins. Bars. Crosses encrusted with jewels, reliquaries, ecclesiastical treasure."

The pair was transfixed.

"You kill my wife, kiss it good-bye. You'll just have to kill me, too, because I swear to God, I'll *never* talk after that."

"Five *tons*? Buried on the cay?"

"Take out the hook and promise not to hurt her, and I'll tell you where it is."

A hesitation. And then Cordray withdrew the hook a few inches from her flesh. "Start talking."

"I can't think with that damn hook so close. Take it away."

"How do we know you're telling the truth?" said Cordray.

He seemed a little less irrational than his wife. And the question gave Gideon another idea.

"All right. I wasn't telling you the whole truth. We already found it."

This had the both of them openmouthed. Amy turned to look at him. "Mark—" she began.

"Some of the treasure's right here on the boat," he added.

"You *dug it up*?"

"There's way too much, we had to leave almost all of it. We have to bring a bigger boat. But we took as much as we could. I'll make you a deal: let us go and you can have it. Take the boat, take everything. Just let us go ashore."

"Where is it?" cried Linda.

"In the galley. Hidden in cupboards behind the food supplies. Bars of gold, crates of doubloons."

He glanced at Amy, who was staring quizzically at him. Slowly and deliberately, he moved his eyes to the gaff hook in Cordray's hand, its long, razor-sharp tip gleaming.

"Jesus Christ, *go look*," said Cordray to his wife.

But she was already on her way, pushing past them on the narrow deck, into the pilothouse and down the companionway to the galley. The lights were still on from the previous search and Gideon could see, through the pilothouse windows, her climbing on the dining table and opening the cupboards, pulling and tossing foodstuffs out of the cabinet.

Cordray was distracted. He kept looking in the window. "Is it there?" he shouted.

"Give me a fucking chance." More stuff came flying out of the cabinet. Now even the two naked pirates were staring in the windows.

Gideon could now see Linda trying to get through the wood panels in the back of the cabinet. She got off the table, grabbed a kitchen knife out of the drawer, climbed back up, and began stabbing and prying at the wood. Meanwhile, Cordray watched her eagerly, his eyes fixed on the window. The gaff hook was in his right hand, forgotten, the hook pointing inward toward his own belly.

Now or never . . .

Gideon lunged forward, checking Cordray's upper arm and body with his shoulder, a sharp, hard blow. The check did exactly what he hoped—thrust the gaff hook deep into Cordray's abdomen.

With a piercing scream he fell back, instinctively trying to pull back on the hook and tearing himself more in the process, blood spurting over the deck. In an instant Amy exploded into action. With one deft move she twisted around, raised her tied hands, and hooked them over the bloody, protruding edge of the gaff hook, slicing off the plastic bonds. She then fell upon Cordray, grabbing the end of the hook.

At the same time, there was a crash in the galley as the woman jumped down from the table, scrambling up the companionway, gun drawn. The two pirates, taken off guard, scrambled backward, raising their guns but unable to fire into the tangle of people.

"Don't move or I pull this hook," Amy said, her voice remarkably calm. "Drop your weapons or I'll gut him."

"No!" screamed Cordray. "Manuel, Paco, *no se mueven!*"

The two pirates froze.

Following Amy's lead, Gideon sliced off his own ties and advanced on the men. They stepped back, guns leveled.

"*Baja las armas!*" Amy cried, starting to pull the hook.

"*Baja!*" cried Cordray. "You too, Linda! Oh, Christ, the blood, *look at the blood!*"

After a hesitation, the men tossed their guns on the deck. Gideon picked them up and backed away, keeping Pirate and Mustache covered.

"You too," Gideon said, pointing a gun at Linda, who was in the door of the pilothouse, frozen, staring at the hook in her husband's belly. "Or Amy pulls."

She dropped her gun.

"Oh, my God!" shrieked Cordray. "I'm bleeding to death!"

Amy let go of the end of the hook and backed up, snatching a proffered gun from Gideon. She pointed it at the two pirates. "*En el agua.* In the water."

The naked men needed no further encouragement. They dove into the water and began swimming as fast as they could back to the *Horizonte.*

She gestured at the wife. "Put your husband in the launch and get out of here."

"Yes. Yes." Linda was trembling all over. Cordray was moaning, holding his stomach with blood-soaked hands, the hook still inside. She tried to help him up, but he couldn't rise. He was sobbing.

"Look at all this blood," he moaned. "God, it hurts . . . Please, *get* me to a hospital—"

"Get in the launch *now*," said Amy, firing the gun into the air.

Gideon took Cordray by the arm and hauled him up, helping him to the stern, while he screamed piteously, the wife stumbling along, through the stern gate, onto the platform, and into the launch.

He pointed his gun at them. "Now get the fuck out of here."

The wife started the engine, Cordray lying in the bottom of the boat, doubled up, gasping. They moved away into the darkness, toward the *Horizonte*. Gideon could see the two pirates now climbing over the side, into the boat.

"We're still within small-arms range," said Amy. "Go cut the anchor rope. We'd better get out of here."

Gideon went forward. He could see the two pirates, and two other crewmen, helping Cordray and his wife onto the *Horizonte*. And then one of the crew went to the foredeck, where he pulled a piece of canvas off what Gideon had assumed to be storage crates or equipment—exposing a large mounted gun.

24

"OH, *SHIT*," SAID Gideon. He sawed through the anchor rope as he heard the engines of their own boat fire up. The *Turquesa* leapt forward just as the rope parted, the dual jet drives blasting a huge roll of water behind as the boat surged.

As they roared into the darkness the deck gun erupted behind them with incredible noise, a column of white water stitching toward them. The *Turquesa* veered abruptly, so hard that Gideon was thrown into the rail and almost went into the water, the rounds zipping past their stern, then whipping around again. The boat jerked once more, zigzagging, the hull almost coming clear of the water with each turn, Gideon clinging with both arms to the rail, his legs dangling over the side. There was a sudden eruption of water at the bow and the sound of rounds smacking into fiberglass and Kevlar. But the *Turquesa* was moving fast, and soon the gouts of water kicked up by the gun were going ever more wild.

They surged out of the bay and hit the swells coming around the point—a rough sea that almost swamped them. Amy slowed slightly, to stabilize the vessel, but it was still leaping and pounding through the swells. Gideon managed to climb back through the rail and crawl into the pilothouse.

"Damn," said Amy, staring at the radar. "They're coming after us."

Gideon grabbed a pair of binoculars and looked back. The *Horizonte*, brilliantly lit, was indeed following them. Fast.

Amy reached down and slapped a bunch of circuit breakers with the palm of her hand, dousing all the lights on the boat. A moment later the *Horizonte* also went dark.

"They can't outrun us," said Gideon.

Amy stared at the radar. "I'm not so sure about that."

"That tub?"

"That *tub* is going thirty knots and getting faster. It must have monstrous engines. And it's a much heavier boat—it can plow this sea better than we can."

Even in the darkness, Gideon could see blood running down her leg and pooling on the deck. "Amy, you're hurt. That hook—"

"Superficial. Didn't pierce the peritoneum."

"We need to stop the bleeding. It can't wait."

"It has to wait. A storm is coming. As the sea gets rougher, they're going to gain on us."

"I'll take the helm while you take care of that wound."

"No."

"I insist—"

"*You'll obey my orders*." She said it quietly, but with such conviction that Gideon knew it was pointless to argue.

"I'm going to treat you right here, then."

She didn't reply. Gideon went into the galley, clinging

to everything as the boat lurched through the rough sea. Feeling around in the darkness, he brought up a first-aid kit and some water in a squirt bottle. She didn't stop him while he opened her pajama top, sponged out the wound, and examined it. The hook had made an inch-long cut. He cleaned it with Betadine, spread on some antibiotic ointment, taped the wound shut, and applied a dressing.

The boat continued to leap through the dark sea. He could see nothing around them but darkness, broken only by the faint gray outlines of streaming whitecaps. But the *Horizonte* was visible on radar, a green blob half a nautical mile directly behind them.

"They're gaining," said Amy.

"What's the range of a 50-caliber machine gun?"

"Two thousand yards."

He peered at the radar screen. "They're only a thousand yards out already."

"In a sea like this, both of us moving the way we are, they can't aim."

"They'll put a lot of lead in the air and try to take us down that way. Those rounds'll go right through our Kevlar hull."

As if in response, he heard a distant, rapid-fire burst from behind. Fifty yards to port, flashes of white water indicated where the rounds had hit. More fire, more white water, this time to starboard.

The boat thundered on, banging and leaping off the waves. Gideon could hear stuff crashing about in the galley.

Amy changed course. "We're not going to outrun them," she said. "Find us a plan B."

"Plan B?"

"It's all I can do to drive this boat."

Gideon's mind raced through a dozen possibilities, rejecting them all. There was another fusillade of fire from the *Horizonte*.

"Gideon—!"

"Okay, okay. I have an idea. We'll light up our launch like a Christmas tree, send it off, use it as a decoy while we escape in the darkness."

Amy rolled her eyes. "They have radar. They can tell the difference between a dinghy and a yacht."

Gideon fell silent.

And then Amy said: "No, wait. It *could* work."

"How?"

"Radar reflectors. In the rear storage chest."

"Radar reflectors?"

"Metal objects you hang from the mast in a fog to make yourself more visible to ship's radar."

"That would make the launch look as big as the *Turquesa?*"

"Yes. Hang them on the launch as high as possible."

"Got it."

Gideon exited the pilothouse, staggering, holding on to whatever he could find. The wind roared around his ears, the boat shuddering and slamming through the sea. He unlatched the storage chest and there—between coiled ropes and other assorted equipment—were two round metal objects with crosspieces inside them, attached to wires. As he pulled them out, he heard another burst of machine-gun fire. Gouts of water swung past the stern.

The *Turquesa's* launch, an eleven-foot Zodiac, was hanging on davits at the stern, swinging violently. There was nothing sticking up he could hang the reflectors on . . . and then he noticed the rod mounts on either side.

Deep-sea fishing rods . . .

Lurching down into the cluttered galley, Gideon threw open the rod cabinets, quickly assembling the two biggest marlin rods he could find, tying the radar reflectors onto their ends. Back on deck, he climbed into the Zodiac, which was pitching madly, and managed to insert the rods into the mounts, securing the handles in place with duct tape from the storage chest. He set one hurricane lamp in the bow and another in the stern. Then, after a moment's thought, he pulled the extra gas tank from its berth and hauled it into the Zodiac as well.

More gunfire from astern.

Now he had to lower the Zodiac into the water, with the boat going thirty-five knots in a heavy sea. This was going to be fun.

Climbing out of the launch, he rummaged in a rear cargo box, finding a long towrope. He fixed it to the front bow eye of the Zodiac and wrapped the other end around a rear cleat on the *Turquesa*. Slowly—stabilizing himself as best he could to ensure he wasn't jolted overboard by the heavy swells—he switched on the hurricane lamps and then lowered the boat from the davits. But when it hit the water, it spun off the davits like a leaf and almost flipped over, saved only when Gideon released a good ten feet of rope.

The Zodiac stabilized and was now planing behind the yacht, riding its wake. Slowly, carefully, he let out more rope, until it found a stable place in the wake about fifty feet back. Then he tied it off and went into the pilothouse.

"Everything's set," he said.

"When you release the launch, I'll execute an immediate escape maneuver—a course change."

"We need to go the way they'd least expect," he said.

"Leave it to me."

Another burst. A couple of rounds clipped through the side of the pilothouse at an angle, showering them with splinters of fiberglass.

"Son of a *bitch!*" Without hesitating Gideon scrambled back to the stern, reached out, and cut the towrope. "Done!" he called out.

The Zodiac skipped and slowed, and almost immediately dwindled to a tiny speck of light in the murk. There was more gunfire. Amy did not change course.

"I said, *done!*" Gideon cried, hurrying back into the pilothouse. "Change course!"

She shook her head. "The *least* obvious move is *not* to change course."

That made sense. "It won't be long before they realize they were duped," he said.

"It only needs to work long enough for us to get out of radar range. We're in a big sea—that's a lot of sea return for radar—and this boat has a low profile. I think three thousand yards should do it."

Gideon stared at the radar screen. He could see the green blob that was their Zodiac, apparently motionless. The blob that was the *Horizonte* was approaching, slowing, turning.

Once again, the sound of gunfire, burst after burst. Staring astern, he saw the dim light suddenly brighten. The Zodiac, no doubt, set afire. There was a puff and a ball of flame as the gas tank in the craft went up. The report of the explosion came rumbling toward them across the water. Another burst of automatic weapons fire, another ball of flame: the spare tank.

Every second was precious, taking them farther away from the *Horizonte*, farther into the radar wilderness of sea and wind.

"They're on to us!" called Amy. "They're coming!"

On the radar screen, the faint green blob that was the much larger *Horizonte* was peeling away, moving faster, gaining speed. The Zodiac had disappeared from the screen—sunk. There was still a flickering light aft from the burning slick of gasoline.

"Change course," said Gideon. "Not much, say twenty degrees. Just to test if they can see us or not."

A hesitation. "Okay."

Amy changed course. They waited for the *Horizonte* to alter course accordingly. It didn't. The faint green blob continued straight, and then, having clearly lost them on radar, made a course change. A guess. A wrong guess.

They were out of range.

A minute later, the image of the *Horizonte* had dropped off their own radar.

"You realize," Gideon said, "that the wife, instead of taking her husband for medical help, came after us. I wouldn't be surprised if he bleeds to death."

Amy shook her head. "Treasure hunters—I've had experience with them. Crazy people. We haven't seen the last of her."

"Why do you say that?"

"She's going to be waiting for us at Cayo Jeyupsi. With a dead husband. *Pissed.*"

25

Brock entered the EES lab, pausing in the doorway. It was seven AM, and these early-morning calls were getting more than irritating. Glinn's attitude seemed to be, *If I don't sleep, why should you?*

Two technicians and Garza were bent over a large, obscure machine, cabled to a flat panel that displayed digital photographic strips covered with fuzzy lines. Glinn was behind them, half in shadow, silently observing the proceedings from his wheelchair.

"Thank you for coming, Dr. Brock," said Glinn, turning. To Brock's surprise, he looked almost flustered, unusual for a man of preternatural coolness.

Brock nodded.

"Please," said Glinn, recovering. "Sit down. Coffee?"

"Thank you. Black, no sugar."

Brock took a chair in the little conference area of the lab. Garza and the two scientists paused in their work and swiveled their chairs around to join the meeting.

"So," said Brock, "did you figure out what animal it came from?"

"That's a difficult problem," said Garza. "To be sure, we need to do a DNA analysis. But first, some questions have arisen about the making of vellum that we hope you can answer. It's our understanding that three types of animal skins were normally used in fashioning vellum—sheep, calf, and goat. What about other animals?"

"Well," said Brock, always happy to deliver a lecture, "in the Levant, many Persian and Arabic manuscripts used a type of vellum made from camel skin."

"Interesting. Anything else?"

"Very rarely, the skin of pig, deer, horse, or donkey was used. There are instances where cat skin was used in repairs."

"No others?" Garza asked.

"Not that we know of."

There was a pause.

"By the way," Brock said with a sniff, turning to Glinn, "I must say that this idea of yours strikes me as a dead end. I don't see how the vellum *itself* could be the answer to the riddle."

"Consider the quotation, Doctor. *Respondeo ad quaestionem, ipsa pergamena.* 'I respond to the question, the page itself.' You pointed out that *pergamena* also meant 'parchment' or 'vellum.'" His eyes flickered as he said this. "Think of the sentence another way: the *parchment* itself is the response, the *answer*, to the riddle."

"We've run Eli's conjecture through the language analysis routines of our computer," Garza said. "They predict the likelihood of it being correct at over ninety percent."

That a computer program could interpret medieval Latin struck Brock as preposterous, but he let it pass.

"How could the vellum itself possibly be the answer to the riddle of this map?"

"To know that, we need to discover what kind of animal it came from." Glinn turned to the technicians. "What next?"

Weaver—the lead DNA technician—spoke up. "The only way to solve this question is through DNA analysis. To do that we have to find a clean source of genetic material—ideally from inside a hair follicle. The trouble is, the parchment has been thoroughly scraped and washed."

Brock sighed. "If hair is what you're after, may I make a suggestion?"

"Of course," said Garza.

"You know that all pieces of vellum have two sides, a 'flesh' side and a 'hair' side. The hair side is darker and coarser, with occasional traces of hair follicles. The follicles themselves, of course, will have been destroyed during the initial preparation. However, you might take a close look at the binding edge of the page. The margins of the skins were sometimes less scraped and cleaned than the rest, and often they left a little extra thickness there to hold the binding. You may find an *intact* hair follicle in that area."

"Excellent," Glinn said. "Thank you, Dr. Brock. You are certainly worth your keep."

Brock flushed at the compliment despite himself.

26

THE MORNING DAWNED dirty and rough, with a howling wind and dark clouds scudding low across the sky. They had taken refuge in Bahia Hondita, a huge, shallow lagoon with dozens of islands and coves and patches of mangrove swamp—an ideal place to hide. With the jet drive propulsion their draft was only three feet, and with no need to worry about fouling a propeller they'd been able to get the boat up a watercourse and deep into the recesses of a mangrove swamp, where the larger *Horizonte* could not follow, even if they knew where they were.

Gideon spent the morning cleaning up the mess in the galley and mopping up the blood on the cockpit deck. Amy opened the hatches and examined the engine and boat systems, doing a damage assessment where rounds had struck the boat.

They convened in the galley over espresso one hour before it was time to make a scheduled call to EES. Amy looked gray.

"How's your injury?" Gideon asked.

"Fine," said Amy. "Listen, we've got some damage. A 50-caliber round fragmented and went everywhere inside the engine compartment."

"The boat seems to be working all right."

"For now. We have some damaged hoses, fuel and oil lines, which I can patch or replace. Some shrapnel in the battery compartment, as well, but no leaks there. One bad circuit board. It'll take most of the day. We'll head out to Cayo Jeyupsi tonight."

"You sure the boat's okay?"

"My only real worry is the ricocheting of all those bits and pieces of shrapnel. It's impossible to trace it all or know what might be wrong—until something fails."

"What about the other rounds that hit the boat?"

"They went high, through the pilothouse. One in the forward hull above the waterline. I put a temporary patch on it."

"Oh, dear, we might lose our damage deposit."

Amy managed a wan smile. "That's Glinn's problem, not ours."

"Speaking of Glinn, we've got to give him a sit-rep in an hour. We should talk now about how we're going to present this to him. I also need to write up what happened in the electronic log."

A hesitation. "Gideon, let's not... alarm him."

"What are you suggesting?"

"Look, we don't want him to abort our mission. We're too far into this."

"Okay."

"I'm not suggesting we lie, exactly. We just have to give it the proper spin. An unfortunate encounter. A bump in the road."

"An 'unfortunate encounter'? Amy, a man's dead."

"We don't know that." A beat. She gazed at him intently with her dark eyes. "You want to give this up?"

Gideon hesitated. "No."

"Then pitch your log entry accordingly, and in the video meeting think carefully about how you present things."

"Is that an order, Captain?"

A long silence. "I won't make that an order. Because I know you're with me on this one."

Gideon nodded. She was right.

The meeting with Glinn was short. They made their report, Gideon presenting it as a brief, unfortunate encounter with a pair of crazy treasure hunters, over and done with. It was, in the end, a good thing, as it produced an essential piece of information: the Devil's vomit cay marked on the map. Glinn listened, asked few questions, did not offer any advice, and signed off quickly.

Amy spent the rest of the day below, fixing the engine. She emerged at sunset covered with grease. She took a shower and then sat down at the computer. The wind had picked up further, the mangroves clacking and shaking around them. The tropical depression that had been building beyond the Cape Verde Islands had turned into a tropical storm and was now heading toward the Windwards and northwestward to Haiti. While they were considerably south of its path, it was a large system and, one way or another, they were going to be affected.

Amy seemed pleased. "The worse the weather, the less chance there is of the *Horizonte* surprising us at the cay tonight."

"I doubt they're going to be at the cay."

"I *know* they will. They're treasure hunters. The word *obsession* doesn't even begin to describe them."

"How do you know so much about treasure hunters, anyway?" Gideon asked.

"That question falls into the personal information category. Sorry."

She went back to the laptop in the work area while Gideon prepared an elaborate dinner of seared duck breasts, wild rice, and toasted goat cheese salad. From time to time, he glanced over at what she was working on so assiduously. It appeared she was comparing the Phorkys Map to other old maps—and a bunch of texts in ancient Greek.

"What's all that?"

"Idle speculation."

"Dinner's ready."

She abandoned the computer and sat down at the dining room table. Gideon laid the plates on with ceremony. He poured himself some wine, giving her the glass of water, no ice, that she asked for.

She tucked in and began the usual unceremonious shoveling.

"Whoa, hold on," aid Gideon, laying a hand on her fork hand, staying the scarfing process. "There's no hurry. Can we please have a civilized meal? I worked hard preparing it—you please should slow down and enjoy it."

"You eat your way, I'll eat mine," she said, forking a quarter of the breast into her mouth and chewing, her cheeks bulging like a chipmunk, making vulgar eating noises.

Gideon shook his head. "Jesus, didn't your parents teach you table manners?"

This was met with a sudden, freezing silence. Gideon thought to himself, *More personal information I won't be privy to.*

She finished, pushing her plate away and standing up. "At midnight, we'll start for Jeyupsi. It's thirty nautical miles. I doubt we can make more than twelve knots in this sea, so we'll arrive around two thirty in the morning. We're going to make a large circle of the cay at extreme radar distance, just to see if they're around. Their boat is bigger than ours, makes a larger radar target, so we'll see them before they see us. If all looks good, we go in, try to figure out what was meant by the phrase *Follow the Devil's vomit.* Agreed?"

"Agreed."

"So why don't you go below, get some sleep? I'll take care of the dishes."

"No objections to that."

As he stood up, preparing to head for his stateroom, she laid a hand on his arm. "Gideon."

"Yes?"

"You handled those treasure hunters really well back there—all that talk about a billion dollars in gold. You got them to lose their heads—and that saved our lives."

"Social engineering is my specialty. But your contribution was pretty damn crucial, too."

"And that business with the launch—they fell for it just long enough for us to give them the slip."

"It was your radar reflectors that did the trick."

There was a slightly awkward silence. Gideon sensed that any praise from Amy was praise indeed, so he just smiled and said, "Thanks."

She nodded wordlessly.

And as he turned to leave the galley, he saw her go back to the computer and continue working on the Greek texts and the map.

27

GARZA LOOKED ON as Weaver, the head DNA tech, leaned over a microscope, peering intently into the eyepiece as he moved the stage this way and that with fussy, tiny movements. Two other techs hovered nearby, watching, various tools at the ready. To Garza, the procedure had all the feel of a surgical operation.

Glinn had vanished after the call from Gideon—in his usual way, without taking leave, saying where he was going, or mentioning when he'd be back. Glinn had always been secretive, but it was getting worse. He used to keep Garza in the loop. He was supposed to be Glinn's right-hand man, second in command at EES. But now he was beginning to feel like an errand boy.

"Okay," Weaver murmured, eyes glued to the microscope. "I've got the binding edge of the page in view and it looks like there might be some intact follicles."

All work on the vellum was done at a painstaking, glacial pace; it had taken them most of a day just to prepare for this procedure. A silence settled over the lab as Weaver continued peering into the scope, every now and then adjusting its stage. The minutes ticked by. Garza resisted the urge to glance at his watch.

"Got one that looks good," said Weaver. "Two, actually. Hand me a probe, a sterile number three forceps, and a strip of PCR tubes."

The technicians came forward with the requested articles. Garza watched as—with the utmost care—Weaver extracted first one microscopic hair, then a second.

"Both follicles are intact," he said as he straightened up from the microscope.

"How quickly can you get results?" Garza asked.

"Sterile microsurgery will be required to access the uncontaminated interior of the follicles—with something like this, DNA contamination can be a huge problem. After that, we have to do a PCR on it, and then sequence it. It's time consuming—and a lot depends on whether there's still contamination in the samples that has to be teased out." He seemed to hesitate.

"What is it?" Garza asked.

"I didn't want to say anything before," Weaver said. "But now that I've actually seen these hair follicles and viewed the pattern of pores under the scope, I'm almost certain."

"Certain about what?"

"About what kind of, ah, animal this vellum is from."

"Well?" Garza said. Why was he being so coy?

Weaver licked his lips. "Human."

For a moment, the lab went silent.

Brock laid down his pen. "You can't be serious."

Weaver said nothing.

"I'm sorry, but there must be some mistake," Brock continued. "There are simply no examples of human skin being used for vellum . . ."

Garza glanced over at him. "Are you sure?"

"Quite. For monks to flay a human and use his skin for vellum is unthinkable. No Christian of the time would have done that, even to a pagan enemy. That sort of cruelty wasn't invented until the twentieth century."

"What about Viking raiders?" Garza asked. "Or other pagan tribes of the time, perhaps? Maybe they made their own vellum from the skin of Christian monks." He cast a smirk at Brock.

"Absolutely not. The Vikings didn't read books—they *burned* books. But more to the point, the desecration of the human body after death was not part of Viking or pagan culture, either. They might rape your wife and burn you alive in your house, but they would never mutilate a corpse." Brock paused. "If you want my considered opinion, gentlemen, you are grievously in error."

Weaver looked down at the tiny box of clear plastic that held the two follicles. "Say what you will. I think it's human."

"Get those tests started right away," Garza said.

28

Amy awoke Gideon at eleven thirty. The wind was still blowing, and the weather report indicated worse was on the way. He went through the usual first-mate chores of raising the anchor, arranging the paper charts in their proper order, and checking the electronics to make sure they were working properly. He was pleased at how quickly he had mastered these numerous but relatively simple chores.

At midnight, they eased out of the mangrove swamp into the choppy waters of the bay. It was a dirty night, sand blowing across the water in stinging clouds, neither moon nor stars. It took another half an hour to reach the inlet, which was boiling from the storm surge—and then they were in the open sea.

The swells were suddenly terrifying, great rolling beasts coming one after the other, the crests foaming white, spray and spume blown forward by the wind.

"This is perfect," said Amy, at the helm. She was adjusting the gain on the radar, back and forth.

"Perfect? You're joking, right?" Gideon was already

feeling queasy. During the encounter with the *Horizonte*, he'd been too busy—and too scared—to feel seasick. That wasn't the case at present. This was not going to be a good night.

"The radar's practically green with sea return, and the waves are almost as high as our boat. They're going to have a hell of a time seeing us on their radar."

"If you say so."

The boat plowed through the water at ten knots. Beyond the pilothouse windows, hammered with rain, there was nothing—no horizon, no stars, no sense of orientation, just a thundering blackness. The swell was coming from behind, and each foaming crest shoved the bow down and pushed their stern sideways in a sickening corkscrew motion, Amy fighting the wheel to stay the course. The chartplotter showed them as a tiny black arrow on a sea of white, moving away from shore until their lonely speck was the only thing on the screen. Gideon tried to adjust the gain on the radar as Amy had previously showed him, but there was only so much he could do in a sea like this.

About one o'clock, a strange sound came from below: a kind of stuttering vibration that shivered the hull.

"Damn," said Amy, looking at the dials. The boat started to slew sideways and she fought with the wheel, throttling one engine down and the other up.

More stuttering, and the boat slewed again. Amy worked the controls, muttering under her breath, and then the shuddering stopped.

"Port engine's out," she said. "I've got to go below. Take the wheel."

"Me? I don't know what I'm doing!"

"Listen to me: *don't let the boat go broadside*. Every wave will try to push your stern around—you've got to turn the wheel the opposite way—push it back. But don't overcorrect, either."

She pointed to the dual throttles. "You only have one engine—starboard, the right throttle. Try to maintain twenty-one hundred rpm. You might need to throttle up or down depending on whether you're climbing and descending a wave. Got it?"

"Not really—"

She went below. Gideon grasped the wheel, peering into the darkness. He couldn't even see the waves in front of the bow. But there was a growling sound behind him, and the stern began to rise with the hiss of breaking water. His hands felt frozen on the wheel. The bow was pushed down, down, the nose burying itself in the water. And then the stern was shoved sideways—violently.

"Fuck!" He turned the wheel against the movement, goosing the throttle; the boat began to straighten out, and then abruptly swung the other way, the bow rearing up as the stern sank into the trough. Fighting the wheel to true it up, he could hear things crashing in the galley. He turned the other way, fighting his own overcorrection, easing off the throttle.

That was only the first wave. Now the terrifying process began again.

Even worse, he was about to be sick. Fumbling with the side window latch, he managed to get it open with one hand, the rain lashing in, trying to keep his other hand firm on the wheel. He stuck his head out the window and retched unhappily. He was hardly done heaving when the next crest shoved the boat sideways again, the water sweeping over the stern and jamming the bow down. He pulled the wheel around; the boat skidded, too much yet again, and he quickly swung it back the other way, the boat weaving drunkenly through the combers.

He heard a muffled yell from Amy, below.

The next wave he handled a little better, pausing to puke again between the swells. On the chartplotter he could now make out their destination, ten nautical miles distant, creeping toward them. This was crazy. They should have stayed in the bay, waited for the storm to blow over.

And now something else was happening. He could hear a hesitation in the rumble of the remaining engine—a kind of stuttering sound. The needle of its rpm gauge began to chatter and drop. He throttled up but that only made it worse, the engine faltering. He quickly throttled back down and it seemed to stabilize. But the rpms had subsided to fifteen hundred—and he could feel the power of the sea taking over as the boat's forward motion faltered.

The next wave came harder, bashing the stern around and tilting the boat viciously. He threw the wheel to the left, and the boat came around—sluggishly. The next wave hammered them again, pushing the vessel farther around, almost broadside.

The engine coughed, rumbled, coughed again.

"Amy!" he cried. "What's going on!" But the roar of the wind and sea snatched the words away.

And then the engine quit totally. There was a sudden loss of vibration, a vanishing of the low-frequency throb—leaving only the roar of the sea and wind.

The boat was abruptly shoved broadside, in a nauseating rotating movement, totally in the grip of the sea. Gideon hung on to the wheel for dear life. It was all he could do to stay on his feet. The lights flickered.

Amy's voice came over the intercom, supernaturally calm. "Go forward to the chain locker, deploy the drogue."

"Drogue—?"

"The sea anchor. It looks like a big canvas parachute. Throw it overboard, run the line out a hundred feet, and cleat it off. Then come back and help me."

He abandoned the wheel and exited the pilothouse. Outside, the full force of the storm slammed into him, staggering him, the rain lashing his face, the deck heaving. Beyond, he could dimly see the ridges and foaming peaks of a mountainous sea rising above his head in all directions.

Gripping the rail, he crawled forward to the chain locker set in the bow. The boat was wallowing, each swell tilting it up and throwing it down sideways, almost like a bucking horse, the hull shuddering. Water erupted over the rubrail and surged along the deck. Each time it did, he had to grip the rail with both hands to keep from being washed overboard.

He made it to the bow, undogged the chain locker. With no light, he reached in and felt his way around blindly. There it was: something bulky made of thick canvas, to the left.

A swell burst over him, knocking his body sideways and sliding him over the deck until his legs dangled over the side. With all his strength, he pulled himself back by gripping the rail. As soon as the swell had passed, he hauled the canvas thing out of the locker. It was all folded up and there was no way to be sure of what it was, but it was attached to a rope and he threw it overboard. *Here goes nothing.* It hit the water, the rope running out fast. It burned his hands as he arrested its headlong rush. He managed to tie it off to the mooring post, his fingers feeling fat and stupid.

It was almost like magic. The line went taut; there was a groaning sound; and then the *Turquesa* began to swing around, bow pointing into the wind and sea. In a moment the boat was riding better—much better.

Gideon crawled back into the pilothouse, soaked to the skin, hit by a series of dry heaves. Head pounding from the effort, anxiety, and nausea, he went below to where Amy was working on the engine. The compartment panels were off and she was on her back, her head and torso deep in the mass of machinery.

"What now?"

"Shut down those fuel lines, there."

Gideon turned the levers perpendicular to the lines.

Amy continued issuing orders as she worked. The boat was riding much better, the big combers hissing past on either side. It was terrifying enough, but at least they weren't broadside and spinning out of control.

"Okay," Amy said at last. "See if you can start the starboard engine."

Gideon went up, set the throttle and shift, and pressed the button. A few coughs and the engine roared to life. He felt a rush of relief.

A moment later Amy appeared—covered in oil, her hair matted. She took the helm. "Raise the drogue. Wrap the line around the anchor windlass and I'll winch it in. Leave it cleated in case we need to re-deploy."

Gideon did as instructed and a moment later the motorized windlass was hauling in the drogue. He manhandled it back into the locker.

The boat swung around, a wave slamming over him as he crawled back toward the pilothouse.

"We'd better get back to Bahía Hondita," he said, coughing and shedding water. "Ride it out there."

"We're two miles from Jeyupsi," said Amy, quietly. "Let's finish what we started." She reached down and flipped a batch of circuit breakers, plunging the boat into darkness. The only light came from the dim glow of the electronics.

Gideon stared at the isolated cay on the charplotter, an irregular shape in the middle of nowhere.

"We're going to circle it at a mile, looking for our friends. If they're not there, we go in and turn on the outside floodlight so we can verify it's the right landmark. You'll document it with photographs and video. And identify whatever might be meant by clue seven, the Devil's vomit."

"And if they're there?"

"We turn and run."

"We only have one engine."

"We'll see them before they see us. We'll lose them in this sea. The crests of these waves are higher than our boat."

"Thanks, I hadn't noticed."

The boat rumbled on, thrown back and sideways again and again. They circled the cay, seeing nothing on radar that might be a lurking boat.

"Okay," Amy said. "We're going in."

She brought the boat closer to the cay. As they approached, Gideon could hear the roar of surf, like a continuous barrage of artillery, growing increasingly in volume. And then, dimly emerging from the darkness, a patch of ever-shifting, ever-boiling white.

She slowed, circling until they were in the lee of the cay. The outline on radar sharpened, beginning to take on the approximate shape of the image on the map. Amy slowed still further, keeping the engine going just enough to keep the boat oriented.

"Get ready with the floodlights," she said. "Aim them at the rock. We'll want to do this quickly."

Gideon grabbed the handles of the floodlights in the roof of the pilothouse and maneuvered them toward the vague outline, white with surf. The surf was so violent, the thunder of it shook the very air.

"Now."

He threw the switches, and the bank of lights blazed into the darkness, brilliantly illuminating the cay. It was stupendous—a huge arch of black rock rising out of the water, lashed by surf, streaming white water. A long rocky shore extended along one side, about a quarter of a mile, raging with surf.

But it was the arch itself that transfixed Gideon. With each wave, the sea rushed through the hole in the arch, cramming in and boiling into a violent maelstrom—and then *vomiting* out the other side, leaving a long trail of white spume on the surface of the sea that trailed off in a straight line into the darkness.

Gideon grabbed the camera and began taking photos as the boat moved past, then switched it into video mode.

"That trail of sea foam," said Amy. "It follows the current. And we're supposed to follow it. I'm taking a bearing now—that'll be our new heading." She gunned the engine, the boat swinging around to slip past the cay...

Just as—suddenly, out of the darkness from behind the cay, churning at high speed—there came the *Horizonte*, its 50-caliber deck gun pointed directly at them.

29

AT THE HELM of the *Horizonte*, Linda Cordray gripped the wheel with whitened knuckles. There they were—right where she wanted them. Her men would hold their fire, as she had instructed.

The ruse had worked perfectly. She had positioned the *Horizonte* in the lee of the cay, in a sheltered cove close enough to shore so their radar image would merge with that of the cay itself, causing them to look like just another rock.

As she stared at the *Turquesa*, now turning in an ineffectual attempt at escape, a white-hot rage lanced through her. In the cabin below, wrapped in a blood-soaked canvas, lay her husband's lifeless body. He had bled to death, screaming and sobbing before lapsing into the final coma as they chased the *Turquesa*. Cordray told herself, yet again, that even had she headed straight to the nearest port, he never would have made it. Nothing she could have done would have saved him. She told herself that several times.

They'd shared a unique bond. Living outside the rules,

two against the world. They were remarkably alike in their thirst for adventure, their loathing for the settled life. He was the velvet fist in her iron glove. They complemented each other perfectly. Ironically, the great physical difference between them just cemented the relationship.

Their dream of the past five years had been to find the wreck of the privateer *Compostela*, laden with the fabled Treasure of Coromandel. It had been sunk off the Guajira coast back in 1550, and they'd narrowed down the possible locations to the point where it was almost in their grasp. A few more weeks of sidescanning, and they would have it.

At first, they'd worried that the *Turquesa* was also looking for the Coromandel treasure. There had been others before—it was a celebrated treasure—and they had dealt with them. But during cocktails they realized the two, Mark and Amy, were instead looking for a different prize. A prize that was possibly even bigger than the Treasure of Coromandel.

Five tons of gold.

She realized that they weren't the usual treasure-hunting idiots, out there on a song and prayer, with a leaky boat and some flea-market map. Oh, they had a map, all right—and she knew it was genuine the moment she saw it. Fake maps always looked the same. This one had been unique. Totally unique.

Her man, her partner, was dead in his blood-soaked shroud, but she could still hear his quiet voice in her mind. Advising her what to do. Telling her what he wanted. And what he wanted most of all was to get the map to the Spanish treasure—and then kill Mark and Amy Johnson. In that order. If she merely killed them, sank their boat—which she could do right now if she wanted—he would not approve. More important, Cayo Jeyupsi was big enough that you could spend a year digging on it. She needed that map.

The *Horizonte* bulled through the swell, the deck heaving. Linda Cordray handled the helm smoothly, her instincts for the waves unerring, staring fiercely into the darkness ahead. The *Turquesa* had doused its lights, but she could still see it clearly on radar. It was eight hundred yards ahead, but they were going a lot slower than before. Engine trouble, perhaps—the vessel had taken some rounds.

She had her four men. They were young, strong, instinctual, and merciless. They would board her, take the boat, and incapacitate the Johnsons. She would take over, get the map—this time with no mistakes. And then those two would die. Horribly.

Seven hundred yards. She was close enough to blow them out of the water with the machine gun. But she wouldn't deploy it yet. It wasn't until her men had fired, willy-nilly, on that decoy launch and it went up in flames that she realized how much she needed that map. She'd had a bad moment then, realizing her mistake, thinking the map was gone. She was almost relieved to see it had been a ruse.

She called in the first mate, Manuel. She told him exactly what the plan was for ramming and boarding the *Turquesa*. Manuel listened in silence. His face was dark. He was ready to kill. She explained the stakes. If they pulled it off, if they got their hands on that map, it would make him rich beyond his wildest dreams.

And they would pull it off. They had the bigger boat,

four tough men, and overwhelming firepower. While the *Turquesa* might have some small arms on board, the 50-caliber at short range could obliterate them.

She glanced at the radar. They had now closed to six hundred yards. Any idiot could see the Johnsons were doomed. They were no idiots. Cordray unhooked the VHF mike and turned it to channel 16. "*Turquesa*, this is *Horizonte*."

Silence. She knew they must hear her—it was standard for cruising vessels to keep the emergency channel 16 live at all times.

"*Turquesa*, hove to, or we open fire."

No answer.

"Hove to. We just want the map. Give us the map and no one will get hurt. Do you read?"

Again, no answer.

She gave the engines slightly more power, even though they were running close to the red.

The gap began closing more rapidly. The six hundred yards dwindled to five. A large wave bashed the side of the boat, surging up and over the decks. She had to fight to keep the boat on course. The sea was growing worse. The VHF weather channel had begun issuing a stream of bad news: a tropical storm, passing to the north, was gaining power and would soon be a hurricane. Seas were expected to grow to twenty feet or more.

Another shuddering wave swept over the foredeck, foaming gray-green as it surged through the railing. She couldn't see the *Turquesa*, but she knew it had to be worse for them. The boat was shorter, narrower—and much lighter. It would be tossed around like a cork. It was amazing they were still afloat.

The pursuit continued. They were now edging into the Barraquilla Basin, deep water hundreds of miles from shore. There was nothing out there—nothing.

Cordray didn't care. Four hundred yards.

She picked up the mike. *"Turquesa, this is Horizonte. I repeat: hove to or we will sink you. This is your final warning."*

Nothing. No answer. Three hundred yards.

She called Manual to her side. He had seen everything the sea could throw at a man, and he was still looking pale. "You and Paco, man the gun," she told him in Spanish. "Be ready to fire at my signal. Focus your fire on the two. Keep it high, avoid holing the vessel."

"Sí, señora."

Two hundred yards. One hundred.

The VHF crackled. "Okay, *Horizonte*, you win. We're hoving to."

It was the woman. This was it: the endgame had arrived.

"Lights!" Linda Cordray cried.

The bank of lights atop of the *Horizonte* snapped on, throwing a brilliant glow across the heaving sea, blinding them. And there was the *Turquesa*, swinging around to face them.

The floodlights of the *Turquesa* went on in turn.

She scrabbled at the VHF mike, yanked it down. "Off! Turn those fucking lights off or—!"

The first shot punched through the pilothouse window, spraying plastic slivers across her face. Her brain was only starting to process what was happening when the second shot slammed into her brow, taking off the top of her head.

30

GIDEON REMAINED PRONE in the bow, switching the M4 to automatic and unleashing a blast at the two men manning the 50-caliber machine gun. He was well within range, but the heaving of the deck made it hard to aim, and the burst went wide. Still, it had an excellent effect: it sent both men diving to the deck. And Amy had scored big-time with the H&K sniper rifle.

Now Amy gunned the engine. The *Turquesa* headed straight for the *Horizonte*. Remaining prone on the deck, legs splayed, Gideon held his fire as they surged forward, narrowing the gap between the two boats in a matter of seconds. Confusion reigned on the *Horizonte*: the two men at the 50-caliber were still on the deck; there was consternation in the pilothouse, no one at the wheel, throttle at full speed. The bow turned in to a cresting wave that burst over the forecastle. The two men at the machine gun, clinging to the mount, temporarily vanished in a frothing mass of water.

The *Turquesa* was now just seconds from impact with the *Horizonte*. One of the gunners managed to get on his feet, pulling himself up by the handles of the 50-caliber, swinging the gun toward them.

Gideon fired again as the gunner, for his part, let fly a deafening burst; the brutal stream of fire raked the *Turquesa*, churning up the fiberglass deck like a chain saw as it swept past. The *Turquesa* checked its course at the last minute, blasting past the other vessel with only a few feet of separation and then swerving away. Gideon could see a grenade canister, tossed by Amy, tumbling into the rear cockpit of the *Horizonte*.

The man at the machine gun let loose another desperate blast, the rounds ripping through the aft section of the *Turquesa*—and then came a deafening explosion as the grenade detonated within the *Horizonte*. A ball of fire, orange and yellow and black all rolling together, punched up into the teeth of the storm, the sound of it booming across the water, along with a huge fountain of flaming debris. The initial blast was followed by a string of thunderous secondary explosions, lofting more wreckage into the air. Their fuel lines had ruptured. Within moments the entire superstructure of the *Horizonte* was splayed open, one long mass of fire. As Gideon watched—rooted in awe and horror—the boat wallowed in the foaming sea. There was another explosion, and a comber burst over the listing vessel, obscuring it as it fell into a trough. And as the swell rose again, all that could be seen was a great fiery slick, sprinkled with burning wreckage.

The *Horizonte* had utterly vanished.

31

As the burning swell subsided, Gideon struggled to his feet from his position at the bow and made his way aft, clutching at the rail to avoid being swept overboard. He found Amy at the helm. The lone working engine was making an ugly, coughing sound, and lights flickered. Each wave seemed to push the boat down farther, it rising ever more sluggishly.

"Check the forward bilge," she cried over the roar of the sea.

Another wave slammed into the boat, pushing it sideways and almost knocking Gideon off his feet as he made his way down the companionway. The cabin was a total mess; the 50-caliber rounds had ripped through the foredeck, leaving gaping holes, shattering fiberglass, and wood. The hatch to the bilge, he remembered, was located in the passageway to the head. He found the square piece covering the bilge access, pulled it up, unlatched the hatch, and raised it.

Water was sloshing around a mere inch below the cabin floor. Even as he watched, the boat was shoved sideways, the floor tilted, and water sloshed up and into the passageway. He tried to shut the hatch but the upwelling of water forced it open again.

The lights flickered again and the engine hacked and coughed. There was a strong smell of diesel fuel building in the enclosed space. He pulled out his walkie-talkie.

"The bilge is full, water's at floor level and still rising. Also, a big fuel leak somewhere."

"Get a life preserver and bring me one."

Gideon pulled out two life jackets from a locker, donned his, and carried the other to the pilothouse. Amy was still at the helm, calmly working the controls with her left hand while broadcasting an SOS on the mike with her right.

"Activate the EPIRB," she said. "Instructions printed on the outside."

Gideon exited the pilothouse and located the emergency position indicating radio beacon in its compartment on the outer wall—completely shot to pieces. He raised his walkie-talkie again. "EPIRB's destroyed. Do we have a backup?"

"Not that I know of."

"I'm calling Glinn. We need a rescue." Gideon leaned in toward the sat phone, flipped on the switch.

Nothing. A closer inspection revealed a bullet hole that bored straight through the phone's innards.

"*Shit!*" He pounded the dead device with his fist.

Amy grabbed his arm. "Listen to me. Get some drysacks, fill them with water, food, matches, a knife, two headlamps, portable sat phone, briefing book, two handguns, ammo, food, rescue dye, binoculars, shark repellent, medical kit, quarter-inch line. Pull out as many life preservers as you can, bring them on deck, tie them together, and tie the drysacks on."

"It's done." Gideon stumbled below again. The water was now up to his calves, covered with floating debris and trash. The boat was sinking fast. He grabbed two drysacks and began wading about, filling them as quickly as he could. The boat was getting heavier, lower in the water, totally at the mercy of the thunderous sea. Each swell pounded the hull, threatening to shake it apart. Cabinets were crashing down; light fixtures had come loose and were swinging from their wires.

And then the lights went out. Simultaneously the engine quit with a strong shudder.

Gideon put on one of the headlamps and kept collecting gear. The boat spun wildly, throwing him into the water. He struggled up, clinging to whatever he could, trying to keep the open drysacks above water. Throwing open the gun cabinet, he pulled out some ammo to match the handguns they were already carrying, and tossed in a couple of grenades for good measure. In went the briefing book, some line, two fixed-blade knives with sheaths, half a dozen liters of water, several boxes of granola bars.

The water was now past his knees.

The boat shook as an exceptionally powerful wave struck the hull. He heard cracking and a sudden spray of water, more cabinets tumbling down.

He sealed the drysacks. Now for the life jackets. He pulled out a mass of them from an emergency compartment and, looping a rope through their armholes, tied them together and dragged them up the companionway. Another massive wave hit the boat, tilting it sideways.

It did not swing back. The vessel wasn't recovering. It was about to go under.

"On deck now!" he heard Amy cry.

Water was surging over the deckrail and pouring into the cockpit as the boat canted. Gideon struggled up the now cockeyed stair, against a rush of water, hauling the bundle of life preservers and the drysacks.

The *Turquesa* began to slide down into the sea sideways. The rush of water through the pilothouse door became a Niagara. It was perhaps the most sickening feeling Gideon had ever experienced. They really were going down.

"*On deck!*" screamed Amy.

Struggling with his burdens, he rammed them through the companionway door and, falling sideways as the deck became vertical, scrambled along the pilothouse windows. The boat had rotated and was lying on its beamends, going down by the stern, the bow rising higher and higher as water continued to surge through the door, the stern now completely underwater.

A great wave slammed the boat, throwing Gideon into the rising water. He struggled to find his footing. He couldn't see Amy in the howling darkness, but he could hear her voice.

"*Get out now!*"

But the pilothouse door was completely underwater, the stern sinking fast and the boat vertical, its bow pointing straight up. He was trapped in the pilothouse, a row of sealed windows above him. There was no way he could swim underwater and out the door—not with the life preservers and drysacks.

Where was Amy?

He heard a deafening crash and a flash of light, then another and another. The far pilothouse window exploded into fragments of Plexiglas and in the flashes he could see Amy astraddle the mooring post, .45 in hand, firing through the windows to create an escape route.

The air rushed out of the gaping windows with a sigh and the water rose still farther, carrying him upward. He maneuvered the bundle of life preservers to the hole, where, with another great sigh, the rising water forced them through, pushing him underwater at the same time. He followed them up and a moment later found himself on the surface of the water, clinging to the mass of preservers.

Seconds later the bow of the *Turquesa* vanished beneath the waves. As he watched, the bottom of its hull appeared like a rolling whale, upside down.

"Amy—?" he began to call.

"Right here."

He could see her dark outline bobbing in the water. A few strokes brought her over to the makeshift float. A great hissing wave rose over them, the comber at its top sweeping over their heads, pushing the float under for a moment. They rose again, shedding water. Gideon took a gasp of air, sputtering.

"Thank you," he managed to say.

Another great wave towered above them, and they were buried again under the foaming crest.

Gideon clung to the makeshift raft for dear life, gasping for air. The only thought going through his mind was: *One hundred and sixty miles from land.*

32

T HE DAWN WAS little more than a smear of mud along the eastern horizon. The storm continued unabated, mostly wind, roaring over the sea and roiling up gouts of spume. Gideon and Amy clung to the mass of life pre-servers, too exhausted to speak. It seemed to Gideon their lives had been reduced to a kind of ghastly sea-rhythm: the rise, rise, rise on each swell; the growing hiss of the approaching comber; then the sudden boiling of water, pushing them under while they clung for dear life, often gripping each other, then clawing back to the surface, gasping for breath—and then the awful sinking into the trough, with a sudden silence and cessation of wind, to be followed by the inevitable rise that repeated the terrible cycle all over again. The air was so full of water it was all he could do to breathe. The seas and wind were driving them westward at a tremendous rate.

At least they had drinking water. Gideon managed to open a drysack and get one bottle out, at the cost of the bag shipping seawater. They managed to pass it back and forth, draining it. Gideon immediately puked it all back up.

Slowly, slowly, the day rose. The wind didn't abate, but at least the sea became more orderly, the great march of waves going in the same direction as the wind and currents. Periodically, bands of rain came lashing down in torrents, the sky split with lightning. The heavy rain seemed to flatten the chop and lessen the wind, and Gideon finally ventured to speak. He could see Amy's dark hair and small face, drawn and pale, as she clung to the other side of the makeshift float.

"Amy?"

She nodded.

"You . . . okay?"

"All right. You?"

"Good."

"More water."

Gideon waited for a wave to pass, and then he unsealed the drysack and pulled out another liter bottle. More water slopped in as he resealed the bag. He waited, cradling the water bottle protectively as another wave crushed them, and then handed it to Amy.

She opened the top, drank deeply. Another wave passed and she handed the half-empty bottle to him. He finished it. Thank God—this time the nausea passed and he managed to keep the water down.

All day they fought the sea, enduring the endless cycle of up and down, wind and water, the half drowning with each passing wave. Toward evening, Gideon could feel his arms growing numb. He would not be able to hold on much longer—certainly not for another night.

"Amy, we need to tie ourselves on," he gasped. "Just in case we can't—"

"Understood."

Gideon struggled to get the rope out of its drysack, and then, with numb fingers, managed to loop it through his belt and through the rope holding the life preservers together, and then through Amy's belt, keeping it slack but not so slack they might become entangled.

The wind began to abate as night descended, and once again they were surrounded by the thundering blackness of the sea. They had now been in the water eighteen hours. In the darkness, with his eyes open, Gideon began to see shapes, in brown and dull red, flickering about. At first they were mere blurry lights, and he told himself they were delusions. But as the night wore on, with the terrible rhythm of the sea never ceasing, he began to see a face—a devil's face, mouth opening wide, wider, like a snake, vomiting blood.

Hallucinations. He closed his eyes but the shapes only grew worse, crowding in. He quickly opened his eyes, tried to slap his own face to give himself a taste of reality. Hours had gone by and he hadn't spoken a word to Amy. Was she even there? But, looking over, he could see her pale face. He sought out her cold hand, gave it a squeeze, and felt the faintest pressure in return.

Another wave buried them; another spluttering rise. He realized that, even with the water at around eighty-five degrees, he might be suffering from hypothermia. Or salt poisoning—God knew he'd swallowed enough seawater. And now, in the roaring, hissing, and boiling of the water, he could hear voices: whispering voices, cackling voices. Devil's voices.

He squeezed his eyes tight shut, waited, and opened them again. But the Devil was still there: the vomiting Devil, mouth opening, showing its hideous pink cavernous interior, the rotting teeth, the sudden eruption of blood and bile....

"No! Stop!"

Had he spoken? He thought he heard Amy say something. His head was spinning.

"...fight against it...fight...."

"Amy!" he cried. "Look!"

"Help!" he screamed. "We're over here!"

He felt a terrible desperation. How could they be seen in this darkness, this howling watery wilderness?

"Amy, a ship! Over there!"

He felt her hand gripping his arm, cold and hard. "Gideon. There's nothing. No ship."

"There is, there is! For God's sake, *look*!"

Now he could see it clearly, and by God it was as large as the *Titanic*, a huge cruise ship, lit up like a Christmas tree, all sparkling yellow, rows of windows, black shapes of people on deck silhouetted against the warmth. It was amazing what Glinn had done.

"Amy! Can't you see?"

"Fight it, Gideon." The hand tightened.

The ship let out a long, booming steam whistle, then another.

"You hear that? Oh, my God, they're going to miss us. Over here——!"

A wave came over them, burying them, pushing them down into roaring blackness. Gideon struggled without air, clawing up, having sucked in water with his shouting. It felt like he was under forever. And

Fight what? And then he saw it, out in the water. A light. A real light. Glinn's rescue mission.

But she didn't seem to respond.

then they broke the surface, coughing, spluttering. He looked around wildly.

"It's gone!"

"It was never there."

"Come back!" Gideon screamed in the extremity of desperation.

"Gideon!" He felt fingers tightening around his own. *There was no ship.* But if you'll just shut up for a moment, there is something out there. Something real."

Gideon stopped shouting and listened. All he could hear was the sound of wind and sea.

"What?" he asked.

"Surf."

Gideon strained to listen, to ignore the odd shapes shifting in front of his eyes. And then he did hear it: a faint susurrus of thunder below the howl of the sea. The wind and waves were pushing them steadily toward the sound.

"An island?"

"Don't know. Could be brutal."

"What can we do?"

"Nothing to do but hold on and ride it in." A pause. "We'd better untie ourselves, or we could get all tangled up."

Gideon fumbled with the knot, but his hands were not working.

"Knife," Amy gasped. "In the bag."

Now the roar was getting louder. They were being driven toward it at a tremendous rate. The seas were growing steeper, the breaking tops more violent. Gideon fumbled with the latches on one of the drysacks, finally got them open, reached in, pulled out a knife. He could barely hold on to it, but somehow managed to slice himself free of the rope. He passed the knife to Amy.

A wave buried them. The drysack was open, full of water. And now, on a rise of wave, Gideon could see a vast band of white surf, with blackness before and beyond.

"Fuck," he said.

"Just hold on, don't fight, ride the waves in."

The waves were looming bigger, terrifyingly steep, smooth and glassy. The roar ahead sounded like a hundred freight trains. Up, up they rose, and a great curl of water loomed above them, over them.

"Hold on!"

Gideon felt himself flipped over, then engulfed in a tremendous, violent, boiling blackness, which instantly ripped the preserver raft out of his hands. He tumbled and thrashed in the darkness, disoriented, with no way of knowing which was up, down, or sideways, the water tugging at his limbs and almost tearing them out of their sockets. His powerlessness in the grip of the sea both terrified and stunned him.

Suddenly—just when he felt his lungs would burst—he broke the surface, gasped, sucked in salt water, and was thrown back into the maelstrom, whirled about, utterly at the mercy of the sea. The faces appeared, now grinning, vomiting over him, and he struggled to thrash free, to no avail...And then a strange peace stole in, slowly, slowly, and the sea and the waves and the faces all vanished into a warm, lovely dark.

33

As consciousness slowly returned, the lovely dark gave way to a sickening, nauseating feeling of pain and exhaustion. Gideon coughed, his chest and lungs feeling like they were on fire. He opened his eyes. There was still the close roar of surf, but he realized he was lying on wet sand. It was still night.

With great effort he managed to get his arms underneath himself and sit up. His skin felt raw and cracked. He was surrounded by a dim, featureless beach, vanishing into darkness in all directions.

"Amy." His voice came out as the merest croak.

The beach was empty. He struggled to get to his feet, head pounding, and was immediately overwhelmed with dizziness. Falling to his knees, he vomited salt water, again and again and again, until nothing remained but dry heaves. A few deep breaths and he collapsed, falling to the sand, curling into a ball, and losing consciousness once again.

After what seemed like an eternity, he slowly swam back to consciousness. He opened his eyes. Day. Again. A dull, zinc light suffused everything. He looked about through bleary eyes, at the empty beach, the dark gray ocean, the thundering parade of surf, a dark line of limp jungle. How he possibly could have ridden through and survived boggled his mind.

The wind had died away, and the clouds above had taken shape. The storm was clearing. His head was still pounding, but he felt a little better. He rose to his knees, and then lurched to his feet, fighting a wave of nausea and vertigo. In the light of a filthy dawn, he could now see where he was: on a deserted coast, the gray beach stretching in either direction as far as the eye could see, a few tattered palm trees, the land receding into jungle-clad hills. No sign of life; no sign of Amy; no sign of the raft or their drybags of supplies.

He had to find Amy. Or, at least, her body. And he had to find the bundle of life preservers and the drysacks with their water.

A raging thirst had taken hold. His lips were cracked and bleeding. His tongue was swollen. He felt so weak he could barely stand.

It took all his willpower to take a step, and then he fell once again to his knees. Despite every effort, he was unable to get back onto his feet. He continued slowly on, crawling down the hard sand until he could go no farther. He lay down. He wanted badly to sleep—or, perhaps, to die. He closed his eyes.

"Gideon."

He opened his eyes to find Amy bending over him. She looked awful—pale, thin, wet.

"*Amy*...thank God..."

"Let me help you up." She grasped him under the arms, and he rose to his feet even as she staggered with the effort.

"Water..."

A bottle appeared and he fumbled for it, unscrewing the top with trembling hands, jamming it into his mouth and sucking down the liquid so desperately it spilled over his shirt.

"Easy, easy." She laid a hand on the bottle. "Wait a minute."

He waited, trembling. He could feel an immediate surge of energy from the water. "More."

"Pace yourself."

He drank more, swallowing just a little bit at a time, until the liter bottle was gone.

"More."

"Sorry, we need to ration."

It was amazing how quickly the water helped him regain strength and alertness. He looked about, breathing slowly and deeply. There, a few hundred yards down the beach, was the sodden bundle of life preservers. He could see Amy's footprints in the sand.

His tongue and mouth were becoming rehydrated, and he found he could speak without croaking. "How did you survive?"

"Just as you did, I got washed up on the beach. I don't quite know how. Karma."

"Where are we?"

"The Mosquito Coast of Nicaragua. I'd guess we're about twenty miles north of Monkey Point."

"How far to the nearest settlement?"

"We don't have a local map. This is one of the loneliest coastlines in the world. Can you walk?"

"Yes."

"I'm a little weak myself. Give me your arm."

They walked down the beach, supporting each other. She led him into a grove of palm trees along the verge of sand. There were the drysacks, with various items laid out and drying on banana leaves—their two weapons, knives, the satellite-phone case, the briefing book with its wet pages laid out, a dozen granola bars, bottled water—and, to Gideon's surprise, the mysterious computer printout of a Greek manuscript Amy had been looking at on the boat, sealed in a ziplock bag that had nevertheless suffered some leakage. She sat down on the sand, and Gideon collapsed next to her.

Even in his weakened state, he couldn't help feeling annoyed at the sight of the printout. She must have taken it with her when they abandoned the *Turquesa* and put it in a drysack at some point while they were on the raft. "Of all the things you could have saved—maps, GPS—you rescued that computer printout? What's the big deal with it?"

"It's just something I've been working on."

"What?"

A shake of her head. "Later. We both need to rest. And eat."

Gideon felt utterly spent, but now a hunger was taking hold. Amy picked up two granola bars and passed one to him.

He lay back, peeling off the wrapper and stuffing the bar into his mouth. The clouds were breaking up, and a single ray of sun came streaming through them, illuminating a spot on the sea. The granola only seemed to

make him hungrier, but he could feel his strength returning.

They lay on the beach, barely moving, barely talking,
slowly recovering their strength, as the day passed. As
the afternoon merged into evening, the last of the clouds
cleared away. Gideon now felt nearly himself again, strong
and alert, unhurt save for a kind of dull and universal
ache—but the passage of time had him confused. How
much time had elapsed since their vessel was scuttled?
Forty-eight hours? Seventy-two?

"Does the sat phone work?" he asked.

"I think so. Container's waterproof."

"Then we'd better call Glinn," he said.

Amy nodded. She finished her granola bar, then took
up the sat-phone container, unlatched the seals, and
opened it up. The phone appeared intact. She took it out,
turned it on. The LED screen popped to life.

"A miracle," said Gideon.

"Yeah, but the battery's run down. We've only got five
percent juice."

"Christ." Gideon shook his head.

She glanced at him. "I'll do the talking, if you don't
mind."

"Be my guest."

She put it on speaker and pressed the FASTDIAL key to
connect with EES headquarters. A moment later Glinn
himself answered. He wasted few words.

"Where are you and what's happening?"

"Had a run-in with some treasure hunters. They shot
up the boat."

"Life raft?"

"Destroyed."

"Launch?"

"Gone. Look, it's a long story. We were able to sink the treasure hunters in a storm but the *Turquesa* went to the bottom as well."

"Position?"

"My best guess is eleven degrees forty-four minutes North, eighty-one degrees one minute West. We're on the Mosquito Coast maybe twenty miles north of Monkey Point, Nicaragua."

"Do you have food and water? We'll get a rescue vessel out to you just as soon as we can."

"We don't need picking up."

Gideon looked at Amy, startled. She held up her hand, asking for his silence.

"I don't understand," came Glinn's voice over the sat phone.

"We're right where we want to be. I know where we have to go next. We can get there on foot."

Gideon listened. This was nuts. He grabbed for the radio, but Amy held it out of his reach.

"On foot?" Glinn's voice crackled over the radio. "I'm extremely concerned about the situation you're in. You've been shipwrecked on an unknown coast. How are you going to finish the mission? We're going to outfit a second boat for you, bring you some crew. I'm looking at the map as we speak. If you can head toward Monkey Point, there's a lagoon just north where we can rendezvous, refit the expedition, and get you back on your feet."

"Your concern is appreciated—but misguided," Amy said firmly. "We're on track. The next landmark on the map is ten miles from where we are, maybe less—I know it."

"How do you know it?"

A silence.

"Gideon," said Glinn, "are you there? Do you agree with this plan?"

Gideon glanced at Amy. She was staring at him. He hesitated and then said, "Yes."

A long silence. "All right. I'm going to trust you. But I want regular updates. Twice a day, morning and night. Do you both understand?"

"We may have to make them less frequent than that," said Amy. "I'm getting a low battery signal."

They disconnected. Amy looked at Gideon, a smile breaking over her pale face, producing dimples he'd never seen before. "Thank you for backing me up."

"I only did so because I expect an explanation from you."

"You'll just have to trust me for a little while longer—"

"No. I want an explanation *now*."

This was greeted by silence.

"Christ, Amy. Here we are, castaways on a deserted coastline with nothing but a few granola bars and half a dozen liters of water. How do you know we're still on track?"

Amy picked up the sodden briefing book and opened it to the Phorkys Map. The picture showed a flat line rising into a sharp line pointing toward a rounded line. The clue simply said, *aquilonius*.

"You showed me that before. What does it mean?"

"Stand up and look inland."

Gideon did as he was told, and was immediately staggered by the two hills in the near distance: one with a sharp peak, the second rounded. "Oh, my God."

"Yes. Oh, my God. *Aquilonius* is one way of saying north. So we go north, looking for the next clue."

"Damn it, Amy, it would've been nice if you'd shared this with me earlier. And why hide it from Glinn?"

"Because I've discovered something even more incredible. It has to do with that printout I've been dragging around."

"What is that damn printout, anyway?"

"*The Odyssey*, by Homer. Perhaps you've heard of it?"

34

Is THAT THE one where this guy who's really lost ends up in a cave with a hot enchantress?" said Gideon.

"Very funny. I'll tell you what I've found, but first, let's build a fire, dry out our clothes, and try to bring a little comfort and civilization to this god-awful place. Then we can talk."

Half an hour later, they were both sitting in the sand by a small fire. The sun had set in a glory of vermilion, and the stars were coming up in the sky. A breeze rustled the leaves of the palm trees above them.

There was something rather glorious, Gideon decided, in simply feeling dry. "All right," he said. "Let's hear it. And it had better be good."

Amy began by declaiming something in a language unknown to Gideon.

"What is that?" he said. "Are you still gargling salt water?"

"It's ancient Greek."

"Sorry, but my ancient Greek is a little rusty."

"I just wanted you to hear the sound of it. It's the most

beautiful language in the world—and I don't just say that because I was a classics major. You can't truly appreciate Homer in English. ἄνδρα μοι ἔννεπε, μοῦσα, πολύτροπον, ὃς μάλα πολλὰ Πλάγχθη. 'Sing to me of the man, O muse, that wily hero who traveled far and wide'—Sorry, the English just doesn't cut it."

Gideon shook his head. "Here we are, lost on an un-known coast, and you're quoting Homer."

"There's a point to all this." She tapped the damp pages of the printout.

"Which is?"

"Let me start at the beginning, so you can understand my reasoning. We already know the Phorkys Map was based on an earlier Greek map. Glinn said as much. That map was discovered by the monks of Iona, among their stores of old vellum."

Gideon nodded.

"Which means that the Greeks got here first. The Greeks 'discovered' the New World."

"Glinn told us that, too."

"But that begs an obvious question: Who was the Greek Columbus? And how did he get here?"

Gideon waited.

"In 1200 BC, the Greeks laid siege to the city of Troy—the famous Trojan War. Which they won, of course, by tricking the Trojans with the hollow horse filled with Greek warriors."

"Beware of Greeks bearing gifts and all that."

"Exactly. Now let's turn to the Phorkys Map." She flipped the pages of their briefing book, with each clue en-larged. "Here it is, the first clue. Ibi est initium, it reads.

And look at the little drawing of a horse. Remember? That was the clue old Brock back at EES couldn't figure out. And it says: 'There is the beginning.' The beginning of what?"

"I haven't the faintest idea," Gideon said.

"Of the voyage of Odysseus."

"The voyage of…" Gideon stopped. "Are you saying that the *Odyssey* should be taken literally? I don't know what's crazier—that, or the idea that he traveled all the way to the New World."

"It isn't crazy. And I'm not the first to propose it. A group of dissident Homer scholars have argued precisely this point for years. They've been ridiculed and marginalized."

"With good reason," said Gideon.

"Because they didn't have the proof we now possess—thanks to your theft of that page from the Book of Kells." Amy's voice was low, quiet, but full of conviction. "I've been comparing the Phorkys Map with the *Odyssey*. It all fits. After the defeat of Troy—using a wooden horse, recall—Odysseus and his men left in six ships. They were caught in two incredibly violent storms: one that drove them westward for three days, and another for nine days. It's obvious to me now that he was driven, first across the Mediterranean, and then across the Atlantic—all the way into the Caribbean. That's how the Greeks discovered the New World. And that, in turn, is how the Phorkys Map was created. It was based on the earlier Greek map of Odysseus's voyage. That's the map the monks found among their old stores of vellum. And *that* is how the monks of Iona were able to reach the New World. Odysseus was the Greek Columbus."

"If you hadn't been a classics major yourself, you'd never have dreamed this up. It's totally far-fetched."

"No, it isn't. It took Odysseus ten years to get home. All those islands he visited, all those adventures he had—they all took place here, in the Caribbean. The key text is right there." She flipped through the printout. "This is from Book Nine of the *Odyssey*. I'll translate as I go along."

A deadly current and howling winds forced us westward, past Cythera. For nine days we were helplessly driven over the deepest ocean. On the tenth day we reached the land of the Lotus Eaters, people who eat a delicious fruit, which is said to give health and heal all manner of infirmities, but at the expense of mind and memory. On that desolate coastline we found water and ate a hasty meal. Once we'd eaten and drank I sent some of my men ahead, two soldiers and a runner, to see who might live there. They left immediately for the north and found the Lotus Eaters, who accepted them in peace and gave them the lotus to eat. Those who ate of it were healed of their wounds of war, but forgot all about home and their companions, and did not care to return to the ships or even send back a message. All they wanted was to stay with the Lotus Eaters and eat the sweet fruit, lost in their dreams, forgetting everything. They wept bitterly when I forced them to come back with me. I had to lash them to the rowing benches.

Amy lowered the printout. "Most scholars think Cythera was an island off the Greek mainland. But here's the catch: Cythera *was* also an ancient name for the Straits of Gibraltar. In other words, they were blown past Cythera into the Atlantic—the 'deepest ocean.' From there they were driven nine days westward, carried by high winds and currents."

"Nine days to cross the Atlantic?"

"The main route of tropical storms goes southwestward from the Cape Verde Islands straight across into the Caribbean. In such a storm, he would have been driven along by the effects of wind, reinforced by the powerful Main Equatorial Current. This is exactly the route mariners took in times past. In reasonably favorable winds they could make the crossing in twenty days. There are many instances of ships caught in storms making the crossing in as little as a week—if they survived."

Gideon fell silent. He felt skeptical—and annoyed. "So you strand us here on this desolate shore, refuse help, place us both in jeopardy—just to prove this ridiculous theory of yours."

Amy sighed with impatience. "Haven't you been listening? If Odysseus had been pushed across the Atlantic in a storm, his ships would have been subsequently caught in the Caribbean Loop Current, which connects to the Main Equatorial Current. And that would have brought him right here." She hesitated. "That's the research I was doing on the boat before we were attacked."

"Why did you keep it such a big secret?"

"Because I was afraid of exactly the negative reaction I'm getting from you now."

Gideon shook his head. It all seemed so speculative. He couldn't bring himself to believe it.

"There's something else in the *Odyssey*—something

you might find more persuasive." She read again from the printout: " '. . . a delicious fruit, which is said to give health and heal all manner of infirmities, but at the expense of mind and memory.' What does that remind you of?"

"I suppose it could be a reference to the medicine we're looking for."

"Of course. Can you imagine a clearer description of the *remedium* Glinn has sent us searching for?"

Gideon stared into the fire, thinking. He was beginning to feel weary again—too weary to be angry. If this were all true, it could be further proof the medicine was real . . . and might actually help him. Immediately he was seized with the foolishness of this line of thought and pushed it out of his head. He had to stop dwelling on this false hope, which would only bring him disappointment and grief.

"Consider the Phorkys Map. 'Follow the Devil's vomit.' We've done exactly that. The spume trail leading out from Jeyupsi Cay naturally followed the Loop Current, which fetched us right up here. This is precisely where we're meant to be—right where the next clue is. Right where Odysseus and his men landed three thousand years ago."

Gideon tossed a stick into the fire. "When did this first occur to you?"

"I was familiar with the speculations of the dissident scholars. When I heard Glinn's theory about the Greeks reaching the Caribbean, when I saw the Phorkys Map, I began to recall certain passages from the *Odyssey*. That's when I began my research in earnest."

For a moment Gideon was silent. Then he shifted before the fire. "I'm not saying I buy into any of this. But for the time being, it looks as if I have to go along. So what next?"

"*Aquilonius.* The unusual Latin term for 'northerly.' Which is where we must head to find the next clue—the very last clue. We're almost there."

"What is that clue?"

She pointed to the page. The drawing on the map showed a partially twisted rectangle without a bottom. The Latin inscription read: *Trans ultra tortuosum locum.*

"*Tortuosum locum.* Twisted place. *Trans ultra.* Beyond the beyond. That's what we're looking for, 'beyond the beyond of the twisted place.' Which should be a little north of here. And"—her eyes glittered in the dying light—"when we get there, we'll be in the land of the Lotus Eaters."

35

Hıs thirty minutes in the whirlpool bath was up. Using the powered platforms and the robotic arm, Eli Glinn raised himself with painstaking slowness—his narrow body dripping water perfumed by soothing herbs and oils—and transported the platform to his dressing alcove. It was the work of another difficult thirty minutes to dry and dress himself.

After the accident, Glinn had spent a great deal of time finding the kind of clothes that were most comfortable and easy to put on and remove. He had ultimately settled on warm-up pants of ultrasoft Persian cotton with an elastic waistband—tailored precisely to his needs by Jonathan Crofts of Savile Row—and mock turtlenecks one size too large. He now had several dozen pairs of each, and he used them as both daywear and nightwear.

The arduous process completed, he clicked the remote to extinguish the candles, lowered himself into the wheelchair, and rolled out of the bathroom, through his bedroom, and into the main living area. As was his custom, he maneuvered the wheelchair through the spare, cool-gray space to the massive window overlooking the Hudson. Glinn slept very little, and he often sat here for hours, reading poetry or simply gazing out over the landscape, his thoughts far away.

The monks used this secret alchemy and were able to heal themselves of "grievous wounds, afflictions, diseases and infirmities." Was it really true? Was there a secret arcanum—or was it just another primitive legend, born of a crude and imperfect understanding of the world? Perhaps Brock's skepticism was rubbing off on him.

But then there was the evidence of the skeletons. That was real.

His thoughts turned to Gideon and Amy. He felt a most disquieting mix of concern and uncertainty over the pair . . . and over the direction the project had taken. Their boat had sunk; they were marooned on the Mosquito Coast—and yet Amy had refused help. It was consistent with her Quantitative Behavioral Analysis. At the same time, they had not anticipated an attack from treasure hunters. They were in uncharted territory. Another item of concern lay in the team's sat phone, which Amy had reported as being low on batteries. Ongoing communication with the two was of vital importance.

His selection of Amy for this project had been one of the more extensive and arduous headhunting tasks EES had ever performed—and the Quantitative Behavioral Analysis tests on her had proven most interesting. EES was in the business of failure analysis as a means of preventing failure—and her QBA had indicated that, during this mission, she would fail. Yet ironically, the failure would be vital to the mission's success.

But that failure was not supposed to take place this

early, or take such a form. Curious—and most disturbing. For the time being, however, Glinn realized he would simply have to take her report on faith.

His thoughts were interrupted by the low chiming of the telephone. Glinn glanced at the clock: five thirty AM. He pirouetted the wheelchair, reached for the phone.

"Yes?" he said.

"Weaver. I wonder if you could get down here. As soon as possible." The technician's voice was tight with anxiety—or, perhaps, fear.

"What is it?"

"It would be easier to show you in person, Mr. Glinn."

"I'll be right there." Hanging up the telephone, Glinn aimed his wheelchair at the elevator and whirred slowly over the expanse of polished slate.

36

Garza arrived in the lab at a quarter to six, bone-tired and sick to death of dramatic, early-morning confabulations.

Weaver, the tech, looked weary and drawn. But on top of that, he looked tense, unsettled. Brock was standing in a far corner, hands crossed over his chest, equally put out. Glinn sat beside him, motionless, his face betraying nothing.

"The DNA test on the two follicles is complete," Weaver said, and then seemed to falter.

"Go on, man," Garza said.

"Remember how I told you my belief that the vellum on this page might be made from human skin?"

Garza nodded.

"It turns out I was wrong."

"Exactly what I predicted," said Brock, primly.

"And right."

Garza said, "Just get to the point."

The tech took a deep breath. "According to our analysis, the DNA sequences of these hair follicles match up with human DNA about ninety-seven percent. Yet there are significant sequences that do not match up with the human genome." He looked around the room. "That's why I say I'm both right and wrong. It's humanoid. It's *almost human*. I mean, it's one percent less than a chimp-and-human match, but two percent more than, say, orangutan-and-human." Weaver swallowed, plucked at his collar. He seemed to be downright frightened by the results.

"What rot!" Brock cried. "You've had the greasy fingers of unwashed monks turning that page over for a thousand years—no wonder it's permeated with human DNA."

"We were very, *very* careful. And we got the same results from both samples. We took the sample from the binding edge of the page, which presumably was handled less. And we ran controls for contamination. That doesn't appear to be the case."

"It doesn't matter!" Brock retorted. "It's been bound and rebound many times! There's human DNA all over it." He turned to Glinn. "Human skin simply wasn't used for making vellum. It's nothing more than animal skin—I would guess pig—that's been badly contaminated."

Ignoring Brock, Glinn came forward slightly in his wheelchair. "You say you obtained similar results from both follicles?"

Weaver nodded.

"*Almost human.*" Garza had to make an effort to keep the skepticism out of his voice. "Weaver, this makes no sense. I'm with Brock. It's contamination."

"No hasty conclusions, Mr. Garza," Glinn said quietly, then turned back to Weaver. "How, exactly, do you check for contamination?"

"We use a standard technique called BLAST—Basic Local Alignment Search Tool."

"How certain is it?"

"It's not one hundred percent."

"There it is," Garza said, with a wave of his hand, his irritation beginning to crest—especially at Glinn's solicitous reception of this nonsense.

"Are there other ways to check for contamination?" Glinn asked.

"Well...there's a new technique we developed for our Swiss client last year, a hybrid version of the BWA-SW algorithm. We could run the sequences through that. Unfortunately, it's much slower than BLAST."

"How does it work?" Garza asked.

"The Burrows-Wheeler Aligner. Basically, it's an algorithm for aligning nucleotide sequences against a referent, with the intent of uncovering any sequence contaminants. The variation we developed can work with longer query sequences, and with a higher toleration for error, than the original."

"Get started," Glinn said.

Weaver nodded.

Garza spoke. "While you're at it, do another run or two on those samples. Let's see if you get the same results." This all seemed unnecessary to him—but he knew they'd make no further progress until Glinn himself was satisfied.

"I'd also like to know," Glinn said quietly, "assuming there is no contamination—what that three percent difference represents."

"We could try to match it up with the genomes of any other species."

"Exactly. And see if you can extrapolate from that to see what sorts of anatomical differences those genes might represent. I want to know precisely what kind of creature we're talking about. What it looks like, what its capabilities are—if we're indeed dealing with a new hominid species."

Weaver's face—already pale—turned a shade paler. No doubt, Garza thought, he was mentally counting up the additional hours of sleep he was about to lose.

37

Twenty-four hours later, Amy and Gideon had managed to get all of five miles northward. It had been anything but a "walk on the beach." Gideon was soaked and sore from wading and crawling through the endless mangrove swamps and lagoons that punctuated the coast, each one humming with noxious, bloodsucking insects and quaking with expanses of stinking mud. There was no way to go around them: they had to slog, wade, and swim across, one after the other.

The sun was beginning to set over the endless jungle when they decided to halt. Gideon walked into the ocean to wash the muck from his clothes, feeling like some time-traveling Robinson Crusoe, fetched up on a prehistoric shore. They had seen no signs of human life: no footprints or tracks on the beach, and no boats offshore. Glancing back, he saw that Amy was busy cleaning her handgun, so he quickly stripped to the buff, rinsed his clothes, wrung them out, and then put them back on.

He came back to camp. Amy was just putting her .45 back together.

"Make a fire, please. I'm going to get us some protein." She slapped the loaded magazine into place and disappeared into the twilit jungle.

Gideon found a level area among the palms and began gathering dead leaves, twigs, and driftwood. He doubted Amy would be able to shoot anything with that .45 and resigned himself to another granola bar dinner. The sky was clear, but the sea was still a continuous roar, the march of rollers unceasing.

He heard a couple of shots, and ten minutes later Amy emerged from the jungle, holding a dead armadillo by the tail. In her other hand she carried a bunch of plantains.

"Armadillo? Is that the best you could do?"

She laid the armadillo down on a banana leaf. "You clean it."

He stared at the creature, with its ridiculous-looking head and bony armor. "Me?"

"I shot it. Now it's your turn."

"What . . . do I do?"

"I thought you were the gourmet cook around here. You think I've ever cleaned an armadillo before?" she said. "It's all yours . . . First Mate." She flashed him a wry smile.

"Excuse me, but the last I checked, your ship had sunk. You're no longer captain."

A silence. "Fair enough. But you're still going to clean that armadillo."

Gideon began working on the animal with his knife, turning it over, slitting open the belly, and pulling out the entrails. It was disgusting work but he was so hungry he hardly noticed. Working the knife between the outer plates and flesh, he was able to carve out the meat, split it, and lay it out in the coals of the fire. As the smell of roasting meat wafted up, he felt a ravenous hunger take hold and he could see the same gleam in Amy's eyes as she stared at the sizzling carcass. They pulled it out of the fire and cut it up on banana leaves. Although it was almost too hot to touch they began devouring it with trembling hands.

It wasn't long before a scattering of gnawed bones lay on the greasy leaves. Gideon felt human for the first time in two days. He glanced over at Amy, who was looking over the text of the *Odyssey* again, comparing it to the Phorkys Map, her face reflecting the firelight.

"Any more revelations?" he asked, trying to keep the cynical tone out of his voice.

"Nothing dramatic." She laid down the text. "But I'm more than ever convinced we're following in Odysseus's footsteps."

Gideon lay back, his hands behind his head. "Tell me the story of Odysseus. It's been a long time since I read it."

She eased back next to him. The fire crackled and the stars were coming out. "It's the first thriller. It's got everything—monsters, gods, demons, witches and sorcery, adventure, violence, shipwrecks, murder, and a love story. Best of all, it has a hero who is sort of the anti–James Bond, who gets his way not through brute force, but through tricks, deceptions, disguises, and deceit."

"The first social engineer."

Amy laughed. "Exactly."

"Sort of like me."

She looked at him. "Maybe a little."

"Anyway, go on with the story."

"I'll stick to the salient parts. After the fall of Troy,

Odysseus and his men took off with their booty and sailed westward. Ultimately, they got caught in a terrible storm. That's the storm I told you about earlier, which blew them 'past Cythera' and for another nine days across the 'deepest ocean.' On the tenth day, they came to the land of the Lotus Eaters. Here was where three of his men, sent to contact the natives, end up wasted from eating the lotus fruit. Odysseus had to drag them back to the ship and tie them up to get them away. They sailed through the night and came to the land of the Cyclopes."

"Cyclopes? The one-eyed giants, right?"

Amy nodded. "Cyclops is plural, Cyclops is the singular."

"Duly noted."

"There were two islands side by side, a big one and a little one. They first landed on the big island, where they feasted on wild goats. Then they made their way to the Cyclopes' island. Here they found a cave with stores of milk and cheese. This is where Odysseus blew it. Instead of stealing the food and hightailing it, he decided to stay and meet the owner. The Cyclops arrived a while later, an ugly brute by the name of Polyphemus, son of Poseidon. Polyphemus sweet-talked them at first, lulled them into dropping their guard—and then snatched up two of Odysseus's men, bashed their brains out on the walls of the cave, and ate them raw while the others watched, horrified."

"Greek canapés."

"Polyphemus imprisoned the rest in the cave for future eating, rolling a huge boulder over the entrance. The next morning he left them penned up while he went out to tend his flock. When the giant returned, Odysseus got him drunk. He told Polyphemus that his name was Nobody. When the giant finally collapsed in a drunken stupor, Odysseus heated up a stick in the fire and drove the sharpened end into his eye. Polyphemus woke up shrieking that he was being killed, but when his distant neighbors called out to ask who was killing him, he responded 'Nobody is killing me!' and so they didn't come to his aid, thinking he was just drunk."

"Cunning little bastard," said Gideon. "I'll have to remember that trick."

"But they were still trapped in the cave. When morning came, the now blind Cyclops had to release his sheep to graze. He rolled the boulder back and let the sheep out one by one, feeling their backs to make sure Odysseus and his men didn't escape by riding them. But unbeknownst to the brute, Odysseus and the rest were clinging to the *undersides* of the sheep—and that's how they escaped. They stole the Cyclops's sheep and departed in their ships. Once at a safe distance, Odysseus called out to Polyphemus, mocking him: Yo, motherfucker, this is what happens when you eat visitors to your cave! And if anyone asks who put out your eye and spoiled your charming looks, you can tell them it was Odysseus, son of Laertes, from Ithaca."

"How do you say 'motherfucker' in ancient Greek?" Gideon asked.

Amy spoke a word, then traced some letters in the sand: ἀναγής.

"Really?"

"Well, with certain poetic liberties."

"I like this Odysseus. He's my kind of guy."

"But Polyphemus, being the son of Poseidon, swore

vengeance against his new enemy. And his father obliged, making Odysseus's journey that much more difficult. Finally, driven along by Poseidon's incessant storms, they found themselves blown all the way to Hades—to Hell itself. They had to ask Tiresias, the blind prophet, for directions home."

"All the way to Hades? That dude was *lost.*"

"Exactly my point. It sure doesn't sound like he was wandering around a few Greek islands in the Aegean Sea, does it?"

"What happened when he finally got home?"

"He found his household full of idle suitors trying to seduce his wife. His solution to getting rid of them all was just as—how can I put it?—*unusual* as his method of escape from Polyphemus." She picked up a plantain and began peeling it. "I hope I'm not boring you."

"Not at all. It's a great story."

She finished the banana, tossed the peel into the darkness. "You know, there's something else I just realized. Homer mentions cannibalism many times in the *Odyssey.* But cannibalism was completely unknown in the Mediterranean in ancient times. It was, however, widespread in the Caribbean."

"Very interesting."

She looked at him. Silence fell. The fire crackled, and a breeze rustled the leaves of the palm trees above them.

He looked at her firelit face. "You are beautiful."

She flushed. "Where did that—?"

He leaned forward to kiss her, but Amy pushed him away.

"What's wrong?" he asked.

"We can't complicate our assignment, or our relationship, like this."

Gideon looked at her. "You mean that."

"Yes, I do." She fumbled a little with the printout. "Now let me get back to my work here, and you...you go jump in the water or something, cool yourself off."

38

They spent the night under the protection of a group of palms. The next morning, a broiling sun rose over the glossy sea, bringing with it a suffocating blanket of heat and swarms of sandflies. Gideon went for an early-morning swim in the ocean, trying to escape the biting insects. When he returned to camp, Amy had built a smoky fire to try to drive them back.

They ate leftover armadillo meat in silence, shooing the flies away from it. They were running low on water and had begun to ration it. As the heat continued to rise, Gideon felt his thirst returning.

"We'd better get going," Amy said, repacking their meager supplies in her drysack.

"Aren't we supposed to call Glinn with a sit-rep?"

"Remember, the sat-phone battery is almost dead. I think we better leave it off in case we have a real emergency."

"Okay, but Glinn will go nuts if we don't call in soon."

Amy shook her head, considering this with a half smile. "Too bad for him."

"You don't like Glinn, do you?"

"How'd you guess?"

Gideon watched Amy carefully roll up the *Odyssey* printout and store it in her drysack. In the light of day, her theory felt more outlandish than it had the night before, as she told the story by firelight with conviction and enthusiasm. He felt a twinge of irritation at her excessive care with the printout, mingled, perhaps, with a sense of embarrassment at his impulsive gesture and the rejection that followed. And why was she so eager to refuse Glinn's help?

They trudged down the beach until they came to another lagoon inlet. This one presented a nasty surprise. It was wider than the earlier ones—three hundred yards at least—and a swift tidal current of brown water was flowing out to sea. Looking inland, Gideon could see that the lagoon was enormous, almost like an inland sea.

"I was afraid of this," said Amy, setting down her drysack. "This must be the Laguna de los Micos, a big lagoon I recall from the charts."

"If we try to swim across, we'll be swept out to sea," Gideon said. "And we can't circle around—it's too vast."

Amy was silent.

"Why not take Glinn up on that offer of a new boat? This lagoon would be a good rendezvous point."

Amy shook her head. "We're almost there." She rummaged in her drysack and brought out the binoculars. Wading into the inlet, she glassed the shores of the lagoon, which swept away from them in a long crescent into the hazy distance. Bugs swarmed about and one buried itself into Gideon's ear canal, buzzing frantically. He used his finger to pry it out. As they remained motionless the cloud of noxious insects thickened, swarming into his eyes, mouth, nose, and ears. Swatting at them was like trying to push back the tide.

Amy lowered the binoculars. "I think we should wade along the shore. Where the lagoon widens, the current drops and we might swim it."

"Whatever we do, let's keep going. I'm being eaten alive."

They waded along the muddy shores of the lagoon, on the edge of an impenetrable tangle of mangrove roots and trees. The water was about three feet deep, with a bottom of muck that sucked them down with every step. It was slow, exhausting work, and the vast insect population of the swamp followed along with them, with more arriving every minute.

As the inlet broadened, the current lessened until they were wading through dead, smelly water the temperature of a warm bath. The heat, humidity, and insects enveloped them like a steam blanket.

"We could try swimming," said Gideon, eyeing the far shore of the lagoon, which now looked to be about a mile away.

Amy squinted. Again, she took out the binoculars and scanned the shore ahead of them. Suddenly she stopped, drawing in her breath.

"What is it?"

She handed him the binoculars. "About half a mile farther. Take a look at that white thing."

Gideon took the binoculars and peered at it. "I think it's a boat."

Wading faster now, they slogged along the verge of the mangroves until the boat came into better view. It was a battered wooden canoe, half filled with water, which had drifted into a tangle of mangrove roots. At least ten coats of brightly colored paint were flaking off its side, giving it a psychedelic air.

"Let's bail it out, see if it floats," said Gideon.

They began bailing with cupped hands, flinging the water out. In ten minutes the boat was floating, with only a trickle seeping back in through cracks in the bottom. They put their bags in the boat, sorted through the driftwood piled up against the mangrove roots, and found a couple of pieces that could serve as paddles. They climbed in and, kneeling in the bottom, began paddling. As the canoe moved away from the mangroves, Gideon could feel, with relief, a faint movement of air that began to push away the cloud of insects.

"My God, I thought I was going to go crazy back there," he said, waving away the last of the swarm. "Just think, we could be relaxing in the cabin of a five-million-dollar yacht right now. All we have to do is call Glinn."

Amy grunted. "Be quiet and keep paddling."

"Whatever you say, Captain Bligh."

Slowly the far shore drew closer, another mass of mangrove swamp. As they approached, Gideon examined it with the binoculars and noted a channel in the mangroves leading to what looked like a sandy beach.

Less than half an hour later, they had landed and pulled the boat up on a muddy beach at the far edge of the swamp. As Amy was hauling out the drysacks, Gideon saw a movement in his peripheral vision.

"Um, Amy? We have company."

She straightened and turned. Six men had appeared

seemingly out of nowhere and were standing in a semicircle about twenty feet away, spears in hand.

"Uh-oh," Gideon murmured.

For a moment the two groups just stared at each other.

"Let me handle this," said Gideon. He rose with a big smile. "Friends," he said. "*Amigos*." Forcing a smile, he held out his hands, palms open. "*Somos amigos*."

A man, apparently the leader, hawked up a gobbet of phlegm and spat on the ground. The stillness seemed to grow. Gideon took the moment to observe them. The men were all dressed in similar fashion: dirty shorts, T-shirts, tattered flip-flops. Many wore necklaces of odd bits of trash from civilization—bottle caps, plastic costume jewelry, tin spoons, and broken pieces of electronics and circuit boards. The leader wore an old iPhone around his neck on a leather thong, with a hole punched through it. The glass front of the phone had an image scratched on it of what looked like a monkey's grimacing face.

"*Somos amigos*," Gideon tried again.

The iPhone man stepped forward and spoke angrily in an unknown language, gesturing at the dugout canoe with his spear. He went on for some time, shaking the spear and pointing at them, at the canoe, and then across the water from where they had taken it.

"I think iPhone is accusing us of stealing," said Amy. "Tell them we're sorry."

Gideon racked his brains. His Spanish was limited to what he'd picked up from living in New Mexico. He turned to Amy. "I thought you were the linguist."

"Yeah, in classical languages. Too bad they don't speak ancient Greek."

More angry gesturing. The man with the iPhone finally said, "*Ven. Ven.*" He gestured at what looked like a trail through the mangroves.

"*Ven*...I think that's Spanish. He's telling us to come with him," said Gideon.

To emphasize the point, iPhone leveled his spear and gestured again. "*Ven!*"

They followed iPhone along a sandy trail that wound among the mangroves, finally leading into thick jungle. It grew brutally hot and humid, and once again clouds of insects flowed out of the verdure to surround them. Even iPhone, Gideon noted with a certain satisfaction, was slapping and grumbling as he strode at a fast pace along the trail, the rest of his men bringing up the rear.

After about five miles, Gideon heard the faint sound of surf. Palm trees began to appear, the vegetation thinned, and he caught a whiff of salt air. A moment later they emerged at a tiny settlement: a few shacks made of driftwood and corrugated tin set about haphazardly in a grassy area, shaded by palms. They could hear but not see the ocean through a thick screen of jungle.

In the center of the settlement was an open area with a fire, where a group of old women stirred something in an enormous, dented enamel pot sitting on the coals. Two posts stood at either end of the hamlet, carved like totem poles with grinning monkey faces not unlike the one on the iPhone. To one side stood what looked like a kind of shrine, a miniature house built of finely shaped driftwood with a grass roof. Inside, Gideon could make out some old human skulls, brown with age, carefully arranged along with other bones.

The leader let forth another burst of talk, indicating

that they should sit on a log to one side. The women continued to cook as if nothing was happening. A group of children materialized out of the surrounding forest to stand and gape at the strangers in silence.

"Do you have any idea who these people are?" Gideon murmured.

"Since this is the Mosquito Coast, I'd assume they are Miskito Indians."

The group of tribal elders huddled, speaking animatedly, iPhone taking the lead. It was all too obvious they were discussing what to do about the intruders, with iPhone leading the group of naysayers. Finally, he detached himself from the group and went up to Gideon, reaching out for his drysack. "*Dar!*"

"No," said Gideon, pulling it back. "*Dar!*"

The man leveled his spear and made a jabbing motion while holding out his hand. "*Dar!*"

"Keep in mind," Amy murmured, "you've got a loaded .45 in that bag if you need it."

"Mi," said Gideon, stepping back.

The man lunged for it, at the same time swiping at Gideon with his spear.

"Son of a bitch!" cried Gideon.

More angry words and gesturing with the spear tip.

"If you take out the gun," said Amy, "maybe that'll shut him up."

"Not a good idea," said Gideon. "At least, not yet."

The man yelled at him again, shaking the spear.

Gideon stepped forward, almost walking up to the spear point, and began to yell. "Put that spear down! *Baja!* We are visitors!" He racked his brains, trying to dredge up what little Spanish he had. "*Somos amigos! Visitantes!*"

The Indian paused, taken aback by Gideon's vehemence.

"*Lo siento!* I am sorry about the boat. *Muchas gracias. Nuestro barco, baja en agua.*" He gestured, showing how their boat had sunk and pantomiming how they swam to shore. With exaggerated and comical gestures he communicated how they were forced to wander about, looking for food and water, how they were starving and thirsty.

The group of men had stopped arguing and were now listening.

"We need help. You understand? *Socorro. Comprende? Ayuda. Alimento y agua.*" He made eating and drinking gestures.

iPhone shook his spear again. Gideon slapped it away, then stepped forward and bared his chest. "You want to stab me, go ahead! If that's how you treat visitors, get it over with!"

This occasioned some murmuring among the older women, who were watching now with beady black eyes.

iPhone, enraged, placed the tip of the spear roughly against Gideon's chest, drawing blood.

"I'm not so sure your strategy is working," said Amy, reaching into his bag for the .45. "I think it's time to show these people we mean business."

39

"W AIT," WHISPERED GIDEON. He smeared his left hand across the trickle of blood welling up on his chest. Then he drew two streaks of blood down his face—one on either side of his temples—and drew a third slash across his forehead.

The effect was immediate—and startling. With a gasp, iPhone drew back, pulling away the spear. A burst of hushed whispering came from the women.

Suddenly the door flap of the nearby hut was flung open and a wizened old man came out: bow-legged, moving painfully, his back bowed into a hump. Unlike the others, he was dressed traditionally, in a loincloth.

The group of arguing men fell silent as the old man stopped before them, eyeing them fiercely. Then he spoke a sharp word at iPhone. Next, he turned to Gideon and launched into a long, incomprehensible speech in his native tongue, accompanied by much histrionic gesturing. The old man did not look happy about them being there, but at least, it seemed to Gideon, he wasn't going to kill them. Finally the man broke off, indicating that they should sit down on a log near the fire.

"What was that all about?" Amy murmured. "Your smearing blood all over your face?"

"I needed a makeover."

She frowned and he hastily added, "Actually, I don't know why they reacted like that. I was just imitating *that*." He nodded toward the closest totem pole. "Look at the one-eyed figure on top. I just copied the decoration on his face."

Amy shook her head. "A gun would've been simpler."

"You take out a gun and things get *real* complicated, *real* fast. I go for the social engineering route—like your pal Odysseus."

Bowls of stew arrived and were placed before them. They smelled heavenly. It was all Gideon could do to keep from burning his mouth as he ate. They ate self-consciously—the only ones eating—while everyone else looked on, crowding around and staring at them—men, women, and children.

"I don't think I've ever tasted anything quite so delicious," said Gideon, spooning the thick broth into his mouth.

Amy was slowly stirring her stew and fished out something that looked like a rat's tail. "I wonder what's in it."

"My advice? Eat with your eyes closed."

They finished the stew. "Now what?" Amy asked. "What do we say to these people?"

"One thing I've learned is that people are the same everywhere," said Gideon. He rose and seized the old man's hand, giving it a vigorous shake. "*Muchas gracias*," he said. "*Muchas gracias!*" He went through the entire crowd, first the men, then the women, shaking their hands with a grin on his face. While this was received with a certain amount of bewilderment, Gideon could see that the good cheer and friendliness were having a positive effect.

"And now," he said to Amy, "I'm going to give a speech."

"You've got to be kidding. They won't understand a word."

"Amy, don't you get it? We've got to act a certain part. Visitors worthy of respect. And what does a visitor worthy of respect do? Give a speech."

Amy shook her head.

"And give gifts." Gideon climbed up on a stump and raised his hands. "My friends!" he cried out.

A hush fell over the group.

"We have come a long way, across the sea, to be with you today . . ."

He continued grandly, in a big voice, while the crowd listened intently, not understanding a word. Concluding after a long interval, Gideon rummaged in his drysack and pulled out a gift: a flashlight. With great fanfare he walked up to the old man—and presented it to him.

The old man looked exceedingly displeased. He switched it on and off, clearly familiar with its use, totally unimpressed, and then handed it to one of the children.

A tense silence ensued. All the goodwill generated by the speech seemed to dissipate.

"Oops," murmured Amy. "Looks like the natives aren't accepting beads anymore."

Reaching into his bag again, Gideon thought fast. What could he give them better than a flashlight? His hand closed on the grip of the .45. No way. There were some knives…but they already had plenty. Granola bars, briefing book, matches, medical kit…he could feel the sweat trickling down his face.

The old chief was looking restless and irritated. It was obvious he felt condescended to in public by being given a flashlight as if it were a gift from the gods.

Gideon pulled out one of the grenades.

Amy stared at him. "Gideon, are you *crazy*—?"

With a flourish, Gideon presented it to the chief. A great murmur rose up. The chief received it in both hands, examined it with a professional eye, and then hooked it on his sash by its lever. Clearly, he knew what it was and highly approved. He gave Gideon's hand a vigorous shake. The other men followed, shaking his hand. All was well.

Now it was the chief's turn. He gave a long, windy, incomprehensible speech in his native language, with many favorable glances thrown Gideon's way, which held everyone spellbound. When the speech was over, the chief went into his hut. There was a long, anticipatory silence.

"Here comes the comely daughter," Gideon muttered to Amy.

Instead, the chief emerged with a small, polished wooden box. He handed it to Gideon. The box was of exquisite workmanship, beautifully hand carved of some dark, exotic wood, with a likeness of the same god or demon who graced the top of the totem pole. Gideon opened it to reveal some dry grass padding. A delicious smell of honey and cinnamon wafted up. Gideon drew aside the grass to reveal, nestled within, a strange-looking object, a dried flower bud perhaps—black, wrinkled, about an inch in diameter. He took it out.

Everyone began talking at once. Clearly it was something of enormous value.

He looked at Amy. "What is this—some kind of drug?"

Amy was staring at the object with great intensity, and then her eyes shifted to Gideon. "I believe these people are the Lotus Eaters. And they've just given you a lotus."

40

Aмy тоoк тне thing out, cradling it in her hand, its intense smell rising in the heat. Gideon felt temporarily stunned, staring at the thing, which looked like a dried pod or bud of some kind. Was this really the lotus—the healing *remedium*? He felt a rush of hope, immediately followed by doubt.

"Gideon?" Amy said, sotto voce. "Hello? Aren't you going to say something?"

"What? Oh." He turned to the chief. "We thank you very much for this gift! *Muchas gracias!*" He gave a low bow.

"Find out where it comes from," said Amy.

"Yes, absolutely. Ah, *donde, donde*…My Spanish is no good…" He held up the thing. "*Donde?*"

The chief's eyes opened. He pointed toward the invisible ocean. "*Isla,*" he said. "*Isla Tawaia.*"

"*Isla,*" repeated Gideon. It came from an island.

Everyone was now crowding around, pushing and shoving. The chief led them to a smaller hut off to one side, pulled open some hanging palm leaves covering the entrance, and—with much talk and gesturing—indicated that this was where they were to sleep: on woven mats laid on the ground, with tattered supermarket sheets and a polyester child's blanket decorated with Tweety Bird.

"Thank you," said Gideon. *Gracias.*" He indicated they wanted to go inside and rest. The sun was now setting, casting a golden glow through the jungle foliage.

The chief left and Amy threw herself on one of the mats. "I'm exhausted."

"I want to reconnoiter," said Gideon. "I want to see if we can identify this Isla Tawaia where the lotus came from. I'm going down to the ocean. You coming?"

"Of course." Amy got to her feet.

As soon as they were out of their shack, iPhone came over. He spoke rapidly, making gestures of help.

"I think you have a new friend," said Amy.

"We're going to the ocean," said Gideon. *A la mar. We're going swimming.*" He made a swimming motion. iPhone nodded his understanding. He pointed to a small opening in the brush that indicated a trail.

Gideon began heading down the trail, Amy at his side. He was glad iPhone wasn't following. As they walked, the sound of the sea grew in intensity, until they passed through a mass of sea grapes and there—through a scattering of palm trees—was the ocean. A golden light lay across the water, and a heavy sea was running.

Amy stopped, staring at a faint blue cluster of mountainous islands in the great distance offshore. She took the binoculars out of her bag and peered through them for a long time. Finally, in silence, she handed them to Gideon.

The distant islands were spectacularly rugged, steep volcanic peaks that thrust almost vertically from the ocean, soaring a thousand or more feet high. Their flanks were black, ripped with landslides, the tops covered in lush green jungle, gilded in the light of the setting sun. A single cloud hovered over the nearer, higher island, glowing vermilion in the dying light. But the thing that caught Gideon's attention was a lone spire of crooked rock before the island cluster, surrounded by boiling surf. It stuck out of the sea like a black corkscrew.

"The Twisted Place," said Gideon, staring at it.

"Incredible. *Tortuosum locum*. And those islands behind are the *trans ultra* of the clue. 'Beyond the beyond.' That's our final destination."

Gideon lowered the glasses. "How the hell are we going to get there?"

"Our friends will take us." She pointed to a row of dugout canoes hauled far up on the beach.

"Cross that sea in a dugout? No thanks. It's time to call Glinn, take him up on that offer of a fresh boat."

Amy paused. "Let's wait on that."

Gideon looked at her. "I don't get it. Why are you so opposed to accepting Glinn's help?"

A long silence. "I don't like his controlling methods. And I'm not sure bringing a big yacht in here is going to help us win the trust of the locals."

"We are working for him, after all."

She lowered the glasses and looked at him. "No. We're working for the project."

For a while they looked out at the mysterious islands, and then Gideon said: "I'd like to take a swim, if you don't mind. I'm sweaty and covered with bug bites."

"I'll join you."

"Well, um, I obviously don't have a bathing suit."

"Who cares? Neither do I."

Gideon shrugged and pulled off his filthy clothes, then ran down the beach and into the ocean. It was wonderfully refreshing. The water was relatively calm, inside where the waves were breaking farther offshore. He swam about, rinsed himself off, and came out. He shook off as much water as he could, spread his shirt on the sand, and sat down. Amy returned a moment later and he found himself admiring her body, which was just about as buff as he'd imagined.

She sat down next to him. "A gentleman does not stare at a naked woman."

"Sorry." He colored, turning his back.

A light breeze came off the water, drying them off. They remained awhile in silence.

"I've been meaning to tell you something," Amy said at last. "Glinn told me about how you managed to steal that page from the Book of Kells. That was some very, very slick work."

"Thanks."

"I don't know how I feel, though—having an art thief for a partner."

"I grow on people," Gideon said.

"I'll bet you do. Like a fungus."

Gideon shook his head, laughed.

"Did you ever get caught?" Amy asked.

"Nope."

"So you were never in jail?"

"Yes, I was. Once. Mistaken identity. I was arrested for a hit and run. Spent the night in a cell, and they caught the real guy the next day."

"What was that like? Being behind bars, I mean."

Gideon shrugged. "I read poetry."

"Poetry?"

"There was an old, battered anthology of poems in the holding cell. It was either that or *The Watchtower*."

They began to dress. "I hate putting these dirty clothes back on," said Amy.

"Think boat. Think showers. Soap. Fresh linen. Clean sheets. Soft bed. Hot espresso."

"Espresso..."

"If we want to explore those islands, we're going to need a boat, we're going to need maps and a GPS. We won't need the trust of the natives. Tomorrow, we've got to call Glinn."

Amy was silent a long time, and then she sighed. "All right. Tomorrow morning." She smiled. "I could really use an espresso..."

41

This time, there were only three of them in the conference room: Garza, Glinn, and Weaver, the chief DNA tech. The atmosphere was tense, like a newsroom in which a big story was about to break.

Weaver—who had in past meetings looked apprehensive—now seemed haggard, at the limits of exhaustion. It had been days since his last report. This time there were no papers before him, no reports or documents of any kind.

"Let's have it," Glinn said simply.

The tech ran one hand through his sandy hair. "We reran the DNA analysis, as requested. In fact, we've done not only a second run, but a third as well, all with fresh genetic material. We sampled several hundred sequences along the genome. The gene sequences among all three runs have been linked and cross-matched. They agree beautifully: the runs have proven functionally identical. Also, the BWA-SW hybrid routine has completed its analysis of the sample: the level of contamination is roughly 0.04 base pairs, well below statistical relevance." He fell silent.

"And?"

"All runs pointed to the same thing. The DNA is primarily human—with some major differences. There were a few sections of the DNA that belonged to no recognizable species. There are sequences that appear to be pongid, that is, ape-like."

Garza shook his head. This was getting more bizarre by the minute.

Weaver cleared his throat. "And then there were a number of key sequences that we were able to identify as"—here his voice dropped almost to a whisper—"Neanderthal."

What? Garza said.

"Neanderthal," Weaver repeated.

"That's preposterous!" Garza blurted out. "How could you know what the Neanderthal genome even looks like?"

"As it happens, the Neanderthal genome was fully sequenced by the Max Planck Institute in Leipzig a few years back. The analysis was done on ancient DNA taken from Neanderthal teeth found at sites in Europe. But we couldn't believe it, either. So we went ahead and sequenced the entire genome of the creature that this vellum came from."

Glinn frowned. "The entire genome?"

"It's the best way. Once that was complete, we ran the results through our gene frequency analysis machine."

"What is that?" Garza asked.

"It's a dedicated computer—series of linked computers, actually—that can take an organism's genome and then, in essence, reconstruct or re-create its possible morphology, behavior, and other attributes." Weaver hesitated. "I have to warn you. We're dealing with a species nobody has seen before. A cousin of the Neanderthals, yes, but...quite different in some ways."

"How so?"

"The unusual genes of this creature fall into the areas involved in aging, size, robustness, and some areas of visual processing. Its hemoglobin shows an unusually high carrying capacity for oxygen. Its respiration and metabolic rate appear to be abnormally low, and our analyses indicate it has the ability to alter these rates at will in times of environmental stress, thus preventing oxidative damage to tissues."

"What does it mean?" Glinn asked. "Can you be more specific?"

Weaver looked from Glinn to Garza and back again. "Yes. There are powerful genetic expressions in the growth and growth hormone sequences. It would appear this organism is large. Much larger, for example, than its Neanderthal cousin."

"How much larger?" Garza asked.

"Hard to say. Fifty percent larger, perhaps."

"So, you mean, like nine feet?"

Weaver nodded. "All factors indicate an extremely robust, moderately intelligent, and highly aggressive beast."

"Aggressive?"

"Yes. There's a whole suite of genes involving the fight-or-flight response, hormonal changes involving the control of emotion, and areas of the brain used in processing fear and aggression—all significantly enhanced. In the same way that it's unusually adaptive to its environment, it also appears to be well developed to defend that environment."

"So we're talking about a large, primitive hominid," Garza said. "Intelligent, aggressive, powerful. Well adapted to its environment."

"Did you determine the age of the vellum?" Glinn asked.

"Yes. It carbon-dates to about fifteen hundred years ago. In other words, this species didn't become extinct until sometime after 500 AD."

Glinn shifted in his wheelchair. "That's remarkable. Tell me more about the visual processing genes."

Weaver glanced at him. "I was wondering when you'd ask. That might be the strangest thing of all . . ."

42

First thing the next morning, Gideon and Amy took the sat phone down to the beach, where they would have the best chance for reception. Amy turned on the unit. As it warmed up, the LED screen flashed with calls received and messages left. There were several—all from EES. Gideon felt a twinge of nervousness: they hadn't called Glinn in days, and the man was not going to be happy.

Amy set the phone to speaker and put in the call. It was answered immediately—by Glinn. The voice wasn't, as Gideon expected, excited or angry. It was cool, formal, measured.

"It's been too many days since I heard from you," Glinn said. "Would you care to explain yourselves?"

"We have to talk fast," Amy said. "We're down to four percent battery power, and no way to recharge."

"Then talk."

Gideon listened as Amy launched into an explanation of her discovery related to Homer's *Odyssey*. But Glinn almost immediately interrupted her. "I've heard enough.

This is irrelevant. Listen to me please—and listen well. We're aborting the mission."

"What the hell are you talking about?" Gideon asked.

"There's new information that needs to be evaluated."

"*What* new information?"

"We solved the riddle. No time to go into the details, except to say that the vellum was made from the skin of a Neanderthal-like hominid."

"Wait. What are you saying?"

"This new information has thrown off our computer models. In addition, there is a consensus here that you can't be left on your own any longer—we've got to re-group, reanalyze, and plan a revised mission. I'll be sending a boat to pick you up and bring you back to New York. I commend your fine work and I look forward to debriefing you both—"

The battery indicator on the sat phone started to blink red.

Amy reached over and shut off the phone.

Gideon stared at her. "What are you doing?"

Amy turned her dark eyes on him. "Is that what you want to do? Abort the mission? After all we've risked, *all* we've done?"

"No, I don't."

"How about *no frigging way!* We're twenty miles from our goal." She gestured toward the distant islands. "It's right *there.* We can *see it.*"

Gideon stared at her. "Okay. I hear you."

"I hope you're going to do more than just hear me. All we have to do is get to those islands, explore them, identify the source of this medicine—which I have little doubt is the very 'lotus' these natives gave you—and bring it back."

"Going against Glinn may have consequences. He might try to stop us."

"He doesn't know where we are," she said.

"He can make a pretty good guess."

"The only thing I want to know right now is this: are you in or not?"

Gideon took a deep breath. He still had his doubts about her theory—but the appearance of the Lotus Eaters had gone a long way toward quelling them. He'd never seen such conviction or such fearlessness before, in man or woman. "I'm in."

Amy smiled, leaned toward him. "You know, I could kiss you for saying that."

"Go ahead."

"Not right now. We've got work to do."

He started to laugh. "If not now, when?"

"You'll know it when it happens." She packed the satellite phone back in the drysack and stood up, brushing off the sand. Then she paused, looking out to sea.

Gideon followed her gaze toward the nearer of the mountainous islands, lying on the horizon at the very edge of visibility, its vastness cloaked in purple haze, so distant and mysterious. A lone cloud clung to the highest peak. Was it possible—even remotely possible—that a cure for his terminal condition might be found in that mythical-looking land?

43

W HEN THEY RETURNED to camp, iPhone was there to meet them. He invited them to sit by the fire and partake of an unappetizing breakfast of gluey maize pudding with mashed green plantains. After they had eaten, Gideon motioned iPhone over. *"Isla,"* he said, pointing out toward the invisible ocean. *"Vamos isla."* He pantomimed rowing a canoe and pointed again in the direction of the islands. "We want to go to island. Okay?"

iPhone seemed put out by the suggestion. He frowned, shook his head. Gideon persisted. *"Vamos isla. Importante. Vamos ahora."*

More shakings of the head and negative murmurings. Finally iPhone got up and went into the chief's shack. A moment later the chief came out, a somber expression on his face. He sat down with them.

"No vamos isla," he said, wagging his finger like a schoolmaster. "No."

Gideon took a deep breath. *"Porque?"*

"Isla . . . peligroso."

Peligroso. What the hell did that mean? Once again

Gideon found himself rummaging around his brain for his high school Spanish. "*Peligroso? No comprende*."

"*Peligroso! Malo! Difícil!*"

Difficult. He got that last word at least. Problem was, the chief's Spanish didn't seem much better than his own.

"*Vamos in canoa.*" Gideon made rowing motions.

"*No. Isla sagrada.*"

Sagrada. Another damn word he didn't know. He turned to Amy. "Help me out here. You know Latin. What the hell is *sagrada*?"

"It sounds a lot like *sacra*. Sacred. And *peligroso* sounds a lot like *periculosum*. Dangerous."

"So the island is sacred and dangerous. But they must go there, or how else would they get the lotus?" Gideon turned back to the chief. "*Cuando . . .*" He pointed at the chief and pantomimed the rest of the question. When *do you go to the island?* After a few false starts, the chief finally seemed to understand. With broken Spanish and much gesturing, he conveyed the general impression that they went there for some sort of ceremony of thankfulness.

"*Gracias,*" said Gideon.

The chief left, and Gideon motioned to Amy. "Let's go for a walk on the beach."

They walked through the brush and came out on the broad beach. There were the canoes, still pulled up on the sand.

"Maybe we should steal a canoe," said Amy.

"We'd never survive. Just launching a canoe in that surf requires incredible skill—someone who knows exactly what he's doing."

"So what are we going to do?"

"We'll take a page from your old friend Odysseus."

"Like what? Poke a stick in iPhone's eye?"

"No. I'm talking about some good old-fashioned social engineering."

"How?"

Gideon explained his idea. He would feign sickness, which would require them to administer the lotus to him. He would be healed, and then they would have to have the ceremony of thankfulness.

Amy stared at him. "Gideon, that's a terrible idea. How do you know the lotus isn't poisonous?"

"One can only hope."

"Hope, right. And how do you know this is a thanksgiving ceremony? That old man's mumbling and gestures could have been describing anything."

"You saw him putting his hands together and bowing. Looked like thankfulness to me. And anyway . . . I want to try the lotus."

She looked at him curiously. "Why?"

"Just to see."

"See what?"

Gideon fell silent.

They spent the next half hour discussing other ways to persuade the natives to take them to the island. But they kept coming around to the one, intractable problem: they went to the island only for the ceremony. Finally Amy gave in. "But I'll only agree if you promise me one thing: I take the lotus."

More arguing, but Amy was adamant.

They returned to camp and sat down around the fire again. While Gideon messed with the medical kit, Amy ate a second breakfast—another bowl of thick maize pudding and mashed plantains. It almost made Gideon sick just watching her cram so much food in her mouth. She gestured for a coconut to wash it down. iPhone brought one to her, hacking off the top with an expert swipe of a machete and gouging a hole for her to drink from. She drank and passed it to Gideon, who drank and set it beside himself. Surreptitiously, when no one was watching, he took a small bottle of ipecac he had palmed from their medical kit and poured the contents into the coconut.

Amy called for coconut milk and he passed it back to her. With a knowing glance at him, she drank deep.

And immediately began vomiting.

Everyone leapt up in horror as she continued retching and heaving, bringing up her enormous breakfast. As she puked, she hammed it up, writhing on the ground and shrieking between bouts of the heaves.

The effect was electrifying. While Gideon rushed over and made a show of trying to help her, at least half the settlement fled into the jungle in a noisy panic, taking with them the children. The chief came over, followed, very reluctantly, by iPhone.

"I'm dying!" Amy shrieked. "Dying!"

"*Muerte!*" Gideon cried, dredging up another Spanish word from his schooldays. The dry heaves had passed—ipecac was very short acting—but she continued to scream, rolling her eyes, clawing the sand, and feigning convulsions. It was so hideous that even Gideon felt his gorge rise. Most of the rest of the village edged farther away, with more fleeing into the jungle.

But the chief and iPhone bravely stayed put, trying to help her. The chief started chanting and laying on hands while iPhone attempted to hold her down.

Gideon pulled the carved wooden box out of his dry-sack, opened the lid, and took out the lotus. "Give her this!"

This suggestion was greeted with a cry of instant approbation. The chief leapt up and fetched some boiling water from the fire, while iPhone whipped out his machete and began mashing and chopping the pod into tiny pieces, then crushing them with the flat of the blade. A foul scent rose from the crushed plant and Gideon had a bad moment, thinking it might be poisonous. But they didn't look like poisoners and were clearly concerned with her illness. When iPhone had reduced it almost to a powder, it went into the pot of boiling water.

Amy screamed one last time, and then—with a final rolling of the eyes—flopped out, unconscious.

The chief and iPhone worked frantically, boiling the lotus in the water, then straining it through a piece of pounded bark. A bad-smelling rose-colored liquid resulted, which they cooled with some fresh water. Talking rapidly, they gestured to Gideon to prop Amy up so she could drink. Gideon managed to get her up, her head lolling back, spittle drooling from her lips. He couldn't believe what a good actress she was.

The chief, carrying a coconut cup with the foul beverage, knelt in front of her and gave her a couple of hard slaps. Her eyes flew open. He put the cup to her mouth. Making a face, she drank down the concoction.

She fell back, once again unconscious. Gideon eased her down.

A minute passed while she lay motionless. The tension

and anxiety from the chief and iPhone were palpable. They stood over her, wringing their hands, their faces distorted with worry.

And then, suddenly, Amy opened her eyes and looked around a little groggily.

A great cry went up from the chief and iPhone. The others who had retreated to the edge of the jungle now shuffled forward to see what was happening.

Amy raised herself onto her elbows and glanced up at the onlookers, blinking.

More hubbub and excitement. People were still hanging back, but the relief was tremendous.

Slowly, gingerly, Amy rose to her feet. The retching and convulsions had passed. She thanked first the chief, then iPhone. People began to crowd around. Amy looked awfully tired, swaying slightly on her feet, but nobody seemed to notice as they came back out of the bush, eyes wide in wonderment at the miracle, making a great noise of thankfulness, gesturing to the sky as if praising the gods.

And then the chief seized Gideon's hand and raised it in triumph. He gave another incomprehensible speech that seemed to be full of praise for Gideon and his wisdom. At least, that's what Gideon hoped it meant—since that had been his intention all along.

Clapping his hands, the chief began calling out instructions. The village children began chasing around a goat, finally capturing it and tying it up. iPhone came over with his machete and, to the sound of much horrible bleating, cut its throat.

The chief was beaming. He clapped again. *"Fiesta!"* he said.

"*Fiesta*," murmured Amy, as if from a long way away.

"*Fiesta*."

As they prepared the feast, Gideon took Amy down to the beach to clean off the dirt and flecks of vomit. That evening, at the feast around the fire, they consumed barbecued goat. The chief made what seemed like an important announcement, greeted with applause. After much questioning, Gideon was able to decode it. It was exactly what he'd hoped: The next morning, they would be making the journey to the island of Tawaia, apparently to give thanks to the gods of healing and to the spirit of the lotus.

After the feast, late that night, Gideon and Amy finally were able to retreat to the darkness of their hut. Gideon lay down on his mat, his hands behind his head. For a while they lay in silence, Gideon listening to the distant sound of the surf and the murmuring of voices around the fire.

"Amy, your performance was amazing."

A quiet snore. Amy, it seemed, was still under the influence of the lotus flower. It had seemed to take her every effort to remain awake during the feast.

"Amy?"

"Mmm?"

"You were horrifyingly effective. It scared the shit out of everyone—including me."

A long pause before the bleary response came. "Long ago, at a very foolish time in my life, I studied Method acting."

"Ah! A clue to the real Amy finally emerges. You put it to good use."

"Your idea." And Amy began to breathe softly again.

Gideon looked over. Every other time he'd seen Amy asleep, there had been a frown on her face. It was as if she was forever struggling with something—what, he could not imagine. Now, however, there was a smile on her sleeping face: a smile that practically radiated serenity and bliss.

44

They put Gideon in the bottom of one of the canoes and Amy in the other. Gideon made sure to bring their drysacks with them. The men ran them into the water, leapt in, and began paddling like mad as the canoes shot out into the surf, bashing through the breaking waves. Gideon was instantly soaked and thoroughly terrified by the time they reached calmer water beyond the break.

Even beyond the breakers it was a nerve-racking journey. The sea was running high, the long canoe riding up and down the great swells while the men, their bare, muscled backs glistening with drops of water, paddled in unison to a rhythmic chant. The wind blew straight into their faces but the canoes moved fast, cutting through the water at five miles an hour. The early-morning sun rose over the distant islands, throwing a brilliant golden light over the sea, limning the mountain peaks in purple.

The landforms slowly rose up as they approached. Gideon could make out three of them. A massive, initial island thrust steeply out of the sea, rising more than a thousand feet into the clouds. A smaller but even steeper and taller island lay beyond it. Right in front of them was the twisted place: a volcanic sea stack or eroded plug that stuck up like a witch's finger, a black, bent spire of rock.

They headed for the closer island, just behind the twisted stack. As they approached, Gideon could see the white cream of surf, and beyond it a narrow beach of black sand, ending in steep volcanic cliffs hung with vegetation and pierced by caves.

The two canoes raced into the surf and were carried through the breakers and into the calm water beyond before grounding on the sand. The men leapt out and hauled the canoes up beyond the high-water mark.

They had arrived. Gideon watched as Amy came over.

The men were busy securing the canoes.

"Feels like the lost world," said Amy, looking around.

The others approached, led by a strange, wizened old man whom Gideon hadn't seen prior to the canoe journey. He was wearing only traditional garb, not the Western clothing of the others, and he carried a tall staff topped by a carved eagle and other, fanciful creatures. His fingers had multiple rings; a dozen heavy necklaces circled his neck. The other men treated him with great deference, casting their eyes to the ground as he walked past.

Now the man walked up to them and stopped, looking at them both. His wrinkled, craggy face, pendulous lips, and gleaming black eyes gave him the air of a man of mystery and power. This man, Gideon thought, must be a spiritual leader or head shaman.

After examining them intently, in dead silence, he gestured to iPhone, who seemed to have become their companion and general factotum. iPhone bustled over, and the man spoke to him.

iPhone turned toward Amy. Gesturing and pointing, and offering the odd Spanish word or two, he communicated that she was to stay with him—she would be separated from the rest. The ceremony was not for her.

Amy began to protest, but Gideon made a calming gesture. "Go with the flow," he said. "We'll have our chance to explore later."

Glaring at him, she nodded. iPhone led her away down the beach, and they were soon gone.

In complete silence, the priest raised his staff as the other men fell in line. He positioned Gideon to walk directly behind him. They proceeded in solemn fashion down the beach for a few hundred yards until they came to a crevasse in the volcanic walls, with the faintest of trails heading up. The priest began to climb, Gideon following with the rest. For an old man the priest was remarkably spry, and Gideon had trouble keeping up with him.

As they gained altitude, tremendous vistas opened up—the great expanse of sea, the waves thundering on the beach far below, and the distant mainland, like a blue-green sea of its own, flat along the shore but rising into steep mountains farther inland. A pair of eagles, disturbed from some nesting place in the cliffs around them, wheeled about over their heads, their cries piercing the air.

Gideon looked everywhere but could see no plant that produced pods or buds that resembled the lotus. He wanted to ask about it but decided it was better to go slowly and see how things developed. He sensed the great solemnity of the moment and was intimidated by the silence of the men.

The trail grew steeper. The priest continued on, climbing with both hands, his staff now tied to his back. Gideon had to push back against his own fear of heights as dizzying spaces opened up below. Still the eagles circled and cried.

And then, abruptly, the trail came over the lip of a broad ledge. Gideon was so relieved to be away from the cliff that he almost collapsed in gratitude. The other men came up and the priest led them along the broad ledge, around a column of basalt—to the mouth of a large cave. Huge, ancient flowering bushes hung down from its ragged upper edge like so many green scalp locks, in some places almost obscuring the entrance.

But there was no more time for speculation, because the others were already silently filing in.

Inside, the cave was low-ceilinged, with a smooth, sandy floor. They walked about a hundred feet in and paused. Gradually, as Gideon's eyes became used to the darkness, he saw that strange pictographs in deep red and blue were painted on the walls. Several men now fetched brands from a pile leaning against the wall and, with an expert striking of flints, lit them ablaze. They continued deeper into the cave.

Gideon's breath quickened when he saw, just ahead, a massive black rock that seemed to be some kind of altar—and painted on a slab behind it was an ancient pictograph, faded by time, depicting the grotesque figure of a monster being, covered with hair, with enormous muscled arms, jutting chin, huge knobby feet—and a single, gigantic eye in the center of its face, surmounted by a massive brow.

He turned to ask the priest a question about it, but the priest gave him a blazingly hostile gaze and made a gesture of silence before he could speak.

Brands burning, they approached the altar, the men fanning out. The priest walked up to it and—so suddenly it startled Gideon—broke out into a loud, nasal chant, which was answered by the men, repeated by the priest, and answered again, in a call and response. The cave echoed with the strange sounds of their half-singing, half-spoken voices. This, Gideon reasoned, must be the beginning of the ceremony of thanksgiving.

The men planted their brands to form a circle around the flat altar. Only then did Gideon notice that the altar was actually a box, with a stone lid. The men moved forward in unison and, still chanting, removed the lid.

A foul odor wafted out. Similar to the lotus, only much, much stronger.

The chanting accelerated as the priest reached in and removed what looked to Gideon like a bundle of small, black, twisted cheroot cigars. He counted out several, carried one to Gideon and placed it in his hand; the rest he solemnly distributed to the others, keeping the final one for himself.

Gideon stared at the thing. It looked like a dried root of some kind, or perhaps a fungus. The smell was fearful, like a combination of dirty feet and bitter almonds.

They retreated to the sand before the altar, sitting down cross-legged. The priest slid the stone lid back into place while several men fetched wood out of a stack in a corner of the cave and set up a bonfire. When it was done the priest set fire to it with his brand. The flames leapt up, filling the cave with flickering light.

In the firelight, Gideon could see things even more clearly. The altar was beautifully polished—gleaming like black ebony—the depiction of the creature behind disturbing in its detail, despite the stylized, geometric nature of the design.

One man went around, placing a polished, flat stone in front of each person, upon which he placed a mortar and pestle carved of lava, along with a stone cup full of water. The priest took up a position at the head of the circle, sitting on a raised stone, and lifted his implements as if to have them blessed. The others did likewise, and Gideon followed suit.

The head priest then poured a little water into the mortar, broke off a piece of the root, dropped it in, and began grinding it, all the while keeping up a rhythmic chant. The others did the same and so did Gideon, pounding and grinding, making a mush. A foul smell arose.

When the fungus-thing was completely turned into a kind of gruel, the priest lifted the stone cup to his lips and drank deeply. The others did the same and Gideon, hesitating, at last followed suit. It tasted hideous and it was all he could do to swallow it. Was this the real lotus? What they had given Amy back on the mainland seemed to be a pale comparison to this powerful-smelling root.

The chanting increased. Gideon wondered what effect the concoction might have. Frightful scenarios out of Carlos Castaneda came to mind. He tried to tell himself that everyone had taken it, so at least it wouldn't kill him. In his wild youth he'd had more than a little experience with drugs, and he figured that, whatever was in store for him, he'd ride it out. He was reassured that this was a ceremony of thanking the gods. He'd been right after all.

In a few minutes, the queerest feeling began to creep over him—a dreamy sense of peace and well-being, a glow that encircled and surrounded him, growing stronger little by little, until he felt swaddled and cocooned, as if a babe in his mother's arms again. He had never felt such peace, such acceptance. And then a strange thing happened. While he normally didn't dwell on his troubles—his horrible childhood, his father's murder, his loneliness, his terminal disease—he did nevertheless carry the burden of them always, unseen. But now, as the drug took hold, that burden was lifted. He forgot—or rather, ceased caring—about those things that blighted his life. With this burden lifted, he felt free, at peace, at home with himself in a way he never had before. It all dropped away, everything—his childhood, his long-gone father and mother, his cabin in the mountains of New Mexico, everything disappeared in a lambent sea of forgetfulness, and time seemed to cease altogether...

45

THE CHANTING SEEMED to come and go, like the waves of a sea. Gideon lay back in the sand. He felt absolutely wonderful and fully alive. The firelight flickered warmly on the cave walls, burnishing them into gold riven with dancing shadows. The sand was soft and luxurious as he smoothed it with his hand, idly clutching it and feeling the tickling sensation as it ran through his fingers. There was a rich smell of stone and sand, overlaid with the perfume of wood smoke. The crackling and popping of the fire filled him with an overwhelming sense of warmth and re-assurance. Most lovely of all, the glow of heat soaked into his skin and seemed to warm his very bones: a warmth more than mere heat; a warmth of spirit and of life itself.

As he lay there, he saw that the men around him had risen, unsteadily, smiling blissfully like him. But they seemed to have some kind of purpose, these wonderful friends of his. They came over to him and he felt himself being lifted up, carried, their strong, muscled arms bear-ing him along—deeper into the cave.

The warmth of the fire began to fade, as did the firelight, but Gideon didn't care: it was all good, whatever they were doing. A clammy, wet sensation wafted over his limbs as they proceeded, their progress lit by a single brand, but the wonderful thing about it was that Gideon still knew that wherever they were going, all was good. The dark mystery of the cave thrilled him, and he knew he would be taken care of by these good, kind people.

The men began to chant, a low, soft, mournful chant that touched him in his very soul with its primordial beauty.

The cave tunnel broadened into a somewhat larger chamber. Gideon wondered if it was real or a dream. Maybe the whole thing was a dream. But no: it was far too powerful to be a dream, far too deep an experience to be in his mind. Despite the sluggishness of his limbs, the delicious sense of somnolence, he nevertheless felt a clarity of mind and a curiosity about what would happen next.

The men laid him down on a raised stone slab, almost like a bed. The mournful chanting increased. Another fire was built, which chased away the clammy damp and threw a welcome warmth about the cavern. The high priest appeared above him with a clay jar, which he dipped his hand into, perfumed oil dribbling down his fingers—and then Gideon was anointed with it. The other men gathered around and Gideon felt the deep honor of their attention, felt their concern and kindness toward him, thankful and gratified by their consideration.

He looked around at the chanting men, now slowly revolving in a sort of slow dance, their hands moving strangely, winding around the cavern and into a dark recess. Then from that dark recess was borne a wooden pallet, carried by eight men on two thick timbers, and on the pallet rested something large and white: a skull. A strange skull, massive like a gorilla, only bigger—with a single, dark, vacant eyehole under a thick ridge of bone.

Gideon stared. Was this some kind of sculpture? But no, this was a real skull—very old, worn, cracked, and almost human. Except for that mysterious, single eye socket. It was the same creature as the pictograph, a one-eyed giant. How interesting... How fascinating... This creature had once existed... The lotus had taken over his being, and he had gladly yielded... He stared at the skull, mesmerized.

Lotus. Lotus Eaters. Odysseus. And then, even in his drugged state, the connection came to him like a bolt of lightning. He thought back to what happened to Odysseus right after he left the land of the Lotus Eaters. On the next island, he came to the land of the Cyclops.

Cyclops.

He was staring at a Cyclops skull. The Cyclops of the *Odyssey* had once actually existed. And here was the proof of it, right here in front of him—in this skull that the natives treasured, preserved, and worshipped.

The ancient skull of a Cyclops.

Gideon stared, transfixed. How beautiful, how fascinating, was this huge skull, with its immense jaw, long interlocking canines, and massive bony crest. And what a tremendous discovery this was for science. Gideon lay back. Science? It didn't seem important now. He didn't care.

And now the skull was taken down from the pallet and placed on a stone plinth, and the chanting morphed into a kind of spoken song, like wind moaning about a forest. The old priest approached and, from a wooden trencher, plucked up an armful of pods—dried lotus pods—which he scattered about and on top of Gideon, followed by drops of shaken oil. And now the priest was kneeling close, and a long, beautifully flaked obsidian blade had appeared in his hand and was hovering over Gideon's face, coruscating in the firelight.

Gideon tried to make sense of it, tried to find his voice, but could not. Never mind: it was all good, whatever it was they were doing, his lovely friends. More wood was thrown on the fire and it leapt up, sparks ascending into the darkness, the crackling of the wood echoing in the chamber.

The blade descended, touched his neck where it met the base of one ear.

A small, very small part of Gideon's brain seemed to be sounding a distant alarm. Strange that he felt no pain, even as the blade began to bite, even as he felt the warm trickle of blood....

46

Suddenly an explosion went off in the cave, impossibly loud. A voice screamed out: "Get away from him!"

The knife froze in place. The voice was distantly familiar. A woman. Who was it, and why was she interrupting this fine ceremony?

Another thunderous explosion. The singing had stopped. The knife remained poised. And then a figure came bursting in, ramming the high priest aside, his obsidian knife flying. A recognizable face came into Gideon's field of view: short black wild hair, flashing eyes. He knew this woman.

She seized him roughly. "Get up!"

When he tried to pull away, she slapped him viciously across the face, first once, then again. Why was she being so mean? The men, his dear friends, had backed away and were raising their hands in the air, angry, yelling.

He feebly tried to fend her off, to return to the peace that he craved, but now her arm was around his neck and she hauled him to his feet. A gun was clutched in her other hand.

"Stay back!" she cried, the gun bucking with another loud explosion. "Gideon, for God's sake, wake up and help me!"

He stood, confused and unsteady. He still couldn't speak and was surprised he had the ability to stand.

"Move your goddamn feet!"

Gripping his arm, she backed up out of the cave, pulling him along with her. She seized a burning brand from its rude sconce and continued on. He tried to mumble a protest but she ignored him. Now they had turned a corner in the stone tunnel and she dropped behind, shoving him ahead. "Run, damn it!"

He tried to run, stumbled. She caught him, grabbed him by the hair, and hauled him up, giving him another slap across the face.

"Move!"

He ran, slowly, his mind full of regret, terrible regret and loss, a longing to return to that beautiful place. "Did you see—?" he began.

"Faster!" This was accompanied by another hard shove.

A moment later he could smell fresh air, hear the ocean, and they came out on the broad ledge. It was night; the sea rumbled below. The fresh air revived him somewhat, began to clear his head. But his vision was abruptly arrested by the starry night sky. "My God, how beautiful..."

Another hard shove reminded him that the angry woman was still there. He had a recollection, a distant memory, of this woman. What was her name? "But look at the stars..."

"Forget the stars. Keep going!"

He stumbled forward and came to the edge of the trail,

which started down through a cleft. He swayed, looking at the white edge of surf below, the dark ocean, the cliffs hanging with vegetation. Now he recalled the trail, their ascent. He had to go back the way he had come. How unfortunate.

"Pay attention! Face out, go slow."

Gideon began heading down the trail, placing one foot gingerly in front of the other. After a few steps, he halted.

"Let's go back . . ."

This was answered with another whack across the top of the head. "Down!"

It seemed easier to obey than to argue, and he continued. He stopped to enjoy the cool, fresh night air flowing up from the sea, and was struck again on the top of the head, so he continued climbing down. Finally, the trail reached the black beach and Gideon fell to his knees, running his hands through the sand. Even this small pleasure was rudely interrupted by the woman, who grasped his hair again and pulled him up.

"To the canoe."

He stumbled down the beach. She grabbed their drysacks from the beach and threw them in.

"Help me pull it into the water."

Reluctantly, he grasped the rope and helped drag the long wooden canoe into the shallow water.

"In."

He got in and felt a paddle thrust into his hands.

"Paddle."

He stood up, laying the paddle down. "Go back for just a little while . . ." He tried to stand up to get out.

The woman pressed him back down onto the rough wooden bench of the canoe. He watched as she lashed him to the bench with some loose rope. She pushed the canoe out and hopped in.

"*Paddle,* damn it!"

He put his paddle in the water, pulled, and repeated. Sitting behind him, the woman was paddling like mad. He tried it a few more times, slowly, until she told him to pull harder.

He couldn't understand why she was so angry, why she had tied him to the seat, but he obeyed. The canoe moved sluggishly toward the roaring break about a hundred yards offshore.

"Harder!"

He pulled strongly. The combers came in, striking the prow and breaking over them. He paddled harder as they came into the heavier surf, the waves curling toward them. The prow burst through the first wave and the canoe was thrown upward. The second wave hit them, spinning the canoe sideways, and a third wave swamped them. Gideon felt the water pushing them down, but the canoe seemed to survive it, half filled with water, and then they were beyond the breaking surf.

And now, for the first time, he felt a twinge of fear.

"Bail! Use your hands!"

Gideon began splashing water out of the canoe, and the woman did the same. But even as they bailed, water kept slopping in over the sides as the canoe rose and fell on the rough ocean.

The soaking, the wind and water, began to clear his head. The woman who was ordering him about—her name was Amy. That's right: *Amy.* He put his hand to his throat and felt the shallow cut, the sting of salt water on it. Those men back in the cave…they were going to kill him. They were going to cut his throat. And he was just going to let them. And then there was the ancient skull of a Cyclops... But that was obviously a hallucination, a side effect of the drug. He shook his head. Strange how the mind played tricks.

He bailed with redoubled effort, splashing the water out of the half-swamped canoe with both hands. He felt a headache coming on.

"Good! Keep it up!"

They were caught in the grip of a massive current, which was carrying them past the island and out to sea. As the canoe swept alongside the island, the smaller, more distant island came into view behind it.

"They're coming after us," Amy said.

Gideon turned. There were bobbing lights on the water—men holding torches in the other canoe as others paddled furiously.

What had happened to him was slowly starting to emerge from the fog of forgetfulness. They'd given him a drug and they'd been about to sacrifice him on an altar to their god. A ceremony of thankfulness... and *sacrifice*.

"Amy, you saved my life."

"You can thank me later. Just keep bailing!"

He bailed like mad. In the grip of the current, their canoe was carried toward the outer island, about a mile away. He could see its black silhouette against the starry sky. It was even more rugged, surrounded by sheer cliffs on all sides rising from the water to a broad, flat top, covered with dense jungle.

They were finally making progress with the bailing, even as Gideon could see the lights of the other canoe, catching up fast.

"Good work. Now paddle."

Gideon obeyed, paddling hard now. The canoe shot forward.

"We've got to land on that island," Amy said. "It's our only hope. We'll never outrun them otherwise."

"Okay, I get it . . . But where? There's no beach."

"When we get closer, maybe we'll see a place."

The island approached, a great black form blocking out the stars. As they neared, Gideon could hear a roar of surf, and then, emerging from the darkness, the whiteness of violent seas crashing directly into the base of the cliffs.

"I don't see anywhere to land," said Amy.

The canoe was being borne onward, the irresistible currents and waves pushing it straight toward the cruel cliffs rising vertically from the sea.

"We're going to be driven right into those cliffs," she said.

The black rocks loomed closer, the surf roaring louder. The other canoe was behind them and pursuing relentlessly, lights bobbing on the water.

Amy tossed him one of the drysacks. "Put that on your back. I'll take the other. Be ready to grab hold."

He slung it over his back by the shoulder straps and tightened them down. His head was now painfully clear, with a throbbing headache.

They were now just beyond the breaking surf.

"Listen," said Gideon. "We'll let the waves carry the canoe up to the cliff face, and at the last minute jump free and get a handhold. We have to time it just right."

"Right. Count of three."

A breaking wave caught the canoe and carried it in toward the rocks, like a surfboard.

"One, two, *three!*"

They both leapt. Gideon hit the rock face hard and was able to grasp a handhold on the craggy rock, scraping his hands and barking his shins. He held on, feet flailing in the air before finding their own holds. A wave dashed against the cliff and swept over Gideon, almost plucking him from the rock. He held on for dear life as a second wave smashed the canoe against the rocks just below him, the surge washing again over Gideon's lower body, the shattered hull of the canoe just missing him.

When the water subsided he looked about in a panic and was relieved to see Amy, dripping wet but clinging to the nearby rock, pale and strained.

"Climb!" she cried.

They climbed. It wasn't quite vertical, but close enough to be terrifying. At least, he thought, there were plenty of handholds. Amy, an experienced climber, moved fast and soon got ahead, and then above him. "Follow me," she called down. "Use the same hand- and footholds I'm using."

"Okay."

"Always keep three points on the rock. Don't overgrip. Keep close to the wall."

Gideon could see, a few dozen feet below, the canoe filled with men approaching along the edge of the cliffs, the men paddling but staying well out of the break. They didn't dare get in close. The canoe was moving fast, the men shouting unintelligibly. A single arrow clattered harmlessly off the rock below them, and then the canoe was swept past in the strong current.

They climbed a few hundred feet, the dizzying heights filling Gideon with dread.

They reached a shallow cave, little more than a lava tube in the side of the cliff, with just enough space for the two of them. Gideon hauled himself up over the edge and collapsed on the floor of the cave, gripping the rock, relieved to be away from the terrifying drop. Amy slumped beside him.

He glanced at her again, then started up. "Hey. What's this?" A dark stain was spreading on her shirt, in her side. "Christ, you're hurt!"

"Yeah, I'm going to need a little help here."

Gideon unbuttoned the shirt, pulled it back. A nasty-looking wound was visible in her side.

"Back in the cave," she said, breathing hard. "A spear…"

"Okay, I'll dress it right now." He opened one of the drysacks and took out the medical kit and a flashlight. He shone it on the wound. It looked messy, but at least wasn't too deep, thank God.

"I'm going to fix you up. You just take it easy." He tore open a gauze pad and dabbed, cleaning around the edges of the wound, examining it. The ocean had largely rinsed it clean, but he sponged it out with fresh water from a canteen. It appeared to need stitches, but there were none in the kit. He sterilized the wound with Betadine, closed it as best he could with strips of surgical tape, and dressed it. Rummaging about, he removed a bottle of amoxicillin and gave her a tablet, along with a couple of ibuprofen.

"How does it feel?"

"Hurts. I feel a little light-headed. I think I lost some blood."

"I can't believe how tough you are—everything you managed to do, and with that wound—!"

She waved a hand. "Sleep. I need to sleep. Tomorrow, we've got a major climb ahead of us."

"You aren't going anywhere with that wound. We'll stay here until you're better."

She lay back. "If we stay here, we'll die. It's as simple as that."

47

GIDEON AWOKE. The rising sun streamed into the little cave on the cliff face. He could hear the cries of seabirds wheeling about. Amy was still sleeping. She looked flushed.

He sat up and clutched at his brow. His head was pounding, and there was a terrible taste in his mouth. He drank from one of the canteens and took stock. They had two liters of water, the last two granola bars, and two pieces of pemmican-like food, wrapped in banana leaves, given to them by the Indians. The medical kit still had plenty of bandages, antibiotics, and painkillers.

He crept to the edge and peered over. They were perhaps two hundred feet above the sea. But from the vantage point of the cave it was impossible to see upward. From the silhouette he had seen of the island the night before, it was at least a thousand, maybe fifteen hundred feet high.

When he turned, Amy had awoken. He put a hand on her forehead. It was warm.

"How do you feel?"

"Not bad," she said.

Gideon didn't believe her. He gave her the canteen, and she drank deeply.

"Let me take a look at your wound."

She lay back. He unbuttoned her shirt and pulled it aside. The bandages were already dark with fluid. She winced a little as he removed them. Gideon tried to hide his fright and concern. The wound was still closed and he didn't dare remove the surgical tape, but he applied more Betadine and some topical antibiotic ointment and put on a fresh dressing.

"Thanks."

"Amy, you got that saving my life. How can I thank you?"

She just shook her head.

"How did you know to rescue me?"

She took a deep breath. "iPhone took me down the beach to a cave. But it was iPhone's behavior that tipped me off. He seemed to get more and more nervous. When it started to get dark, I tried to question him and he was evasive. That's when I began to fear something bad was going to happen to you. I confronted him, and while he denied it, he really started to sweat. So I pulled my gun out of the bag and tied him up. And then I went looking for you."

"Thank you."

She said, "Did you see that huge skull?"

Gideon stared at her. "You mean, you saw it, too?"

"Damn right I did. It took me a moment to real-ize—that it was the skull of a Cyclops."

"And I thought it was just a hallucination."

"*Hic sunt gigantes.* 'Here there be giants.'" The map

didn't lie—there were Cyclopes living here once. They were going to sacrifice you to the Cyclops god."

"I was so zonked, I was ready to have my throat cut without protest... I feel like such a fool."

"You were drugged."

"They gave me a black root to consume. That's got to be the true lotus. It was incredibly powerful, made me forget everything, made me feel so wonderful I never wanted it to end—just like what happened to Odysseus's men."

"So what was the pod they gave us?"

"A fake lotus, a ceremonial substitute? Or maybe the aboveground part of the plant."

Amy licked her dry lips. "There's something else—something I should have realized earlier... You know this Phorkys Map we've been following? Phorkys was a minor Greek god of the sea, a son of Poseidon. Just as Polyphemus was supposed to be the son of Poseidon. In other words, Phorkys was the brother of Polyphemus, the Cyclops. If that doesn't connect Phorkys to Odysseus and the Cyclops, I don't know what does..."

She was rambling, sweating, her forehead beaded. Gideon felt it again. "You're running a temperature."

"I know. As soon as possible—before I get any sicker—we need to finish this climb. Because I *am* getting sicker."

"You can't climb in your condition."

"I can do it now. In another six, twelve hours, maybe not. I'm coming down with a fever. It's getting worse. We can't stay here. There's almost no food or water. We've got to shoot for the top right now. Otherwise we'll die here."

She struggled to sit up, grabbed her drysack.

"This is crazy," Gideon protested.

"Crazy, yes. Our only option, yes. Just follow my lead. We'll climb fast and free."

Gideon looked at her. This was one determined woman. Nothing was going to change her mind. And as he mulled over the problem, he realized she was probably right. They had no other choice.

In silence, they ate the last of the granola bars and drank some more water. And then Amy started climbing up the rock above the cave.

The pitch was terrifying, an almost vertical face of volcanic rock, but with plenty of cracks and bubbles that made for good hand- and footholds. Gideon followed below her, watching where she put her feet and hands and trying to follow suit. He asked a few times how she felt until she told him to shut up. She was doing well, it seemed to him: climbing steadily, silently. The birds cried, the surf thundered below, the wind swept over them. And still they climbed. As they rose, the difficulty varied, depending on the verticality, but the dizzying space below became only more terrifying. Five hundred feet, he judged; six hundred, eight. He tried not to look down, but it was necessary in finding footholds. They couldn't see up; there was no way of knowing how much farther it was to the top. Gideon's arms ached and he wondered how Amy could do it. He could see a dark stain spreading on her side, staining her shirt. The wound had opened again and was bleeding.

She began to slow down, fumbling longer for hand- and footholds.

The clouds started rolling in, and there came a rumble of thunder. It began to rain. Several times Amy slipped, rocks tumbling as she hung by both hands for a moment while her toes sought a purchase. The rain came down harder and began streaming down the sides of the cliff, adding a slipperiness to the climb, carrying water and debris pouring over them, getting in their faces and eyes every time they tried to look up.

Amy slowed further. Even in the easy stretches she began to struggle, and at times she stopped and swayed. There was nothing Gideon could do. He was deeply frightened for her—but she was right: they had to keep going.

They finally came to a large, horizontal crack, which Amy crawled into and immediately collapsed. Gideon followed. They were soaking wet and water was now pouring down the cliff face in miniature waterfalls, the wind lashing the rocks.

Gideon saw Amy's face for the first time in hours. She looked awful—pale as ivory, her lips blue, her eyes clouded and jittery.

"Rest," she muttered. "Rest. And then more climbing. Must be . . . must be close to the top."

It was clear to Gideon that Amy wasn't going anywhere. He said nothing but reached out to feel her forehead.

She drew away. "I'm fine!" She shivered again. "Rest. Then climb."

Gideon laid a hand on her forehead anyway. She was so hot it frightened him. He rummaged in the drysack and removed the medical kit, took out some ibuprofen and offered them to Amy.

She took them.

Next he brought out the bottle of amoxicillin. There

was another antibiotic in the kit, labeled azithromycin. Should he give her both? Or would that have an adverse effect? Was the wound getting infected? Or was the fever some kind of bodily response to the injury? God, he wished to hell he knew more about medicine.

He gave her both. She took them with trembling hands and then seemed to lapse into a kind of half sleep.

What a place to be, Gideon thought: jammed into a little crack barely three feet deep on an exposed cliff face maybe twelve hundred feet above the ocean, unable to move, lashed by rain and wind, with a companion who was sick and growing sicker. The sky darkened further and a peal of thunder roared above them. More rain, lashed down, developing into a massive downpour. It was like sitting behind a waterfall. Gideon fished out the canteens from the drysacks and filled them with the dirty water now streaming down the sides of the cliff. Amy began to shiver uncontrollably and he took off his shirt and forced her to put it on, despite her feeble protests.

She was going downhill. He took out the sat phone. There was very little battery left. Shielding it from the rainstorm with his body, he turned it on. The screen came on, the SEARCHING FOR SATELLITES legend appearing.

The searching went on and on. They were clearly in a bad position, jammed into the cliff. He tried to hold it out, chancing the soaking, but the searching didn't stop. The battery symbol began to blink red, fast. The display dropped from two percent remaining to one percent. And still the phone couldn't locate satellites.

He quickly shut off the phone. He would have to make the call from the top.

"What … are you doing?"

He squeezed her hand and tried to smile. "Trying to call Glinn. No luck—we're too close to the cliff."

Ten minutes went by in silence as the rain poured.

"I'm frightened," she whispered.

This admission scared him more than almost anything else.

Her face was small, her eyes burning and moving restlessly about, her lips white and trembling. Her reserve of determination, the stoical mask of self-assurance that never left her, had crumbled away. She looked terrified—as well she might. There was no way she could keep climbing in her condition—she was stuck in this horrible little crack of rock. They were in a lethal situation. He needed to think, try to work out the options.

"What do we do?" she asked, almost plaintively.

Gently, Gideon spoke to her. "You rest—let me worry about it."

There was silence for several minutes. She squeezed his hand. "Talk to me. Please."

"It's going to be okay, Amy." He felt lame saying it. He was pretty sure it wasn't going to be okay.

"My name isn't Amy. It's Amiko. Stop calling me Amy."

"Of course. Amiko."

She let out a long, shuddering sigh, her eyes closing, opening, as if in slow motion, her hand clutching his like a frightened girl. "My father was Japanese. My mother, Swiss German. I was . . . born in Japan."

"You don't have to tell me all this, not now—"

"I have to talk," she said. "I *need* to talk. I want you to know some things. If I die."

"All right."

"My father had three sons from a previous marriage.

All pure Japanese. He was very traditional, very old-fashioned. My mother was . . . a cold, cold woman. When I came along, I just wasn't what my father was looking for in a daughter, I guess. I tried, I tried so hard to earn his respect and love. I did it all. But no matter how many karate courses I took, or ikebana, or music lessons, no matter how many A's I got in math, no matter how many Vivaldi concerti I played on the violin . . . It wasn't enough. I was a girl. And I wasn't Japanese. Not in his eyes."

She paused, breathed hard.

"When I was twelve, my father was transferred to . . . a job in America. My older half brothers, all successful with their own careers, stayed in Japan." She paused again. "I always felt out of place in Japan. Now, in the US, I felt even more out of place. And my father . . . he didn't understand America. He was a fish out of water. Things went downhill. We never seemed to have any money, although my father seemed to have a good job. My mother left—just walked out—I never knew why. And then, one day, I came home from school to find my father dead. He . . . he'd killed himself."

"Amiko, how awful. I'm so sorry."

"And then it came out. He'd been laid off eighteen months before. To save face, he continued to leave the house dressed in a suit every morning, not returning until the evening, spending his days in libraries, employment offices, and finally in parks and other public spaces. That was it for me. I was seventeen. I think maybe I wanted to die, too. I just left everything behind. Worked my way through college, by myself . . . That's when I tried acting. I was good, but that was no way to make a living . . . Went to graduate school. That's when Glinn found me. I did a few black-bag jobs for him, researching treasure maps with my knowledge of ancient languages, and then...following up on what I learned. And here I am."

She closed her eyes, opened them again.

"And your mother?"

"Card on my birthday...Gift certificate for Christmas...Never saw her again."

Gideon felt terrible for her. And all this time he'd been feeling sorry for himself, thinking he'd had a rough childhood. No wonder she'd been forced to overcompensate, show a thick veneer to the world.

"Water...I need water."

Gideon put the canteen to her lips, and she drank. He felt her forehead. It was burning hot.

And now it was growing dark. Night was coming on. The rain poured, thunder rolled across the waters, illuminated by flashes of lightning. The roar of the sea filtered up from far below, the cliffs shuddering even here with their great power as they struck the rocks.

"Talk," Amiko whispered. "Please."

Gideon hesitated for a minute. "I've got a terminal condition."

Her reddish eyes swiveled toward him. "What?"

"It's called an AVM. This big knot of veins and arteries in my brain."

"Can...can it be operated on?"

"No. Inoperable. Incurable."

"How long until...?" Her voice trailed off.

"Ten months, give or take."

He didn't know, exactly, why he was telling her this. It wasn't as if the mood needed to be any bleaker. Somehow, it was all that was coming into his head.

"Oh, Gideon," Amiko murmured.

"It's okay. I'm reconciled to it." Maybe, in some strange way, it would make her feel better—knowing she wasn't the only one of them bearing a secret burden.

"So that's why you wanted to be the first to try the lotus," she said.

"Yes."

They fell silent for a moment.

"Don't let me sleep," Amiko pleaded.

But she sank into a fitful sleep anyway, shivering and moaning, her head tossing back and forth. Gideon looked out over the darkening ocean, a feeling of despair washing over him.

48

As the earth darkened into night, the rain lessened into a fitful drizzle. Amiko's fever remained high. Gideon hoped that when she woke up, she'd be stronger, but as the night wore on and her fever only got worse, he realized this wasn't going to happen.

Only one possible solution presented itself: he would have to finish the climb solo, rig a line, and then come back for her and try to haul her up somehow. He could call Glinn from the top, but a rescue would take a few days at least and by then, jammed in this crack, exposed to the elements, she'd be dead. He had to get her to the top, into some kind of shelter, with a fire.

He went through both drysacks and combined the ropes. By measuring them out, he figured there was about a hundred feet. It wasn't climbing rope, but it was sturdy marine nylon and it seemed like it would hold the weight of a human.

He racked his brains, trying to figure out just how this would work. Amiko was now beyond doing much for herself. He couldn't just drag her up the rough rock. He had to make a sling of some kind, like a seat, and pull her up that way. He would have to climb to the top, estimate how far it was, fashion a sling, set up a top-rope, climb back down, and put her in it. Climb up, haul her up.

Emptying one of the drysacks, he packed it with the rope and essentials and strapped on one of the headlamps. The battery was good, the light bright. Amiko was still sleeping. He decided to let her sleep, wake her up on his return. He quickly scribbled a note, *I'll be back*, and tucked it in the crook of her arm.

He took a deep breath. He hoped the note was true—that he would be back.

Loaded down with the single drysack, he edged out of the crack and looked up. In the darkness and rain the headlamp could only illuminate about ten feet, but he picked what looked like the easiest route, mentally registering the hand- and footholds and pre-visualizing the climb. Then, with another deep breath, he pushed his way out onto the cliff face.

In the dark and the rain, without Amiko, it was more terrifying than ever. The wind roared up from below, carrying with it the sound of the surf. Confused raindrops lashed about in the beam of his headlamp. The worst was not knowing how far he had to go—one hundred feet? A thousand?

The rock was crumbly, friable, and wet. He lost his footing at one point and ended up dangling in space, holding on by his hands alone. He got a foothold back just as one of the handholds gave way, a bunch of rocks peeling off from the cliff, and he swung by a hand and foot for a moment as the rubble plunged down. He recovered his grip—and then, distantly, heard the clatter of the falling rocks as they struck far below. The near-fall left him utterly paralyzed with fear, clinging to the cliff. He couldn't move. His heart was galloping, he was hyperventilating, and his head seemed ready to explode in the storm of terror.

Ride it out. Get yourself under control.

Slowly, he came back to himself. Staying put was not an option. He had to go up. *Up, up, up.* He repeated it with each breath. That was the only way he and Amiko would survive. But the fear was still with him, like a monkey on his back now. And he was going to have to come back down, and go up again.

Don't think about that now.

He resumed climbing. Shift a hand. Then a foot. Transfer weight. Detach the other foot. Find a new foothold. Move the other hand. Begin again. It was like a slow mantra.

The rock was becoming increasingly rotten. Another foothold gave way as he transferred his weight and he dangled again, his arm muscles screaming with the effort before he found a new purchase. This could not go on much longer. And then—just when it seemed he could go no farther—he came through a notch in the lava and saw just ahead a mass of dripping vegetation. He pulled himself up, seized a tree trunk, and scrambled into the welcoming cocoon of the forest, throwing himself down on the forest floor—blessedly, wonderfully, safely flat.

He lay there for a while, trying not to think about what he had to do. First, the good news: that last climb had been no more than a hundred and fifty feet. If he could somehow lengthen his rope with vines, he could haul up Amiko. And the jungle around him looked rich with hanging vines and creepers.

He sat up, breathing hard. He didn't have time to waste. She was soaked, she was jammed into that crack, she had a fever—but she was, he hoped, conscious. It would be infinitely worse if he had to haul up an unconscious body.

Rising to his feet, he took off the drysack and carefully marked where he had come up over the edge. He would need at least two hundred feet of creeper rope.

He cast about and noticed a number of very thin, whip-like creepers hanging down from the branches of nearby trees. They were only about an eighth of an inch in diameter, but they could be woven into something stronger. He began pulling them off the trees, shaking and yanking them down, until he had dozens of varying lengths. Laying them side by side, but staggered, he created a length of some two hundred feet. And then he started at one end, twining them together in a double braid, six strands' worth. When one strand ended he wove the loose end in tight where it wouldn't slip and continued with another.

It took about an hour to finish the makeshift rope. Then he carefully tied the actual rope around his legs and waist, making it into an improvised sling for Amiko. When it was done, he stepped out of it, leaving it intact. He would have to get it around her. She could help. Maybe.

He lashed the end of the makeshift rope around a tree trunk and lowered its full length over the edge of the cliff. Praying that it would be long enough, he began the descent.

The descent was another level of difficulty from the ascent. But he had one advantage—he had one hand on the rope. With every downward step he prayed it would not part or break.

In half an hour he reached the crack. He had thirty feet of rope to spare. Amiko was there, awake, sitting up, her face pale. "Where have you been?"

He briefly explained his plan.

"You climbed to the top…and back?"

"Yes."

She sagged back, confused. "Why?"

"I'm going to haul you up."

He pulled on the loose end of the rope and brought up the makeshift sling. Amiko stared at it. "That's no good." She pulled it in, quickly untied it, and then—staggering to her feet and standing with much difficulty at the very edge of the crack—lashed it in a sling around herself. "We call that a Swiss seat," she said when she was finished, her breathing hard and flushed.

"How do you feel?" Gideon asked.

A silence. "I'll make it."

"Sit down. I'll climb back up, haul you up."

She nodded, sat down.

He positioned her in a safe place. Putting everything into the other drysack, he shrugged it onto his back. Then he began climbing again, using the rope as a guide. This time it was easier and he was on top in another half hour.

He took off the second drysack and placed it on the ground. Now, using two trees as friction brakes, he started to pull Amiko up, slowly, slowly. His greatest fear was that the rope would snag up somewhere on the jagged lava rock. And, after about fifty feet, it did. No matter how much he maneuvered, moved this way or that, it was caught.

He heard a feeble shout from below. Tying off the rope, he went to the edge of the cliff. He couldn't see Amiko but could hear her voice.

"It's caught!" she said.

"Where?"

"About twenty feet above me."

There was only one option: to descend and work it loose.

He went back down yet again, following the rope, until he reached the snag. The vine rope was hooked under a jagged, projecting rock. Examining the problem, he realized he would have to get beneath it and unhook it from below. Twenty feet down, Amiko was dangling in free space. She looked awful, her face gray, translucent.

"Gideon, that's too hard a maneuver . . ."

He ignored her. Climbing down slowly, he managed to work his way underneath. The handholds were very poor. Clinging to the rope with one hand and the rock face with the other, he edged out under the overhang, and reached out to unsnag the rope. He grasped it, tried to shake it loose.

Stuck.

He shook harder, and then harder still. It suddenly came free, the rope jerking, causing him to lose both footholds. As his body came off the rock, he grabbed the rope with both hands, sliding and burning, splinters from the vines going deep. He was able to arrest his fall. Now he, too, was dangling in midair.

"Gideon, *swing!*"

With a terrific effort he swung his body, once, then again. The improvised vine-rope groaned under the weight of them both and, with a sudden jerk, dropped a few inches, starting to unravel.

Gideon threw himself onto the rock face, grabbing at a single pocket handhold, taking the weight off the rope. In a panicked scrabble he managed to find a hold for his feet. He looked back at the rope. With the excessive weight gone, the unraveling had stopped.

He climbed back up, the muscles of his arms jerking and quivering with both strain and anxiety. Making it to the top—just barely—he rested only a moment, then resumed the slow work of bringing up Amiko and the sling. Finally, just as dawn was breaking in the east, he managed to haul her up over the lip of rock and into the protection of the jungle.

Amiko stumbled over and collapsed on the ground. She tried to sit up, coughed, lay down again. "You…saved my life."

"That makes us even," he gasped. "Rest. Don't talk."

She lay back, her breathing shallow, her face pale and bathed in sweat. Gideon looked around the dripping jungle, so thick it enveloped them in twilight despite the rising sun.

He would have to build a shelter.

49

Kneeling on the ground, Gideon went through the drysacks, emptying out all the contents he'd managed to salvage and spreading them out to dry. The granola bars were gone, but there were two pieces of pemmican left, both damp. A single handgun, some ammo, knives, cups, lighters, four liters of water, med kit. And the sat phone. He would call Glinn as soon as possible—there might be just enough juice left for one more communication. But for now, he had to make sure Amiko was taken care of.

Struggling to his feet, he grasped a knife and began cutting down some large, flat, glossy leaves, spreading them out to make a dry ground cover. He helped Amiko onto it, making her a pillow out of a bundle of leaves.

He lit a small fire—with great difficulty, as everything was damp—and used a Sierra cup to boil a small amount of water.

"We're going to change your bandage," he said.

She nodded her thanks. She was flushed, her eyes bloodshot, her fever high.

He unbuttoned her shirts, pulled them aside. The bandage was soaked with blood. He removed both it and the dressing underneath, exposing the wound. It was no longer closed, the tape having come loose in the struggle up the cliff. The wound was bleeding.

Using clean gauze pads from the medical kit, dipped in the boiled water, Gideon cleaned the wound, rinsed it with sterile water and some Betadine, then applied antibiotic ointment and reclosed the wound with surgical tape. He bandaged it, then crushed an amoxicillin tablet in water, along with a tablet of the second antibiotic. Amiko took them both.

"You need to eat," he said.

"Not hungry."

Gideon took out the two pieces of pemmican, which Amiko finally ate.

"We made it," she said, struggling to smile. "We're here. You saved my life. And I'm feeling a lot better."

"Good." She did look better—but the wound was awful. She had to get to a hospital.

He picked up the sat phone. "I'm calling Glinn. We need a rescue."

She struggled to sit up. "Wait, Gideon. We made it. Let's explore the island first."

Gideon shook his head. She really was half crazy. "You're injured and you need a doctor."

"We've got bandages, antibiotics, all we need."

"No way. I'm making the call." He picked up the cell phone and unlatched the box. Amiko watched as he opened it, checked the battery. Still at one percent.

He turned it on.

It took a while, searching for satellites, while the battery meter blinked red. As soon as it locked on, he made the call.

It was answered instantly.

"Gideon?" It was Glinn.

Gideon interrupted him. "Battery's almost dead. We need to talk fast."

"I told you this mission was aborted and ordered you—"

"Enough! We need a rescue. Amiko is hurt."

"Badly?"

"She needs immediate medical attention."

"Very well. Give me your coordinates."

"We're on an island about twenty miles offshore," he said. "I'm not sure exactly where."

"I'm locking in on your satellite signal. I'll have it in a minute."

"We succeeded. We found the medicine. It grows here, on this island group. Another thing: this area was once inhabited by large, one-eyed hominids—Cyclopes. The natives worship its skull. It all backs up Amiko's theory about the *Odyssey*."

A brief silence. "Extraordinary. We're almost there with your coordinates . . ."

Amiko held out her hand. "Let me talk to him. Now."

Gideon handed the phone over. She grabbed the phone box, turned it upside down.

"What are you—?"

She yanked out the battery and gave it a mighty heave over the cliff.

50

W HAT THE *FUCK!*" Gideon jumped up in time to see the battery go sailing off into blue space. "Are you nuts?"

She stared back at him, her eyes glittering with defiance. "I will not walk away from this. Not now. Not ever."

Gideon stared at her. He could think of nothing to say. He should never have given her the phone. She was crazy, feverish—not in her right mind.

"Do you really think Glinn will let us finish what we started? No. He'll put together a new team. The government of Nicaragua will have to be involved, because I'm pretty sure this is part of their territory. It'll turn into a scientific circus. There won't be any role for us."

"You need medical attention. You could die."

"I'm recovering. We need to see this through."

He stared at her. She really did seem better. Or maybe it was just the flush of determination.

"We're almost there," she said softly. "We need to explore this island, identify the lotus plant—and bring it back. Only then will we be done." She lay back, gazing at him intently, her face flushed and beaded with sweat, but her eyes clear. She was rational and serious.

Gideon stared back at her. What she said was undoubtedly true—if Glinn pulled them out now, their role would be over. And they were so close. All that remained was finding the plant, and how difficult could that be? He realized that he, too, wanted to see it through. More than that: he wanted to save his own life. How long would it take for the lotus to be developed into a drug and reach the market? The process took years. He didn't have the luxury of time. It was a long shot, but why not? He had nothing to lose.

"All right."

She smiled. "I knew you'd come around. You and I—we're not so different."

He shrugged. "I'll see what I can do about finding us some grub. You rest and recover." He picked up the .45, checked it, then stood up, shoving it into his waistband. He had to grasp a vine while a wave of dizziness washed over him. The top of the island, seen in the dark from below, looked like it might be a few miles across. There seemed to be a lot of wildlife—he could hear birds calling and flitting about in the trees above, along with noises and cries he couldn't begin to identify.

He picked up an empty drysack, thrust in a canteen and the ammo, and then set off, pushing into the jungle. It was incredibly thick, dense leaves and forest litter underfoot, along with an almost impenetrable understory of big green leafy plants. All around, tall, smooth tree trunks reached upward. And yet, when he looked up, he couldn't see the sky—just a shifting green dome flecked with gold and brown.

It would be easy to get lost. But as he slashed his way through the jungle with the inadequate knife, he realized he would be able to follow his trail back. Progress was agonizingly slow. He stopped from time to time to scrutinize a plant, pluck a leaf off, and crush it in his hand to check its scent. But there was nothing remotely like the smell of the lotus, either the pod or the root.

Suddenly, as he reached for one odd-looking plant, he felt the ground crumble beneath him and—seizing a nearby branch—just managed to stop himself from sliding into what appeared to be a deep sinkhole or ancient lava tube. After that, he moved much more cautiously. The island, he realized, was riddled with such holes and pits, interspersed with outcroppings of jagged volcanic rock jutting out of the jungle floor, dangerously camouflaged by heavy stands of ferns and undergrowth. At one point he heard a thrashing far above as a troop of monkeys passed over in the treetops, screeching down at him, the invader. He tried to get a bead on one of them with the .45, but the treetops were too dense and the monkeys moving too fast.

Suddenly he came out onto a path—a large-animal trail, beaten down from long use. He looked about for sign or scat, something that would give him a clue as to what kind of animal had made the trail, but could see no telltale sign. This was encouraging—maybe. Whatever it was, it was big. It might be good eating. It might be good if he could hit it with a .45.

He continued along the trail, relieved not to have to thrash through the undergrowth and risk falling into another pit. The rising sun beat down on the high treetops, turning the wet jungle into a steaming green oven. He continued to check various plants at random, realizing that finding the lotus might be a bigger challenge than he'd anticipated. At one point, he came to a bush covered with round, burgundy-colored fruits, not unlike small plums. Cautiously tasting one, he found it was deliciously sweet, and he stripped the bush and put the fruit in the drysack.

The trail forked, and he took one branch at random. It wound its way about, passing another bush full of a different but equally delicious fruit. The island was starting to feel like a tropical paradise, a lost world. The plants were almost all unfamiliar—but then again, he'd never been to this part of the planet before. He wished to hell he had spent more time studying the botany books in the boat's library.

There were all kinds of strange rustlings in the bushes, and once a family of small hairy tusked pigs—javelina, perhaps—burst out of the undergrowth and barreled across the trail to disappear on the other side—again, too fast for him to shoot.

The trail seemed to head toward a lofty volcanic outcropping, and as he approached, he saw that it led straight into a large cave—a lava tube.

Gideon crept warily up to the entrance. Clearly it was some kind of lair. But for what animal? Bison didn't live in caves, but bears did. Jaguars? He ventured to the opening and stepped inside. There was an animal smell, a smell of dung and wet fur. It didn't seem like a good idea to keep going.

He looked around the floor of the cave for tracks. And there, in the dry sand, he found a confusion of them. They belonged to an odd-toed ungulate, probably a tapir.

Their library on the boat also had a section on the mammals of Central America, and he vaguely remembered the animal's odd hoofprint and the fact that tapirs were nocturnal and created trails in the jungle. And that they were prized by the locals as good eating.

He now had a goodly amount of fruit, and so he decided to head back to camp. Amiko was still lying where he had left her, sleeping. She looked so pale, so sick, his spirits sank.

Rekindling the fire, he made some more tea. She woke up and drank the tea. He asked how she felt and got an annoyed look in return.

"I'm going to rig up a shelter in case it rains again." She started to rise.

"Damn it, you stay put," said Gideon. "You need to get better."

Laboriously, Gideon cut some stiff poles with the knife, and used them to create an improvised lean-to, lashing them together with creepers. A set of thin sucker rods made the skeleton of a roof, and this he covered with huge leaves. He paved the floor with more of the same. He helped Amiko in, and she lay down on a bed of leaves. He placed the sack of fruit next to her.

"I'm sorry I'm so useless," she said.

"While you rest, I'm going to do a more systematic exploration of the island."

She staggered to her feet. "I'm coming."

"No, you're not."

"To hell with you." She got up but swayed on her feet.

"You can hardly stand up."

"A little moving around will help."

Gideon felt a wave of anger with this impossible

woman. "Listen. You trashed our sat phone—your last chance of getting medical help. So you *owe* it to me to get better. That means staying right here."

She stared at him, the old defiance glowing in her eyes. But after a moment she faltered. "All right. But look for the lotus."

"I wish to hell I knew what to look for."

She eased herself down, wincing. "And shoot us some meat, will you? I could use a steak."

Gideon outfitted a drysack for his jaunt, taking some extra ammo, water, and a headlamp. Maybe later, he thought, he'd go back to the cave and try to ambush a sleeping tapir.

He followed his old route to the tapir trail and took it in the opposite direction. This time he moved more slowly, making mental notes, observing the plant life, occasionally crushing a leaf or pod to check the scent. The forest trails forked again and again, in seemingly random directions, but using the position of the sun he maintained a westward-trending route that, in about forty-five minutes, brought him to the other side of the island. He could see light through the trees—and then, suddenly, he found himself on the edge of a precipice, looking out toward the horizon of the open ocean. It was a magnificent view, the sun-dappled water far below, puffy white clouds sailing along, the faint sound of surf. The cliff was just as sheer as the one they had climbed up. Gideon wondered how, when the time came, they were going to get off this fortress of an island.

The trail continued along, close to the cliff's edge. The surrounding jungle appeared to be full of strange and exotic creatures: brilliantly colored spiders (which he hoped weren't poisonous), odd crested lizards scurrying away, and multicolored birds crying raucously in the trees. Another monkey troop approached with a huge amount of noise, different from the first. He quickly stepped off the trail into dense vegetation, ready to take a shot. These monkeys had white heads, and he recollected from the briefing book that they must be white-headed capuchins. But he didn't recall the streak of yellow on the hind legs, like stockings.

Hoping that they weren't rare and exotic, apologizing to the gods, he waited silently. .45 at the ready, as the troop worked through the treetops closer to him. They were feeding with great gusto on fruits, the discarded pits dropping down around him. Slowly, he took a bead on the biggest monkey and aimed. It was a tough shot, over a hundred feet. He let his breath run out, then squeezed the trigger.

A loud explosion. The monkeys erupted in a deafening screeching, the trees thrashing as they raced off, including the monkey he had tried to shoot, with a large amount of loose dung falling around him as a sort of good-bye gesture.

"Son of a bitch," he muttered to himself, tucking the .45 back into his waistband, flicking a piece of monkey shit off his shoulder, the foul stench rising up around him. He moved carefully back to the open trail.

Behind him, he heard a sound, a rushing—and then a terrifying roar. He spun around, fumbling his pistol out, but before he could raise it a hideous, terrifying creature came charging down the trail, its pink mouth open and bellowing. It was gigantic, humanoid, with a massive oversize head in which stood one huge, glistening, yellow, saucer-like eye.

A huge hairy arm swept out and Gideon felt a bone-breaking blow to his side, knocking him a good ten feet into the violent embrace of the jungle. He lay dazed and in excruciating pain as the furious creature, with another grotesque and spine-freezing roar, bore down on him with a slab-like hand, and struck another mighty blow...

51

Through a veil of pain, awareness slowly returned. Gideon found himself in semi-darkness. He drifted in and out of consciousness, vaguely aware that someone was with him, apparently tending to him. Slowly, bits and pieces of what had happened came back to him. He tried to move and felt someone raise his head, lift a gourd of water to his lips. It was Amiko.

"My God . . . What a nightmare . . ."

"I'm so glad you're coming to."

"It hurts—"

"I know. Drink some water."

He drank again. "Where . . . ?"

"We're in a cave."

"And you—how are you—?"

"I'm good. Almost all better."

"How long have I been out?"

"About twenty-four hours."

Gideon laid his head back. Nothing made sense. How could she be better? Why were they in a cave?

The attack. The creature. Was it a nightmare? Or real?

"I had this nightmare. I dreamed I was attacked by . . . by some kind of monster."

"It's no nightmare. It's real. We're his prisoners."

"Prisoners?" He tried to sit up but a lightning pain shot through his head, and he winced and lay back down. "What happened?"

Amiko set aside the gourd. Gideon tried to focus on her in the dimness, but his head kept swirling.

"After you left, I started to get worse. Much worse. The wound was becoming infected. My fever spiked. I couldn't move from the spot where you'd left me. I felt like I was burning up, I became delirious, and I guess I was shouting or mumbling. And then this . . . one-eyed *creature* appeared. I thought I was hallucinating. It, or rather he, circled about warily, grunting at me. God, you can't believe how frightened I was when I finally realized . . . *this isn't a dream.* I think what saved my life was that I was obviously too sick and weak to be a threat. He came closer, roughed me up a bit. Slapped me, prodded, yanked my hair. I tried to scream. He made a horrible sound, struck me harder. Opened the wound again."

"Bastard . . ."

"Gideon, I think that monster is an honest-to-God living Cyclops."

"Impossible. They must have died out thousands of years ago."

"Listen to the end of my story, then. I figured this monster was going to kill me. But he didn't. He seemed more apprehensive than aggressive. I tried to think what to do . . . and then I had an idea. I spoke to him."

"*Spoke* to him? What did you say?"

"I spoke the ancient Greek word for 'friend.'"

Gideon tried to wrap his head around this.

"In the *Odyssey*, the Cyclopes could speak. I figured, if Odysseus came here, and the Greeks after him, maybe this thing was really a Cyclops and knew some words of Greek."

"And it understood?"

"When I spoke that word, he stopped cold. Stared at me with that awful eye. I repeated the word, spoke a few others. It was my impression he understood a little, but couldn't speak in return. But I kept trying, one word after another. For the longest time he remained, listening, as if in a trance. It almost looked like he was remembering…" She paused. "I kept repeating that I was a friend, that he could trust me —soothing words, spoken softly. But then I lapsed back into the fever. After that I don't really remember much. He carried me to the cave. I sort of remember seeing you. I was getting even sicker. The wound got swollen, bloated, purple, and all this foul fluid starting coming out, and I really felt like I was going to die. I can't remember much except that he forced me to drink a terrible-tasting gruel."

"The lotus root."

"Yes. And it did to me what it did to you. I'd never felt so peaceful. And when I came out of it, I was a lot better. The fever was gone. The wound was healing fast. Incredibly fast. Look at me now. *He saved my life.*"

"And then what?"

"The creature was gone when I came out of it. You were lying there, on the ground, all bloody. At first, I thought you were dead. That he'd killed you. I looked you over, found you were alive—but I think you've got some broken ribs and a possible broken arm, not to mention a nasty head wound—maybe a concussion."

Gideon lay back, his head spinning, body racked with pain. This was too crazy.

"The thing rolled a boulder over the mouth of the cave. We're his prisoners."

"What does he want?" Gideon managed to say.

"I have no idea. You're in bad shape. We've got to get you the lotus. We've got to convince him to help you like he helped me."

Gideon tried to concentrate on what he had just heard. It seemed incredible. He glanced around but had a hard time focusing his eyes. He realized several bones were broken; he could feel the ends grating against each other, and the terrible pain, when he tried to move in certain ways. They were in a rough lava cave. Faint light filtered down from a narrow fissure in the ceiling. A dying fire lay upon the rude sandy floor. "Convince that monster? I doubt it. We need to get the hell out of here."

"No. We need his help. Otherwise, you won't make it."

At that moment there was a sound—a scraping and rumbling.

"He's coming back," Amiko whispered. "He's moving the boulder."

Another rumble, and now Gideon could hear footsteps—a heavy tread that seemed to shake the ground. He turned warily toward the sound—and there, emerging from the darkness, was the creature that had attacked him.

Gideon could hardly believe what he was seeing. The creature was huge—maybe nine feet tall, with a massive head on a thickly muscled neck. In the middle of its face glistened a single, glossy eye the size of a plate that looked this way and that, exposing bloodshot whites. It had a huge nose, flat and glistening, flaring nostrils, and a wide, fleshy mouth with dry, leathery lips, which drew back to reveal a rack of sharp yellow teeth and pink gums. A mat of silvery hair sprang up from the top of its head and fell in long, tangled tresses, almost like dreadlocks, to its waist. The monster's body was the color of sand, covered with pale fur that looked as soft as mohair. Despite this, the skin beneath displayed many ragged purplish scars, old wounds, marks, and puckered flesh. He was wearing an old animal skin tied around his waist, with a leather sack hanging from it. The creature looked like some hideous species of ape.

Except for its weapon. In one massive, ropy arm he carried a giant wooden spear with a flaked stone point.

Without a doubt, it was the living version of that hideous skull the natives worshipped. Amiko was right. It was, indeed, a live Cyclops.

The Cyclops stopped and stared at Gideon with that large, yellowish globe of an eye. It scowled, the eyelid narrowing. Then, with a guttural roar, it raised the spear menacingly and advanced with it pointed at him, apparently about to run him through. Gideon, his head still swimming, tried to move, but the pain was so massive, and his head so thick, he could barely turn aside.

Amiko cried out, rose to her feet, and stepped in front of Gideon, speaking to the Cyclops in ancient Greek, rapidly, quietly, soothingly. Her words seemed to give the creature pause…but only momentarily. It growled again, pushed her aside with its arm, stepped forward, and placed a bare, horny foot on Gideon's chest. The pressure against his broken ribs sent a wave of pain coursing through him and he screamed.

"No!" Amiko cried. "Please!"

The creature placed the point of the spear against Gideon's chest.

More rapid talk from Amiko, urgent, desperate. The creature stared down, his face distorted with what seemed like hatred and fear. Gideon could feel the tip tear through his shirt fabric and pierce his skin. He felt helpless. "No...no..." He tried to twist away but couldn't. He was too weak, and the pain was truly unbearable.

Amiko pleaded, her voice getting louder. The pressure on the spear increased, the tip biting through the flesh, pushing against his breastbone.

"Stop it!" Amiko cried in English. "For God's sake, stop!" She rushed at the creature and attacked it with her fists, flailing away. "Don't hurt him!"

Taken by surprise, the creature stepped back and grabbed her in one of its massive arms. She flailed about, clawing at its eye. It thrust her aside with a gentle movement, but with still enough force to send her sprawling on the sandy floor. She tried to get up, yelling in Greek.

The creature removed the spear from Gideon's chest and then, with an irritated noise, walked to the wall of the cave, and leaned it against the stone. Then he displayed his empty hands to her in a clear gesture of acquiescence.

Amiko continued speaking in Greek until the Cyclops made a violent gesture at her with a loud barking roar. Amiko fell silent, trembling in fear.

Gideon lay there, in so much pain that he almost hoped it would soon be over.

"I think the Cyclops is going to try to kill you."

"Your gun...," Gideon gasped, "get it out."

"I can't. He saved my life, Gideon... And if I kill him, you won't get the lotus. We have to find another way."

Gideon gasped as another wave of pain wafted over him.

"He's very suspicious of you. It's clear to me he's been hurt by people before."

The creature squatted at the hearth and, taking some dry sticks from a pile nearby, placed them on the dying coals and blew up a fire. The cave filled with a flickering light. Gideon could hardly take his eyes off the monster. It was like something out of a B movie, a huge, muscled Neanderthal, stooped, with a sloping forehead and a beetling brow over that single monstrous eye. The fire going, the Cyclops squatted and, untying the leather sack from his waist, opened it and removed a large iguana. He rammed a stick through it and propped it to roast next to the fire.

Gideon felt his head swim. He felt like he was going to pass out.

Amiko started speaking again, pointing at Gideon and gesturing. The creature ignored her for a while, then growled menacingly, but she continued to press the issue. Even as she spoke, Gideon felt the pain growing—unbearable pain—and his mind clouded, swimming. He struggled to stay conscious, but despite his best efforts things drew farther away... very far away indeed... and he lapsed back into unrelieved darkness.

52

Three days had passed. Three strange days. They had gone by in a dream-like fugue state, as Gideon passed in and out of consciousness. Fragments of it came back to him later: the Cyclops growling and prodding him hard; the Cyclops stretched out in the sand, sleeping by the fire; Amiko feeding him a cup of foul gruel, similar to what he'd tasted at the ceremony, while the Cyclops looked on, scowling. He remembered anew that wondrous feeling of peace and contentment he had experienced before, followed by a second vicious hangover.

And then, when his head cleared at last, he felt better. Much better. He was still weak, and in some pain, but incredibly enough the broken bones appeared to be well on their way to knitting, the cuts were healing, and his head no longer hurt. The restorative power of the root was truly remarkable.

For the first time, Gideon felt a wave of actual hope. Real hope instead of hopeless speculation. He might have a future after all. For all he knew, the vein of Galen defect in his brain might be healing up along with his broken bones. But then...it wasn't an injury. It was a congenital defect. It might be beyond the reach of even the lotus.

The only problem was that they were still prisoners of the Cyclops.

Gideon lay by the fire, watching Amiko grill the carcass of some small animal—evidently a rat—a string of which the Cyclops had brought back to the cave and hung on the wall.

"Yum," said Gideon, looking at the roasting, popping rat, its little claws flaming into stumps, dripping fat into the fire.

"Almost done. You're going to love it."

"I actually think I will. I'm starving."

Amiko removed the rodent from the fire and propped it on its improvised stake to cool. After a few minutes she pulled apart the roasted animal with her hands, laying a piece for Gideon on a large banana leaf. He tucked into it.

"You realize, Gideon, we now have all the proof we need. Both of us, cured by the lotus. We've got to identify the plant—and the Cyclops is the key to that."

"How?"

"You're the one who's good at social engineering. Think about how we might persuade the Cyclops to show us the plant."

"The last time I tried social-engineering a Cyclops, it ended badly. Do you know why he's keeping us?"

"Fear," Amiko said. "I believe he's terrified of humans and thinks that if he lets us go, we might come back with more of our kind."

"He's probably right."

"I'm serious about the social engineering, Gideon. I've

tried everything. I can't break through his suspicion. And you know . . ." She gave a little laugh. "He's kind of dumb, actually. In a sweet way. He might be easily manipulated—if you could just find the right way to do it."

Gideon sat back, thinking. Successful social engineering always exploited a basic need. Odysseus had gotten Polyphemus drunk and put out his eye. Aside from the fact they had no wine, hurting the creature was out of the question. The Cyclops had injured them—but it had also saved both their lives. They had not gained its trust, however . . . only its forbearance. And that was a tenuous thing indeed.

They needed to make friends.

The Cyclops was gone for the present, the rock rolled over the mouth of the cave. Gideon noticed that their drysacks had been thrown into one corner. Crawling over to his, he rummaged through it, then finally dumped the contents onto the sand. Knife, gun, miscellaneous junk. Friendship started with an exchange of gifts. He couldn't give away the gun; besides, the creature wouldn't know how to use it. The knife? He needed that, too. And he'd noticed that the Cyclops already had an array of beautifully made stone knives with bone handles.

"If you're looking for a gift," Amiko said, "I thought of that. We don't have anything he would want. We forgot the beads and mirrors."

"One of the headlamps?"

"He seems to see perfectly well in the dark."

Gideon thought for a while. Social engineering always began with understanding the target's deepest needs and desires. What were a Cyclops's basic needs? Food, water, sex, shelter, fire . . .

Gideon suddenly had an idea. He explained it to Amiko.

She thought for a moment and said, "Worth a try."

"Fetch one of those spears and climb on my shoulders."

Amiko grabbed a spear and climbed up. Unsteadily, ignoring the pain, he managed to raise her. Taking the butt end of the spear, she reached upward, jammed it into a crack in the ceiling, and started prying.

"Don't start a cave-in."

"I'm trying not to."

"When a rock comes loose, give a shout."

She pried back and forth with the pole, loosening a chunk of lava from the ceiling. Suddenly she gave a shout and jumped off his shoulders; he threw himself sideways as a large chunk of lava came down with a crash, landing with a thud in the sand near the fire, showering them with smaller rocks, one of which glanced off his forehead, leaving a nasty cut.

Gideon wasted no time. He gathered up some of the smaller rocks and artfully dumped them on the fire, scattering a few around, adding some sand. They then rolled the big rock on top, effectively putting out the fire. They brushed away marks in the sand around the fire, hiding the evidence of what they had done and arranging it to look like a small, natural cave-in. Smoke came trickling up from around the rocks for a few minutes, and then stopped.

"Damn cave-in," Gideon said with a smirk. "It put out the fire. Wonder what our friend's going to do about it?"

A few hours later they heard the Cyclops return, rolling the rock away with much grunting and then entering, two enormous, gutted iguanas over his shoulder. He walked in and stopped, staring at the fire. Then he looked up at the ceiling, looked back down, and hastily began pulling the rocks and sweeping the sand from the fire. Fetching some small twigs, he placed them in the dead coals and knelt, blowing steadily. Nothing happened. The fire was dead.

He stood up with a roar of anger, staring at them and gesturing toward the fire. Amiko shrugged. Another roar, the spittle flying from his lips. He gestured again at the fire, staring fiercely at Gideon, as if it was his fault.

Gideon shrugged.

Another roar of frustration.

Gideon took the lighter from his pocket and offered it to the Cyclops. The creature came over, stared at it, took it, smelled it, and then tossed it aside with an irritated growl.

With a smile, Gideon retrieved the lighter. The Cyclops watched him with deep suspicion. With an elaborate flourish, and making sure the Cyclops was paying attention, Gideon flicked it on. The little yellow flame jumped into life.

The Cyclops's single eye flew wide, his hairy brow arching up. He issued a sharp grunt, hesitated, took a step forward, and poked his finger at the flame, pulling it out when he appeared satisfied it was really fire.

Now Gideon, slowly and with exaggerated motion, picked up the bundle of twigs on the dead fire and applied the lighter; they crackled to life. He laid them back down, added larger sticks from the nearby pile, and in a few minutes the fire was burning merrily.

The creature stared, amazed.

Gideon offered the lighter to him again. Cautiously,

the Cyclops reached out and took it, tried to flick it on, but his hands were clumsy and it slipped from his grasp and fell. Gideon picked it up, flicked it on a few times while the Cyclops watched, and then placed it in his hands and, modeling his fingers, showed him how to scratch the wheel to make fire. After half a dozen fumbling tries he got it going, his saucer-like eye growing large with wonder.

Gideon turned to Amiko. "Tell him it's a gift."

Amiko spoke a few words in Greek. The Cyclops flicked it on a few times, and then reverently placed it inside his leather bag. He sat down at the fire, grunting softly to himself and glancing from time to time at Gideon.

Amiko turned to Gideon. "Okay, I'm curious. How did you figure out he didn't know how to make fire?"

"I watched him. He tended that fire like a baby. It never went out. He carefully banked the coals at night and lit a new fire from them in the morning. I never saw him use any fire-making tools—and there aren't any in his supplies."

"You think his kind has been tending the same fire for thousands of years?"

"Perhaps."

"Nice work, Prometheus."

"The gift of fire. Greatest gift to mankind. And Cyclops-kind."

Amiko hesitated. "You know what I think?"

"What?"

"I think he's lonely. We haven't seen any other Cyclops. Maybe he's the last of his kind. And that could be another reason he's keeping us here—for companionship."

"And we haven't introduced ourselves. You know: me Tarzan, you Jane."

"You're absolutely right," said Amiko. "Do you think he even has a name?"

"Only one way to find out." Gideon stood up and, swallowing his apprehension, stepped toward the creature. It raised its shaggy head and stared at him with that frightening eye.

Gideon put his hands on his chest. "Gideon," he said loudly.

The creature stared.

"Gideon." Then he turned and placed a hand on Amiko. "Amiko." "Back to himself. "Gideon."

Then, with a certain trepidation, he opened his hands and pointed toward the Cyclops.

The creature merely stared.

Gideon went through the whole elaborate charade again, but the Cyclops greeted this fresh round with a puzzled growl and either didn't appear to understand or found the whole thing annoying.

"Wait. Let me try." Amiko stood up and, walking over to the Cyclops, reached out and touched it. She said something to it in ancient Greek.

The reaction of the creature was striking. It seemed to cease all motion, cease breathing. Its eye widened slowly, slowly, as if a memory was returning to it after a long absence.

Amiko repeated the word.

The eye opened wider. The Cyclops looked almost comical in his expression of astonishment. A great stillness fell. And then the creature reached out a trembling hand and touched her shoulder. It repeated the word in a deep, rumbling, awkward, and tentative voice.

Good God, it can speak, Gideon thought in astonishment.

She said the word a third time, and the creature repeated it again. And then an extraordinary thing happened. The great, horrible, saucer-like eye glistened and welled up, and a large tear coursed down its ragged face.

And then it spoke another word. Another tear came, and another, and then the creature placed its hairy, broken hands over its face, and wept.

"What did you say?" Gideon whispered.

"I spoke the name Polyphemus."

"And what did it say in reply?"

"An archaic Greek word that means 'begetter,' 'ancestor.' Or more like 'father of all.'"

53

T HE JUNGLE WAS alive with life: a green, steaming, roaring hothouse full of insects, lizards, and invisible animals all contributing their chirps, croaks, tweets, rasps, and drumming to the general din. Gideon had been following the Cyclops through the jungle for several hours now. The morning after they'd exchanged names, the Cyclops had left the cave—after a halting "conversation" with Amiko—with an ambiguous gesture to Gideon that seemed to be an invitation to follow. The creature was apparently involved in a search of some kind, and Gideon hoped beyond all hope it was a hunt for the elusive lotus. But so far the Cyclops, despite a most diligent search, had found nothing.

Once again, Gideon was powerfully impressed with just how beautiful and unique the island was. The sheer variety of life on the island-top was staggering—the massive clusters of blooming flowers, orchids cascading down like brilliant waterfalls, the giant ferns, the ancient tree trunks covered with moss, the hanging vines and mysterious, shadowy understory. And everywhere he looked came the sounds of life and the rustle and flash of hidden creatures, along with an incredible variety of butterflies and brightly colored lizards.

It was also hazardous. The top of the island, which appeared flat from afar, was in reality a collapsed volcanic cone, the ground riddled with pits, sinkholes, and extinct fumaroles carpeted over with vegetation so thick it obscured the openings and fissures, turning every step into a potential trap. While Gideon was no botanist, he was amazed by the bizarre and exotic plants he saw: giant pitcher plants full of water; an orchid with enormous purple blossoms that smelled like rotting meat; vines that formed impassable nets; gigantic tree roots that looked like melting cheese.

But nothing that could be the lotus.

Gideon followed the Cyclops along ever-smaller trails through the forest. It was hard to believe such an ungainly creature could move so gracefully, with such silence and stillness. It made its way along almost invisible trails without rustling so much as a leaf. Gideon, half its size, blundered along, pushing through branches, tripping on roots, and generally struggling to keep up.

The previous evening—the episode with the lighter, the introduction of the name Polyphemus—had changed everything. While the creature hadn't exactly become friendly, it finally offered them their freedom, rolling away the stone and indicating with gestures that they were free to go. Or stay, as they wished. They had decided to stay for another night, and then move camp the following morning.

After supper, Amiko had tried to learn more from the Cyclops about the history of his people on the island. It was long and frustrating, with many misunderstandings and false starts, and it indicated to Gideon that, despite their common hominid ancestry, there was still a great gulf between them in terms of comprehension and intelligence. Amiko had gleaned—or thought she had gleaned—that Polyphemus was an ancestor who seemed to be revered, about whom there seemed to be numerous stories. The Cyclops did not himself have a name, it seemed, or at least not one he chose to reveal. He was very old, but just how old was hard to determine. With many gestures indicating the passage of days and seasons, Amiko had estimated his age at centuries at least. While Gideon found that hard to swallow, the creature certainly looked ancient, scarred, and—above all—weary. He had the air of having seen and suffered much. Amiko had not been able to find out any information about other Cyclopes on the island. On that subject, he seemed sadly silent.

It was getting close to noon, with the jungle turning into a steaming green oven, but the Cyclops had still found nothing. The speed with which the beast moved through the forest, combined with the heat, was gradually wearing out Gideon, who was still weak from his injuries.

All of a sudden the creature halted. Dropping to its knees, it began sniffing around with its big, flat nose in a most comical manner, gently probing the ground with the tip of its spear as if to release some kind of scent. Slowly, the Cyclops moved off the trail into the incredibly dense understory, and Gideon followed gingerly, also on his hands and knees, as it was the only possible way to proceed. But the Cyclops moved faster than he could, disappearing into the thicket, and Gideon in a panic hurried to follow.

"Wait!" he called, knowing well that the Cyclops not only didn't understand him, but couldn't care less. He tried to stand, got tangled in the understory, dropped to his knees again, and pushed forward, listening for the creature's movements. As he moved along, a shower of ants fell on him from the leaves above, disturbed by his passage, and he felt them crawling down his shirt and into his hair, biting him and releasing a smell of formic acid.

"Son of a *bitch!*" He crawled forward, slapping and cursing. Just as he was thinking he had lost the Cyclops, he broke through a wall of vegetation to find the creature in a small opening, on his hands and knees, digging furiously with the wooden end of his spear.

A few moments later a black, root-like thing was exposed. With a start, Gideon realized it wasn't actually a root at all—it remained unattached to any sort of plant—but an underground fungus of some kind, perhaps something not unlike a truffle. It even released a powerful, truffle-like scent: a combination of dirty socks, earth, and a cinnamon-like spice.

It was the smell of the lotus.

With a reverence and care that astonished Gideon, the Cyclops carefully brushed away the dirt and lifted the fungus out of the hole. He removed a piece of leather from his sack and spread it on the ground, laid the lotus on top, and proceeded to clean it more thoroughly with twigs and leaves. Then he carefully wrapped it in the leather and tucked it in his bag.

He turned his face to Gideon and stared, then made a gesture with his hand that Gideon didn't understand.

"Good work," said Gideon, giving him a thumbs-up and a smile. As usual, the creature didn't seem to understand him, either. But then, it seemed to Gideon the creature gave a fleeting grimace—was it a smile?—and tied the sack back around his waist. The creature turned away and proceeded back through the forest, Gideon struggling once again to keep up. Soon they were back on the trail and, in twenty minutes, had returned to the cave, by byways so obscure, with twistings and turnings so confusing, that Gideon could never have retraced it.

Amiko was there, tending the fire. The Cyclops sat down at the fire, removed the sack, and opened it.

Gideon caught Amiko's eye.

"A lotus?" she asked, her voice hushed.

Gideon nodded. "He dug it up. It's not a plant—there's no aboveground growth. I think it's some kind of fungus."

"This is incredible," she said in a low voice. "All we need is to get it."

They watched as the Cyclops carefully unwrapped the root-like thing, the smell of it drifting through the room. With a glittering obsidian blade, the Cyclops carefully began slicing the lotus into long slivers, releasing more of its powerful scent.

"What is he doing?" Amiko asked.

"No idea."

"I hope he isn't going to eat it."

But that was exactly what the Cyclops started to do, first toasting the slivers on a hot, flat rock by the fire and then eating them with his fingers while they watched. His actions had a reverential air to them, and for a while he made a strange humming noise that might have been some sort of chant or prayer. When all was gone, he retired to his sleeping area—a patch of soft sand in one corner—and curled up.

Amiko darted out and swept up the remaining peelings and strings, wrapping them in a piece of plastic and packing them in a container in her drysack.

She came back and sat next to Gideon, speaking in a low voice. "You realize this is it." Her eyes glowed. "We've found the last piece of the puzzle. And just consider what we've found! An extraordinary healing plant. *And* a living Cyclops—with ties to the historical Odysseus. This is going to change the world. And *we* did it."

Gideon said nothing. For a while, certain thoughts had been growing in his mind. They were not good thoughts.

"What's wrong?" said Amiko.

He shook his head. "We haven't thought this through."

"What do you mean?"

"What do you think is going to happen to the Cyclops when we report back to civilization?"

Amiko stared at him. "Well, it's an incredible discovery: an ancient hominid-like creature, perhaps a cousin to the Neanderthal, an honest-to-God living Cyclops."

"*Living* is the operative word. You didn't answer my question: what's going to happen to *him?*"

"I . . . I'd imagine some kind of wildlife sanctuary would be established here, you know, with visitors carefully controlled."

Gideon shook his head. "With a powerful, lifesaving, miraculous, trillion-dollar drug hidden on this island?"

"The lotus would be cultivated elsewhere."

"First, it's an underground fungus, like a truffle. Despite the fact that truffles cost thousands of dollars, no one's ever been able to cultivate one. Second, it took the

Cyclops six hours of searching to find that one lotus, using all his knowledge and powerful sense of smell. Six hours. There can't be many left. And now we know he *eats* the root. He's one of the Lotus Eaters himself! Maybe that's why he's so incredibly old. He's dependent on it. His whole existence, his very life, depends on this island remaining exactly as it is. But will it? Once this knowledge gets out? I hardly think so."

Amiko fell silent, and finally said: "I hadn't considered all that."

"Lastly, this island would appear to be Nicaraguan national territory. So as soon as we report this, it's out of our hands. The Nicaraguans will be in control. God only knows what they'll do."

Amiko glanced over at the sleeping creature. Gideon followed her gaze. It lay on the sand, curled up, its hairy sides rising and falling in rhythm to its breathing, its big horny toes with their broken nails twitching, looking for all the world like a dog having a dream. His single eye was covered by a large wrinkled lid. There was a certain strange "otherness," for want of a better word, about the Cyclops. He seemed to show kindness, in his way—but at the same time he could be violent and unreadable. He was sort of human—sort of an animal.

"I'm growing fond of the old brute," Amiko said.

"And I think he might be, ah, developing feelings for you."

"Don't even joke about that."

"I'm not joking. He won't give me the time of day. He only took me lotus hunting because you pretty much harangued him into doing it. You're the only one he responds to. And I've seen the way he looks at you."

"I don't believe it. This isn't *King Kong*."

Gideon took her hand. "Anyway, we've got a much bigger problem. We can't just walk out of here and tell people what we've found. Because if we do, all hell will break loose—and then that Cyclops is lost. Look at him. He may look fearsome, he may look strong—but, in reality, he's totally vulnerable."

54

THE FOLLOWING MORNING, the Cyclops went out at dawn and returned with a baby armadillo. He roasted it upside down over the fire and then, with his flint knife, carved out the meat as expertly as a surgeon and silently shared the pieces. Gideon noticed that he saved the biggest, juiciest piece for Amiko.

Gideon watched him eat. He wasn't exactly fastidious, shoving the dripping pieces of meat into his mouth with greasy fingers, chewing noisily with his huge rack of yellow teeth, stripping the bones with much grunting and sucking and then spitting them out. But there was something, Gideon thought, about the sharing out of food that was uniquely human. This strange, ugly creature was, on a certain level, human like him—not just an intelligent ape. He felt a responsibility for him, a sense even of affection. This creature had no idea what kind of world was out there, or what would happen to him if that world ever learned of his existence—but he had known enough to be agitated and fearful of their arrival.

Amiko, too, was silent and troubled. They consumed

the armadillo without conversation. When it was over, the creature rose and, with a rumbling sound, gestured brusquely for them to come with him. This time the gesture was not ambiguous.

They followed him out of the cave and into the early-morning light. He proceeded down one of the main trails on the island, again moving with amazing silence and speed. Gideon kept up more easily now—the ribs were almost completely mended, thanks to the marvelous healing powers of the lotus. The trail branched several times and then, abruptly, they found themselves on the edge of the cliffs, staring out to sea. The morning sun was still low in the sky, laying a dazzling path of light across the water. The Cyclops barely paused before disappearing over the edge.

Gideon peered over and saw that there was, in fact, an almost invisible trail of sorts plunging down through a fissure in the rock. The Cyclops was moving swiftly and surely down the trail, so steep it was almost a staircase of lava. Gideon scrambled to follow, with Amiko behind. He descended quickly, trying to ignore the dizzying heights.

The faint trail wound down among pillars of lava, caves, overhangs, and steep rockfalls. It appeared to be a very old path, much worn with use, the edges of lava rock polished smooth by the passage of many feet. After they had descended perhaps two hundred nearly vertical feet, the trail made a hairpin turn, followed a tight horizontal ravine, and then entered an unobtrusive opening in the rock.

Very quickly the passageway opened into a large tunnel, evidently an old lava tube, heading into the heart of the island. The floor was of solid rock, the central portion worn and gleaming, again as if polished by the passage of countless feet. Gideon glanced at Amiko but said nothing.

As the light from the entrance became dim, the passageway opened up into a large, domed cavern, with a roof a hundred feet above their heads. The Cyclops halted. At the far end of the cavern stood a crude stone door, made from lava rocks fitted and stacked, with a shaped block forming the lintel. A mysterious, pale light spilled from beyond the door. Now the Cyclops shuffled forward on his large feet, moving slowly and with what felt to Gideon like a certain hesitation—or perhaps reverence—toward the entrance.

They stepped through the door, entering a cavern even bigger than the last. Gideon stopped in astonishment. Behind him, he heard Amiko gasp out loud. The walls of the cavern were encrusted with crystals—clusters and sprays of milky white, some four to five feet long. A spear of sunlight streamed in from a distant hole in the ceiling above them, striking a crystal array on one wall, which refracted it, spreading a soft, ethereal light throughout the cavern. The floor was covered with pure white sand. On the far wall, the lava had been polished smooth and was decorated with many designs, like petroglyphs—animals, spirals, suns, moons, and geometric people.

Gideon glanced at Amiko and saw the astonishment in his eyes reflected in her own. Neither spoke; the cathedral-like atmosphere and the hushed movements of the Cyclops seemed to call for silence.

The Cyclops continued walking through the cavern, past the crystals, toward the wall of petroglyphs. There were other drawings here, and with a start Gideon recognized a picture of a ship with a sail and what looked like rows of oarsmen.

"That," whispered Amiko, "is a Greek pentekonter. The ship of Odysseus."

With a grunt of annoyance the Cyclops hurried them along toward where the cavern closed in to a narrow yet tall passageway. As they left the brightness of the crystal cavern behind, the full dimension of what they were seeing in the dimness beyond slowly began to take shape. The high walls were honeycombed with niches, shelves, and small openings. From every dark nook came the faint gleam of white—the white of bones. It was a catacomb, Gideon realized: a vast necropolis carved into the lava, on which rested massive skeletons—skeletons of Cyclopes. From where they were standing, they could see dozens, if not hundreds, in the walls all around them and in the corridor ahead, stretching into full darkness.

The Cyclops moved forward, much more cautiously. As they penetrated deeper into the catacombs, darkness closed in, but the Cyclops kept on. At one point Amiko stumbled in the dark and the Cyclops, with a soft noise, took her hand and led her along. Gideon realized the large, single eye was indeed some sort of adaptation to darkness, as the creature could evidently see far better in the darkness than they could. They followed the sounds of his movement.

Then he stopped. Gideon could hear him breathing. And suddenly there was a *click* and the Cyclops stood there, lighter flicked on. The wavering flame cast a dim yellow glow all about. Now they were literally surrounded with shelves and holes full of bones, a vast city of the dead, but the Cyclops was standing in front of one niche in particular. This one was different from the rest. It was larger, the opening framed with carefully shaped blocks of stone. Inside were laid large crystals, apparently offerings to the remains within. As Gideon peered in, he saw that behind the crystals were laid out various grave goods—flint knives, spears, and a much-corroded bronze helmet.

An ancient Greek helmet.

The Cyclops spoke. His voice was rough, guttural, but nevertheless reverential, and it boomed through the dark spaces of the cave. Gideon jumped.

The Cyclops spoke again, repeating the word.

Gideon recognized the word from before: *Polyphemus.*

Could this be his tomb?

The Cyclops reached into the tomb and grasped the slab lid of an ancient, stone container sitting near the skeleton. He slid the lid off and reached in, removed a handful of dried lotus, and showed it to Gideon, who stared down at the wrinkled store of brown fungi. Once again, he had the impression that the lotus was more rare and precious than gold.

Then the tall form slid the lid back on, and turned away. They silently followed him out of the catacombs of the Cyclopes.

55

THEY RETURNED TO the dwelling cave later that day. The Cyclops built up the fire in the cave and then disappeared out the door, carrying his spear, leaving Amiko and Gideon behind. It was the first time they'd had a chance to talk since seeing the Cyclopes' necropolis. Even though they doubted the Cyclops could understand any English, they had both been reluctant to discuss their situation in front of him.

Amiko spoke first, the words pouring out. "My God, Gideon. Do you realize what that necropolis means? These Cyclopes—they aren't just a bunch of cavemen. They have a culture. A history. A sense of the afterlife. *Religion.* That art—it indicates a symbolic understanding. In other words, they have something we might call civilization. And they've been here a very, very long time."

"And that single eye," said Gideon. "It's an adaptation to darkness."

"Exactly. This island is riddled with caves. This is their homeland. In a way, like *Homo floresiensis,* the 'hobbits' in Indonesia. This group of islands is where they evolved.

And he may well be the last of his kind. I think he's been alone for a long time—maybe hundreds of years."

"Kept alive by the lotus."

"We've got an obligation to protect him," Amiko said. "Otherwise, he'll end up in a zoo or a lab…or worse. Here's what we'll do: we'll get some of those dried lotus and bring them back. That was the mission Glinn tasked us with. But we'll keep secret the existence of the Cyclops and the location of the island. Nobody needs to know that. Mycologists might be able to cultivate the lotus, or perhaps chemists will be able to isolate and synthesize the active ingredients."

"That may be difficult," said Gideon. "The compounds in the lotus must be incredibly complex to have such a profound effect on the human body."

"If that's so, we've really got a problem on our hands."

"And then there's Glinn. He knows about the Cyclops. And he knows our general location."

"He has no idea we found a *live* Cyclops. And he doesn't know the location of the island. We'll lie. We'll make up a cover story, say we were on another island. Say we only saw bones—old bones."

"Glinn's a hard man to deceive," said Gideon.

"Then we won't deceive him. We just won't *tell* him. We'll keep silent. And if he insists on the details, we'll be vague. We were sick, the details are fuzzy. I mean, how many times has Glinn kept us in the dark? Turnabout's fair play, right?"

"So what now?" Gideon asked after a moment.

"We're done here. We need to get back to civilization. With the lotus."

"Easier said than done," Gideon said. "We're stuck on a

volcanic peak walled in by sheer cliffs, in the middle of the sea, with no boat and no phone. Not to mention a mainland populated by people who are seriously pissed off at us."

They fell silent, the fire burning low, casting flickering shadows about the walls of the cave. Beyond the entrance, the afternoon sun streamed through the vegetation, and the faint calls of birds and frogs could be heard drifting back. Gideon could feel the spell of the moment enveloping him as he thought back on what they'd seen and experienced: the lost-world magic of the island; the ancient Cyclops, apparently the last of his kind; the crystal mausoleum hidden in the cliffs; the ancient petroglyphs of the Greek ships. It was all so fantastical, so otherworldly. He looked at Amiko, her face, pale and beautiful, staring into the dying fire, the faint, earthy smell of the lotus lingering in the air like a musky perfume. Gideon extended a hand to her, and she turned her face toward him. He gently drew her toward him and their lips met. This time, he could feel the willingness, the eagerness of the contact. They kissed quietly, slowly. He pulled her closer, felt her breasts against him, and their kisses became faster, more urgent—

Suddenly a shadow fell over them and they sprang apart. The Cyclops stood in the entrance to the cave, a bloody howler monkey hanging from a stick. His single eye stared at them, black brow furrowed in displeasure. Slinging the dead monkey aside, he advanced at Gideon with a growl.

Gideon stood up, facing the creature and realizing what a colossal mistake they had made. He could feel the air congeal with tension.

The Cyclops halted a few feet from him, staring him

down with his single, bloodshot eye. He was gigantic, towering over Gideon by a good three feet. Gideon could smell the creature: the sweat and dirt, the crushed jungle foliage. He could see that the Cyclops was flushed, the skin under his coarse hair mottled red, the muscles of his long arms jumping with nervous tautness. He sensed he was moments from being torn apart. But he stood his ground, feeling intuitively that to turn and run, or try to talk his way out of it, would only set off the explosion he still hoped to avoid. The Cyclops, although clearly enraged, his veins pulsing with anger and jealousy, seemed uncertain what to do next.

Gideon waited for a sign, a signal, some sort of indication how to defuse the situation. But he could think of nothing.

Amiko tried to speak—a few halting words of ancient Greek—but the Cyclops silenced her with a terrifying roar, brown teeth snapping.

Slowly, a hand rose up and closed around Gideon's throat. Gideon grasped the wrist with both hands and tried to tug it away. But the Cyclops was unbelievably strong, the wrist like a steel bar.

"Don't. Please." He glanced over at his bag. The gun was in there. Amiko could use it. She followed his eyes and seemed to understand.

The grip tightened.

In a smooth and easy motion, Amiko reached out, grasped the bag, removed the gun, and pointed it at the Cyclops.

He ignored her, the fist tightening, Gideon could feel his air being cut off, the blood thrumming through constricted arteries.

Amiko spoke again in Greek, but the Cyclops didn't appear to hear, so focused was he on Gideon. Still grasping Gideon by the neck, the creature lifted him off the ground.

Gideon could no longer breathe. He felt himself starting to black out and struggled to cry out to Amiko. She had to shoot. *Now.*

The ground suddenly shook. A faint rumble like thunder rolled through the forest. The Cyclops jerked, startled, dropping Gideon and staring about wildly.

Coughing, tugging at his neck, Gideon scrambled to his feet and backed away. Amiko was still pointing the gun, but the Cyclops was ignoring both of them, completely focused on the sound. Another rumble, the ground shaking. This was clearly something the Cyclops had never heard before, and he was becoming more agitated than they'd ever seen him. In a flash he loped to the entrance of the cave and peered out with his huge yellow eye, surveying the jungle.

"Thunder?" Amiko asked.

"No," Gideon replied in a strangled voice.

Now another sound reached them: the *thwap-thwap* of chopper blades. In an instant the Cyclops vanished into the forest. Gideon exited the cave with Amiko and stared up in time to see a shape passing over them: a large single-engine helicopter, which Gideon recognized as a Sikorsky S-70, was passing over the trees. A column of smoke was rising into the pristine sky from the far end of the island-top. Even as they looked, there was the roar of another explosion, along with a wash of overpressure that lashed the jungle canopy. Another ball of fire rose into the sky, billowing into black smoke.

"What the hell?" Amiko cried.

"Napalm!" yelled Gideon, over the roar. "They're clearing a landing zone!"

"They? Who?"

As the S-70 passed overhead, Gideon could see no identifying logos or marks—only a call number. But even as he watched, the chopper slowed and the cargo door slid open. Just before the chopper disappeared over the trees, Gideon could have sworn that the man standing in the door, wearing plain jungle camo, was Manuel Garza.

56

T HE HELICOPTER HAD vanished, but Gideon could still hear the thud of its rotors. It sounded like it was going into a hover near the middle of the island, no doubt to rope down personnel to finish clearing the LZ.

"*Glinn*," said Amiko, in a low voice.

Gideon swore. "I guess he got a better fix on us than we realized."

For a long time, neither said a word. The thump of the chopper blades rolled through the trees, the smoke billowed upward. Soon that was joined by the sound of chain saws.

Gideon looked at Amiko. He could see the disbelief, the shock and anger, in her eyes.

"We need to stop this," she said.

"Yes. We need to confront Glinn, find out what's going on."

They went back into the cave, threw some supplies into a drysack. Without exchanging a word, they set out toward the rising smoke and the outraged buzz of chain saws, following the web of trails toward the far end of the island. As they moved on, the sounds grew louder: the crashing of a great tree being felled, the whines of multiple chain saws going at once, the shouts of men, the crackle of radios—and now the rumbling of a massive diesel generator.

They burst into the clearing. One chopper was coming in while a second had already put down. A third was hovering nearby. It staggered Gideon how much had been done in so little time. A crew was busily cutting up and hauling off a litter of great trees that lay on the ground, while others went around with fire extinguishers putting out the last of the napalm fires that had devoured the thick brush and understory. Still others were erecting metal poles for tents and establishing an electrified perimeter fence.

At one side, a massive metal cage was being erected.

At the sight of this, Gideon stopped. It was impossible. They hadn't told Glinn—hadn't even known themselves—that there was a live Cyclops on the island.

"The son of a bitch," breathed Gideon. "How did he know?"

Amiko said nothing.

Nearby stood a large wall tent, already erected and staked out, with a small gazebo adjacent to it. After a moment's hesitation, Gideon walked toward it, Amiko following. He pulled aside the flap and there, as he expected, was Glinn, sitting in an all-terrain wheelchair, wearing light safari clothing, a young blond man in camo standing at his side, holding an M16. Nearby stood Manuel Garza, his face like stone.

"Ah, Gideon and Amiko," Glinn said. "I was expecting you. Come in."

"What's that cage for?" Amiko asked quietly.

"Won't you sit down?"

"Answer my question."

"You know some of it already. It all started with the vellum. *Respondeo ad quaestionem, ipsa pergamena.* 'I, the very page, answer the question.' It turns out that the 'very page'—the parchment itself—was the solution. It was made from the skin of an animal—but not any sort of animal normally used for parchment. We did a DNA analysis of the sample. As I've told you, we identified the creature that the parchment was taken from. Neanderthal. But there was a twist. This Neanderthal-like hominid was different. More robust. Bigger. Fiercely aggressive. And in one area, this creature's genetics are completely different from Neanderthals—and modern humans. And that is in the area of sight. The creature of the vellum had a very different way of seeing, a single, large optic nerve, a single area of the brain for optic processing—and what's more, *a single eye.* When you radioed that you'd seen the skull of a Cyclops, we knew exactly what this creature was. And when we ran this information through our proprietary QBA programs, we got a most interesting result: that, given the remote location of this island group and lack of contact with the outside world, *there was no good reason to think the Cyclops had gone extinct.*"

"And the cage," said Amiko. "That's for...capturing one?"

"While the lotus is our prime goal, the scientific opportunity to study a living Neanderthal-like creature must not be missed."

Gideon stared at him, then glanced at Amiko. She was

looking at him with intensity, communicating some meaning.

Gideon managed an easy laugh. "That's ridiculous. We've been on the island now for days. We haven't seen the slightest indication of any Cyclopes. You might as well send that cage back to where it came from."

Glinn seemed to pierce him with his one gray eye. "You're an excellent liar, Gideon, but you can't fool me."

"Meaning?"

"Meaning I shall keep the cage ready and waiting, because you have just confirmed what I suspected: that there are Cyclopes on this island."

Amiko finally spoke. "Wrong. There's *one* Cyclops. A very old one. The last of its kind."

Glinn arched his eyebrow. "Indeed?"

"So you see," said Amiko slowly, "there's no way you can put the last one in that cage. It would be a crime against nature."

"I'm sorry, Amiko, but we're going to be working to recover the lotus. Our activities will be disruptive to the Cyclops's habitat. The creature will need protection."

Amiko's voice rose a notch. "You need to call this whole thing off. Right now. You're wrecking the island. It's a unique habitat. This isn't the way to recover the lotus!"

"I am sorry," said Glinn, "but it's the *only* way to recover the lotus."

Amiko said, "You'll kill him if you put him in that cage."

"Him?" Glinn's one eyebrow raised slightly.

"Yes, him."

"So you've made contact?"

"Yes."

He lapsed into silence. Finally he sighed and extended one claw-like hand in a gesture of conciliation. "May I speak?"

Amiko said nothing.

"There are two issues here," Glinn began, his voice mild, reasonable. "The first is that we've discovered a medicine that will change the lives of every human being on this planet. It's that significant. Of much less importance, but still extraordinary, is our discovery of a living hominid—"

"*Our* discovery?" Gideon said acidly. "You had nothing to do with it."

"*Your* discovery of a living hominid, a relative of our species, a variant of *Homo neanderthalensis*. That this creature lives in the same place as the miracle drug and apparently feeds on it is unfortunate. By landing here, by identifying the plant and obtaining samples, we can bring the drug to humanity. By studying the creature, we can learn much about our origins. Two birds with one stone. That is why we're here. And truly, the Cyclops needs to be protected, if only from itself."

"You're not going to put him in that cage," Amiko said. "We need to create the right habitat for him."

"Habitat," Amiko repeated. "You mean, zoo?"

"He can't be turned loose just anywhere to fend for himself. Certainly you can see that. We will find a suitably appropriate habitat for him to live out the rest of his days."

"Amiko's right," said Gideon. "He'll die in a cage."

Glinn continued on, his voice infuriatingly calm. "Mr. Garza and I ran countless scenarios on this. We chose the route with the highest probability of success. That route requires us to go in fast and hard, get the lotus, and get out. To establish a Cyclops preserve, we'd have to enter into negotiations with the Nicaraguan and Honduran governments—for whom this island is disputed territory. That would mean going through our State Department and diplomatic channels—a sure route to failure. We're here, we've taken possession, and by the time anyone finds out, we'll be gone. The Cyclops is in the way. We will do all we can to save it. But the lotus comes first. We'll be doing God's work in bringing this miracle to the human race."

"God's work?" said Amiko. "You really are crazy."

"Not at all. This medicine is not for the benefit of one corporation, one nation, or one socioeconomic class. The goal of our client is to use this discovery to benefit the world."

"Your goal is right, but not like this! That Cyclops saved my life! And Gideon's!" Amiko's voice was on the verge of breaking.

"It's the only way."

"It's *not* the only way. *You can't do this.*" She swallowed. "Wait until you see him, you'll understand. He's a person, he's almost a human being. But even more than that, he's the last of his kind. You can't take him away from his home. Please, Eli, let him live out his last days here, in peace, in the place he knows and loves, where all his memories are."

"I am indeed sorry, but that can't happen."

"*For the love of God, don't put him in that cage!*"

"The cage is only temporary—"

In one smooth, practiced motion, Amiko pulled the .45 from the drysack and pointed it at Glinn. The aide raised his M16, but Glinn made a sharp gesture for him to put up the rifle.

"I'll kill you before you put him in that cage," Amiko said. "I swear to God."

Glinn contemplated the .45 with a steady gray eye. "I already know you won't use that on me."

"You son of a bitch, I will!"

"Then do it."

Amiko raised the barrel and fired it into the air, the massive pistol giving off a deafening boom, then lowered the muzzle again. Glinn continued looking at her. A group of soldiers burst into the tent, but Glinn again held up his hand. "Let me handle this." He glared at Amiko. "I'm still waiting to see if you're a killer. You want to stop this? You can do it by pulling the trigger."

Amiko stared at him, her chest heaving, the gun shaking in her hand. Suddenly she rushed at him, swinging the gun like a club. The aide launched himself forward to tackle her, grabbing for the gun, but she was too quick, spinning around and striking him in the head with her foot. The two soldiers threw themselves into the struggle, one punching her hard in the face. Seeing this, Gideon joined in without thought, tackling one soldier and sending him sprawling into the side of the tent, while kneeing the other solider in the diaphragm. The tent came down around them with a tearing of canvas and clattering of poles. Others joined the fray and in a moment it was over. Gideon found himself jammed facedown on the ground, knees pressed into his back. He could hear Amiko amid the wreckage of the tent, screaming like a wild woman.

"Clear this mess away," came Glinn's cool voice.

The tangle of torn tent fabric and bent poles was

whisked off, leaving Glinn sitting, unscathed, in his wheel-chair. Amiko was pinned by two men, her nose bloody, screaming at Glinn.

"Let Gideon up," Glinn said.

They released him and Gideon stood up, spitting blood from a cut lip.

"You bastard," Amiko screamed at the top of her lungs.

"You won't just kill him, you'll be responsible for the ex-tinction of his species!"

"You *are* a bastard," said Gideon, staring at Glinn, and then at Garza. Garza hadn't participated in the melee. His face was a hard, neutral mask.

"You won't get away with this," Amiko continued yelling. "The world will know! You cage that Cyclops, you'll pay!"

Glinn shook his head. "You are thinking with your emotions."

"Go to hell!"

"Please take her away until she's rational."

She was hauled away, cursing and spitting. Glinn turned his gray eye on Gideon. "You seem...confused."

"I'm not confused about the way you're treating her. It's outrageous."

"I want you to understand why I'm doing what I'm do-ing. Give me credit for caring what you think."

Gideon stared at him. He could still hear Amiko out-side, yelling, screaming, and threatening. He didn't quite know what to make of her outburst, pulling the gun. The intensity of her rage, its extreme suddenness, shocked him. Glinn, on the other hand, almost appeared to have expected it.

"As I was saying, this is the best—and the only—way

to succeed. If we let the local governments become involved—even if they don't destroy the island in their squabble over it—they will seek to monetize the discovery. They will cut an exclusive deal with a multinational pharmaceutical company to bring the drug to market. The end result is that the drug will be expensive and available only to the privileged. And they'll put the Cyclops in a real zoo and monetize that as well. The way to stop this is to do what we are doing now. A preemptive strike. Our client, who is completely trustworthy and a man of goodwill, will found a nonprofit organization that will breed the plant and distribute it free to any qualified research group, government, and pharmaceutical company that wants it. In this way, the drug will come to market at the lowest possible cost."

He paused again and eyed Gideon with peculiar intensity. "I'd think you, *of all people*, would want to see this drug developed."

Gideon said nothing. Glinn had touched him where he was most vulnerable. But caging the Cyclops remained an ugly, *ugly* decision.

Glinn went on in his reasonable voice. "The logic is inescapable. We will do all we can to help the Cyclops, but it cannot remain on this island. According to our computer simulations, we have twenty-four hours before our presence here is discovered and investigated. If we don't have the lotus by then, we will fail."

Gideon winced slightly as Amiko, outside, let forth another shrill outburst. "As always," he said, "you make everything sound so inevitable. But I want no part of it."

"And you shall have none. Neither you nor Amiko. Tomorrow morning, Manuel will fly you both to Managua, and from there you will return to the States. Your work is done. And exceedingly well done, if I might say so, despite the contretemps at the end." He gestured toward the sound of Amiko's screaming. Glancing in her direction, Gideon could see that the two men holding her were having a hard time; she was amazingly strong for someone so small.

Suddenly a thunderous roar came from the wall of jungle. Gideon turned his head in time to see an extraordinary sight. The Cyclops came bursting from the foliage, his yellow eye fiery with rage, his mouth open, exposing long, yellow canines, his gigantic, muscled frame radiating ferocity, his silver hair streaming behind him. He carried a club in one massive hand and a spear in the other. He rushed straight at the men holding Amiko, who were so stunned they seemed momentarily paralyzed. He swung the club, which literally exploded the skull of one of the men, and grabbed Amiko.

"I want it alive!" cried Glinn.

Several men rushed forward, Tasing the creature with flashes of blue light, the crackling sound mingling with his terrible roars as he swept them aside with a massive arm. The Tasers only seemed to enrage him more. Now other men rushed up with a metal net, which they flung over him. Thrashing maniacally, the Cyclops clawed it apart with his hands, the metal strands snapping and twanging like guitar strings as he tore the net to pieces, Amiko fighting to help free him from the entanglement.

Men with rifles were hastily taking up positions, leveling their guns.

"No!" screamed Amiko, "don't shoot!" But the rifles went off with popping sounds—tranquilizing darts. Half a dozen stubby syringes buried themselves in the Cyclops's back and side. He gave another jungle-shaking bellow and flailed about, pulling them out and flinging them away.

"Again!" Glinn ordered.

"*No!*" Amiko screamed, trying to place herself between the Cyclops and the shooters.

A second round of well-aimed shots hit the Cyclops. The soldiers backed off as he came to a staggering halt, his great eye rolling grotesquely, his mouth distorted, spittle drooling out. He flailed about hopelessly for a moment, and then collapsed on the ground, his guttural cries dying into a choking sputter before going silent.

In five minutes, the soldiers had loaded his gigantic body onto a dolly and rolled him into the cage. Amiko, who had been tackled and recaptured, had finally stopped screaming and fallen silent.

Glinn turned to Gideon. "The creature came to rescue her. Impressive. Now that we've captured the Cyclops, we can get moving on phase two—finding the lotus." He gestured at the headless body of the man lying in the wet ashes of the clearing. "That was unfortunate. Manuel, could you please have it taken care of?"

Garza went off in silence and soon was directing a group of men removing the body. Glinn gestured for Amiko to be brought to him. Her hands cuffed behind her back, held by two burly men, she was led forward.

"It's over," Glinn said. "There's nothing you can do for the creature now. If you promise to behave, I'd like to release you."

Silence. And then Amiko said, in a strange, cold voice: "You can release me."

The two men undid her cuffs and let her go.

"The men will stay with you, however, until you de-part."

"You've overlooked one small fact," Amiko said.

"And what is that?"

"You won't find the lotus—without *his* help."

57

G IDEON AWOKE BEFORE dawn, bleary-eyed and deeply discouraged, unable to sleep due to the miserable roaring of the Cyclops, which had gone on for most of the night. The bellowing had finally died down, and he had managed a restless hour of sleep before being awoken for the flight home. As the sun rose over the treetops, Gideon and Amiko—with her two armed guards—were standing to one side while the chopper sat in the landing zone, warming up, ready to take them away.

Amiko looked like a ghost, pale, her bloodshot eyes set in pools of dark skin.

"Are you all right?" Gideon asked, taking her arm.

She silently pulled away.

The soldiers indicated it was time to board. Garza was in the pilot's seat, his face set, unreadable.

For a moment, Gideon hesitated. Where was Glinn? All their hard work and sweat, the dangers they'd endured—and now they were being hustled back to civilization. It all felt wrong. It made him angry. He glanced back in the direction of the security enclosure. The Cyclops had started bellowing again.

One of the soldiers gestured with his weapon. With a sigh, Gideon hoisted his drysack over one shoulder and climbed up into the chopper after Amiko. The soldiers shut them in.

He settled into his seat, buckled in, and put on the headset. A moment later the Sikorsky lifted off, rising above the jungle canopy, Garza at the controls. As the chopper gained altitude, Gideon could see the top of the island, floating high above the sea like a green paradise, but now marred by the scorched LZ, the camp, and several other brutally fresh clearings hacked out of the jungle. Directly below, he could see the Cyclops, shaking the bars of his cage and staring upward with that hideous eye.

He glanced over at Amiko. Her face was dark and strange. It chilled him how she had gone from pleading with Glinn, to a sudden eruption of furious violence, to this cold and forbidding silence.

The chopper banked over the canopy, flying along the spine of the island. But instead of winging out over the sea, when the chopper reached the end of the island it began to slow. Then it swung around and abruptly descended toward a rough clearing EES had cut out of the jungle on the far side of the tabletop. A moment later they landed.

"What's going on?" Gideon asked.

Garza turned around in his seat, taking off his headset and indicating they were to do so as well. "I'll tell you what's going on," he said over the whine of the engine. "You've been hearing Glinn talk about his 'client.' I'm surprised you haven't figured it out yet. There *is* no client. Or rather, the so-called client is Glinn himself."

Gideon stared at Garza.

"From the very beginning of this project," Garza said, "I've been concerned about Glinn's behavior. He was so secretive, holding his cards close, never revealing the name of his client. I'm his right-hand man; I've always had a place in the inner circle. Not this time—it was an inner circle of one." He paused, frowning. "I've seen Glinn go off the deep end before, and I've begun to see the signs of it again. He's after the lotus to heal *himself*. And he's not going to give it away. He plans to make big money on it."

"Do you know this for a fact?"

"I know it because I know Glinn. I've been through this before, with the meteorite business."

"Meteorite? You mean, the one you mentioned in the bar?"

"Exactly. This is a continuation of that same story. When we talked before, I never told you what the meteorite was, exactly. Now you need to know. It was a seed."

Gideon stared at him. "A *what?*"

"You heard me. It was Panspermia on a grand scale, a huge alien seed, floating through space for God knows how long. It fell to earth a few thousand years ago and was lying dormant on a frozen island. Eli collected it for the Lloyd Museum, but the project failed, the ship sank, and it went to the bottom of the South Atlantic. Planted. Where it found the ideal conditions it needed to sprout. *And grow.*"

"My God."

"It's Eli's white whale. He prided himself on never failing—and on that op, he failed colossally. He thinks that whatever is growing down there threatens the earth—that it's his fault, and his responsibility to kill it. That project has always been in the back of his mind. But he's estimated that he needs a billion dollars to mount an expedition to kill that thing. I believe this drug is how he's planning to finance it."

"So all that talk of giving the drug to the world . . . is a lie?"

"Oh, he'll give it to the world—for a price. On top of that, the drug is also for himself. To cure his injuries. Glinn believes he must lead the expedition, and in order to do that he has to be able to walk and have use of his limbs."

Gideon felt stunned. All along, he'd been thinking about what the lotus might do for him. He'd never considered that Glinn had his own agenda. It was so obvious, once it was pointed out.

"Glinn is going to get all of us killed," Garza said. "I've seen it before. I saw one hundred and eight people die when the *Rolvaag* sank, and I never want to see anything like that again."

Gideon looked at Amiko, then turned back to Garza.

"So what's your plan?"

"Simple. We bypass Glinn, get the lotus, and get the hell out of here ourselves. *We* give it to science, freely, for the benefit of mankind. What Glinn was claiming to do, but we do it for real. It's up to us to pull this off."

"How?" Amiko suddenly asked.

Garza turned to her. "You said something back there that struck me. You said we wouldn't find the lotus without that creature's help. Is that really true?"

"Yes," said Amiko.

"Can you control him? Keep him in check?"

"I think so," Amiko replied.

Gideon looked at her in surprise. She was looking steadfastly at Garza with an expression of dark intensity.

"To release the Cyclops," Garza said, "you'll have to get past the electrified enclosure. I've got the codes to its cage." Garza pulled a piece of paper out of his pocket and gave it to her. "He came to rescue you. He trusts you. You free him and get him to dig up a lotus and bring it back here. Then we'll set him free and take off with the lotus. We've got six hours before Glinn expects me back. Think you can do it in six hours?"

"You know I can."

"Gideon, you in?"

Gideon said nothing for a moment, and then spoke slowly. "A stash of lotus is hidden in a cave near here, below, in the cliffs."

Garza stared at him. "You never said anything about that."

"It's true," Gideon replied. It seemed a more prudent course than freeing the Cyclops.

"Then that's the answer to all our problems," said Garza. "I'll wait here while you two go get it." He removed his .45 and handed it to Amiko. "You may need this."

She took it, shoved it in her waistband, and rose up from her seat. "Let's go," she said to Gideon.

58

GIDEON SCRAMBLED DOWN the dizzying trail to the crack that led into the necropolis, Amiko following. Once again the beauty of the necropolis—its lofty dignity, its mysterious light—was overwhelming. Here was proof the Cyclopes once had a culture, spiritual beliefs, a civilization. Anger at Glinn rose in him afresh. But he pushed those thoughts out of his mind, striving to focus on getting the lotus and getting out. There was nothing he could do about the rest of it—nothing. At least Garza was on their side. He had badly misjudged the man.

They entered the dark recesses of the necropolis, its silence overwhelming after the noise of the camp and the roar of the Cyclops. They quickly located Polyphemus's grave. There was the stone box . . . and there was the lotus. Amid the strange and powerful scent that rose from the box, Gideon scooped as many pieces up as he could fit in his drybag. They turned and emerged from the necropolis into brilliant light, making their way up the treacherous trail.

At the top of the cliff, Gideon turned in the direction

of the chopper, but Amiko paused. "What about the Cyclops?" she said.

Gideon hesitated. "What about him?"

"What do you mean? We've got to free him! We can't leave him in that cage. And he *needs* the lotus. He's dying."

Gideon looked at her steadily. "We can't do anything for him. He's surrounded by a dozen armed soldiers."

"I've got the codes. And I've got a plan. Now give me the bag with the lotus."

"Wait, Amiko...Garza needs the bag."

She stared at him, her face darkening. "The Cyclops saved your life. He saved mine. And you're just going to leave him there, in a cage, to die in misery?"

"I don't like it any more than you do. But there are bigger things at stake here. Like this." And he lifted the bag.

"Give me half. I'll take it to him. You can take the rest and go with Garza."

"We don't know how much will be needed for analysis. We can't risk it. Look—"

Quick as a striking snake, Amiko lunged for the bag, seizing it. Gideon yanked back and for a moment they struggled over it before it tore open, scattering the lotus. She abruptly released the bag, sending Gideon off balance, at the same time plucking the .45 from her belt and, turning it butt-first, striking him on the side of the head. He hit the ground and all went black.

Gideon felt like he was swimming back up from the bottom of the ocean, and the journey seemed to take a very long time. He struggled to sit up, his head throbbing, and looked at his watch. He'd been out about fifteen minutes. He cursed himself for not seeing this coming.

He glanced around. The lotus roots, which had been lying everywhere, were gone. Except for one that she had left for him, shoved in his pocket. She had taken all the rest.

Blood oozed from a cut on his temple, and his head pounded so that he could hardly think. He pulled the lotus from his pocket, wrapped it in a leaf, and tucked it back. Slowly, he rose to his feet. As he tried to clear his head, he heard the thunder of a distant explosion. A moment later he saw a ball of fire rise above the canopy, roiling into red and black, in the direction of the base camp.

Amiko.

He sprinted through the jungle, bashing through the vegetation, ignoring the pain in his head, until he reached the waiting chopper.

"Where were you?" Garza cried. "Something's going on at the camp." His radio had burst into frenzied chatter, everyone speaking at once over the frequency:

. . . it's loose . . . killing everyone . . . that woman . . . fire suppression now . . . Oh, my God! . . .

And then, as if to underscore all this, a distorted bellowing came from the radio, drowning out the babble of voices, dissolving into a roar of static—and then, suddenly distinct over the radio, a scream of human agony, cut short by the sound of ripping flesh.

"Son of a bitch!" Garza cried, and then stared at Gideon. "What the hell's happening?"

"Amiko," said Gideon. "She knocked me out. Took the lotus. She's freeing the Cyclops."

Garza looked at him. "*Took the lotus?*"

"All except this one." He pulled it out of his pocket and gave it to Garza.

"Get in," said Garza, snatching it. "Let's get the hell out of here. And let's pray to God that one root will be enough."

Gideon hesitated, his foot on the threshold.

"Get in, damn it!"

Gideon shook his head. "No. No, I can't."

"Why the hell not?" Garza was already powering up the rotors.

"It's a catastrophe. I can't go while that thing is killing people and . . . while Amiko's in danger."

Garza grabbed the controls. "If that's the way it is, I hope you survive. Sayonara." The door slammed and locked. Gideon retreated at a crouch as the chopper ascended into blue sky, then accelerated westward, toward Managua and home.

As Gideon watched it disappear, another massive explosion shook the forest.

59

GIDEON SPRINTED TOWARD the camp along the makeshift road that EES had slashed through the forest, the great trees cut and bulldozed aside like so many matchsticks, the shoulders banked with a confusion of ripped vegetation, broken trunks, crushed flowers, and tangled vines.

The camp was in chaos. The main generator and its fuel tanks were burning ferociously, smoke and flames leaping into the sky, threatening to set afire a second set of tanks supplying the backup generator. Several men battled the fire with fire extinguishers. Three horribly mangled soldiers lay scattered on the ground, two obviously dead, while medics worked on the third, who was shrieking in pain. The electric perimeter fence had been torn apart in several places, and the remaining soldiers were spooked, shooting in panic into the dense wall of jungle every time they thought they heard a noise or saw movement.

Almost immediately Gideon found himself surrounded by angry-looking soldiers.

"I want to see Glinn," he said.

The soldiers searched him roughly, handcuffed him, then shoved him toward Glinn's tent. Drawing back the flap, they pushed him inside.

From his wheelchair, Glinn was briefing a pair of armed commandos along with another incredibly bulked-up man, with massive shoulders, a neck as thick as a tree stump, wearing camo and a Rambo-style wifebeater, with a shaved head and goatee. Ignoring Gideon, Glinn continued speaking to the men. "You have your instructions. Track it with the dogs. Don't engage it—drive it back this way. Keep in radio contact. We'll be ready. Understood?"

"Yes, Mr. Glinn," said the beefy man.

"Dismissed."

Only now did Glinn turn to gaze at him coldly. While still preternaturally calm, he was breathing rapidly and shallowly, and there was a look in that gray eye Gideon had not seen before. In the background, he could hear the barking of dogs.

"What happened?" Glinn asked brusquely.

Gideon told him everything. Glinn listened, his face expressionless. When Gideon had finished, he was silent for a moment. Then he shifted in his wheelchair.

"Garza initiated this?" He thought for a moment. "I'm not sure if I should shoot you or free you."

"I'd rather it was the latter."

Glinn turned to the soldiers. "Remove the handcuffs."

They complied.

"So the mysterious client is *you*," said Gideon. "And you lied. You're going to sell the drug, not give it away."

"Yes, I am the client. But that changes nothing. And Manuel's wrong about the money. I've set up a foundation that will still get the drug to the general populace for virtually nothing, with only a small percentage to be set aside for the use of EES—"

A *crump* sounded beyond the tent, temporarily drowning out Glinn's voice, the yellow glow of fire penetrating the side of the tent. There was more shouting outside, a burst of automatic weapons fire.

"Your partner showed up," Glinn said. "She set our fuel dump afire, destroyed the primary generator, and disabled the backup. In the chaos she freed the Cyclops. The creature then went on a rampage. You saw the carnage. And after it had killed without mercy, it grabbed her and took her off into the jungle. I would have said she was a hostage, except that she showed no signs of struggling." He stared at Gideon. "Now: what are you doing here?"

"I came back because I'm partly responsible."

"With that I would agree."

"I don't mean in that way. If you hadn't come here, set fire to the jungle, caged the Cyclops—none of this would have occurred."

"The killings occurred because Amiko freed the creature."

"How, exactly?"

Gideon waved this away. "I'm not going to argue with you. There isn't time. I'm here because I can make things right."

"The creature isn't a brute animal—it *can* be reached. If I go out there, alone, unarmed...I might have some influence. And Amiko will listen to me. Together we might calm him down, bring him in with the lotus."

Glinn stared at him, his face shut down like a blank mask. "It will destroy you."

"I'll take that chance."

For a moment, Glinn went entirely still. Then he shifted again in the wheelchair. "We're so far outside our strategic predictions that anything is worth trying, even a plan as feeble as yours. I will allow it on one condition only: you go armed."

"I won't kill him."

"Take it anyway." Glinn gestured to his aide, who grabbed an M16 from a nearby rack, along with a couple of extra magazines, and silently handed them to Gideon. Gideon grabbed a headlamp, then nodded and turned to leave.

"One other thing."

Gideon glanced over his shoulder.

"Don't make the mistake of trusting it—*or Amiko.*"

60

GORDON DELGADO HAD started out as a dog handler in Iraq. Several tours and many citations later, he was honorably discharged and went to work as a crack dog trainer for the FBI. He had seen a lot of shit in his career, but when he'd arrived on the island the day before, he couldn't believe his eyes when he saw that monster in the cage. And when it got out and went berserk, that was something beyond even his worst nightmare: worse than Iraq, crazier than any movie. He could still vividly see, in his mind's eye, that monster with its dreads flying, bellowing, cavernous mouth open like a giant funnel, exposing rotting teeth and a ropy tongue plastered with foam, its furry hands swiping open a man's belly with no more effort than scooping butter out of a tub, that loping sideways run—and that eye, Mother of God, that eye, a pinpoint of black surrounded by bloodshot piss-yellow, big and shiny as a saucer, rotating crazily in its orbit. During its rampage, the thing had looked at him for just a moment—one soldier in each massive paw—a look that he would never shake as long as he lived. He hoped to hell he never had to look into that eye again.

They had left the camp behind, which he'd been glad to do. The fences were down while the backup generator was being repaired, the men jumpy and firing at nothing. The dump fire was at least getting under control, or so it seemed, and thank God for that, because if it spread into the thick jungle, there was no telling what might happen.

The dogs had picked up the creature's scent trail along the newly cut road to the other side of the island and they were following it rapidly. Holding their leashes, he moved along the path that had been freshly hacked out of the jungle, the two soldiers behind him, left and right point. Delgado knew quiet competence from braggadocio and half-assery, and these were two good men. He himself carried a .45 and an M4A1 carbine. His radio was clipped to his belt, its channel kept open to the camp's main frequency. The idea was to track the monster and circle him, then drive him back toward camp, where an eight-man squad was set up in an L-ambush, ready to take him out. The girl, if she was with him, was to be captured, or—if that was impossible—neutralized.

Delgado had never worked with this kind of dog before, an Italian breed used for sniffing out truffles. But while they weren't killer dogs, they were clearly intelligent, alert, steady, with no lack of guts. And anyway, against a monster like that a mastiff would be as useless as a terrier. These animals immediately understood what they were to do and had not lost their minds in terror.

The dogs paused at the wall of jungle next to the road, indicating that the scent trail went that way.

The plan seemed simple enough, and likely to succeed. But Delgado couldn't get out of his head the speed and ferocity the monster had displayed in its tear through the camp. As they left the road, pushing into the thick vegetation, he understood that there would be little warning if the creature decided to rush them.

Almost immediately the dogs' leashes started getting hung up.

"Hold it," he told the soldiers as he knelt over the dogs. They were eager, tense, their flanks quivering with excitement. "Gotta unleash the dogs."

The soldiers said nothing. He liked that. Soldiers joking and talking trash at the beginning of an op were only displaying their fear.

The dogs, unleashed, understood they were to stay close to him. All the better. He would know when they were closing in on the monster by their behavior. These were damn good tracking dogs, he decided, quiet and focused. Dogs, cars, guns, and women—the Italians did well where it counted.

It was hard to move through the jungle without making a racket. It was hot and green and overpoweringly humid, and Delgado was soon soaked. The monster would hear them long before they would become aware of him—except for the fact that the dogs would act as a kind of early warning. What he worried most about was their own rear. He didn't know how intelligent the huge creature was, but even a dumb-ass Cape buffalo knew enough to circle around and come up on its trackers from behind. They had to expect anything.

As they penetrated farther into the jungle, everything became very quiet. The sounds of the camp disappeared.

The jungle seemed devoid of life. Delgado found it spooky.

The island was small. It wouldn't be long before they closed in on the creature. He could already see they were getting nearer from the behavior of the dogs: their heightened tension, their quickened movements. He signaled to the soldiers, and they nodded their understanding.

They moved slower, more cautiously, hyper-aware of every little sound.

And now the dogs began to tremble. They were tense, frightened, but still in control. And then suddenly Delgado realized he could smell it: a thick, cloying odor with a foul human component he found nauseating. But it was good news: if they could smell the monster, because of the wind direction, it couldn't smell them.

With a hand signal, Delgado indicated to the soldiers that they were to make a ninety-degree turn. This would be the beginning of the stalk and circle. They moved off the scent trail, the dogs whining and reluctant to go but obedient in the end. Moving slowly, he led the soldiers two hundred yards to the nine o'clock position, and then began the clockwise circle to noon. He had done this more than once with insurgents in Iraq, and it was a move that tended to confuse and frighten them, causing them to retreat along the six o'clock line. He hoped it would have the same effect on the monster.

They reached the twelve o'clock position, and he signaled to the soldiers to stop. He figured that the monster should be about three hundred yards due south of them. Now the time had come to drive the creature toward the ambush salient. With additional hand signals he readied the group; they raised their rifles and awaited his signal.

The dogs, sensing something was about to happen, went rigid with tension.

Delgado raised his hand, paused—then brought it sharply down.

The soldiers charged forward, discharging their weapons in burst mode. The dogs joined in immediately, leaping ahead of the soldiers with hysterical barking. Delgado brought up the rear, firing his .45 into the air, the massive ACP rounds sounding a deep thunder to the chatter of the M16s. Shock and awe—enough to terrify anything and send it fleeing.

Then came something like a gust of wind, a disturbance in the leaves, a sudden blur, followed by the brief shriek of a dog. Then nothing. Delgado halted in sudden confusion. Both dogs were gone. And then he saw it: a long streak of gore clinging to the vegetation, going off in a perpendicular path into the dense jungle—blood, ropes of intestines, meat, fur, a pink tongue still twitching, a floppy ear.

All was silent.

It took a moment for Delgado to process what had happened. The monster had crossed their path at right angles and swept up both dogs, utterly dismembering them in passing, and then vanished again.

61

As he walked along the hacked-out road, Gideon heard the sudden burst of firing, the hysterical barking. He stopped and listened. It sounded like it was about half a mile away, but it was hard to tell in the thick foliage. The shriek of a dog—and then, abruptly, there was silence.

It was, he thought, unbelievably foolish for them to think they could meet the Cyclops on his own ground, in the dense jungle, and survive. How right Garza had been: Glinn, in his obsession, had lost his judgment. All his computer models and quantitative behavioral analysis were for naught in the face of an unknown creature like this. It would be a miracle if anyone got off the island alive.

He wondered what was going through Amiko's head. The Cyclops wouldn't kill her, he was sure of that. But where was she, what was she—what were *they*—doing? Was she a willing participant, or was he holding her against her will? She, too, had all too clearly lost her judgment. In retrospect, it didn't completely surprise him; not given the story of her father, her early life, and her strange attachment to the Cyclops. But he couldn't worry about that now. Judging from the sounds, he could estimate the Cyclops's current location, and this would help him get into position without being detected.

Gideon jogged down the road until he reached the LZ where Garza had dusted off an hour or so before. Pushing into the jungle, he arrived at the cliff's edge and descended the dizzying trail to the necropolis. He squeezed through the opening and made his way through the caverns, past the crystal room, to the burial caves in the rear.

The niche containing the bones of Polyphemus stood on the lower part of a vast series of small caverns and hollows containing bones. The stone box containing the last of the lotus stood where he had left it, lid closed. He went in, took out the few lotus pieces left, and put them in his pockets. Gideon turned and scanned the opposite wall, selecting a niche high up and slightly to one side. He climbed up, trying not to leave marks of his passage, and crawled into it, pushing aside the bones and dried, mummified remains of a Cyclops. Behind him, the niche narrowed into a tunnel that sloped steeply downward; there would be no ambush from that direction. Lying down, he sighted through his scope, using a broken hip bone as a brace, hoping that wouldn't be necessary—he would fire only to save his own life. He carefully moved the mummified remains in front of him to create a kind of screen.

The Cyclops had been wounded, he was sure of that. Gideon felt certain that the wounded creature would eventually take refuge in this necropolis—bringing Amiko with him.

He settled in, waiting. He had a feeling it wouldn't be long.

* * *

"Son of a bitch," whispered Delgado, staring at the pink tongue, which had finally ceased twitching. He looked into the faces of the two soldiers. They were shocked and frightened—but still in possession of their faculties.

"Okay," said Delgado quietly. "This wasn't a good idea. We're out of here—straight back to camp, weapons free, burst setting, *go*." He stabbed his finger in the direction of camp.

Neither man needed persuading. They set off at a jog, pushing through ferns, jumping mossy fallen trunks, tearing aside vines, weapons lowered and ready to fire. Delgado had never seen an attack as swift and violent as that one—from man or animal. He now knew this was a terrible mistake.

Another burst of foul-smelling wind; a sudden eruption of vegetation; and the soldier to his right went down with a massive meat-tearing sound, his weapon firing in a crazy burst that raked the canopy above before falling silent. Delgado and the other soldier halted and crouched, instinctively turning back-to-back, scanning the forest as leaf tatters fluttered down like rain all around them, but the creature had vanished. Blood and matter from the soldier dripped steadily from the leaves, making a pattering sound.

Delgado, his back pressed to the remaining soldier, could see no sign of the monster. Yet it had been there, leaving the body of a soldier on the ground like some dreadful calling card, the torso almost completely separated from the hips. It had all happened so quickly the man was dead before he could even cry out.

More absolute silence. And then, coming from everywhere and nowhere at once, he heard a long, deep-throated wail, climbing in pitch to a scream and then dropping down the scale to a shuddering, moist rumble—a sound simultaneously animal and human. It was the most terrifying thing Delgado had ever heard.

"Clear three sixty full auto," he whispered urgently to the soldier, "then *move!*"

They both leapt up, firing on full automatic mode, raking the jungle in a complete circle around them, sending up a storm of leaves, twigs, and splinters—and then they ran, firing ahead and behind. His magazine empty, Delgado ejected it, slammed in another on the run, resumed firing. It was as if they were moving through a storm of shattered vegetation. Nothing could approach without getting riddled.

He ejected another empty magazine and slammed in yet another. He had two more; they'd better last. He flicked the lever on the M4 to burst mode in order to save ammo. Running like mad, his face and body torn by sharp vegetation, he continued firing around him in three-round bursts.

The creature suddenly popped up in front of them—like some hideous jack-in-the-box rising straight out of the ground. He swung and fired but it was already moving at lightning speed. A hairy, ropy arm flashed around like a bullwhip and took the last soldier's head off, as easily as a knife but not nearly so cleanly, blinding Delgado with the spray of blood. Delgado fired anyway, shouting incoherently, shaking the stuff out of his eyes even as he smelled the stench of the beast.

Through the red fog he could now barely see. The

monster was standing right before him, towering, chest swelling with his poisonous roar, and suddenly Delgado felt a physical jerk so violent it was as if he'd literally been turned inside out. He looked down and saw that he had.

62

GLINN REMAINED IN his tent, surrounded by communications equipment, his aide at one side. Over the open radio channel, he had heard everything that happened to the dog team: the conversation, the shooting, the roaring of the beast, the gruesome sounds of dismemberment and death—and then silence. He also heard some of it directly through the jungle: faint, delayed, like an echo.

It was happening all over again. A single unexpected factor, impossible to foresee, had overturned all his carefully calculated models. It was exactly what had occurred five years before, with the meteorite that turned out—against all odds—to be something else. The failure, sudden and complete, was unraveling around him, in real time. Now they had a completely unpredictable hominid, neither animal nor human, filled with a murderous and vengeful rage, to contend with. Unleashed by a person they had failed to fully understand. Glinn knew, with brutal clarity, that his determination to succeed at all costs had affected his judgment and led them into disaster.

Now they were in uncharted territory. He had lost his

right-hand man, Garza—a loss he felt keenly. He had not treated Garza properly; he saw that now. It had been a serious mistake to deceive him. His QBA of Garza had always indicated a thorough pragmatist, a careerist, a man who looked after number one. But now Garza had displayed an unexpected, altruistic side.

Glinn shook his head. These were all lessons he would have to carefully ponder at some later date. But not now. Now, the first order of business was the survival of his men and himself against the fury of this extraordinary creature.

He pressed the TRANSMIT button on his comm unit and spoke to the eight men waiting at the ambush sallent. "It's over. Delgado's team is gone. Assemble the squad in here for a briefing. Now."

Moments later the eight soldiers entered the tent. They were frightened but still steady. Glinn had chosen them well.

"The Cyclops," said Glinn, "is coming for us. Here. In camp."

"What makes you think—?" began the squad commander.

"He's wounded. We've ruined his island. He doesn't care if he lives or dies. I believe he's going to take as many of us out as he can before the end." Glinn noticed, in passing, that he was now referring to the Cyclops as *he*, not *it*. That was his mistake from the beginning: thinking of him as an animal.

"Yes, sir."

"What's the status of the electric fence?"

"With the backup generator running again, it's up and juiced."

"He'll go right through it. Now, listen carefully. *He knows.* He was here, he watched, he saw who was in charge. He'll be coming for me first."

"Yes, sir," said the commander.

"So I'm the bait you will use. Understand? You set your men up to nail him when he comes for me. It's got to be subtle. That thing is no animal. He's nearly human and he can *think.*"

The squad commander nodded.

"Dismissed."

They exited the tent, leaving Glinn with his aide.

Glinn turned to him. "Bring me my Glock."

"Yes, sir." The aide fetched it, checked the magazine, handed it to him. He took it with his shriveled hand and racked a round into the chamber, setting it down in his lap. The Glock 19 was light enough for him to fire with his crippled hand, and it had good stopping power. But he didn't fool himself into thinking that, if it came to that, the pistol would do much good.

"Open both flaps. I need to see—and so does *he.*"

The aide complied.

The men had disappeared. Glinn could see no evidence of where they were hidden, waiting for the creature. Good. Another group of men were putting out the last of the fire, and the backup generator was humming. A stench of diesel and burnt plastic and metal hung over the camp. Two remarkably dismembered bodies still needed to be taken care of. Later. The air conditioner in his tent had finally cooled things off. But Glinn didn't like the noise; he wanted to hear.

"Shut off the A/C."

"Very well, sir."

His aide stood at the opening, M16 in hand, quiet, serious, waiting. A good man. All his men were crack, the squad commander the best there was. They would know what to do, how to set up the ambush. He told himself he didn't have to worry. The Cyclops was big, it was remarkably powerful, but it could be killed like any other living thing, and it was already wounded. Glinn was sure of that. Perhaps it was even dying.

That was a comforting thought.

He realized he was afraid. Not of his own death—but of the failure that would follow. Glinn calmed himself down, used the techniques he had learned to slow his heart rate and breathing, clear his head. He felt a new sensation, one he wasn't used to. It was not exactly fear. It was more *apprehension*: concern that he would not be able to complete his work in the South Atlantic. No one else could do it but him. It would be a great tragedy for the world if he perished now, on this island, before having completed his true mission.

Any minute now it, or rather he, would be there. And even as Glinn thought this, he heard him, right on schedule: a brutal, maddened roar that seemed to shake the very fabric of the tent.

Then, silence.

Not a shot was fired. That was good. It meant the men were still in possession of themselves. No point in firing stupidly into the wall of jungle, giving away their locations.

Another long, shuddering, wet roar, this time from a different direction. *Wet.* Was he shot through a lung? It was like the roaring of lions in the African night.

He wondered what Amiko's role in this was, if she was

even alive. Was she . . . *advising* him? The thought was inconceivable, and he dismissed it immediately. Amiko was no killer. She had lost control of the creature.

The roars went on for another ten minutes as the brute circled the camp. Glinn had to admire his patience, his use of psychology. It was bloody unsetting; he had to admit. And it occurred to him that the circling might also be a form of reconnaissance, using sight and smell. He wondered just how the commander and his men had set themselves up, if the Cyclops could discern what they were up to.

His aide stood in the opening, his keen blue eyes roving this way and that. Even he, the most taciturn and composed of men, was sweating.

Now the roars ceased. Glinn was surprised to find the sudden silence even more unsetting. His respect for the creature increased.

His thoughts turned to Amiko again, and then to Gideon. He wondered what Gideon was up to, assuming the creature had not killed him already. Gideon was one of the most competent human beings he had ever encountered, but a man who was very unlike him, who operated on almost pure, seat-of-the-pants intuition. Glinn had never been dismissive of intuition—it was a powerful tool, albeit dangerous—but this notion that the Cyclops could be reasoned with, turned, tamed, somehow domesticated, was wrong, and Gideon would not survive any such attempt.

The silence became prolonged. The tension increased.

It started with a rush, an explosion of vegetation at the edge of the jungle, exactly opposite his open tent. The creature burst straight out in a swirl of leaves and bits of branches, hit the fence with a crackle of electricity; the wires sprang apart like broken piano strings, the alarms going off.

Glinn noticed that—horrifyingly—the creature carried a drysack in one hairy paw. Was it Gideon's? He did not want to speculate how the Cyclops had gotten possession of it.

Even as the torrent of gunfire came pouring out of the tents surrounding him, the creature made a sudden turn, then another, moving extremely fast, the rounds kicking up geysers of mud and dirt all around him, some hitting home, and now he was moving laterally with a hideously rapid lope, faster than any runner, moving randomly while the converging lines of fire followed him.

And then Glinn saw that his movements were, in fact, anything but random. As he raced past the secondary fuel tanks and backup generator, the fire fell off abruptly—but not abruptly enough. Rounds slammed into the metal tanks, spraying fuel everywhere, and—Glinn could hardly believe his eyes—the Cyclops reached into the drysack, held out a *lighter*, flicked it on... and the entire secondary fuel dump erupted in a wall of flame.

And here came the Cyclops, *on fire*, heading straight at him, items tumbling out of the drysack and hitting the dirt behind him, emitting a bellowing roar, his huge gray tongue hanging out, that fearful, bloody, awful eye looking straight at him.

The aide let loose a burst of fire but his reactions weren't fast enough. The creature slammed into the tent, flame suddenly everywhere. Glinn had his Glock up, and as the Cyclops charged toward him he fired point-blank into the creature's flesh, the heavy wheelchair absorbing most of the blow of the creature's massive arm. Just as fast as he was there the thing was gone, no scream this time...and Glinn found himself sprawled on the ground, his wheelchair smashed, blood and smoke and fire everywhere.

63

Dᴇᴇᴘ ɪɴ ᴛʜᴇ necropolis, Gideon could hear nothing. Slowly, his eyes had adjusted to the dimness. He had chosen a good spot, well hidden, with a clear view of the entrance and the opposite niche holding the bones of Polyphemus—and the last of the lotus. The movement of air came from the opening into the cavern: he was downwind of the entrance. For that reason, he hoped the Cyclops would not be able to smell him.

Lying on the cool stone, he played out various scenarios in his head. It was impossible to predict what would happen when the Cyclops arrived, but arrive he would. The big question was Amiko. He would have to play it by ear.

He waited, listening. At the edge of audibility, he thought he heard something far away—a faint rumble of explosions or gunfire? After a moment it seemed to fade away.

Still he waited. Minutes passed.

And then he heard something else. At first he wasn't sure what it was, or even if it was. Perhaps it was just in his own mind. But then he heard it again: something low, faint, close. A breath? The soft sound of a footfall in sand?

He had arrived.

The sounds became more distinct as the creature approached, still unseen, in the huge antechamber outside the central necropolis. He could hear the sound of stertorous breathing, wheezing—then, diffusing through the still air, he smelled a vile mixture of diesel fuel, burnt hair, and animal foulness. The creature was wounded, struggling. He heard the sounds of eating, crunching, and then the faint smell of the lotus reached him. And a voice—a soft voice.

Amiko.

She was with him. She was helping him, caring for him. He listened as they rested in the antechamber, Amiko speaking softly.

Gideon made up his mind what to do. "Amiko?" he called out.

A sudden grunt of fury; a cough; then Amiko's soft voice soothing the beast, talking to him in Greek, calming him down.

"Gideon," she said in a low, sharp voice. "What are you doing here?"

"I came to help save the Cyclops. And to find you."

A silence. Then: "It's too late."

"It's never too late. Please talk to him. Glinn knows he screwed up. We can work things out now so the Cyclops can stay on the island."

"You don't understand. The Cyclops will kill you. He's killing everyone. I can't control him. Get out, now."

"You have to make him understand. Listen to reason. I want you to help me reach him."

"It's too late."

"I've got a weapon. If he comes through that door, he's dead. Tell him that—"

His talking was interrupted by a roar, a cry so laced with hatred and fury that it turned Gideon's blood cold.

"Just get out now!"

More angry sounds came from the Cyclops, growls of repressed fury, with Amiko's urgent voice suddenly raised in warning: "Gideon! He's coming for you—!"

A flash in the doorway, and the Cyclops came tearing through. Gideon had aimed at the opening, but despite all of Amiko's warnings he found himself hesitating to kill. It was only for a split second—but it was enough to miss the opportunity. The creature was moving so fast that by the time Gideon had repositioned the rifle it was already below him, climbing up the stone face with long hairy arms, coming for him with a howl. He fired as the Cyclops vaulted into the niche, slamming violently into him, tumbling him backward into the vertical shaft, and they fell together, in sudden free fall, through a dark void, the Cyclops roaring and clawing at the air.

I'm about to die, Gideon thought with what seemed like remarkable clarity. *I'm about to die.*

They landed in water, ice-cold, and Gideon thrashed about in pitch black, his head below the surface. He felt himself dragged down by the rifle, a current plucking him along. He managed to free himself of the gun, sending it to the bottom as he clawed his way up, breaking the surface and gasping for air. He could hear a bellowing, choking sound as the Cyclops fought the water.

He can't swim, Gideon thought.

It seemed they had fallen into some kind of underground river. The water was flowing faster now, and he could hear, growing in volume, another sound: the sound of a waterfall.

Unable to see, Gideon instinctively swam crosscurrent and moments later hit the rough, volcanic wall of the underground stream. It slid past his fingers as the current carried him along with increasing speed. He grabbed at it desperately, caught a ledge, managed to seize a rough projection with his other hand, and pulled himself out of the water onto the rock face. Muscles in spasm with the effort, he managed to find two decent footholds and a handhold in the rough lava, which allowed him to fumble his headlamp from his pocket, turn it on, and pull it over his head.

Son of a bitch. The Cyclops was clinging to the wall not twenty feet from him. He looked shattered, one leg dangling uselessly, skin burned raw, his flanks torn and bleeding from several bullet wounds—but still coming for him, his yellow eye gleaming murderously. Even in his ruined state the creature was preternaturally agile; in a matter of seconds he had gotten close enough to Gideon to reach out with a massive hand, broken nails sharp brown daggers, swiping at his neck.

There was nothing for it: Gideon leapt back into the water and allowed it to sweep him downstream, the creature bellowing in fury.

He swam to the other side of the river and tried to grab at the wall, now flying past in the accelerating current, the roar of the falls almost upon him. Scrabbling at it, tearing his hands on the rough lava, he managed to get a purchase and haul himself out. Once secure on the rock, he again shone the light around. The Cyclops was nowhere to be seen. It had not followed him into the water.

Gasping for breath, he took stock of his surroundings. The underground river was barreling along, boiling down toward a dark hole—a devastating waterfall, bounded by walls of razor-sharp lava. His light showed what looked like an opening above him, a brutal crack that led upward, seamed and riddled with holes, one of which might lead to a passageway out.

Gideon knew that he had to get out as quickly as he could. The Cyclops would undoubtedly know these caverns well, and even wounded as he was, he had the agility and eyesight to hunt down and to kill, quickly and efficiently. Gideon no longer had a weapon—not even a knife.

He started climbing up toward the crack. He managed to reach it, pull himself into it via improvised hand- and footholds, find a lava tube leading off from its steep flanks, and drag himself in. He collapsed onto a patch of sand, breathing hard. His hands were lacerated and bleeding from the sharp lava he'd climbed. Everything hurt.

And somewhere in these caverns was a murderous Cyclops, bent on his destruction. He turned off the headlamp and listened. Over the sound of water he could hear, somewhere, the rumble of labored breathing, the sounds of movement.

It was still out there, still coming for him.

64

Eli Ginn lay in the sand as two medics pulled the wreckage of his wheelchair off from on top of him, cut away his shirt, and undertook a quick examination. He was vaguely aware of his injuries, but he felt detached from them, distant, as if all this had happened to someone else. He struggled to make an inventory of his condition. His shoulder, broken. His crippled arm, lacerated and bleeding. A cut on his head, with perhaps a mild concussion. Burns. They hurt already; very soon, they would hurt much more.

He could hear the roar of the fire, see its angry glow through the ruined and tattered tent fabric. This was far worse than before. There would be no controlling this fire. He could already hear the popping sounds as it moved into the jungle, branches crackling, seedpods bursting, treetops erupting in noisy flame. Fanned by a rising wind.

Painfully, he turned his head to one side. His aide lay on the ground, in three pieces, connected only by strings of tissue. The man's surprised blue eyes stared into space.

The man's body, and Glinn's wheelchair, had absorbed the blow. It was a miracle Glinn was still alive.

The medics finished fitting a neck brace on him. They lifted him gently, then placed him on a stretcher.

"We're going to get you on the chopper," the chief medic said.

"Not ahead of the others."

"I'm doing the triage around here," the chief medic said tersely as they headed for the door.

"I said *no.* I'm stable now. Set me down. Take the others out first. I'll go with the last group."

A hesitation, and then the medic nodded. "Okay, Mr. Glinn. Have it your way." He disappeared out the door.

Glinn raised his head from the stretcher, looked around, spotted a soldier. He beckoned him over. "You're my aide now. You'll relay my orders."

"Yes, sir."

Glinn grasped the man's collar, pulled him close. "I want an immediate general evacuation of the island. First the wounded, then the others. We have two choppers left—it'll take four trips. The mission hospital in Puerto Cabezas, south on the mainland, will be our destination. There's a helipad there. Do it quickly."

"Yes, sir."

"Second order: abandon the firefighting effort. It's too late. The remaining soldiers—*everyone* left on the island—are to maintain the perimeter, defend against the creature, until the evac is complete. Is that understood?"

"Understood."

"Good. Now *go*."

"Yes, sir." Glinn released his hold on the man's collar.

The soldier jumped up and immediately disappeared around the corner of the tent.

Glinn lay back on the stretcher, on the ground, staring upward at the canvas, bright with the light of the fire. According to Gideon, Garza had gotten one lotus root out. Just one. He hoped beyond all hope that it would be enough.

65

GIDEON FORCED HIMSELF to sit up, his head spinning. He had to get the hell out of here before the Cyclops found him. There would be no communication between them, no mercy. Glinn was right about that, at least: he'd been a fool to think otherwise.

He strained to listen. Save for the low rush of water, a deep silence had descended. Gideon waited in the darkness, trying to catch his breath. And then a slow growl came rumbling out of the black tunnel: a howl of hatred, fury, and pain. It grew in volume until it ascended into an ululating wail.

Staggering to his feet, gripped by panic, Gideon flashed the light around briefly, saw nothing, and ran down the passageway, a lava tube with many branches. He took one at random, then another, sprinting as fast as he could, using his headlamp in his hand and turning it on and off just enough to keep from running headlong into the walls. He had lost all sense of direction. He had no idea where he was. His only desire was to get away from the beast.

Silence—and then another, low growl. It sounded like

it was ahead of him. Could the creature really have moved that fast? Had he himself, in his panic and confusion, doubled back? Stopping abruptly, almost tumbling into the sand, Gideon turned and ran back the way he had come, veering down a new tunnel, scrambling over the fallen rocks of a cave-in. He paused to listen again. Where the hell was it?

He could hear, faintly, the Cyclops moving: huge hoary feet biting into the sand. Again it seemed to be ahead of him. He could feel it, feel the electricity of the creature's hatred, its desperate need to kill. And then—quite suddenly—he could smell it.

Looking around, he saw an opening in the ceiling of the lava tube and he leapt for it, pulling himself up and climbing fast. One hand found a horizontal passage leading off from the pipe and he climbed into it and paused to reconnoiter. The tunnel was small—perhaps too small for the Cyclops.

He crawled down its length for a hundred yards, cutting his knees on the rocks that jutted up from the sandy floor. He could make out a dim light ahead, a faint smear of white. As he approached he saw it was the glow of the crystal cavern, framed by a rough opening.

...And then, suddenly, the black silhouette of the creature appeared against the light, blocking his way. With a cry, Gideon fell back. The Cyclops was playing with him—torturing him. Scrambling backward, he noticed a vertical hole to one side of the narrow passage. Shining his light down it, he saw that, after a few feet, it leveled out and widened. He climbed down and found himself in a dark passageway, apparently some rear section of the necropolis. There were ancient bones everywhere, crumbling into dust, along with crude stone tools, polished pieces of obsidian, and other artifacts. But Gideon was too panicked to pay much attention. He sprinted down the passage, chose another branch at random, then another, and another, the beam of his flashlight streaking wildly across the walls.

He forced himself to stop and listen. *Get a grip*, he told himself. He had to think about what he was doing, not just run in panic, willy-nilly. If he could only get to the surface, he might be able to reach the relative protection of Glinn's camp.

As he waited, listening in the dark, he heard a new sound: a faint calling. It was Amiko, calling for the Cyclops. Searching for it. Pleading with it. Calling it in.

He began moving again, taking a fork in the passage that seemed to head in the direction of her voice. As he ran, he could hear—overlaid by Amiko's voice—the creature's grunting sounds of pain as it loped along. Where was it? The confusing system of passageways, with their echoes and re-echoes, made it hard to tell. Gideon paused, uncertain whether to advance or retreat, fighting back the panic that tried to bubble its way to the surface.

A minute went by, then another. Amiko's voice had died away. Gideon hardly dared breathe. And then he heard other sounds—that same stertorous breathing, that same growl of hatred, the same slow sounds of movement. And this time, there was no confusion: they were coming from the unknown darkness *behind* him. He spun around just as the thing came shambling out of the darkness into the beam of his flashlight, bloody eye staring.

Gasping in fear, scrambling backward, Gideon dove through a random hole in the lava tube, tumbled down a sandy slope, and rolled out into a huge space—the crystal cavern. He ran toward its exit, the Cyclops grunting and dragging itself behind him. Gasping for breath, he gained the outer cavern, ran through the entrance, and burst out through the crack in the stone into the blinding sunlight.

His momentum almost carried him off the cliff and he scrambled desperately at the edge, rocks falling away into sheer space, before pulling himself back. He raced up the trail, the Cyclops directly behind him. At the very lip of the cliff, the creature's arm whipped out and seized his calf from behind. With a brutal roar of triumph, he plucked Gideon up from the face of rock and swung him out over blue space, preparing to fling him off the cliff. Gideon cried out as he hung upside down in the massive fist, staring at the crawling blue ocean a thousand feet below.

"No!" came Amiko's cry as she suddenly appeared just above them on the trail. "Stop!"

The Cyclops hesitated, dangling Gideon over the precipice. Then, slowly, it looked up, toward Amiko...and past her. Its eye widened with apparent horror at what it saw. Despite his desperate plight, Gideon followed the creature's gaze—and saw it, too.

The island was on fire. A massive firestorm swirled upward in a spiraling tornado of flame: leaves, twigs, entire burning branches lofted on the updraft, shaking the very air. As he stared, momentarily forgetting even his own predicament, a chopper flew overhead, speeding for the mainland. The fire was consuming everything, advancing at a furious pace, fueled by the wind blowing toward their end of the island. Even as the Cyclops stood, paralyzed at the sight, animals escaping the fire came flying off the cliff, wild pigs and big cats and creatures Gideon had never seen before racing out of the jungle and tumbling into the sea below with cries and yelps of terror, twisting in the air as they tumbled into space.

There was no hope for the island—none.

Staring at the conflagration, the Cyclops lifted his head and bellowed out a roar of impotent rage. It was as if his horror at seeing the final end of his world, his centuries of loneliness and pain, were all rolled up into that one horrible cry. He seemed to have forgotten Gideon, still dangling from his massive arm.

"No," said Amiko, stepping toward him with a strange air of calm. "Please, no."

Gideon clawed the air, trying to catch hold of something, in a perfect terror of the dizzying heights.

Amiko stood there, and the Cyclops stared at her, at the all-consuming fire, at Gideon, and then back to her. Gideon stopped struggling. Some sort of communication seemed to take place between Amiko and the creature—an understanding that almost transcended language. And then, gently, the Cyclops drew Gideon back from the brink and released him to the ground.

Gideon collapsed on the rock, breathing hard.

Amiko stepped over to the Cyclops. They turned their backs to Gideon, to the island—and stared out toward the infinite blue horizon.

The Cyclops took a step toward the cliff face. He was a ruined creature, burned, bloody, his leg shattered, blood streaming down his back. Above, the fire crackled and roared. More animals went driving and falling past them, their screams whisked away by the wind.

There was a brief moment of stasis. And then, with

a motion that was almost graceful, the Cyclops joined them, leaping from the cliff. Gideon rushed to the edge and stared down. It took a long time for him to fall. At the end his body made a flower in the water...and then the blue sea smoothed over and it was gone.

Gideon retreated from the cliff face and glanced back, across the clearing to the wall of jungle. Now he could see the fire advancing in its full fury. A sucking updraft was developing as the smoke and burning detritus whirled into the sky in a tornado of flame. A tapir came charging past him, zigzagging, making a high-pitched sound of terror, before disappearing over the edge.

The Cyclops had realized it was the end of his world. Vengeance, rage, struggle were useless. There was nothing more he could do. And somehow—maybe with Amiko's help—he had reached within, found that human core of mercy, and spared Gideon's life.

He turned. Now Amiko, following in the footsteps of the Cyclops, was also approaching the cliff edge. As he watched, she took a slow, deliberate step—and then another.

"Wait," said Gideon, a terrible realization dawning within him. "No. No, don't."

She looked at him sadly. "There's no place for him in this world. And none for me, either."

"For God's sake, Amiko—!"

She stepped to the edge of the precipice, preparing to follow.

"Amiko," Gideon said in desperation. He reached out a hand to stop her, then withdrew it; he sensed that any physical contact would result in her immediate plunge. He gasped, forcing himself to think. She stood there, toes over open air, glancing down at the foaming rocks that had already claimed the Cyclops.

"Do you remember that book of poetry I told you about? There was a line that stuck in my brain, from a poem by Delmore Schwartz."

She had paused. She was listening.

"He wrote: *Time is the fire in which we burn.* That line has always haunted me—all the more so now, when I have so little time left."

She did not turn; did not make any indication of having heard. But neither did she jump.

"I've got ten months. You've got the rest of your life. And you're going to throw away all that gorgeous, wonderful time, time that I would love to have—but can't. For what? Because you say there's no place for you? Because you're afraid?"

She seemed to sway a little, teetering on the edge.

"But you *aren't* afraid. You're the bravest person I've ever met. The way you handled those pirates with the gaff hook. The way you rescued me from the sacrifice to the Lotus Eaters, and took a spear for your pains. The way you climbed the cliff face with a raging fever." He took a ragged breath. "Sometimes it takes courage—maybe all the courage you've got—to just live life. Every morning I wake up and the first thing I think is: *Oh, shit, I'm dying.* And that makes me want to make my time *count.* My condition may be the worst thing that's ever happened to me, but it's also done something good: I've learned the value of time. And here you are, about to throw your life away. Don't do it. Listen to a man who knows the preciousness of time."

She remained still, body quivering with anticipation, swaying out over the uttermost edge of the cliff.

"You have the courage to face death. But do you have the courage to face life? Do the most courageous thing of all. Step back from the edge. Turn around. And come with me. Please."

For another moment, she remained motionless. And then—slowly—she turned around and took an unsteady step toward him, and another. Quickly, Gideon grabbed her hand, pulled her in, and hugged her tightly as if to prevent her changing her mind.

Clutching her to him, he turned away, looking back toward the conflagration. The island was being utterly consumed by the firestorm, sweeping away everything in its path. It was leapfrogging from tree to tree, gobbets of burning debris starting to drop around them like snow, starting fires everywhere. It would be on top of them within moments. Where could they go? Back down the cliffs into the necropolis? But the fire had cut off that route of escape and was now closing in on three sides, backing them up against the cliff. The minutes he'd spent convincing Amiko not to hurl herself over the edge had eaten up precious time. Already the heat of the fire was becoming unbearable and he could hardly breathe...

...And then he heard a thudding sound above the roar of the fire. The shadow of a chopper appeared, low and slow. It went into a hover; a rope ladder dropped. Gideon grasped it and pushed Amiko up ahead of him even as the flames swirled around. Just before they pulled him in after her, he glanced back and got a final glimpse of the island: it had turned into a rotating tower of flame.

Epilogue

GIDEON KNEW THAT the chopper that had brought him to his remote cabin in the Jemez Mountains of New Mexico would eventually return. And almost a month later to the day, it did. Just as he finished preparing his single meal of the day—roasted wild goose breast in a ginger and black truffle emulsion—he heard the *thwap* of rotors.

Turning off the heat, he went to the door of his cabin. Coming in over the trees, the helicopter settled down in a nearby grassy meadow, flattening the long grass. The door opened and a wheelchair lift lowered Glinn in his all-terrain chair onto the ground. Garza appeared a moment later, and they both crossed the meadow to the cabin door.

Gideon held open the door.

They entered in silence. Glinn rolled over to one side while Garza took a seat in a leather chair. Gideon seated himself at the table. He was surprised to see Garza back with Glinn, but said nothing.

Glinn finally said: "How was your latest visit to the doctor?"

Gideon glanced down at his hands as he shook his head.

"Nothing at all?"

"They don't know why I keep going back, asking for one MRI after another. They think I'm a little crazy." He paused. "The lotus may work on broken bones and damaged limbs. But maybe not on a condition like mine. What I have is congenital—it can't be undone."

"Have patience—and faith."

Gideon said coldly: "And you? I saw you gnawing on that lotus in the helicopter while we were evacuating the island. Where'd you find it, anyway?"

"When the Cyclops returned to the camp a second time, it had your drysack in one hand. A few specimens fell out as it was attacked. I rather selfishly took one for myself."

"Lot of good it did you."

A moment passed. Glinn and Garza exchanged looks. And then—slowly, rather painfully—Glinn rose from the wheelchair, took a step, and another, gripping onto the table for support, and made his way without further assistance to an empty chair. He eased himself down into it, grimacing slightly.

"Oh, my God," Gideon murmured.

"Yes. I'm feeling stronger—and healthier—by the day. And that resulted from my one crude and selfish attempt at self-medication. Now some of the best minds in the world are working on the drug. They've been able to propagate the lotus, they've sequenced its DNA, and now it's only a matter of time before they isolate and analyze the active agents in it. It's a unique organism, eukaryotic, very ancient, evidently a type of myxogastrid or slime mold that lives part of its life cycle as a single cell and part as a complex multicellular organism. They feel confident they will eventually crack the code."

"I'm happy for you," Gideon replied in an astringent tone.

A pause. "Gideon, I owe you a most profound apology."

Gideon remained silent.

"I'm responsible for this disaster. I ask your forgiveness for . . . the unforgivable."

"The unforgivable," Gideon repeated.

"Yes. I blame myself for—"

All of a sudden, the rage, the frustration, all the feelings that he had spent the last few weeks trying to put behind him, came boiling to the surface. "You selfish bastard," he said with quiet vehemence, rising from his chair and stepping toward Glinn, hands unconsciously balling into fists. Garza moved to step between them, but Glinn motioned him to stay where he was.

"After the way you screwed up that meteorite job, sinking a ship and causing the death of over a hundred people, a normal person might have taken stock. Reconsidered his assumptions. Maybe even have acquired a little humility. But not you. You're too egotistical, too sure you're right. You've no appreciation of your own shortcomings or the basic unpredictability of things. Oh, you're a champ when it comes to plotting out a course of action. But your system is hardly fail-safe. You're too arrogant to consider your failings. This time, instead of sinking a ship, you destroyed an island. You killed a being, the last of his kind, and caused the extinction of a race. Because of you, more people died. And here you are: back again." He paused and said: "God *damn* you."

Gideon stood there, staring at Glinn. The man's face was, as usual, unreadable. A blank. But then it slowly paled, the lines wavering.

"A perfect example of this," Gideon said, in something closer to a normal voice, "is what happened to Amiko. Last I heard, she was running an Outward Bound program in Patagonia. After that, she fell off the map."

"We're trying to locate her," said Glinn, weakly. "We want to help her."

"Help her? You did this to her," said Gideon bitterly. "You knew about her inner turmoil when you hired her and leveraged it against her. When you killed the Cyclops, you killed part of her. She *loved* that creature. But the human condition cost didn't matter to you. Just like you used my own condition against me, allowing me to hope against hope that the mission might cure me. But guess what? The *thing's still in here!*" He pointed at his head. "You've never learned. *Never.* And you never will."

Gideon halted, breathing hard. Glinn's face had undergone a remarkable change—white, beaded with sweat, creased with anguish.

"You're wrong," Glinn replied. "I've spent the last month coming to grips with my crimes. I made terrible mistakes, did terrible things. The death of the Cyclops. The destruction of the island. Lost lives, ruined hopes. It has been an agony for me to accept what I've done."

Gideon said nothing.

"Somehow, ironically, my starting to heal made me face up to who I am. Face my own fallibility, my own weaknesses. My basic philosophy was wrong. No amount of computing power or predictive work can kill the Black Swan. There's always something impossible to predict. Like a live Cyclops. I've been an arrogant fool."

Gideon looked at him. The leader of EES did indeed look stricken.

Glinn raised his eyes again. "Gideon, I failed—but the project did not. This drug will change the world. We succeeded. It was messy and cruel. But it worked. And the fact is . . . we still need you."

Gideon waited. He knew this was coming.

"The time has come. For our final project."

"The meteorite."

"Yes. The meteorite was a giant seed. I planted it. And now I must uproot it. It's an alien life-form that threatens the earth. The time to act is now."

Gideon turned to Garza. "And you? What's your take on this?"

"I'm in," Garza replied in his gruff voice. "Eli's telling the truth: he's a changed man. Otherwise I wouldn't have signed back on. This seed is as dangerous as Eli says it is. I'll be mission co-leader. No more secret orders, no more vetoes from on high, no more my-way-or-the-highway. This is to be a team effort."

"What about the funding?" Gideon asked Glinn.

"You recall I told you EES was going to take a small percentage of profits from the drug in lieu of a royalty? We worked out another deal with the foundation. Instead, we accepted a single, onetime payment: just one percent of what the foundation estimates will be realized in the first year of the drug's distribution. Financed by a generous benefactor who wishes to remain anonymous."

"And how much is that?"

"A little over a billion dollars."

Gideon shook his head.

"We have the money," Garza said. "We have the knowledge and the technology. We're the only ones who have a hope of defeating this thing. And we'll be doing it as partners—you included."

"Why me?"

"You know why," Glinn said. "You're the yin to my yang. You don't know why you do what you do, you have no discipline, you don't think things through, and you ignore logic. And yet you always seem to make the right choice. You're an intuitional genius. Temperamentally and intellectually, you are my exact opposite—and that is precisely why we need you. Or we will fail. We have no time left. We need to move. I want you to come with us right now."

A very long silence ensued. It stretched into a minute, two minutes. Finally, Gideon stood up, went to the stove, picked up the pan with the beautifully prepared goose, and dumped it in the garbage. Despite all he'd been through—despite the heartbreaks and danger and suffering and mortification he had tried so hard to put behind him—somehow he had known this would happen; that Glinn would be back . . . and that he would be ready.

He grabbed his coat. "Lead the way."

Acknowledgments

We'd like to thank the following for their support and assistance: Mitch Hoffman, Sonya Cheuse, Eric Simonoff, Jamie Raab, Lindsey Rose, Claudia Rülke, Nadine Waddell, and Alicia Gordon.

Two of the central concepts in the novel, the nature of the vellum and what creature it came from, were proposed by Isaac J. Preston, for which we thank him most sincerely.

About the Authors

The thrillers of DOUGLAS PRESTON and LINCOLN CHILD "stand head and shoulders above their rivals" (*Publishers Weekly*). Preston and Child's *Relic* and *The Cabinet of Curiosities* were chosen by readers in a National Public Radio poll as being among the one hundred greatest thrillers ever written, and *Relic* was made into a number-one box office hit movie. Coauthors of the famed Pendergast series, Preston and Child are also the authors of *Gideon's Sword* and *Gideon's Corpse*. Preston's acclaimed nonfiction book, *The Monster of Florence*, is being made into a movie starring George Clooney. Lincoln Child is a former book editor who has published five novels of his own, including the huge bestseller *Deep Storm*.

Readers can sign up for The Pendergast File, a monthly "strangely entertaining note" from the authors, at their website, www.PrestonChild.com.

When a murdered corpse appears on his doorstep, Special Agent Pendergast discovers an ancient family secret—and a conspiracy that can only end with his own death...

Please see the next page
for a preview of

Blue Labyrinth

1

THE STATELY BEAUX-ARTS mansion on Riverside Drive between 137th and 138th Streets, while carefully tended and impeccably preserved, appeared to be untenanted. On this stormy June evening, no figures paced the widow's walk overlooking the Hudson River. No yellow glow from within flowed through the decorative oriel windows. The only visible light, in fact, came from the front entrance, illuminating the drive beneath the building's porte cochere.

Appearances can be deceiving, however—sometimes intentionally. Because 891 Riverside was the residence of FBI Special Agent Aloysius Pendergast—and Pendergast was a man who valued, above all, his privacy.

In the mansion's elegant library, Pendergast sat in a leather wing chair. Although it was early summer, the night was blustery and chill, and a low fire flickered on the grate. He was leafing through a copy of the Man'yōshū, an old and celebrated anthology of Japanese poetry, dating to ad 750. A small tetsubin, or cast-iron teapot, sat on a table beside him, along with a china cup half-full of green tea. Nothing disturbed his concentration. The only sounds were the occasional crackle of settling embers and rumble of thunder from beyond the closed shutters.

Now there was a faint sound of footsteps from the reception hall beyond and Constance Greene appeared, framed in the library doorway. She was wearing a simple evening dress. Her violet eyes and dark hair, cut in an old-fashioned bob, offset the paleness of her skin. In one hand she held a bundle of letters.

"The mail," she said.

Pendergast inclined his head, set the book aside.

Constance took a seat beside Pendergast, noting that, since returning from what he called his "Colorado adventure," he was at last looking like his old self. His state of mind had been a cause of uneasiness in her since the dreadful events of the prior year.

She began sorting through the small stack of mail, putting aside the things that would not interest him. Pendergast did not like to concern himself with quotidian details. He had an old and discreet New Orleans law firm, long in the employ of the family, to pay bills and manage part of his unusually extensive income. He had an equally hoary New York banking firm to manage other investments, trusts, and real estate. And he had all mail delivered to a post office box, which Proctor, his chauffeur, bodyguard, and general factotum, collected on a regular basis. At present, Proctor was preparing to leave for a visit to relatives in Alsace, so Constance had agreed to take over the epistolary matters.

"Here's a note from Corrie Swanson."

"Open it, if you please."

"She's attached a photocopy of a letter from John Jay. Her thesis won the Rosewell Prize."

"Indeed. I attended the ceremony."

"I'm sure Corrie appreciated it."

"It is rare that a graduation ceremony offers more than an anesthetizing parade of platitudes and mendacity, set to the tiresome refrain of 'Pomp and Circumstance.' " Pendergast took a sip of tea at the recollection. "This one did."

Constance sorted through more mail. "And here's a letter from Vincent D'Agosta and Laura Hayward."

He nodded for her to scan it. "It's a thank-you note for the wedding gift and once again for the dinner party."

Pendergast inclined his head as she put the letter aside. The month before, on the eve of D'Agosta's wedding, Pendergast had hosted a private dinner for the couple, consisting of several courses he had prepared himself, paired with rare wines from his cellar. It was this gesture, more than anything, that had convinced Constance that Pendergast had recovered from his recent emotional trauma.

She read over a few other letters, then put aside those of interest and tossed the rest on the fire.

"How is the project coming, Constance?" Pendergast asked as he poured himself a fresh cup of tea.

"Very well. Just yesterday I received a packet from France, the Bureau Ancestre du Dijon, which I'm now trying to integrate with what I've already collected from Venice and Louisiana. When you have the time, I do have a couple of questions I'd like to ask about Augustus Robespierre St. Cyr Pendergast."

"Most of what I know consists of oral family history—tall tales, legends, and some whispered horror stories. I'd be glad to share most of them with you."

"Most? I was hoping you'd share them all."

"I fear there are skeletons in the Pendergast family closet, figurative and literal, that I must keep even from you."

Constance sighed and rose. As Pendergast returned to his book of poetry, she walked out of the library, across the reception hall lined with museum cabinets full of curious objects, and through a doorway into a long, dim space paneled in time-darkened oak. The main feature of the room was a wooden refectory table, almost as long as the room itself. The near end of the table was covered with journals, old letters, census pages, yellowed photographs and engravings, court transcripts, memoirs, reprints from newspaper microfiche, and other documents, all arranged in neat stacks. Beside them sat a laptop computer, its screen glowing incongruously in the dim room. Several months before, Constance had taken it upon herself to prepare a genealogy of the Pendergast family. She wanted both to satisfy her own curiosity and to help draw Pendergast out of himself. It was a fantastically complex, infuriating, and yet endlessly fascinating undertaking.

At the far end of the long room, beyond an arched door, was the foyer leading to the mansion's front door. Just as Constance was about to take a seat at the table, a loud knock sounded.

Constance paused, frowning. They rarely entertained visitors at 891 Riverside Drive—and never did one arrive unannounced.

Knock. Another rap resounded from the entryway, accompanied by a low grumble of thunder.

Smoothing down her dress, Constance walked down the length of the room, through the archway, and into the foyer. The heavy front door was solid, with no fish-eye lens, and she hesitated a moment. When no third rap came, she undid the upper lock, then the lower, and slowly opened the door.

There, silhouetted in the light of the porte cochere, stood a young man. His blond hair was wet and plastered to his head. His rain-spattered features were fine and quintessentially Nordic, with a high-domed forehead and chiseled lips. He was dressed in a linen suit, sopping wet, which clung to his frame.

He was bound with heavy ropes.

Constance gasped, began to reach out to him. But the bulging eyes took no notice of the gesture. They stared straight ahead, unblinking.

For a moment, the figure remained standing, swaying ever so slightly, fitfully illuminated by flashes of lightning—and then it began to fall, like a tree toppling, slowly at first and then faster, before crashing facedown across the threshold.

Constance backed up with a cry. Pendergast arrived at a run, followed by Proctor. Pendergast grasped her, pulled her aside, and quickly knelt over the young man. He gripped the figure by the shoulder and turned him over, brushing the hair from his eyes, and feeling for the pulse that was so obviously absent beneath the cold flesh of the neck.

"Dead," he said, his voice low and unnaturally composed.

"My God," Constance said, her own voice breaking.

"It's your son Tristram."

"No," Pendergast said. "It's Alban. His twin."

For just a moment longer he knelt by the body. And then he leapt to his feet and, in a flash of feline motion, disappeared into the howling storm.

2

Pendergast sprinted to Riverside Drive and paused at the corner, scanning north and south along the broad avenue. The rain was now coming down in sheets, traffic was light, and there were no pedestrians. His eye lit upon the closest vehicle, about three blocks south: a late-model Lincoln Town Car, black, of the kind seen on the streets of Manhattan by the thousands. The license plate light was out, leaving the details of the New York plate unreadable.

Pendergast ran after it.

The vehicle did not speed up, but continued at a leisurely pace down the drive, at each cross street moving through one set of green lights after another, steadily gaining distance. The lights turned yellow, then red. But the vehicle continued on, running a yellow and a red, never accelerating, never slowing.

He pulled out his cell phone and punched in a number as he ran. "Proctor. Bring the car. I'm headed south on Riverside."

The Town Car had almost disappeared, save for a faint pair of taillights, wavering in the downpour, but as the drive made the slow curve at 126th Street even those disappeared.

Pendergast continued on, pursuing at a dead run, his black suit jacket whipping behind him, rain stinging his face. A few blocks ahead, he saw the Town Car again, stopped at another light behind two other vehicles. Once again, he pulled out his phone and dialed.

"Twenty-Sixth Precinct," came the response. "Officer Powell."

"This is SA Pendergast, FBI. In pursuit of a black Town Car, New York license plate unidentified, traveling southbound on Riverside at One Hundred Twenty-Fourth. Operator is suspect in a homicide. Need assistance in motor vehicle stop."

"Ten-four," came the dispatcher. And a moment later: "We have a marked unit in the area, two blocks over. Keep us posted on location."

"Air support as well," Pendergast said, still at a dead run. "Sir, if the vehicle operator is only a suspect—"

"This is a priority target for the FBI," Pendergast said into the phone. "Repeat, a *priority target*."

A brief pause. "We're putting a bird in the air."

As he put the phone away, the Town Car suddenly veered around the cars idling at the red light, jumped the curb and crossed the sidewalk, tore through a set of flower beds in Riverside Park, churning up mud, then headed the wrong way down the exit ramp to the Henry Hudson Parkway.

Pendergast called dispatch again and updated them on the vehicle's location, followed it up with another call to Proctor, then cut into the park, leapt over a low fence, and sprinted through some tulip beds, his eyes locked on the taillights of the car careening down the off-ramp onto the parkway, the screech of tires floating back to his ears.

He vaulted the low stone wall on the far side of the drive, then half ran, half slid down the embankment, scattering trash and broken glass in an attempt to cut the vehicle off. He fell, rolled, and scrambled to his feet, chest heaving, soaked with rain, white shirt plastered to his chest. He watched as the Town Car pulled a U-turn and came blasting down the exit helix toward him. He reached for his Les Baer, but his hand closed over an empty holster. He looked quickly around the dark embankment, then—as brilliant light slashed across him—was forced to roll away. Once the car had passed, he rose again to his feet, following the vehicle with his eyes as it merged into the main stream of traffic.

A moment later a vintage Rolls-Royce approached and braked rapidly to the curb. Pendergast opened the rear door and jumped in.

"Follow the Town Car," he told Proctor as he strapped himself in. The Rolls accelerated smoothly. Pendergast could hear faint sirens from behind, but the police were too far back and would no doubt get hung up in traffic. He plucked a police radio from a side compartment. The chase accelerated, the Town Car shifting lanes and dodging cars at speeds that approached a hundred miles an hour even as they entered a construction area, concrete barriers lining both shoulders of the highway.

There was a lot of chatter on the police radio, but they

were first in pursuit. The chopper was nowhere to be seen.

Suddenly a series of bright flashes came from the traffic ahead, followed instantly by the report of gunshots.

"Shots fired!" Pendergast said into the open channel.

He understood immediately what was happening. Ahead, cars veered wildly right and left, panicking, along with the flashes of additional shots. Then a *crump, crump, crump* sounded as multiple vehicles piled into each other at highway speed, causing a chain reaction that quickly filled the road with hissing, ruined metal. With great expertise, Proctor braked the Rolls and steered into a power slide, trying to maneuver it past the chain reaction of collisions. The Rolls hit a concrete barrier at an angle, was deflected back into the lane, and was hit from behind by a driver who rammed into the pileup with a deafening crash of metal. In the backseat, Pendergast was thrown forward, stopped hard by his seat belt, then slammed back. Partially stunned, he heard the sound of hissing steam, screams, shouts, and the screeching of brakes and additional crashes as cars continued to rear-end each other, mingling with a rising chorus of sirens and now, finally, the *thwap* of helicopter blades.

Shrugging off a coating of broken glass, Pendergast struggled to collect his wits and remove the seat belt. He leaned forward to examine Proctor.

The man was unconscious, his head bloody. Pendergast fumbled for the radio to call for help, but even as he did so the doors were pulled open and paramedics were pushing in, hands grasping at him.

"Get your hands off me," Pendergast said. "Focus on him." Pendergast shrugged free and exited into the sweeping rain, more glass falling away as he did so. He stared ahead at the impenetrable tangle of cars, the sea of flashing lights, listening to the shouts of paramedics and police and the thud of the useless, circling chopper.

The Town Car was long gone.

VISIT US ONLINE AT

WWW.HACHETTEBOOKGROUP.COM

FEATURES:

OPENBOOK BROWSE AND
SEARCH EXCERPTS

•

AUDIOBOOK EXCERPTS AND PODCASTS

•

AUTHOR ARTICLES AND INTERVIEWS

•

BESTSELLER AND PUBLISHING
GROUP NEWS

•

SIGN UP FOR E-NEWSLETTERS

•

AUTHOR APPEARANCES AND TOUR
INFORMATION

•

SOCIAL MEDIA FEEDS AND WIDGETS

•

DOWNLOAD FREE APPS

BOOKMARK HACHETTE BOOK GROUP
@ WWW.HACHETTEBOOKGROUP.COM